KAJI
WARRIORS

SHIFTING STRENGTH

KAJI WARRIORS

SHIFTING STRENGTH

Kelly A Nix

Ignited Publishing

First Printing, 2020
Book cover design by germancreative.

Kaji Warriors: Shifting Strength
Kelly A Nix
www.kellyanix.com

ISBN 978-0-578-67395-0 (paperback)
ISBN 978-0-578-68464-2 (ebook)

Ignited Publishing LLC
750 E US Hwy 80
STE 200-527
Forney, TX 75126

www.ignitedpublishing.com

I dedicate this book to the strongest woman I know. Her strength of character is unmatched, and she throws a mean reverse punch. Thanks, Mom.

PROLOGUE

A Kajian female stands in the middle of a field just outside the planet's capital city. Hidden by the tall crops fluttering in the wind around her, she searches the night sky as the shifting clouds eclipse one of the small moons. Her mind swirls with the consequences of recent decisions, and her chest tightens around her heart from the pain of loss. She knows it's dangerous to be here, probably a trap. But he will be gone soon, and she will be alone. Alone but for the billions of souls looking to her to lead them. She is many things to her people; above all else, she is a warrior. So with a warrior's determination, she frowns, clenches her fists, and stands firm against the storm raging in her heart and mind.

The warrior's calloused hands pull the black hooded wrap tighter as a cool breeze brushes against her. Although unable to dull the amber shine of her eyes, the cover conceals her movement and shape as she taps her foot and waits. Finally, a transport shuttle slips out from behind a cloud and descends upon her location. The warrior stares up at the massive construct in confusion as a hint of anxiety takes root from the implications of the star ship's presence. Wind from the vehicle bellows, bending the tall grass to its will while the warrior darts her gaze around to satisfy her paranoia. With a huff of impatience, she watches the trespassing ship land, ignoring the growing smell of exhaust and burnt grass.

She narrows her eyes at the thought of the stealth ship slipping unseen past her planet's defenses. The anxiety rooted deep inside her sprouts tiny sprigs, but a building storm of rage threatens to smother it. When the bay doors open, the warrior's molten gaze snaps to the familiar figure

1

exiting the shuttle. A bestial growl bursts from her chest as anger and betrayal rages within the warrior. She stomps toward the awaiting female with a nasty snarl and a dangerous word engulfing the warrior's mind.

Traitor.

The traitor steps from the shuttle's dock onto the familiar ground and sighs with relief to breathe in the scent of home. Seeing the warrior striding toward her, the traitor pauses with a sigh, then rolls her shoulders and waist to stretch the muscles that she'll need for this 'discussion.' The traitor plants her feet in the center of the clearing and awaits the wrath of her former packmate. The warrior stops an arm's length from the traitor and, with a fury born of love and betrayal, amber eyes meet traitorous emerald. A silent struggle of wills ensues as the two females express their mutual hatred for one another in distasteful snarls and gnashing teeth. The moons cast a deceptive light on the two lone figures, and a light breeze twirls the black robes around each of the battle-hardened females as they square off. In a deep, resounding voice, the warrior speaks first.

"What do you want?"

The traitor huffs at the expected question and responds in the familiar, silvery voice that grates across the warrior's nerves. "Were you followed?"

"Were you? How did your ship arrive undetected?"

"I have my ways," the traitor says. The warrior narrows her eyes at the flippant response.

"As do I," she says and snatches the traitor by her robes to jerk her close. "Now, why did you contact me? Never mind how you did it."

The traitor does not pull away nor cower to the warrior's rage; instead, she accepts the warrior's pain and anger. In fact, she expected blood by now. Perhaps, the seasons have softened the warrior.

"I have an idea that I'd like to discuss with you," the traitor says.

The warrior slams her fist into the traitor's emerald eyes, and the traitor yelps in surprise at the brutal attack. The punch propels her backward several paces, but the traitor refuses to kneel. She opens one eye as the second swells shut. Still, she manages a menacing glare at the warrior, who crosses her arms with a smug smile.

"It must be quite an idea to risk coming back here," the warrior says.

The traitor snarls at the quip and retaliates. Prepared, the warrior shifts her weight to the left, so the traitor's fist skims past her. Surprised by her lack of contact, the traitor hesitates, and the warrior slams her knee into the traitor's exposed mid-section with a loud snap of a rib. With the wind knocked out of her, the traitor topples forward. Amber eyes show no mercy as the warrior slams her fists into the traitor's neck. The force of the blow sends the traitor crashing to the ground hard enough to crumble the dirt below them. With a satisfied grin, the warrior steps out of the rubble of soil and weeds to watch the traitor groan and struggle back to her feet.

"It must be an impressive idea to show your face to me, again," the warrior says.

She grabs the traitor's hair and wrenches her opponent's head back in a painful hold. The warrior dips her face close to whisper promises of pain.

"What makes you think I won't kill you here and now?"

Grimacing, the traitor glares at her attacker, but the warrior's molten gaze is just as fierce. The traitor clenches her teeth and smashes her forehead into the warrior's nose, producing a satisfying crunch. With a yelp, the warrior releases her grip and jumps back from the traitor to clutch her broken nose. The traitor wipes at the blood that seeps from her damaged forehead and huffs at the minor injury.

"Because we gave our words not to kill each other when we agreed to meet," the traitor says. The warrior rolls her eyes as she cradles her nose in her hands and blood pools in her palms.

"Why should I trust a traitor?"

The traitor sighs, and her emerald eyes dim with pain and regret.

"I'll show you. Wait here."

The traitor returns to her shuttle before the warrior can argue. The amber-eyed female scoffs at her dismissal and splatters blood on the ground around her. The warrior takes a deep breath before snapping her nose into proper alignment. She bites back a painful groan and peers up into the night sky to fight the tears that flood her vision. She smiles at the adrenaline surging through her body. It's been far too long since she's suffered an injury. With dry eyes, she glances back to the traitor's shuttle to find the emerald-eyed female descending the landing with something bundled in her robe.

The traitor hesitates when she sees the clotting blood smeared across the warrior's hands, neck, and chin. The warrior flashes a grim smile that sets an unsettling scene under the moonlight. Noticing the traitor's response, the warrior chuckles at her opponent's discomfort. The traitor frowns at the other female's familiar antics and sighs, before returning an imploring gaze on the warrior.

"I am your packmate, and for the sake of our people, you must trust me," the traitor says. She drags her robes away to reveal six pounds of squirming flesh, wrapped in a bundle of delicate garments. A squeal of delight escapes from the bundle as moonlight gleams off bright fuchsia eyes, and amber eyes widen in surprise.

"Is that –?"

"Yes," the traitor says. She's afraid to let her companion speak the words. Even in the dead of night, someone is always listening, and spoken secrets travel the universe faster than light itself.

"Is it–"

"Yes. She is," the traitor says. Across from her, the warrior throws her hands into the air.

"I don't believe it," the warrior says. "This is why you contacted me?"

The traitor sighs and rocks the small child in her arms as she stares at the warrior.

"Yes."

"Do you understand what you are asking of me? Of the Kaji?"

"Do you?" the traitor asks. "If you don't do this, and he finds out about her? He will destroy us all."

The warrior's eyes harden, and she clenches a fist at the traitor.

"He will try," the warrior says. The traitor retreats a single step from the warrior and cradles the squirming child to her chest.

"You've lost so much already. Are you willing to risk everything?" the traitor says.

The warrior flinches away from the other female she once considered pack. Gathering herself, she sighs and, with great effort, pushes aside her own heartache for the sake of others.

"You know what I want in return," the warrior says. The traitor closes her eyes and exhales as her burden lightens.

"It will be done," she says, opening her eyes. "But it will not last forever."

"How long?" the warrior asks. The traitor shrugs as she watches the infant wiggle in her arms.

"Until she is of age. Longer, maybe," the traitor says.

The warrior notices a small, bittersweet smile slip from the traitor's swollen face when she brushes dark hair from the child's eyes. For a moment, the warrior remembers a time when she expected their offspring to grow alongside each other as they once did. Slipping a protective hand over her midsection, the warrior wonders if that dream may still come to fruition.

"What happens then?" the warrior asks.

"I…I do not know."

"Why do you sacrifice so much for a single child?" the warrior asks. The traitor frowns at the warrior and presses her lips together.

"One day, you will understand. The day you hold a child in your arms and worry for its future."

Snorting, the warrior tilts her eyes up to the moon-filled sky as she considers her options. Once again, she searches the shifting night for an answer and struggles against the storm raging within her. After a few moments of inner debate and perhaps a small amount of reflection, her gaze returns to the traitor.

"I accept. Now, leave the child and go."

"No. You will take the child from my arms," the traitor extends the bundle toward the warrior, "into yours."

The warrior glares at the traitor for a few moments before she concedes and retrieves the child. She peers down at the life she holds and raises an amused eyebrow at the infant's odd coloring. She glimpses up to see the traitor gliding back up the landing of her shuttle. As she reaches the large bay doors, the traitor hesitates and glances back. Emerald eyes, swirling with fear, pain, and regret, meet with innocent fuchsia. Doubt crawls across her mind, and indecision squeezes her heart, but the traitor slams down a steel wall of determination. With the remnants of her honor, she disappears into the shuttle and leaves the warrior to carry the child home.

It doesn't take long for the warrior to slip past the palace guards and into her lavish living quarters. Once the infant is asleep, the warrior pours a hard drink and collapses into an overstuffed chair. Bringing the glass to her lips, she pauses as though just remembering and sets the untouched drink on a nearby table with a sigh. For a long while, the warrior watches the sleeping child, letting her mind whirl around the implications of her decision. When her gaze wanders to her large, extravagant bed, unmerciful despair clenches her heart at the thought of climbing between the cold, empty sheets.

She sucks in a painful breath and turns from the pitiful sight. Suddenly, she needs air and perspective. Leaving the child in the care of a trusted servant, she escapes to her favorite room in the grand palace. Once in the throne room, she places one hand on the cold window that overlooks the entire city and slips the other over her stomach. In the light of Planet Kaji's three suns, the warrior can see every being that wanders

5

through her city. But, under the veil of darkness, she has to imagine them, along with the billions more that she will never meet. Every soul that once looked to him will soon turn to her for guidance.

What can I do? What have I done? How long can I postpone the inevitable?

She stands in silent contemplation for a long time before the rays of Solis break the horizon and announce a new beginning.

I will do what I must.

With a surge of assurance and determination, the warrior straightens and snaps her fingers. One of several guards stationed throughout the throne room lurches to her side.

"Bring me Solum," she says.

"I believe the royal advisor is still in mourning. Shall I interrupt?" the soldier asks. She cringes at the reminder of their recent losses but does not waver.

"Yes. We must postpone our mourning. There is much to be done, and I need Solum here immediately."

"As you command, my queen."

CHAPTER 1

At one time, a giant asteroid entered Planet Kaji's solar system, and its path arched in several directions as numerous gravity wells tugged on it. It took centuries for the new asteroid to settle into a long elliptical orbit that reached far past the outer planets and then circle back to visit the inner worlds. For a millennium, the asteroid danced with the three stars of the solar system, Cerule, Solis, and Sul, in perfect synchronization until its orbit crossed the path of a small spacecraft.

At the outer limits of the system, the ship captain opted to blast the asteroid into oblivion rather than alter his course. His emerald-eyed passenger demanded an expedient and stealthy arrival to Planet Kaji; given the compensation offered upon her safe return, the captain would deliver as promised. So rather than wasting time and fuel, he shot the asteroid with his most powerful cannon. Instead of crumbling into dust, the sturdy asteroid shifted in its orbit and out of the ship's course. With a shrug, the captain continued on his vector to Planet Kaji.

The slight change in the asteroid's orbit inevitably resulted in a slow demise. As the stars and planets continued without pause, the asteroid careened through the solar system on its new path. Planet Kaji orbited the three stars seventeen times before the asteroid swayed too close and plummeted toward the planet's surface. Fortunately for the inhabitants, the Kajian planetary defense weapons are more than capable of destroying most of the asteroid before it enters the atmosphere.

When the planetary defenses first detect the encroaching asteroid, an unperturbed Capital City basks in Sul's diminishing light. A young Kaji warrior-in-training stands in the center of a familiar, overgrown field. Oblivious to the secret deal negotiated just three steps to her right almost seventeen seasons ago, Atae waits with her eyes closed.

I am strong. I am Kaji, she says to herself.

The older adolescent's face twitches from her inner struggle to calm her racing heart as the soft breeze cools the sweat misting her gray skin. She wipes at her forehead to pull the short strands of dark blue hair from her face. She twists her plump lips and strains the muscles across her high cheekbones as she listens to the field around her. Atae wears a simple, black, short-sleeved bodysuit that ends just above her knees. Neither the dark color of her uniform nor the silver Sula Academy logo emblazoned across her chest help to camouflage her amid the golden field.

A Kaji warrior would not stand idle.

Atae sighs but doesn't move. Her task wouldn't be difficult for a purebred, or full-blooded Kaji. A purebred would shift into her second form and track down the enemy. However, Atae is not purebred. Her midnight blue hair contrasts with the red and white of other females, but its thick, unruly strands are typical for all Kaji. Atae's gray skin is too pale compared to the dark chocolate shades of most purebred Kaji. Her short stature and petite build appear too dainty next to the tall, lean physiques of females her age. Atae is a half-breed, a hybrid. But she is still Kaji. And Kaji do not accept defeat.

Atae clenches her jaw and opens her eyes to reveal determination and tenacity swirling within her fuchsia gaze. If nothing else, the youngling's colored eyes mark her as a hybrid, since most Kaji possess black eyes. But Atae doesn't care that she is flawed in the eyes of most purebreds. She cares about the snapping twigs nearby that indicate an encroaching enemy. She scans the horizon in the direction of the noise but finds only the tall swaying stalks of the overgrown field.

She sniffs the air and listens for the rustling of foliage, but the wildlife presence is too strong. She smells nearby creatures and listens to their frantic trampling.

Where is he?

A large hand grabs her right shoulder from behind, and Atae whips around. She uses her right elbow to knock the offending hand from her shoulder and slams her left fist into hard flesh. Atae can't stop the triumphant smile that escapes when a couple of ribs snap under the force of her blow. The purebred Kajian male on the receiving end of her attack grunts from the pain but doesn't retaliate. His broad shoulders cast a long shadow over Atae as he steps toward her with a disappointed scowl. She jumps back and watches him with a wary gaze as she meets his ebony eyes. His shaved head hides a hint of white stubble, but his square jaw and sharp features are clean-shaven. Average height for the Kaji, Solum towers over the youngling with a hard, expectant gaze.

Solum crosses his arms over his chest and stares down at Atae as he speaks in a gruff voice. "You failed."

"No," Atae says. "I reacted the moment I found you." Across from her, Solum shakes his head.

"You didn't find me. I found you. If I wanted, you'd be dead."

"I can do better," Atae says. "I will do better."

"You must if you want to survive the Gridiron," Solum says. Atae snarls, and he smiles at her typical response to challenges. The dark warrior places both hands on the youngling's shoulders and meets her gaze.

"Atae, close your eyes and calm your body," he says.

She nods then closes her eyes before inhaling a deep calming breath. She wills her frantic heart to slow as the adrenaline ebbs from her system. Breathe in, *thump*. Breathe out, *thump*.

"Now," Solum says. "With a silent body, you can hear everything around you. Focus on the grass. Listen to it bend in the wind."

Atae notices the swishing noise from the tall stalks swaying around her, and she smiles.

"Listen to the creatures scurrying along the ground," he says.

She pushes past the noise of the swaying stalks and listens for the tell-tale signs of wildlife. A snapping twig and rustling foliage whisper through the field, and Atae nods. When a light breeze whips past, Solum continues.

"Feel the breeze on your skin and capture the smells it reveals."

Atae sniffs and wrinkles her brow at the odd smells. The scent of wildlife is overwhelming, but Solum's proximity provides a strong sense of sweat and muscle.

Solum jabs Atae in the midsection, and she crumbles to the ground with a surprised yelp. Opening her eyes to face her attacker and struggling to fill her lungs again, Atae squints up to find Solum gone. After catching her breath, she smiles at the new challenge and, again, closes her eyes.

This time, I will win.

It takes a moment to relax her body and spread her senses again. The breeze brushes at her back with the delightful smells of creatures going about their lives but no sign of Solum. So Atae decides to focus upwind and straight ahead. She listens for any sign of a large predator, but as the breeze picks up, so does the deafening noise of billowing grass. She frowns and concentrates past the wall of white noise until a snapping twig breaks through. Atae zeroes in on the sound and waits with bated breath for another. She grins when a heavy foot thumps against the ground.

"I win!"

Her voice triggers a surge of rushing footsteps, Atae opens her eyes to find Solum launching toward her through the tall stalks of grass. She gasps and scrambles out of his reach, then the youngling plants her feet in a defensive stance and guards her arms with clenched fists. In a similar stance, Solum shifts side-to-side, watching Atae's minuscule reactions.

"Are you afraid?" Solum asks.

"I am Kaji. I fear nothing."

Atae launches forward to drive a jab into his chest, and Solum bats her away with a frown. The momentum of her attack pushes her past him, so Atae twirls around to slam a kick into the side of Solum's knee. The joint falters, and the larger warrior yelps as he falls to his knees. Atae continues her attack, but her proximity only allows for an elbow thrust to Solum's face. He catches the youngling's arm in one hand and jabs her in the ribs with his other. The wind knocked from her lungs, Atae stumbles away from the dark warrior and gulps at him.

"I found you," she says. Across from her, Solum raises an eyebrow at Atae as he climbs to his feet.

"You've found me," Solum says. "Now, what? Can you defeat me?"

Atae watches the older warrior step closer as she clutches at her injured side. Solum scowls and lunges for his weakened opponent. When he's within reach, she smirks and sweeps her leg under Solum to knock him to the ground. The larger warrior lands hard on his side, and Atae jumps up, slamming the heel of her foot into the side of his face. She rejoices at the resounding crack of his cheekbone, fragmenting under the force of her attack.

Stunned, Solum lies flat on his back and blinks up at the dimming sky. When he spots another foot descending upon him, the warrior rolls away from the hybrid. Solum leaps to his feet in time to catch another kick aimed for his ribs. Instead, he snatches her leg right out of the air and swings the short youngling around and down. The dirt crumbles under the force of Atae's face and body crashing into the ground.

Solum nurses his cheek as Atae sits up with a groan, then he brushes the grass and dirt from his uniform. Like most adult Kaji, Solum wears a tough bodysuit designed to withstand light training and day-to-day tasks. The latest technology allows for outfits that survive the violence of Kaji shifts, as well as protect against minor temperature changes. While the bodysuit remains a staple of Kajian fashion, recent outside influences created intricate designs that incorporate embroidery, beadwork, and even precious stones. Ignoring the latest trends, Solum wears a simple dark red uniform with gold trim. The sleeveless outfit ends inside his short, heavy boots and remains unharmed after his scuffle with Atae.

"That was better but not good enough," Solum says. He notes the darkening sky through the foliage and Sul's descent over the ever-darkening field. "It's time to go home."

"But," she says. "I'm not done." Atae struggles to her knees, and Solum hides a smile at the youngling's naïve determination. He knows one day her naivety and innocence will be lost in battle, and when she is ready, she will rise to be a great warrior. But not for several seasons still. Until then, it is his job to prepare her. For now, Solum kneels to help her to her feet.

"Yes, you are," he says. Atae leans on him and grumbles.

"One day, I'm going to defeat you, Father."

"But not today. And not tomorrow morning. I must leave early."

Atae nods in acknowledgment as she steps away from him to gather herself. Watching her inspect her bruised face with gentle fingertips, Solum wonders how many times he'll get to use today's tactics before Atae devises a strategy against them.

"What did you learn today?" Solum asks. Despite her tender injuries, Atae smiles at her father.

"Not to let you throw me into the ground." When Solum frowns, her smile falters, and she stands straight before answering.

"Feku, I mean…Elder Warrior Feku lectured about the Ru-Kai crest. He said they are the noblest bloodline in the history of the Kaji Empire. They've ruled the longest."

As they trample through the field and into the nearby forest that will lead them back to the city, Atae stares ahead and imagines her future fighting for the empire. A smile spreads across her lips, and she glances up to find her father watching her.

"One day, I will fight for the empire. I will be a great warrior," Atae says.

When they reach the forest edge, Solum stops and faces his daughter. Recognizing the grave, yet inspired, twist to his face, Atae blows out a breath and prepares for the impending lecture.

"A warrior is nothing without honor, Atae," he says. "It gives you courage and keeps you loyal. It defines you. It haunts you. And it strengthens you. I do not doubt that you are strong, but there are warriors far stronger. And you do not know the true meaning of strength. Not yet."

"I do know!"

"Think, Atae. Imagine the strongest warrior you can, and remember it. Strive to be that warrior. You must always strive to be better. To be stronger. To be Kaji."

Seeing his daughter's look of consternation, Solum nods and waits for her to consider his words. Atae bites her lip as she glances at him, then she closes her eyes with a resigned sigh. It doesn't take much imagination to create a clear image of her strong warrior. He stands in the daylight with a stern expression, unafraid to face numerous enemies. He defeats them with powerful attacks and impenetrable defenses. The mighty warrior cannot be injured and laughs at any attempts to challenge him.

When she opens her eyes, Solum stands across from her, waiting for her to continue on their trek homeward. As a swelling pride builds within her chest, she smiles at her perfect warrior. Solum raises an eyebrow but crosses his arms over his broad chest in satisfaction, then continues onward. Determined to follow in her father's footsteps, Atae crosses her arms and stomps after him.

CHAPTER 2

Solum stands next to the throne room's massive window and watches what remains of the asteroid disintegrate in a bright streak across the sky. The asteroid was detected last night and destroyed this morning when it came within the range of the planetary defenses. Ignoring the busy streets below, Solum peers around the majestic room with a bored sigh. Growing up in the royal palace, he's accustomed to the lavish decoration and sparkling jewels. But of all the castles he's visited throughout the empire, this one is, by far, the most beautiful. It is a testament to the growth of the Kaji Empire.

Images etched into the stone and colored with jewels decorate every wall in the castle. They depict crucial moments or decisions in Kajian history, mostly gruesome battles. Earlier murals portray primitive and barbaric wars amongst the Kaji, but the most recent describe high-tech, but no less savage, conflicts with clashing interplanetary empires. The throne room depicts the ascension of the Ru-Kai family crest to power after Kruot Ru-Ghi led his men to victory centuries ago. He delivered the head of the enemy leader to Princess Skulta Fu-Kai as a token of affection for his new bride. While one wall illustrates the gruesome battle, the other depicts two family crests melding to form the Ru-Kai royal seal. It's one moment in history that combined the two most powerful families into a new bloodline that would rule for centuries.

The Ru-Ghi seal displays a fierce bird of prey with magnificent wings and deadly talons. The Fu-Kai seal illustrates the Kajian second form, a four-legged, massive, fur-covered beast with bladed tails and forelegs, in mid-attack. The two families joined to create the Ru-Kai royal seal. Etched into the stone above the two thrones, the seal depicts the beast in a protective stance with glorious, widespread wings erupting from its back. The Ru-Ghi warrior and the Fu-Kai princess promised to protect and strengthen the Kajian people when they took power. The dedication to that promise has kept the Ru-Kai royal family in power for centuries longer than any other before them.

It is this promise that makes Solum proud to serve his queen and only slightly annoyed at her tardiness. He glances at the two giant marble thrones across the massive room and remembers the secret royal summons that changed everything. Even after nearly two decades, Solum remembers every detail of his conversation with the queen. Seventeen seasons are a drop in the ocean of time that rules the universe, but for the Kaji, this drop was a tidal wave of change. Change is never easy, but Solum and most of the citizens of Kaji recognize its necessity. Others fight tooth and nail to maintain the status quo.

To fend off boredom while he waits, Solum activates his personal hologram and flicks his wrist in a memorized fashion until a small cube assembles in front of him. The head and shoulders of a Kajian female materialize inside the box with her name, Skiska, flashing underneath. The red ends of her course, long hair shim across her shoulders as she tilts her head in greeting, while the white roots frame her round face. With a dark, confident gaze, the holographic spokesperson presses her lips into a tight smile and speaks in a honeyed voice.

"Yesterday, Queen Sula Ru-Kai and her son returned from their two-season campaign across Quadrant Four. Her Majesty's work to systematically restructure the Kaji Empire seems to be proving fruitful as our economy slowly recovers."

The hologram shifts to an older Kajian male with a square jaw and deep-seated eyes. His name, Frack, also appears below him. His dark skin and eyes are typical for purebred Kaji, and his thick, white ponytail points in all directions. The lines of Frack's face form a permanent scowl as he speaks with a loud voice.

"It's her fault the economy tanked, to begin with." He jerks his head to the side and throws a hand into the air. "Queen Sula ended the war with no advance notice. After fighting for generations and building an empire around the strengths of our armies, she just signs a peace treaty and shuts down all our military factories." The hologram reforms to display both commentators side-by-side.

"Well, fifty percent of them..." Skiska says, but Frack interrupts.

"And suddenly, our economy tanks!" Skiska narrows her eyes at her co-host as he fumes before she jerks her gaze back to the audience.

"Queen Sula has made great efforts to rebuild the empire's entire economic structure," she says. "Almost immediately, she decreed the Sula Academy & Research Facility be built in the capital city of her home planet. I think we can all agree on the economic and social success of her first decree as queen regent. The multitude of her decrees that followed had varying degrees of success. Still, they all worked toward the same goal of not only stabilizing the imperial economy but also making it self-sustaining in this time of peace."

"Ha. And how long will this 'time of peace' last? We were at war with the Camille for generations. She can't possibly believe the Kaji will forget the atrocities committed by the Camille?"

"That, my dear Frack, we can agree on. It seems as though our queen's latest policies, while economically beneficial, are detrimental to the Kajian culture. Even as the Camille continue to hide behind their galactic borders, the Setunn, Kips, and Runx have taken up shop on planets throughout the empire at Queen Sula's insistence," Skiska says. Frack snorts and rolls his eyes, but she continues unperturbed.

"According to a recent study, about twenty-five percent of our latest generation of younglings are hybrids. That's the highest it's reached in Kajian history. On Queen Sula's home planet, Planet Kaji, Capital City boasts a youngling population with just as many hybrids as purebred Kaji."

"Which is absurd. We are a race of warriors, not pacifists. I can guarantee that the majority of our viewers feel the dilution of our Kajian blood only weakens us as a species. The hybrids can't shift-"

"For the most part," Skiska says.

"They don't have battle beasts. The few hybrids with alternative forms are not worth mentioning," Frack says. Skiska nods her head with a shrug.

"What do you think viewers? Are the Kaji growing weaker with each hybrid born? Has Queen Sula Ru-Kai done enough to repair the damage to our economy? Be sure to voice your opinions in our comment sections."

"Next time, we'll be discussing the prince's latest debacle and just what we can expect from the Ru-Kai heir in the coming seasons," says Frack. He waves goodbye, and Skiska flashes a sparkling smile.

"Well, that should be a lively debate," she says. "Until next time, right here on the Skiska and Frack channel."

As the holographic image of Skiska and Frack disperses and reshapes into a list of viewer comment posts, Solum waves away the personal hologram. The royal advisor isn't interested in the opinions of other Kaji at the moment. Instead, he reminisces about the intergalactic war that spanned generations and shaped the Kaji Empire. Solum remembers with fondness the battle stories that his father and grandfather told him as a youngling. He idolized them and strived to exemplify their courage and strength during his training. It wasn't until his bid for citizenship that he realized the real merit of his sires. Their stories of ambushes and crafty war strategies fueled his imagination and shaped him into a master strategist fit to advise the royal family. At the side of the king and queen, Solum led fifteen armies of the Kaji Empire against the Camille.

King Uta and Queen Sula led the latest generation to continue the never-ending war. The walls of the palace detailed thousands upon thousands of gruesome battles that cost millions of Kajian lives. Solum doesn't know why his ancestors declared war on the most powerful empire in the known universe and condemned their offspring to the laws of battle. He suspects that no one alive remembers their initial reasons for war, but Solum remembers his reasons for fighting. Even now, Solum struggles to curb his hatred for the Camille as he remembers the destruction of his homeworld. Solum was young and still learning the realities of war when his entire family, all seven generations of his crest, were obliterated, along with three billion other lives. He will never forget what the Camille took from him, and he will never offer forgiveness. But his life no longer revolves around the war. Thanks to his queen, Solum's life now revolves around one fuchsia-eyed youngling, and he couldn't be happier.

With a small smile, he shifts next to the glass wall overlooking Capital City and its surrounding mountains. Early morning light basks everything in a red haze as Solis reigns supreme in the cloudless sky. Bright sparks shower the atmosphere as small fragments of the asteroid break apart and disintegrate in the atmosphere. It won't be long before Cerule's blue light breaches the horizon and begins the morning dance with Solis.

When the large decorative doors swing open, Solum spins in time to watch Queen Sula arrive opposite the grand stairway. Her guards enter first and proceed to their appointed positions throughout the room while scanning the area for threats. Their movements are deliberate and graceful from seasons of repetition. Solum admires their tight formations, expecting no less from the queen's guard.

In the center of the formation, Sula strolls into the throne room with a bored expression plaguing her sharp features. The light from the massive window highlights her high cheekbones and dances across her thin lips. The soft blue outfit, with intricate silver and gold embroidery, complements her dark skin. Her strapless bodysuit embodies the latest fashion trend with long gloves and high boots. Like most Kajian females, Queen Sula has thick, coarse hair. Today, she's wrestled the white and red locks into a long braid that falls across the arch of her back. She uses a silver metal band as an informal crown and to hold back stray hairs from her face. A scar stretches across her collar bone and right shoulder as a reminder to her subjects that Sula Ru-Kai is a warrior above all else.

Ignoring her guards' routine activities, the queen notes Solum's location near the window and ignores her throne to join him. In true Kajian tradition, Solum places his right, balled fist to his chest and his left, balled fist at the small of his back. Solum raises his eyes and face to the crest of Ru-Kai before meeting his queen's unusual amber gaze. A small, amused smile replaces her bored expression as he salutes her

"Solum, it is good to see you," Sula says. He returns her smile and drops the fist at his chest.

"It is good to see you home," Solum says. Sula surveys his battle-hardened form before veering her attention onto the bright window. She stares at the city below, like a mother eyeing a misbehaving child.

"And how is home? Are my subjects still at each other's throats?"

"Things are better." He flicks his wrist to activate a holographic list from which to reiterate. "We now have 352 Setunn citizens, twelve of which are hybrids."

"Good," Sula says. She nods as Solum continues in a monotonous tone.

"The Runx gained 125 citizens, three of which are hybrids. We have 203 Kips, as well. No hybrids." Solum takes a deep breath. "Unfortunately, twenty-five additional people were killed shortly after gaining their citizenship."

Queen Sula whips around to face him and asks a question for which she already knows the answer. "Honor duels?"

With a stern frown, Solum nods his head in confirmation.

"Why so many?" she asks, then shakes her head. "Honor duels are meant to be non-lethal. Have the Kaji completely lost their self-control?"

Sula crosses her arms over her chest and stomps toward her throne. Solum watches her storm away and hides an amused smile at her familiar temper. He reminds her of what every Kaji youngling is taught.

"There is always a chance of fatality in any duel," he says. Sula stops midway to her throne and glances over her shoulder at the royal advisor. She arches an eyebrow at his condescending tone, and he clears his throat before continuing. "The number of honor duels has increased exponentially, especially amongst alien citizens. So more are dying than normal."

Sula continues to her throne and sits with all the regality of royalty. Solum follows after her to stand before the queen.

"Am I right to presume that unhappy Kaji are challenging the aliens due to their new citizenship?" she asks.

"Yes, my queen," he says. "As you know, during the war, newly acquired worlds were expected to function independently from the rest of the empire. They only interacted with other planets for trade and war support. Since the end of the war, you have encouraged, even demanded, integration. Hundreds of creatures and cultures are converging throughout the empire."

"I don't need a history lesson, Solum. I knew this path would be difficult for many of the Kaji, but future generations will thank them. Already, this integration has strengthened our relationships with our allies. Which is why I chose this path. We must maintain the strength of our empire," Queen Sula says. Solum nods in agreement.

"Without the constant threat of Camille hostilities, many of our smaller allies no longer needed our protection," he says. "We would've seen far more rebellions and declaration of secession in recent seasons if not for your incentives to integrate. Now our political and economic ties are stronger than ever. But this process has been very taxing on our people."

Sula throws her hands into the air in irritation at Solum's attempts to remind her of events with which she is already intimately familiar.

"What do you think I've been doing these past two seasons?" Sula says. "I have visited twenty-five Kajian planets and orchestrated the integration of 125 different alien species. I am well aware of the integration process. What you see on this planet is happening throughout the empire."

"Are you aware that the average Kaji on this planet, our homeworld, is still adjusting to the integration, even though it's been fifteen seasons? And now, the aliens that you forced upon them are gaining citizenship and voices in front of the council. How long before they speak out against our traditions?"

"The Runx and the Kips have no qualms with our ways. Their ways are too similar to our own."

"But the Setunn will," Solum steps closer to his queen. "The majority of them are religious zealots that condemn us all to eternal damnation. What will they demand from the council?" Sula huffs at her advisor but nods her head in agreement.

"We must pay close attention to our new citizens, but it would be dishonorable to deny their rights. They are citizens of the empire. They earned a right to be heard. Besides, everyone on the council is Kaji. They will not subject their own kind to the judgment of aliens."

"Agreed, my queen." He nods his head and pushes aside the unease plaguing his mind. Sula crosses her legs and watches Solum with a mischievous smile.

"Now, tell me," she says. "How is your daughter?"

Solum raises an eyebrow at the sudden change in topic, accustomed to Sula's sporadic behavior. He looks down to hide the small smile growing as he thinks of his offspring.

"Atae is doing well. I believe her morning class at Sula Academy will begin at any moment."

Sula jumps to her feet and glides to the large window overlooking her city. "Really? Who is instructing her?"

"Feku has taught her much over the past few seasons," Solum says. He follows at Sula's side to appraise the changes that have swept through his current home.

"My son has a packmate in Feku's class. He is a fine instructor. It seems Feku has settled down a great deal since our glory days."

"I could say the same of you."

Solum chuckles, and Sula smiles at her friend as happy memories skim across her mind. Her smile falters when her memories turn bittersweet and then hemorrhage into sorrow. Slipping her royal mask back into place, Queen Sula peers out over Capital City and pushes back the uninvited emotions. It was easier to ignore the pain and emptiness when she was traveling in space and visiting other planets. But here, on her home planet, in her city, Sula has too many memories. Too many memories of him and their life together.

"King Uta would be proud of what you've done for our people," Solum whispers. Sula closes her eyes and sighs. She basks in the warm light against her face and takes comfort in Solum's words.

CHAPTER 3

In the congested merchant section of Capital City, several people pause in the busy streets to watch the asteroid light up the sky with its demise. Atae hurries past the onlookers in her path, running through the paved roads toward Sula Academy. The youngling's dark blue hair billows around her ears as the short strands struggle against her rushed pace. A decade ago, her smoky gray skin would've been considered odd, but today, she blends into the array of aliens hustling through the streets of Capital City. Her fuchsia eyes, on the other hand, are still considered unique even amongst the oddest of hybrids. But at her pace, it's hard for anyone to notice.

Determined not to be late to class again, Atae dodges between speeding transportation crafts, loaded with goods to be sold at market. Sprinting at full speed and dodging between pedestrians, she doesn't notice when the modest homes lining the streets grow to luxurious businesses. However, she does notice when the foot traffic stops in a massive crowd at the base of a large fountain. Atae stops and sighs in frustration.

Come on, this is ridiculous. Some of us have places to be. Atae complains to herself with a sour frown. A chattering crowd blocks the entire square, and Atae stretches to see above everyone and find a clear path. Her frustration grows when, even on her tiptoes, she cannot see above the crowd.

Her slim, wiry frame stopped growing upward last season, much to Atae's disappointment. Realizing her adult height will leave her a head shorter than the average Kaji female, Atae learned at an early age how to utilize her size. Today is no exception as she drops to her knees and crawls through the crowd.

Move people. One way or another, I am coming through. Atae shoulders aside the shins and feet all around her. She ignores the shouts of protest as she scrambles over toes. Several annoyed Kaji attempt to stomp and kick at her, but she whacks them hard in the shins and chuckles when they cry out in pain.

Halfway through the square, a path opens up, and Atae scurries out of the fray of legs and feet, smashing several toes in the process. One warrior connected to a few of the injured toes kicks at her but only manages to tangle her legs with his. Atae stumbles into the clear path and falls flat on her face.

Smooth. Atae groans against the pavement, more in embarrassment than pain, and closes her eyes against the dirt and debris. She can hear several chuckles as she sits up to a kneeling position, and she struggles to bite her tongue. *Ignore them. Just ignore them.*

"Does your species have no pride? Must you kneel to worship me so openly?"

Atae snaps her gaze to a youngling, maybe a season her junior, leering down at her in the middle of the path. She notices his amber eyes first. She is surprised by the hardness in his young gaze since Atae has only ever seen such guarded expressions on older, battle-hardened warriors. Then, she sees the stray locks of red in his otherwise white head of hair.

Hybrid.

His thick, cropped hair stands on end and contrasts with his caramel skin, giving the youngling a fierce aura. His broad shoulders and thin waist suggest he will grow into a strong warrior. But with a season of growth ahead of him, the male youngling stands equal in height to Atae.

I can't be late.

Atae's eyes shift past the antagonistic youngling to find a clear path through the crowd that leads to a side street past the square. Determined to reach Sula Academy on time, Atae ignores the chuckles cascading through the group at the youngling's remark. Atae grumbles with a dismissive wave as she climbs to her feet.

"Don't flatter yourself. I am Kaji, and I worship no one," she says. The crowd falls into a hushed silence as though waiting for the junior youngling to respond. Surprised by Atae's attitude and her unique eye color, the youngling's hard expression deepens as he replies with a taut voice.

"Watch your mouth, or I'll break your jaw."

Atae huffs at the brutish threat, then strides past him, much to his surprise. She pauses to glance over her shoulder at the angry youngling but stumbles at the sight of two battle beasts trotting to his side. Covered in thick fur, the four-legged creatures bare their sharp teeth in a quiet threat as their bladed tails arch over their backs, ready to strike. Atae notes the strength behind their lean, muscular forms, but also their small stature. These battle beasts are young, maybe a season or two older than Atae. The Kajian second form has several advantages, especially in battle, and many Kaji prefer to travel in their beast form. Battle beasts are common in Capital City, and she isn't impressed by their attempt to intimidate her. In fact, she's insulted, and she snarls at the group of younglings.

"Who do you think..." Atae says, but a high-pitched voice interrupts from across the square.

"I told you to leave my family alone!"

Several heads in the crowd twist toward the female voice, and Atae stretches on her tiptoes again, hoping to catch sight of the speaker. At the outskirts of the square in the direction from which Atae came, she can see the crowd moving and making room for the agitated female. A rough voice that cascades through the group berates the female.

"And we told you to leave the square. We don't want your kind selling to the royal guests. In fact, why don't you just go back to your own planet?"

Atae can't see either figure, but she knows a fight will break out soon. She falls back on her heels and sighs in disappointment.

I don't have time to stay and watch.

Atae stifles a whine as she eyes her path out of the square. The young brute at her side also struggles to see over the taller Kaji around them until he growls and starts pushing his way through the crowd and toward the two arguing citizens. To Atae's amazement, the group gives way to the younger hybrid. People fall over themselves and those around them to make room for him.

They didn't do that for me.

Atae frowns in annoyance and begins to retreat toward her destination but pauses when she realizes only one battle beast followed after the younger hybrid. The second sits in an upright position and stares at Atae with his long snout twisted into a snarl. Without thinking, she responds with an unimpressed sneer then drops the façade when she meets his gaze. His intensely silver gaze.

No way. That means…

Before she completes her thought, the battle beast snorts at her astonished expression and trots off after his packmates. Atae gapes after him in stunned silence until an inner dam breaks. Embarrassment washes over the young hybrid, staining her gray cheeks pink, as she covers her face with her hands to hide her humiliation.

Idiot.

She takes a moment to wallow and berate herself as the crowd surges past her in anticipation of the brewing fight on the other end of the square. With a heavy sigh, she sprints toward Sula Academy with silent promises to tell no one of her faux pas. It doesn't take long for Atae to arrive at Sula Academy & Research Facility, and she pauses a short distance from the building steps. Bending over to catch her breath for a moment, she searches for her friend. Jeqi stands at the foot of the steps with her back to Atae. One of Jeqi's tan hands flickers through the air as though flipping an invisible page.

Personal hologram. She's always working on something.

Jeqi retracts her arm and wraps a finger in her blonde hair while she reads. Focused on her personal hologram, she leans on one leg and props her second hand onto her hip. Jeqi's taller frame makes her lean figure look gawky and awkward, but her deliberate and controlled movements bring a sense of grace and self-assuredness. Like Atae and most Kaji younglings, Jeqi's thick hair is cropped short and points in all directions. In true Kaji fashion, the blonde locks blend into silver after a few inches, proven by the silky, silver tail wrapped around her mid-section. Sometimes, Atae envies Jeqi because, even with her tan skin and blue eyes, she tends to blend in better than Atae.

Working on an assignment at the foot of the building entrance, Jeqi does not notice her friend's arrival. With Jeqi's back to her, Atae sneaks up behind her packmate, sporting a mischievous smile. She shifts into an offensive stance and pounces into the air, flipping over her friend's head and landing with a loud thump in front of the blonde. Intent on surprising Jeqi, Atae's wide grin almost overshadows her sparkling eyes, but it fades when she realizes her packmate hasn't paused in her studies. Jeqi merely shifts to her right, so the hologram, visible only to her, can reassemble around the intruder. Atae frowns and glares at the other hybrid. Then, she wraps her arms around herself to pout.

"How'd you know?"

Without looking away from her private work, Jeqi answers in a crisp tone.

"I heard your foot scrape the ground as you prepared to jump. You always make noise when you shift your stance. You'll never beat Advisor Solum like that."

Atae huffs, and Jeqi glances up from her studies. She grimaces at the sad condition of Atae's face. The youngling's smoky gray skin is bruising over one cheekbone, and her darker lips crack open, revealing bright red blood as she smiles at Jeqi. A breeze twirls her short, blue hair and stings the dark swollen skin around one fuchsia-colored eye. In short, Atae is a mess, even for a youngling in training.

"Your face is proof of that," Jeqi says. She shakes her head as she gathers her things to stand. Her silver tail unwraps from around her waist to dawdle behind her. Despite sucking at her swollen lip, Atae holds her head high as they walk to the entrance of the academy.

"I'm getting better every day," she says.

As always, Atae is oblivious to Jeqi's tail flickering in agitation and the dark annoyance in her blue eyes, so Jeqi snaps at her packmate.

"At this rate, we'll never be allowed to enter the Gridiron."

"I'm more worried about the tournament. Yesterday, Feku said he's assigning us to packs of four. What if we get stuck with someone like Tuk?" Atae asks. She stifles a laugh while Jeqi glares at her.

"The tournament won't matter if we're not allowed to enter the Gridiron. I've held up my part of the deal. It's time for you to do the same. Defeat Solum, and we can enter whenever we choose."

"I know, I know," Atae says.

Since Jeqi's mother is not Kaji, she bares the hybrid label like Atae or any other non-full blooded Kajian. Jeqi has her mother's coloring and gentle nature, although her father's Kajian anger is more prominent at the moment. Jeqi's smaller build and soft upbringing put her at a disadvantage, but she is determined to bring honor to her family. Atae knows how important it is for her to defeat Solum and honor the deal with their parents, so she frowns with a sharp glare at her packmate but holds her tongue. When she notices Jeqi's deep concern with her progress, Atae drops her guilty gaze as they arrive at the classroom.

She's kept her end of the deal. Why can't I?

"Great, we're late again," Jeqi whispers. She shakes her head as she glances around the room. Atae curses and pales when she realizes the already seated class of 200 younglings is staring at the latecomers.

In the center of the large room, Elder Warrior Feku stands fuming at the tardy younglings. He is surrounded by row after row of student stations; each circular row is larger than the previous. The classroom is big enough to fit the entire class of younglings, and one aggravated elder warrior. Framed by an angular face, Feku's black eyes blaze with menace as he clenches his square jaw. He stands tall with broad shoulders and dark skin that contrasts with his choppy, silver hair, and his guttural voice sounds like a growl.

"I assumed you two were eaten by a clamox beast. That is the only excuse for being late. Again."

Atae stares at her feet and squirms under Feku's harsh gaze.

"It's my fault, Elder Warrior. I arrived late, and, as a good packmate, Jeqi waited for me," she says.

"Well, then you've lost two points for your tardiness, Atae," Feku says. The elder warrior touches the holographic screen surrounding him with his dark, muscular hand.

Atae watches as each occupied station receives an alert on their holographic displays, detailing her score reduction and subsequent drop in the class ranking. Jeqi dominates first position with a twenty-point lead, leaving Atae, Marqee, and Sloan to fight over the second position. Atae grumbles, knowing she will have to work extra hard today to regain her footing. Feku notices Atae's irritation and crosses his arms before smiling at her.

"Tell me of this plant, Atae," he says, "and I will award you one point."

Eager to earn back her lost points, Atae glances at the elder warrior with a small smile. Upon seeing his expression, she realizes Feku doesn't expect her to know anything about the plant displayed on every screen. Not willing to give up without at least trying, Atae walks to the center of the room. She stops next to Feku and examines the holographic image. Meanwhile, Jeqi slinks to her station and powers on her screen as her silver tail seeks safety around her waist.

The holographic image reveals a small plant with spotted petals and a stem covered in long, sharp thorns. The hologram lacks the vibrant colors of reality, but Atae recognizes the deep blue petals and the pink spots filled with pollen. Returning her gaze to the elder warrior, Atae's fuchsia eyes sparkle at her chance to shine.

CHAPTER 4

"I don't know its name, but I've seen it before," Atae says. She fidgets in front of the class and glances at Feku. The elder warrior sweeps his hand to signal for her to continue. Whipping around fast enough to rustle her cropped, blue hair, Atae addresses the class with a proud smile.

"I've seen this plant on Mount Tuki after training with my father, Advisor Solum," she says. Mentioning the private sessions always stirs up whispers of envy from her peers. After a moment, Atae continues.

"This plant is beautiful but not vulnerable. Its thorns and pollen are poisonous. One stick can paralyze an enemy for several seconds."

A purebred youngling that sits behind her snickers before speaking in a grating tone.

"What good is that? If you are so desperate in a battle to need a flower to save you, what will a few seconds do except postpone a well-deserved defeat?" the purebred says. Atae sighs at the familiar voice and twists her mouth into an annoyed frown even before her gaze reaches his smug expression.

Sloan. Ugh.

Atae rolls her eyes at the delight he takes from her annoyance. His facial muscles dance across his defined jaw and narrow cheeks as his dark eyes flitter with mischief. The taunting twist of his full lips sends several female hearts to flutter, but Atae only notices his snide, arrogant attitude that grates on her nerves. A season older than Atae, Sloan's lean frame and well-toned figure mark him as a couple of seasons from full maturity.

"Well…" Atae says. She is unprepared for the question, but she doesn't want to lose face to her rival. "I…uh…wouldn't use this in battle. It just isn't practical. But don't underestimate what a few seconds in battle could accomplish. My father told me once that battles are lost and won within just a few seconds."

Unimpressed by the name drop, Sloan arches one eyebrow. The class, on the other hand, hums with excitement at another mention of Advisor Solum. Ignoring the whispers, Atae narrows her eyes at Sloan and walks to her station next to Jeqi. After sitting, Atae notices her packmate's frantic scribbling across her holographic screen. She leans over Jeqi's tan shoulder, trying to decipher her rushed writing. Atae points her finger at a crude sketch of what looks like a fighting glove.

"What is that?" she asks. "Are those spikes?"

"Don't worry about it," Jeqi says. She swats Atae's hand away and pushes the blue-haired hybrid out of her station. Atae smirks at Jeqi's secrecy, knowing her packmate is too much of a perfectionist to discuss incomplete projects. Atae slips into her workstation as the rest of her class settles, and Feku draws everyone's ire by awarding her one point as promised.

"Well done, Atae," he says. Atae's point addition flashes across each youngling's station. Feku continues his lecture on the plant, revealing its name as the Blousq flower. Atae, still listening to the lesson, frowns as she highlights her class rank on her screen. She is one point behind Marqee and Sloan, both of whom are tied for the second position.

Atae peers at the two purebred Kaji across the room and finds them both gloating with smug expressions. Marqee is the same age as Sloan with a similar build, but Sloan's tan skin pales in comparison to Marqee's chocolate complexion. Marqee's attractive bone structure and deep dimples charm quite a bit of attention from the females in the class, especially when he smiles. But he falls short of the seductive allure of his packmate's swagger.

Atae glowers at the males, oblivious to their appeal. Sloan's constant sarcasm and antagonistic remarks over the past twelve seasons at Sula Academy have buried any inclination toward either male. Snarling under her breath, she makes it clear that they won't stay ahead for long. Every day is the same vicious fight for dominance. No one bothers to try to de-throne Jeqi from her top rank, but the second place has been up for grabs for several months. The constant battle has become tiresome, but Atae's Kajian pride won't allow her to give up.

"Don't let them get to you," a quiet voice says. Atae glances to her right to find Jent, a small, meek hybrid. He watches Atae with golden, slit eyes, his third eyelid peeking out as he blinks. Gray feathers cover his body and quiver with his slightest movement. Atae once wondered, with sympathy, if the feathers covered everything but never dared to ask. Kip hybrids are not commonplace, even in Capital City, and some Kaji find the feathers and third eyelid disconcerting. Having known Jent since she began attending Sula Academy twelve seasons ago, Atae is accustomed to his unique physiology.

Today, his third eyelid does not recede all the way, and Atae finds it unnerving. Jent quirks his head to the side with a small avian-like jerk and scrutinizes her with his golden orbs.

"What?"

"Are you feeling okay?"

Jent huffs at her, offended by the question. He blinks hard, forcing his third eyelid to retreat to its customary position, even if it is a bit slower than usual.

"I'm fine."

Jent snaps his attention back to Feku's lecture, and Atae frowns at him. Like some hybrids, Jent takes after his non-Kaji parent with his timid and reclusive tendencies. Atae is unfamiliar with the Kips since Jent is the only one she's met in person. She's uncertain whether his meek personality is a result of his parentage or a quirk. Shrugging off Jent's odd behavior, Atae returns to the lecture.

"So in what region does the Blousq flower originate, Jeqi?" Elder Warrior Feku asks. She pauses in her scribbling, peers at him with her bright blue eyes, and answers without hesitation.

"Region Alpha. Sector 2. Although, because it's stored in the POD, the Blousq flower can be found in several regions."

Nodding his head, Feku allows Jeqi to return to her work and awards her one point. The station of a purebred youngling named Tuk lights red, indicating that he has a question. All eyes are on him when he stands.

"What's the POD?"

"You should know this," Feku says. "You just learned about it last month. Is your mind incapable of storing information longer than a month, Tuk?"

When she sees Tuk pale, Atae lights her station. She waits until the elder warrior signals for her, and then she stands to explain, hoping to earn an easy point.

"It stands for the Protected Organism Database," Atae says.

"And what is it?"

"Well, it's a database. A really big one that stores and catalogs the genetic makeup of significant organisms."

"Significant organisms? What makes one organism more significant than another? Why not store them all?" Feku asks. He crosses his dark arms over his chest and leans against his station as he waits for Atae to tell him what he already knows. Familiar with Feku's teaching methods, Atae pauses to consider the question before answering. She tries to remember previous lectures on the POD.

"Resources?" she says. "It must take time and resources to gather the specimens and record their genetic makeup. And...they get their resources from...terraforming. They sell their terraforming services...which includes the organism's needed to balance the ecosystem."

That's it. Atae's eyes widen in excitement as she connects the ideas humming through her mind.

"They only collect organisms that will sell when they terraform barren planets. That way, the POD funds itself." Atae smiles at her mentor and hopes for confirmation that her hypothesis is accurate. Feku nods.

"That's a fair assessment, but only the Yasp know for sure," he says. The elder warrior motions to his station, and Atae's ranking flashes across everyone's screen with a two-point addition. When her rank jumps in front of her two rivals, Atae grins and glances at Sloan and Marqee. Marqee frowns and sits back in his chair as he grumbles at her. Sloan just flashes a crooked smile, and Atae raises her eyes in acceptance of his silent challenge.

Meanwhile, Jent wonders at something Elder Warrior Feku mentioned. "The Yasp?"

"The Yasp are G3 species. They run the POD and provide the majority of the empire's terraforming needs, including maintenance of the Gridiron," Feku says. He smirks when the level of excitement in the room doubles with the mention of the Gridiron. Dozens of stations light up with eager questions, but Feku eyes one student in particular.

"Tuk," Feku says. "Here's your chance to atone."

Tuk jumps from his station at attention. The brawny youngling is always ready for a fight but hesitates, waiting for Feku's explanation.

"Tell me, what does G3 mean?" Feku asks, and Tuk's face falls. Given the command, Tuk will attack a herd of clamox beasts but ask him to remember information from last month, and he flails.

"Uh…" He glances at his packmate, Jent, for help. But Feku's strict 'no help' policy keeps the feathered hybrid from mouthing the answers. "It…uh…has to do with…it has to do with generations. Three of them."

No, duh. Atae snorts and sits back in her chair. She sighs and glances at Jeqi while Tuk continues to babble onward. Noticing Atae's attention, Jeqi leans close to whisper.

"Why would anyone want him as a packmate? What good is muscle with no brain?"

"I guess, Jent is the brain, and Tuk is the muscle." Atae snickers, and Jeqi smiles at the jab.

"Did you hear that the royal family is back? Maybe you'll get to meet them," Jeqi says. Atae wrinkles her nose at her packmate.

"I doubt it. Solum doesn't tell me anything about his work."

"Do you ever ask?"

"That's not the point," Atae says. She glances back to Feku as he admonishes Tuk for his ignorance. When a thought occurs to her, Atae snaps her attention back to Jeqi.

"Although, their arrival would explain why Father left home early this morning. We didn't even have time for our morning training session," Atae says. Jeqi's eyebrows knit together in concern as she motions to Atae's bruised cheek and split lip.

"Your injuries," she says. "They aren't from this morning?"

"Anyone else care to try an answer? What does G3 mean?" Feku asks the class before Atae can answer Jeqi's question. Most of the stations light up, much to Tuk's chagrin. When Feku motions for Sloan to answer, Atae sits up in her chair and glowers at her rival from across the room. Sloan glances at Atae from the corner of his eye, delighting in her aggravation.

"It means that for every generation of Kaji that is born and then dies, three generations of Yasp are born and die. They have shorter life spans than we do, by about two thirds," Sloan says.

"And how many G1 species exist?"

"Five, Elder Warrior. The Setunn, the Kips, the Runx, the Camille, and, of course, the most powerful and handsome, the Kaji." Sloan flashes a teasing glance at one female student, and she giggles. Feku ignores the youngling's typical behavior and remains focused on his lesson.

"And where does the loyalty of each species lie?"

"Well, they've all signed peace treaties with the Kaji Empire."

"That's not what I asked," Feku says. Sloan's brow falls, and his playful expression twists into a severe frown.

Atae enjoys the irritation crawling across her rival's face, but she's surprised to see it. One of Sloan's most aggravating skills is hiding the expressions and emotions he doesn't want others to see. Atae is never sure if her barbs or arguments affect him because he hides behind a mask of sarcasm.

Why does this question bother him? Atae wonders as she watches him cross his arms over his chest. When Sloan answers Feku, he speaks in a controlled tone with a blank face that sets Atae on edge.

"No one trusts the Camille. The treaty is still too new. The others maintain an allegiance to the Kaji Empire as a whole, but each colony, no matter their species, allies with the crest that fits their needs," Sloan says. Atae bites her lip as she studies Sloan's odd behavior. She's never seen this guarded demeanor from him.

Elder Warrior Feku huffs at Sloan's political answer but adds two points to his class ranking. Atae fumes as her rank slips below Sloan. Expecting her rivals to taunt their victory from across the room, Sloan surprises Atae when he sits back and glares at Feku. Marqee leans toward his packmate and whispers something. Sloan shrugs his shoulders and snaps back in a hushed voice.

Why isn't he celebrating? Why isn't he rubbing it in my face? Atae huffs at their odd behavior.

"The twelve Crests of Kaji rule the twelve regions of the empire," Feku begins but pauses. Sadness creeps into the room as the class recognizes his mistake.

"Eleven," Sloan says. "There's only eleven left now."

"Eleven bloodlines and eleven regions." Feku nods and takes a moment to recollect his thoughts. When he continues the lecture, Atae leans closer to Jeqi.

"What happened to the twelfth one?" Atae asks. Surprised by the questions, Jeqi gawks at her.

"It was destroyed during the war. Hasn't Solum told you about it?"

"No, why would he?" Atae says with a shrug. "The Camille managed to destroy an entire bloodline? One of the crests? How?"

"They destroyed the entire region."

CHAPTER 5

Solum, taking advantage of the cool evening, stands on rocky terrain high on Mount Tuki, a common training ground for young warriors. Several steps away, the rock face drops into a three-story cliff and ends in a valley of jagged stone that once formed the tip of the great mountain. Solum glances at the cliff edge before returning his attention to the wild vegetation across from him. He crosses his arms over his chest and lifts his head with a sigh as he waits. The royal advisor doesn't need to close his eyes nor concentrate on hearing the wildlife around him. With ease, he listens to birds chirping, rodents rustling for dinner, and even creatures ripping into the doomed carcasses of their evening meal. The wilds ignore Solum just as he ignores it until all goes quiet. Even a chattering bird in the distance falls silent, and Solum smiles.

Atae bursts from a small patch of vegetation at Solum's back. In one fluid motion, the youngling lurches from her hiding spot and leaps from boulder to boulder until she reaches her target, then Atae attempts a well-planned jab to Solum's kidney. He is not quick enough to dodge the spry youngling, but he blocks the attack with a well-placed elbow. With speed earned from performing the technique hundreds of times a day for seasons, Atae rebounds from the older warrior. She lands on a nearby boulder, placing her above Solum and just out of reach of a counterattack. The youngling snaps into a defensive stance, causing the stone underneath her to rumble threateningly.

Solum swings his leg around and destroys the boulder with a colossal strike of his heel. Unable to keep her footing as the rock crumbles underneath, Atae flails to the ground and lands in a crouch. Solum flings himself toward his attacker and barrels a massive fist into her abdomen. Anticipating his predictable response, the youngling leaps into the air with practiced ease and, with perfect timing, lands on his outstretched arm. Her weight redirects Solum's momentum, forcing his dark fist into the ground. Atae rolls, returning to a crouch a few steps away. Without waiting for her to recover, Solum lunges for the youngling, and she spins to face him. He lashes out and lands a hard jab to her midsection, knocking the wind out of her. Following up with a punch to her face, Solum forces Atae to stumble backward. He continues with a few vicious strikes, propelling the youngling back with each blow. After pushing her to the edge of the cliff, Solum stops his assault long enough to shift his weight and plant a hard side kick into her ribcage. The force of the attack shoves the hybrid over the precipice.

Atae panics and flails against the cliff wall, trying to slow her descent, but the youngling free falls, flipping head over heel down the rock face and into the valley below. Solum cringes as his daughter lands face down in the jagged pile of rubble. Searching for movement, he peeks over the edge, but Atae lies still at the bottom with a cloud of dust swelling around her.

It won't take her long.

Solum sits on the edge of the cliff to squint out into the bright sky. Of Planet Kaji's three stars, only Sul remains above the horizon at this hour. He enjoys a few moments of relaxation as he watches the red sun persist along its endless journey. A rare smile touches Solum's lips as he remembers how few sunsets he watched throughout his life. He muses over the changes he faced throughout the last seventeen seasons, changes that left him with little time for such trivialities as sunsets. After a few moments, Solum glances down to check on the most significant source of change and finds her gone. He frowns and scans the valley, but the vegetation and boulders make his search difficult.

Focused on finding Atae, Solum almost misses the sound of a large stone shifting behind him. He spins around in time to catch a small, gray leg with his outstretched hand and flings the rest of the youngling over the cliff edge, again. This time, Atae is quicker and snatches the towering warrior's wrist just as he releases her leg. Unprepared for the jolt of her momentum, Solum topples over the cliff with her. He snags the edge with a firm grip, holding himself and the youngling at bay. The larger warrior peers down to see her rosy eyes dance with amusement, despite her one swollen eye. Atae smiles with an open mouth as she pants from the vigorous training session.

"I got you."

Solum snorts at her claim and jerks the arm Atae holds in her grip, forcing her to wobble below him. "You think so?"

Atae giggles at his antics then plants her feet against the wall of the rock face and pulls. Solum's eyes widen as he realizes her intent, but with nothing to grasp for leverage, he cannot stop her. They both tumble down the cliff in a free fall. Atae twists to position her smaller stature above the larger warrior and uses his body to absorb the rough landing. The two Kaji land with a loud crash, sending dust and rubble flying in all directions.

Atae lays sprawled across Solum's massive form with her black uniform ripped and splattered with blood. As the dirt settles, the youngling lifts her head from the older warrior's chest. Coughing, she clears the dust from her lungs and peers down into Solum's face. He groans, and Atae giggles again. Solum cracks an eyelid to see his delighted daughter watching him, and he closes his eye again with an audible sigh.

After a few moments, Atae lays her head against Solum's chest. Content to listen to her father's heartbeat for a time, she closes her eyes and rests her exhausted body. Solum opens his eyes and peers into the sky, no longer seeing Sul dance behind the clouds. Instead, he considers the encroaching changes that the future promises and cringes. Solum slips a protective arm around Atae's back, and she grins.

"Father?" Atae's quiet voice interrupts Solum's thoughts, and he grunts in acknowledgment, still staring above.

"I defeated you," she says.

"Your point?"

"Jeqi and I get to choose when we enter the Gridiron, now."

"That was the deal."

"Will you be disappointed if we don't enter with the rest of our class at Sula Academy?"

"Why wouldn't you compete with your class?" Solum asks.

"Jeqi wants to enter the Gridiron with the prince," she explains. "So, we have to wait to see when he will enter."

"I expect our queen will schedule her son's pledging ceremony within the next few months. We can start planning then."

Atae nods and sits up to free Solum. Climbing to his feet, he watches his daughter sway until she steadies herself with a hand against the ground. She blinks a few times, then stands without an issue, sporting a broad smile. Solum studies her bruised face and the subtle favoring of her side, where he kicked her off the mountain. At her father's odd behavior, Atae's smile twists into a concerned expression, and she drops her gaze, running her hands over her arms.

"What's wrong?" she asks.

"Was this battle too taxing?" he asks sternly.

"No!"

"If our training regimen is becoming too difficult to maintain, how do you expect to survive the Gridiron?" he says. Atae scowls at him and raises her head in defiance.

"I'm fine, Father."

"Sula Academy's Tournament will begin next month. It will be a good indicator of your current abilities. I expect you to perform admirably."

Atae's mouth curves into a smirk as she jams her hands onto her hips. "Admirably? I'm going to win."

Solum chuckles as he leads Atae toward home. He remembers the naïve arrogance of youth and the ruckus it caused within his small pack. Uta, Roga, Sula, Feku, and Solum were quite the troublemakers in their day. That was before the sobriety of war, and before the Camille took everything dear to them. Solum's humorous mood sours with his thoughts. Atae is skilled for a Kaji her age, hybrid or purebred, but she is far more naïve than he would like. Still, he dreads the day her charming innocence is stripped away. The day she enters the Gridiron. The tournament will challenge Atae and help her fine-tune her skills, but the Gridiron will change her. If she survives, that is. If she comes home, she will come back different. She will be a warrior and a citizen of the Kaji Empire. A small pit tightens in Solum's chest, and he frowns at the unfamiliar feeling.

CHAPTER 6

Solis dances alone in the sky, too early for Cerule to enter the galactic stage. Solis' red rays of sunshine warm Atae's bruised skin and dry her already cracking lips. The cool morning breeze rustles her hair as she lies sleeping in the small clearing. Mount Tuki is alive with morning wildlife, but the sounds of the surrounding forest are not enough to wake Atae. However, Jeqi's swift kick to the ribs is more than enough to jar her friend from slumber.

"Argh." Atae jumps up to clutch her side. Jeqi's amused grin twists to concern at her packmate's painful reaction. She crouches to place her hand on Atae's shoulder as the blonde's tail flicks behind her.

"Let me see," Jeqi says. Atae jerks away from her packmate.

"I'm fine. Just a few bruises from last night's training session."

Rejecting her excuse, Jeqi tugs at Atae's uniform until her friend reveals bruised and beaten ribs. Jeqi's tail twitches in curiosity as she analyzes the damage. The blonde notes the dark bruising, the swollen tissue, and the scabbing cuts and gashes over Atae's ribs.

"Tsk." Jeqi rolls her eyes and drops Atae's shirt. "This is minor damage, Atae. I remember when Marqee broke your arm during a sparring session. You still managed to defeat him. A broken rib or two shouldn't even register on your pain threshold."

"Well, it does," Atae says. She climbs to her feet while hiding her discomfort from the other students arriving for class.

"How'd that happen anyway, Atae? Forget to block a sidekick again?" Jeqi asks. She strolls to the edge of the clearing, and Atae scowls at her packmate as she follows her to a large tree.

"No," Atae says. She sighs at Jeqi's crabby tone and impatient attitude, her norm as of late. They both lean against the massive trunk and watch the surrounding students.

"It probably happened when I got kicked off the mountain face last night."

"Side kicked?"

Atae huffs at her packmate's comment but doesn't argue. Instead, she watches in irritation as Marqee and Sloan arrive. Both purebred males saunter into the small clearing with arrogance rolling off them in waves. Sloan raises an eyebrow and winks at a group of female students that catch his eye. They explode into a fit of giggles, and Atae twists her face in disgust.

"Last night?" Jeqi asks, interrupting Atae's thoughts.

"What?"

"Your injury happened last night? It looks fresher than that," Jeqi says. She twirls a strand of blonde hair around one finger as she surveys her surroundings and notes which of her classmates have arrived.

"Does it?" Atae shrugs. "No, it definitely happened last night. No training this morning. Father was gone before I awoke. That's why I was able to get here early for once."

"And fell asleep in broad daylight where any enemy could've found you."

Atae frowns but bites her tongue. She knows that Jeqi is right to scold her. Giving in to any level of exhaustion is inexcusable. Atae doesn't know how she let it happen. One moment she was meditating and listening to the wildlife, the next moment, Jeqi was kicking her awake. Atae remembers being tired but not exhausted. Even now, she takes a deep breath to combat the fog that clouds her mind.

But what should I expect after such a groundbreaking triumph?

Atae hadn't meant to fall asleep, but warriors have died in the Gridiron due to smaller mistakes. She wonders if Jeqi's confidence in her is wavering. In an attempt to reassure her packmate, Atae opens her mouth to announce her victory over Solum. But before she can, Jeqi continues.

"Advisor Solum doesn't miss many training sessions with you."

"Only when something big is happening at the palace or regarding royal affairs. Why?"

Surprised by her packmate's suspicious tone, Jeqi glances back to find Atae watching her.

"I'm just worried that the prince will participate in the Gridiron before you ever defeat your father," Jeqi says.

Atae scoffs and jerks away from her friend. "Why do you insist on participating with the prince anyway?"

Jeqi whips her head around to Atae, and her cool-blue eyes melt into scorching flames. Her tail puffs to twice its size and stiffens with anger. Atae can't help but squirm under the blonde hybrid's attention.

"You may be ready to let the Gridiron decide your fate," Jeqi says, "but I want to be appointed a specialist. You know the best way to do that is to be named a royal companion."

Atae nods, avoiding eye contact, and hunches her shoulders in a submissive posture to appease her packmate.

"And the quickest way to earn the title is to fight by the prince's side in the Gridiron. Got it," Atae says. Jeqi blinks, and her tail relaxes along with the rest of her form. She shakes her head, tucks her tail around her waist, and peers back at the clearing.

Atae watches Jeqi for a moment, concerned about her aggressive behavior. Most Kaji are temperamental and antagonistic, but Jeqi's Setunn pedigree bestows a healthy balance and tight control over her temper. Usually. Elder Warrior Feku should be arriving at any moment to begin class, so Jeqi tugs on the silver studs in both her ear lobes. Recognizing the minuscule reflections in Jeqi's eyes, Atae follows suit.

When Atae activates her visual visor with her own pair of silver studs, a hologram only visible to Atae populates in front of her. The personal hologram analyzes Atae's environment and highlights points of interaction, such as Jeqi's visual visor. The corner of Atae's mouth quirks up as a thought crackles across her mind, and she waves her hands in a memorized pattern that activates her visor's communication app.

A keyboard bursts into existence, but only Atae can see and use it. As she types out a message, Atae shoots Jeqi an innocent look. Then she sweeps her arm to toss the note at the blue-eyed hybrid. Jeqi's visor flashes with confirmation on Atae's hologram, and Jeqi flicks her fingers to open the message now visible only to her:

'I guess it's a good thing that I defeated Solum last night.'

Jeqi's eyes light up with eagerness, and her silver tail jolts to life. "What? You defeated him?"

Atae can see Jeqi's desperate need to confirm her announcement, so she gives a lopsided grin and shrugs. Jeqi opens her mouth to congratulate her friend, but the chatter from the surrounding group of students plummets into silence. Dropping their conversation, for now, Atae and Jeqi glance around to investigate the sudden change. Elder Warrior Feku stops in the center of the clearing, surveying the crowd with his dark, perceptive gaze. He scrutinizes each of his students as his dark skin absorbs the morning light, and his silver hair reflects it. Atae's eyesight is momentarily impaired when every student in the clearing activates their visual visors. Her personal hologram highlights each activated visor as points of interaction. Since the hologram can only identify interaction points within eyesight, visors active within the city walls are not available for communication.

"Why are we here?" Feku asks. Every visual visor in the clearing lights up as eager students hope to earn an easy point. It's Atae's visor that glows gold when chosen to answer via Feku's visual visor.

"To learn, Elder Warrior," Atae says. Anticipating a point addition, she flashes a smug glance to Marqee and Sloan over her shoulder. Marqee sighs, and Sloan nods at her with a sarcastically chipper smile.

"To learn what, Atae?" Feku asks.

Atae furrows her brow in uncertainty and scans the clearing for inspiration. "To learn about wildlife?"

"Not good enough." Feku shakes his head, spearing Atae with disappointment. "Jeqi?"

Atae ignores the snickering from nearby students, specifically Marqee and Sloan, and focuses her attention on Jeqi. The hybrid's blue eyes bounce across the display of her hologram, but when he calls her name, she wipes away her distraction to pay Feku the respect he deserves. Jeqi spouts off the answer as though it were common knowledge.

"We are here to learn how to survive the Gridiron."

"That is correct," Feku says. He nods, and the names of the five top-ranked students flash across everyone's visors with an additional point, further securing Jeqi's top position. Atae only has a moment to take pride in Jeqi's performance before a visor lights up to indicate a question. Feku signals with his visor for Tuk to ask his question.

"But I thought we were preparing for the tournament? It's only a few weeks away. It'll be months before our class enters the Gridiron."

"Anyone care to explain?" Feku asks. Once again, the majority of the visors light up. He chooses a hybrid with green hair to answer, and she speaks in a gravelly voice.

"The Gridiron is our ultimate goal, but the tournament dictates which of us will enter the Gridiron as representatives of Sula Academy. It's like our final exam, and the Gridiron is graduation."

"I doubt your graduation ceremonies from previous courses were this celebrated nor dangerous. Representing Sula Academy in the Gridiron has been a death sentence for a handful of young warriors. Why would anyone want to do it?" Feku asks. The green-haired youngling snaps a hand to her hip and smirks at the elder warrior while Atae bites her lip and struggles to remember her name.

"Because we are the best of the best," she says. Feku chuckles and awards her one point. Atae recognizes her name, Trinka, when it pops up on her visor in twenty-fourth place.

"Does anyone know what to expect from the upcoming tournament?" Feku asks. Again, every visual visor in the clearing lights up with eagerness. A purebred with dark, beady eyes framed by white and red locks, named Debil, answers with a throaty voice after her visor glows gold.

"My brother competed three seasons ago. He said the tournament had four rounds designed to test each participant's strength. The entire class entered, but only the top performers advanced in each round. I think the thirty highest ranked students from round four were chosen that season."

"I heard her brother didn't make it past round two," Atae whispers to Jeqi. She watches Debil slip past a few students to stand next to Sloan and Marqee. Jeqi waves away her personal hologram long enough to glance at the dark female and shrug.

"That didn't stop him from entering the Gridiron along with the Sula competitors."

"Really? You can do that? How did he do?" Atae asks. Jeqi nods at her as she reactivates her hologram.

"It's not recommended," she says, fiddling with her screen. "He didn't have any of the perks that come with representing Sula Academy, and he didn't survive. It's to be expected. If you fail the tournament, you're not likely to survive the Gridiron."

Atae grimaces at the grave news. When she peers back at Debil, Atae notices something odd about her expression. Debil's thin smile seems fragile, and her eyes are glassy with unshed tears. Atae can see the wavering dam holding back Debil's emotions but has no idea how to help or if she should try. Debil isn't her packmate, merely a fellow student. Their recent interactions were limited to competitive maneuvers to earn the most points from Feku. Atae dominated each opportunity and never considered Debil a threat. She certainly never realized Debil's family history with the Gridiron. As Atae considers how this new information should affect her opinion of the purebred, Sloan leans down to whisper something into the dark female's ear, and Debil's smile grows genuine.

Never mind. Atae scowls as her distaste for Sloan spews onto her opinion of Debil.

"That's right," Feku continues. "There will be four rounds, and only the top competitors will advance. All two hundred of you will enter round one, but only the best fifty of round four will represent Sula Academy in the Gridiron. Each round of the tournament is designed to test your limits. It will be the most difficult competition you can imagine, but it will not compare to the hardships awaiting you in the Gridiron."

Debil's dark eyes shimmer, but she sets her jaw and slips closer to Sloan. He flashes a suggestive grin at her, and she returns a coy expression, happy for the extra attention from the attractive male. Unimpressed by Debil's thirty-fifth ranking that flashes across everyone's hologram, Atae glances at the dark female as the remaining class continues with Feku's questionnaire.

The moment she escapes the spotlight, Debil releases the breath she held and sags into a slouch. Even though the class has yet to do anything strenuous, Debil seems tired. Atae furrows her brow but shrugs off her puzzlement when Sloan catches her watching and slips an arm around Debil. Their eyes meet, and Atae wonders at his protective response. Then, as though answering her question, Sloan's expression twists into a steamy invitation that would make any other female blush. When Atae rolls her eyes and flips back to Feku, Sloan chuckles at the expected response and tightens his arm around Debil.

"If the Gridiron is so deadly, why would anyone want to participate?" Feku asks. He glances around the class of future warriors and selects Marqee to answer.

"Well, one reason is for the honor. Only the strongest warriors survive the Gridiron." Marqee flashes a smug smile, and Sloan sneers at Atae. Feku ignores his students' posturing and lifts two fingers.

"And the second reason?"

"The second reason is for citizenship. All survivors are awarded citizenship in the Kaji Empire. Warriors from all over the galaxy participate in the Gridiron in hopes of earning their citizenship."

"Good." Feku rewards Marqee with one point, after which, Sloan gives a congratulatory arm punch to his packmate. When both purebred Kaji eyeball Atae with pleased expressions, she crosses her arms and scoffs at them.

"But what does citizenship mean?" Feku asks.

This time only a handful of visors light up. Even though she is still three points ahead of Marqee, Atae refuses to give up any ground. So she makes sure her visor is among the handful and smiles when Feku chooses her to answer.

"Citizenship opens up a lot of opportunities. It allows warriors to become officers of the empire and to specialize. Citizens are also allowed to submit concerns regarding imperial policies to the royal council. In essence, they have a voice in the empire," she says. The elder warrior nods, and Atae raises a cocky eyebrow at Marqee and Sloan. After rewarding Atae with a single point, Feku continues.

"Why is the Gridiron so dangerous?" He scans the clearing as almost all the visors light up. Feku stops his coal-black eyes on a youngling named Seva. She can pass for a purebred Kajian with her dark skin and blood red hair, too short to fade into white. But her golden eyes reveal a stain in her bloodline. Atae follows Feku's line of sight and notices that Seva's visor is one of the few not lit. In fact, she doesn't seem to be paying attention to the lesson. Seva stands at the edge of the clearing with her shoulders slouched and head hanging low. The only sign that the youngling is conscious is her standing position and open eyes. Even from a distance, Atae can see the dark circles under Seva's unfocused gaze. Seva is the epitome of exhaustion.

Atae watches Feku and expects him to berate Seva for showing such weakness. She anticipates a comment about how Seva would already be dead if they were in the Gridiron. Instead, he shifts his calculating gaze to Sloan. After his visor signals, the tall youngling cocks a hip and answers with a smirk.

"Because of warriors like me."

The entire class bursts into snickers, and the elder warrior sighs at the arrogant youngling before settling a stern gaze on Sloan.

"What is the number one killer in the Gridiron?"

Knowing a serious answer is the only acceptable response at this point, Sloan thinks for a moment. "Hunger?"

"Close. That's the second-highest kill rate. Atae?"

"The wildlife." Atae echoes her first answer with a small, abashed smile.

"And what's so dangerous about wildlife when there are warriors like Sloan running around?" Feku asks.

The class cascades into another fit of giggles while Atae glances at Sloan with a snide answer. "Because warriors like Sloan never learn which wildlife will kill him and which wildlife will save him."

"And that will be our focus today. Each Gridiron is different with unique environments and wildlife, but there are always a few common elements. You're bound to find plenty of Blousq flowers and clamox beasts in every Gridiron. So I'm certain you'll come across them in the tournament," Feku says. He awards Atae a single point, and she beams. The hybrid flashes a smug smile over her shoulder at both her rivals. Sloan shrugs and squeezes Debil's shoulders with a sly smile, while Marqee twists his lips into a pout and snubs the blue-haired youngling.

Elder Warrior Feku signals for the class to follow him through the forest as he discusses plants and animals of importance. Jeqi and Atae fall to the back of the group to observe in silence. Not long into the lecture, Atae notices that Jeqi is focused on her personal hologram as she has been the entire class. She nudges her packmate and whispers so as not to attract Feku's attention.

"What are you doing?"

Jeqi waves her away. "Don't worry about it."

Feeling a sense of déjà vu, Atae shrugs and shifts her attention back to the lesson. She opts to squeeze between fellow younglings to garner a better view. Meanwhile, the group pushes between trees and brushes, passing a rock slab that almost reaches the top of Mount Tuki.

As Atae ebbs closer to the front of the class, the group stops to watch Feku handle a clamox hiding in a cave off the rock slab. Atae slows her pace in an attempt to quiet her steps and refrain from drawing the elder warrior's attention. A misstep lands her on a patch of gravel, and the scrape of the shifting pebbles distracts some nearby younglings, but thankfully, not Feku. Unfortunately, it's loud enough to attract Sloan's attention.

Never one to pass up an opportunity to drag down his competition, Sloan glides forward and swings his right leg under Atae. Focused on remaining silent, Atae doesn't notice Sloan's attack until it's too late. The noise that Sloan makes during his attack is minute compared to the orchestra of sounds and cursing that echoes from Atae. He sweeps Atae's legs out from under her, and she lands face first in the gravel. Feku glances up from his demonstration on the best way to capture a clamox beast just in time to witness Atae clamoring to her feet.

When her visor flashes a two-point deduction from her class ranking, Atae snarls at Sloan. He wiggles his eyebrows as his dark eyes dance over a satisfied smirk. Feeling safe from retaliation due to Feku's proximity, Sloan's sarcastic finger wave adds to Atae's wounded pride, and he chuckles at her aggravation.

Arrogant bastard.

Taking a deep breath, Atae pushes her rage to the back of her mind and focuses on the lecture. She watches as Feku holds a beast three times her size in one hand.

A clamox is a massive arachnid that spends half of every season incubating thousands of eggs. Its eight muscular legs are longer than Atae and meet at the enormous abdomen, which harbors its precious offspring. A thick coat of brown fur protects its fat belly and the sack of eggs snuggled close. The clamox's hairless head features large arachnid eyes and mucus-covered fangs. Horns extend from the beast's boney forehead to ward off enemies aiming for its unprotected neck. With enough muscle and bone to outweigh a small Kaji, a clamox can be a worthy foe to the untrained. Feku holds the creature by the base of its skull at such an angle that the horns run parallel to the elder warrior's arm.

Atae listens to Feku explain the best way to track the creature. She learns that a clamox hide can be used for warmth or shelter, and its meat can feed a Kaji youngling for a few days. The bite of a clamox is venomous with an extremely painful but short-lived toxin. Atae makes a mental note not to let one bite her before a few of her whispering classmates distract her from the lecture.

"My parents saw the ship land in the outer parameter of the city. I overheard them reporting to the city guards," Marqee says, his black eyes flashing with excitement. Debil huffs in annoyance, trying to hide the fatigue behind her dark eyes.

"It's probably just a royal ship transporting the royal family," she says.

"But it wasn't a Kajian spaceship. Why would they travel in an alien ship?" Marqee says.

"It could be an alien race looking to abduct unsuspecting citizens for inappropriate probing..." Sloan says. He offers Debil another playful grin, and she tries to hide her blush with a smile. Next to her, Seva lifts her sagging head and speaks with feverish speed.

"It's probably the Camille planning a sneak attack. I wouldn't put it past that filthy scum. My father told me countless stories of their treachery and dishonor in battle." Seva's energy fades again as Debil slips an arm over her packmate's shoulders.

"There hasn't been a firefight with the Camille Empire since before we were born. Why would they start now?" Debil says.

When no one offers a reasonable explanation, Atae decides to make an important point. "If a Camille ship intent on inciting another intergalactic war landed on the Kaji Empire's base of operations, don't you think every Kajian in the city would know by now?"

Marqee glares at Atae for her intrusion, but Sloan twists his mouth and raises an indifferent eyebrow. Debil, on the other hand, considers Atae's claim.

"Hmm, that's true. It would be the biggest news since the peace treaty was announced." A small, sly smile slips across Debil's face. "What if it's a fugitive from another planet looking for a place to hide?"

"Who would seek shelter on the capital planet of the most feared warriors in the galaxy?" Marqee asks.

"Maybe they crash-landed," Debil says.

"Has anyone thought to ask Jent? His father oversees Capital City's flight plans. Maybe he overheard something?" Atae says. All the younglings listening search the group for the Kip hybrid.

"I don't think he's here," Marqee says.

"I haven't seen him since yesterday," Debil admits.

Before the younglings can discuss the matter further, Feku signals for the class to continue forward. The group obeys, and the elder warrior describes harmless plants on their path through the forest. One such plant is the Jassell tree, and Atae smiles as they pass one, feeling a kind of kinship with the unique tree. She pauses to place her hand on the trunk as the rest of the class continues on their path. Her gray skin almost blends into the dark gray, knotted tree bark. The hybrid notices something small and light brush against her, and she pulls a leaf from her thick mane. Spinning the fallen foliage between her fingers, Atae smiles at the familiar color. As a bud, the leaf shines with a bright blue hue, and with age, it darkens to a shade almost identical to Atae's hair until it falls lifeless from the tree. Atae drops the dark blue leaf as Jeqi steps up beside her.

Atae glances at her packmate and signals for them to catch up. She follows Jeqi's much stealthier lead and squeezes between classmates until they reach the front of the class. Jeqi stops at the edge of the crowd encircling Feku, and Atae peers over her packmate's shoulder. In the center of the circle, a warrior eater hangs above Elder Warrior Feku.

The warrior eater is a flower the size of a small Kaji that hangs at the top of the forest canopy. Its large petals reach between trees and disappear into the canopy, and the center of the flower hosts massive, dangerous thorns. Between them are sprouts of vines that hang to the forest floor.

"The warrior eater, as most Kaji call it, is a carnivorous plant," Feku says. "It impales unsuspecting prey with its large thorns at its stalk and absorbs the nutrients. The corpses of its prey are left behind for scavengers and fungi." The elder warrior points to the enormous plant above then to a few bones lying on the forest floor. A visor to Atae's left lights up and, after Feku signals, Sloan speaks.

"How does it impale its prey if the thorns are way up there? Sparkling dust and happy thoughts of murder?"

Gawking at his packmate, Marqee whispers, "Sparkling dust and happy thoughts? Where do you come up with this crap?"

"It's a gift."

Atae can't help the small chuckle that escapes, and Sloan glances at her with a side smirk before refocusing on the elder warrior.

"Like this," Feku says. He unsheathes his blade and walks directly under the warrior eater. The moment he touches the vines, they wrap around him and drag him toward the thorns above, constricting his arms and legs. Fortunately, no amount of wrapping can keep him from twisting his wrist around and slicing through the vine around his arms. Another swipe of his blade frees his legs, and he falls to the ground moments before the large petals close, ready to absorb the nutrients of its latest prey.

The entire class is in awe of the elder warrior and clamors around him to ask questions. After taking a few moments to explain that avoiding the vines is the best way to elude the warrior eater, Feku signals for them to move on to their next subject. The rest of the day is spent learning about creatures that may or may not be in the Gridiron and the best way to handle them. As Solis and Cerule dip below the horizon and Sul is sure to peak out soon, Feku announces the end of class. The entire group of younglings mosey down toward the base of Mount Tuki and escape to their respective homes. Along the way, Jeqi's silver tail thrashes behind her, and she decides to grill Atae.

"Tell me. How did you do it?"

Atae grins at her packmate, glad to see Jeqi in a better mood.

"Well, do you remember Feku's lesson last week about natural talents?"

"You mean about how some warriors are naturally stronger or faster than others?"

"Right. Well, I noticed that night during our evening training session that Father has natural strength," Atae says. Jeqi peers at her friend with a dubious frown.

"Of course, he has natural strength. Do you think he became the queen's royal advisor because of his personality?"

Atae punches her friend in the shoulder with a scowl.

"Ow." Jeqi rubs her shoulder, and the fur on her tail stands on end. "I mean come on, Atae. You've trained with him every morning and evening since you were two. That's fifteen seasons of personalized training, and twelve of those included lessons at Sula. How did you not know he was an above-average warrior?"

"Shut up." Atae's cheeks burn red with embarrassment, and Jeqi giggles.

"I guess you got suspicious when you were the top fighter in your class?"

"Well, yeah. I mean, I could never get close to Father before. Feku really opened my eyes to different strategies and techniques," Atae says. Her voice radiates with admiration for her lessons instructor, and Jeqi nods in understanding.

"That's when he told you about your natural speed, right?"

"And agility," Atae says. "He said that my technique was based on raw force and power that I just didn't have."

"That makes sense since you learned most of your fighting skills from Solum. He's all about raw force."

"Right, so Feku suggested that I concentrate more on using speed attacks and outmaneuvering my target, rather than overpowering it."

"Well, it sounds like he was right. How did you do it?" Jeqi asks. Atae dives into the incredible tale of her triumph. She makes sure to exaggerate where appropriate and acts out significant scenes as any youngling her age would do. They both giggle in the end when they reach the bottom of the mountain.

Jeqi halts and scans the area around them until she finds a small figure in the distance. She frowns, then dips her head to focus on something flashing across her personal hologram. After a moment, she sighs in annoyance.

"Mother is waiting for me."

"Why? She never picks you up from lessons," Atae says.

"I don't know, but she says that you are to meet with Solum for your evening lessons immediately. She forbids you from stopping or socializing along the way," Jeqi says, reading from the message her mother sent via the visual visor.

Both younglings shrug and say their goodbyes before Atae treks back up Mount Tuki. Heeding Deh's warning, Atae dashes up the side of the mountain, dodging between trees and jumping from boulder to boulder. Upon her arrival at their designated training spot, she expects to find Advisor Solum waiting for her but receives a digital message on her visor instead. She takes a moment to catch her breath, irritated when it takes longer than usual, and curses at her weakness. Atae activates the message with a simple command, and a note from Solum flashes across her holographic screen:

'Warm up. I'll be there soon.'

Atae smirks at the very Solum note, simple and to the point. Knowing that she better be ready to work by the time Solum arrives, Atae switches off her visor and dives into her warm-up.

CHAPTER 7

The next day, Solum stomps through the palace halls with a deep frown. His shadow stretches across a jeweled depiction of a sly assassin slipping past enemy lines. The bloody murder is engraved into the white stoned walls, but Solum ignores the gruesome scene. He squeezes his fists and bites back a growl of frustration. The few servants in his path scamper away at the sight of his angry posture.

It's impossible. Solum halts in front of the throne room doors and pauses to calm his temper and clear his mind. He stares at the winged battle beast engraved into the massive doors. The large crest has always helped to calm his mind and focus on the task at hand. How many times has Queen Sula interrupted his duties for an impromptu conversation?

Too many to count. The corners of Solum's mouth quirk up as his frustration ebbs. Usually, Sula's interruptions are welcomed and appreciated. His work can be tedious and repetitive at times, and Sula can be an entertaining host. But today is not a day for fun and games. Today has been a challenge, and Solum is struggling to control the urge to destroy something. With a sigh, he waves at the guards on duty to open the throne room doors.

Solum finds Queen Sula perched on her throne, holding several metal blades. She twirls one dagger between her fingers and eyes Solum with a mischievous smile. As he strolls toward the wild-haired queen with a respectful posture, she flings a knife at him. Solum doesn't flinch when the blade whistles past him and thumps into a wooden target perched next to the entrance. Sula frowns at her packmate's lack of reaction before releasing another blade. This time the dagger strikes the marble floor a finger's width from Solum's left foot. Again, he doesn't flinch or halt in his advancement toward the throne.

"There was a time when you would have picked up that blade and thrown it back at my face. You just aren't any fun anymore," Sula says. Solum stops a courteous distance from the throne and purses his lips at her.

"That was before you became queen and mother to the future king."

"Oh, yes. You wouldn't want to disrespect your queen, now would you? Instead, you let her die of boredom." Sula lies over the arm of her throne, like she's wasting away as they speak. Solum bites back the amused smile threatening his lips.

"I'm sure there are other ways to entertain yourself, my queen," he says. *Perhaps this break will do me some good.*

"Like listening to rumors of a rogue ship landing on my planet, just outside my city walls?" Sula's cold tone and placid expression slaps Solum like a splash of icy water.

Damn it.

"Rumors," he says. "Unsubstantiated."

"Are you certain?" Sula asks. She sits straight against the back of her marble throne, staring at her advisor with a stern gaze.

"I've combed through all the recent security reports, and I've found no evidence of a breach."

"And what of the rumors?"

"There were several complaints of an unidentifiable ship entering the atmosphere near Capital City, but our scans of the planetary surface were negative."

"So, you think my people are lying?" Sula asks with a dangerous tilt of her head.

"No," Solum says. "I think they saw something. I just don't know what. A ship would have been detected long before it entered orbit. Even if it somehow avoided our defenses, scans of the area would pick out the ship's location within moments. Whatever they saw, it wasn't a ship. It's impossible."

Queen Sula frowns at her packmate's frustration. Solum isn't easily perplexed, and failing to find the rumored ship seems to be infuriating the royal advisor. A wave of familiarity slams into Sula as she remembers the last time a space vessel landed on her planet undetected.

"Not impossible," Sula mutters. She averts her gaze from Solum while she considers the implications. Solum recognizes the sudden shift in his packmate's demeanor and studies her face. He's rewarded with a small glimpse as her royal mask slips to reveal an instant of concern and a hint of anxiety.

"What do you mean? What do you know, Sula?" Solum asks and steps closer.

Hearing her name, the queen shoves her mask back into place and snaps around to face him. Solum jerks back and straightens his posture. At this moment, they are not packmates or friends.

"There is an unidentified ship on my planet. Find it."

"Yes, my queen."

Solum salutes and hurries away, but he halts after a few steps when his packmate's voice reaches out to him.

"Solum."

He pivots to find Queen Sula glancing at several of the guards stationed throughout the room. She watches them for a moment and contemplates her next words.

"I trust you to protect her."

"Sula-"

"I trust you...to protect us all."

They both pause; Solum stares wide-eyed at his queen, and she stares back at him from a cold, royal mask.

"Yes, my queen," he says, then exits.

Inside the throne room, Sula closes her eyes and tries to push back the wave of shame engulfing her. On the other side of the large decorative doors, Solum stops and takes a deep breath. He has several long days ahead of him, but he must find the rogue ship. The sensation of a molten rock settles in his stomach when he realizes that the Queen of the Kaji Empire is frightened.

CHAPTER 8

Once again, Atae bounds through the streets of Capital City. She weaves between merchants and bustling commuters, running as fast as she can toward Sula Academy. Panting, she stumbles while dodging an irate merchant's cart. Atae catches herself in time to avoid a fall but growls at her mistake.

Between last night's pitiful training session and oversleeping this morning, I wouldn't be surprised if Solum disowns me.

Last night, Solum arrived just as Atae finished her warm-up, and he coached her through conditioning activities, like Search and Destroy, Cliff Hopping, and Uphill Rockslide, all of which are fun and motivating but require strict attention. No one wants to slip during a round of Uphill Rockslide and end up covered in a few dozen tons of mud and rock, yet Atae wound up in that exact position. Uphill Rockslide usually consists of Solum throwing boulder after boulder down the rock face and Atae moving fast enough to use the sliding rocks as steps, from the bottom to the top.

This time, Atae fumbled over her feet during each attempt to reach the top of the mountain. Time after time, she slammed headfirst into the rock slab and tumbled back down to the bottom. The other conditioning exercises were similar disasters. After several failed attempts, Solum expressed disgust in her fatigued state and told her that she would have to do much better to survive the Gridiron. Atae went to bed exhausted and ashamed of her disappointing performance.

Atae cringes as she leaps over a long box of goods carried between two merchants. Her ribs are still tender, but she attributes it to her recent tumbles down Mount Tuki. Again she stumbles, favoring her injured side, and slows to a halt at the steps of Sula Academy where Jeqi and her mother, Deh, are waiting. As sweat drips from her bruised face, Atae bends over to catch her breath.

"Rough night?" Jeqi asks. Her eyebrows knit together in concern as she watches her packmate recover.

Unable to speak just yet, Atae nods and smiles at Jeqi's mother, Deh. The Setunn's pale skin and delicate features gleam in Solis' and Cerule's light. Deh's long, blonde hair flows past her hips and surrounds the small creature in an almost heavenly glow. Her deep blue eyes sparkle with concern as her silky, blonde tail curls behind her.

"I fear Solum will push you too hard one day," Deh says. "Why are you here by yourself?"

Atae blinks. "Uh, because I always meet Jeqi here before lessons."

"No, I mean, why didn't Solum bring you? He isn't concerned about you running around unsupervised?"

"No," Atae shrugs. "Why would he?"

Deh huffs, and Atae glances at Jeqi in confusion. The Setunn hybrid sighs and shakes her head, and Atae smiles at her packmate's annoyance. Deh's tail thrashes about in outrage as she throws her hand up into the air.

"Never mind. If Solum chooses to do nothing to protect his offspring, that is his choice. I will not make the same mistake," she says.

Atae steps back and gapes at Deh. It's no secret that the Setunn cares for her offspring and takes, what Kaji consider, unnecessary precautions to protect Jeqi. This is the first time Atae has heard Deh criticize another parent, especially Solum. Before Atae can prod for more information about why Solum should be more concerned for Atae's safety, Jeqi announces her big news with a smile.

"Atae finally beat Advisor Solum in training."

"Oh? Congratulations, Atae," Deh says. Jeqi's silver tail pats the floor as she frowns at her mother.

"Mother? Do you realize what this means?"

"Yes. It means you and Atae will be able to compete in the Gridiron when you feel you are ready."

Jeqi, her tail paralyzed in shock, gawks at her mother. Deh, like most Setunn, never hides her repugnance for the violence that's an everyday affair in Kajian culture. Jeqi sometimes struggles to understand her mother's attraction to her father, a well-known Kaji warrior. She can only conclude that his sense of duty and honor counterbalances his violent nature. At least, in her mother's eyes.

"And you're fine with this?" Jeqi asks.

On more than one occasion, she's forbidden Jeqi from participating in activities considered normal in Kajian culture but unthinkable among the Setunn.

"I told you long ago when this bargain began, as long as you stay top of your class at Sula, you can participate. You've not failed to hold up your end of the bargain. Why would I fail to uphold mine?" Deh tilts her head, peering at her daughter with a patient gaze, but Jeqi frowns at her.

"You're not afraid that I will give into my 'heathen' side and decide I would rather be a warrior than a specialist?" Jeqi asks.

Over the past few seasons, she's grown distrustful of her mother's intentions because Deh uses every opportunity to dissuade Jeqi from warrior training, encouraging her to specialize instead. Jeqi and Atae learned of the Gridiron four seasons ago, which prompted the deal between Atae and her father. Deh used the opportunity to encourage Jeqi to concentrate more on lessons than training, and Advisor Solum used the bargain to inspire Atae to develop her combat skills.

Most younglings do not begin combat training until their fifth or sixth season, focusing more on physical and mental conditioning in early seasons of development. Around their fifteenth season, purebred younglings start their shifting phase, a period in which their bodies learn to shift from their first form into their second and back. Kaji families usually remove their offspring from the public to teach them in private how to control their newly acquired shifting ability. This can take a few days, weeks, or months, depending on the youngling. Even after they return to their regular routines, some may struggle to maintain control.

While all purebred Kaji eventually learn to shift, most hybrids do not have a second form. Therefore, Solum began training Atae in combat at an earlier age. He knew she would be at a disadvantage her entire life, and expert fighting skills could help level the playing field. Deh, on the other hand, used all her resources to ensure Jeqi has the best education and as much opportunity to specialize as possible. Deh smiles at her daughter and caresses her with a softly spoken voice.

"Jeqietta, daughter of mine, I have no doubt that when you see a true battle between Kaji warriors, you will have no desire to join them."

Jeqi's eyes burn, and her puffed-up tail sputters behind her as she glares at her mother. A familiar thought whispers through the dark crevices of Jeqi's mind. It's a thought that always floats to the surface, no matter how hard she tries to drown it.

Am I good enough? Will I ever be a true Kaji warrior? Am I strong enough? Jeqi clenches her teeth, wrestling the dreadful plague of whispers down, deep into the depths of her mind and out of sight.

"Do you think I'm a coward?"

Deh's patient, blue eyes peer into Jeqi's passionate azure, and Deh slips her smooth hands over both sides of her daughter's face. Her words are gentle, and her tone is loving.

"I think you have too much of your mother's blood to be a true Kaji warrior."

Jeqi's eyes fill with tears, but she endeavors to keep them at bay as she struggles against the rekindled whispers that drown her with insecurity. Her lips tremble, and her voice cracks as she speaks.

"How can you say that? I am Kaji. I will serve the empire honorably."

"Of this, I have no doubt, my love. You will bring great honor to our family, as your father has, but not in the same way." Deh wipes her daughter's tears with the tip of her tail, letting the soft fur caress Jeqi's hot cheeks. The whispers slacken their grip on her mind, and Jeqi breathes a little easier. Standing, Deh kisses her offspring on the head with a note of finality.

"One day, you will understand, my dear." She walks away from the two younglings, perhaps, to give her daughter much needed privacy. Jeqi clings to her mother's assurances like a life preserver and gathers her strength to beat back the mental waves of anguish her mind has released upon itself.

After watching the entire conversation and display of affection, Atae stands in awkward silence, oblivious to Jeqi's inner struggle. She spends every day with Jeqi at Sula Academy and visits her home several times a week. Jeqi always displays a strong will and eagerness to earn citizenship, thus honor, as a true Kajian youngling should. And every night, her mother comforts her and encourages her to perform better. Atae is fascinated by the Setunn's unabashed affection for her loved ones and finds herself envying Jeqi once again.

Solum is a fine father for Atae. He is supportive and patient. What he lacks in warmth, Solum makes up for with quality time. Solum is a hardened warrior, and Atae has learned to appreciate the small displays of affection he supplies. A nod of approval, a smile of pride, and, on rare occasions, a verbal compliment. Sometimes, after leaving Jeqi's affectionate home for another challenging training session with Solum, Atae wonders if her mother would have held her and kissed her as Deh does for Jeqi.

Atae watches her friend as Jeqi, lost in her inner turmoil, grasps her soft tail in both hands. It flickers against her face, mimicking her mother's comforting touch. Unnerved by her comrade's display of insecurity, Atae interrupts Jeqi with a soft punch to the shoulder.

"You worry too much," Atae says. Jeqi jerks her head up and drops her tail, a small blush creeping across her face.

"And you don't worry at all," Jeqi snaps. Atae raises an eyebrow at her friend's harsh tone but says nothing. She surveys the Academy building and notices all the arriving students are piling into their respective classes. Not wanting to be late again, Atae signals for Jeqi to follow her inside.

The two hybrids reach their stations as Elder Warrior Feku strides into the classroom. He takes his place at the lecture station in the center of the room and activates his giant hologram, which initiates the student stations. Atae notices that Jent's station is empty and wonders about his whereabouts until Feku directs everyone's attention to the metal object sitting at each station.

Most of the younglings are curious, and some pick up the object to search for identifying marks. Jeqi, on the other hand, squeals in excitement as she holds it with a firm grip.

"What is it?" Atae asks.

"They are weapons. More specifically, your weapons," Feku says. In unison, the entire room bursts into exhilarated chatter, and the elder warrior waits for the group to exhaust their excitement. Soon, the students realize the chunk of metal looks more like the lever on a hovercraft than a weapon, and all eyes find their way back to Feku.

"Jeqi, care to explain?"

Everyone shifts their attention to the blonde youngling, and Jeqi jumps up with a giant grin on her face, holding her weapon out in front of her with both hands. Without a word, a beam of energy erupts from the top of the metal lever, expelling a distinct, high-pitch zing. The energy beam forms a massive two-handed sword with the metal lever as the hilt. Classmates all around Jeqi gasp in surprise, then, without warning, the blade melts into a small dagger and echoes the same distinct zing. As Jeqi waves the shorter knife in one hand, the light from the energy beam creates a frightening shadow across her face. After a few moments, Jeqi deactivates the weapon, and the energy beam recedes into the hilt like it never existed.

"It's an energy blade," she says.

"That's right," Feku says. Almost no one notices the five points added to Jeqi's class ranking as it flashes across all their stations. Every youngling in the room hangs on the elder warrior's next words and hopes to learn how to wield the fantastic weapon.

"Does anyone know what powers it?" Feku asks. He searches the class for anyone who might have an answer. With no stations alight, he asks a slightly different question. "Does it create energy out of thin air?"

"No," Atae whispers. But the quiet room amplifies her musing, and Feku glances at her.

"What was that, Atae?"

"Uh...no. It can't create energy. Nothing can. Energy can only be converted."

"So, what powers it?" Feku asks again. When, still, no one responds, Feku decides to rephrase the question. "How is it charged?"

"I got it. Our uniforms." Marqee jumps up and sends the class into a cascade of smiles and giggles.

"Very good, Marqee. But control yourself long enough to use your station indicator next time you have an epiphany, and you might get more points." The elder warrior smirks as the class giggles again. Marqee's dark eyes dart away to hide his embarrassment, but he smiles at his point addition.

"Like most modern uniforms, your Sula Academy outfit has several capabilities, including weapon holstering. There are many places for you to attach your hilt. Most warriors prefer the hip or along the outer thigh, but feel free to pick whichever site is more comfortable," Feku says. He demonstrates by firmly pressing a hilt against his uniform then releasing it. The silver metal hugs his hip even as he maneuvers around the room. The class explodes into action as each youngling follows Feku's example.

Atae sheaths her sword against her hip then walks around her station a few times to see how it feels. After a few quickdraws, the blue hybrid sheaths the hilt in other positions before settling on the outer thigh of her right leg. Enjoying the alien sensation of the small, heavy object against her leg, Atae smiles at Jeqi. The blonde smiles back with the same excitement, sporting a hilt on her left upper arm, below her shoulder. Feku addresses the class after most of them choose their ideal holster positions.

"What other advantages does your uniform offer?" He motions for Debil to answer, and she offers a tired shrug.

"It's pretty tough."

"Tough, but it's certainly not any kind of armor. There's something more to it. What is it, Sloan?"

"It stays with us during our shift."

"Good, but how?" Feku prods for more, and Sloan wrinkles his dark forehead as he considers the implications before responding.

"It kind of disappears, like my body absorbs it when I shift. Then, when I return, so does it."

"It's biocompatible," Jeqi says. "Your body can't tell the difference between your tissue and the uniform, so it treats them the same."

"Very good, Jeqi." Feku nods. "During a shift, your body will break down unnecessary cells and create the new, necessary ones. When you return to your first form, your body reverses the process."

"So, the uniform becomes a part of me when I shift?" Marqee asks. "That's kind of weird."

"It's either that, or we walk around naked after every shift," Sloan says. He winks at Debil, and she flashes a playful smile at his attention.

"It seems we should all be grateful for Sloan's uniform," Feku says sarcastically. After the elder warrior awards Jeqi and Sloan their earned points, Atae indicates that she has a question.

"If my uniform charges my hilt, what powers my uniform?"

"That's a great question, but only the Bargae know the answer. That particular feature is proprietary and a well-kept secret."

"The Bargae never share any technological secrets with us," Marqee says.

"That's because they make more money exporting the products that we're willing to buy if they are the only ones selling it," Feku explains. "That's basic economics and, while it's a fascinating subject, I bet you'd all rather learn more about your new weapons."

Appreciating his students' enthusiasm, Feku explains that the hilt is activated by a small switch at the base of the small device, but a visual visor is needed to adjust the shape of the blade. This type of hilt is not able to generate projectile weapons, but ranged and shield hilts are available. Then he explains that most weaponry technologies are created and designed by Kaji specialists, and non-weaponry technologies, such as the visual visors, were created by other species or acquired from conquered planets. As the lecture shifts into historical facts, Atae loses focus and glances around the room.

Atae notices an empty station on the other side of the classroom and realizes Seva is absent. Atae ponders Seva's health but dismisses the thought. She knows that few viruses and illnesses affect Kaji. Glancing around the rest of the room, Atae spots Debil, who seems just as fatigued as yesterday but less capable of hiding it. Atae is thankful she isn't the only one dragging today. Uncomfortable with the display of weakness, Atae averts her gaze and lands on Jeqi. The blonde hybrid has been scribbling on her hologram station since putting away her hilt. She peeks over Jeqi's shoulder.

"What are you doing?" Jeqi opens her mouth to shoo her away, but Atae cuts her off. "And don't tell me not to worry about it."

Jeqi closes her mouth and glances at her screen then back to Atae. She frowns but submits to her packmate's curiosity.

"It's a weapon."

Atae blinks then tries to peer around Jeqi to her screen. "What kind of weapon?"

"Don't worry about it." Jeqi pushes her friend away, and Atae can't help but chuckle as she returns her attention to the lecture. She hopes the lesson will include hands-on training with their new weapons.

CHAPTER 9

Surrendering their new weapons to Elder Warrior Feku, the class of younglings piles out of the Sula Academy building at the end of the day. Everyone scatters, heading for their respective homes. Atae and Jeqi say their goodbyes, and the blonde hybrid complains to her mother that she is too old to be escorted around the city by a parent. Atae smiles at her packmate's whining then sets her sights on Mount Tuki. She grimaces at the thought of another pitiful training session with Solum but sprints forward.

Tonight will be better. I will not disappoint him again.

As she reaches the training ground, Atae stumbles over a boulder and drags her exhausted body to a stop. Drained from climbing the tall mountain, she is somewhat relieved that her father is late. Atae hopes to rest a bit before his arrival, but a beeping signal from her visor squashes that thought. Atae leans on her knees, panting, and activates her father's message.

'Push-ups, sit-ups, lunges, and rebounds until I arrive.'

Conditioning is a necessary activity to build strength and endurance, but it's boring. Atae learned long ago that she could accomplish the same conditioning with much more exciting activities, like Search and Destroy, Cliff Hopping, and Uphill Rockslide. After catching her breath, Atae sighs. She understands that this is a form of punishment for her failures yesterday, so she throws herself into the warm-up but finds it a bit more taxing than she expected.

Trying to distract herself from the discomfort, Atae reviews her day and past lessons. She imagines what the tournament will be like and hopes it is similar to what the other younglings at Sula described. She wonders if the Gridiron will be as difficult as Feku and Solum claim. A sting of disappointment zips through her at the realization that she and Jeqi may not compete as representatives of Sula Academy. Not because they might lose the tournament, but because they plan to enter with the prince. Atae wonders when the prince intends to compete in the Gridiron. She makes a mental note to ask Jeqi, confident that her packmate has an acceptable plan of action.

By the fourth round of her warm-up, Atae struggles to focus past the pain and keep her body moving. Unwilling to stop for fear her father would know, as somehow he always does, Atae concentrates on the life around her. She embraces the chill wind that kisses her hot skin, welcomes the scents of plant life intertwining around her, and invites the sounds of rustling wildlife that scurry to their dens for the night. Atae glances to the lone star, Sul, at the peak of its rise. Soon, it will descend and immerse her into a cold night.

Amid her meditation, something in the forest sends the hairs on the back of Atae's neck on end. When the distinct and high-pitch zing of a hilt forming a blade flitters through the wilds and settles on Atae's ears, panic overrides her senses. She launches to her feet and twirls around. Her eyes bounce from one end of the clearing to the other. Atae listens for the sound again, footsteps, heavy breathing, or anything to pinpoint the threat, but the pounding drum of her racing heart drowns everything out. She lifts a trembling hand and clenches her fist with a twisted snarl.

Kaji warriors do not panic and shake at the first sign of battle.

Certain that Solum would never panic like this, Atae closes her eyes and inhales a deep lungful to fight the surge of adrenaline. She wills the rhythm of her heart to slow so that she can hear beyond it. Breathe in, *thump*. Breathe out, *thump*. With a silent and calm body, Atae reaches out into the world around her and opens her senses.

She feels the light touch of a breeze caressing her cheek and sniffs for scents that it tugs along. A foul smell of rot and sweat stings Atae's nostrils, and she cringes. Twigs snap under heavy boots at the edge of the wilds, and Atae opens her eyes. She knows there isn't enough time for her to get up the mountain before the intruder reaches the clearing, and she can't get around him through the trees without being seen. Atae glances at the cliff drop but decides that the loose gravel and dirt would announce her position, as it did during lessons. Refusing to lose the advantage of surprise, Atae darts behind a nearby boulder and waits.

Atae notices Sul has almost reached the horizon, and one of the moons is peeking out through the clouds. Darkness will make everything that much more difficult. Surely Solum will arrive soon. Atae stiffens as the heavy footsteps stop at the edge of the tree line. She waits and fights the urge to tremble again. Breathe in, *thump*, and breathe out, *thump*.

A deep, rumbling chuckle emanates from behind a tree that's covered in moss and vines. The sound races down Atae's back and sends shivers up her spine. Breathe in, *thump*, breathe out, *thump*.

In a deep, rough voice, he says. "Hmm. I can smell your fear. Delicious."

Snapping branches and vines echo across the clearing as a towering figure steps from the edge of the forest. Atae peeps out from behind her boulder for an instant before snapping back to her hiding spot. A pit in Atae's stomach drops, and the unfamiliar sensation of vulnerability and helplessness crawls into her chest. The creature before her is not like anything she has seen before. He is not much taller than Solum but three times as massive with broad shoulders and a colossal chest, rippling with layers of muscle.

Remembering her father's words of strength and honor, Atae glances up to see Sul disappear behind the horizon, and darkness swallows everything around her. Atae knows that Solum would not fear this massive creature, and neither should she, but she cannot stop the tremor in her breath and the sinking abyss in her gut.

I am a warrior. I am strong. I am Kaji.

Breathe in, *thump*, and breathe out, *thump*. Atae hears a hilt deactivate a few steps to the right of the creature and a rough but feminine voice.

"What are we doing out here?"

"I told you. I smelled someone," he says. His heavy footsteps stomp around the clearing as he searches for his prize.

"I don't see anyone. Are you sure that snout of yours is working?"

"She is still here. I can smell her."

Breathe in, *thump*, and breathe out, *thump*.

"Her? What kind of her?" the female asks.

"A youngling."

Atae can hear an excitement in his voice that makes her nauseous. His heavy boots stop in front of her boulder, and she holds her breath. She wills the deafening thumps of her heart not to betray her.

"A youngling? You dragged me out here for that?" the female asks angrily. The heavy footsteps clomp away from Atae's boulder to face the feminine voice, and Atae releases her breath. Breathe in, *thump*, and breathe out, *thump*.

"I didn't tell you to follow me, Salyn. Go back to the ship and wait for Lipson like a good little female," the creature growls. Atae cringes at his remark, but Salyn chuckles.

"But not little enough...Not for your tastes, at least," she says. Atae cannot hear Salyn's silent footsteps, but her voice shifts closer to the creature. He growls, and hatred spews from his voice.

"I could make an exception. I wouldn't mind hearing you scream."

"But Lipson would, wouldn't he?" she asks. The creature growls again but doesn't argue when Salyn continues. "Don't take too long, Kandorq. I'd hate for you to be left behind."

The feminine voice floats closer to the edge of the clearing, where she first appeared. Then her quiet chuckle disappears into the wilds.

"Bitch," Kandorq says. When he is sure that his companion is gone, Kandorq sucks in a sharp breath. He groans deep in his chest, and Atae cannot stop the shiver of disgust or the escaping gasp.

"You smell like fear and sweat. I can't wait to hear you scream, Little One," he says.

As Kandorq's heavy footsteps stomp closer to Atae's hiding spot again, she eyes her escape route. If she were ever going to use it, now would be the time. But Atae doesn't move. She doesn't even breathe. She can't push away the paralyzing fear or think of anything other than the sounds of Kandorq's heavy footsteps coming for her. Her racing heart thumps as loud as Kandorq's steps, and, for a few precious moments, all she hears is her own heartbeat.

Then a hand as big as Atae's head reaches around the side of the boulder and latches onto her neck. Atae sucks in a breath to scream only to have her throat squeezed shut by the giant hand. Kandorq lifts Atae high off the ground by her neck. She scratches and pulls at his heavy hand, if only for a small gasp of air. Kandorq is unrelenting as he admires his catch then settles his gaze onto Atae's face.

Even in the darkness lit only by the moons, Atae can see the creature's pale white and scarred skin. At the top of his head, two large black horns wrap the sides of his face. His strange grin reveals black and decayed teeth that emanate a smell that, in any other situation, would make Atae ill. His red eyes blaze with an evil Atae could never imagine. She struggles against his grip by scratching at his bald head and pulling at his powerful arms, but she can't tug her gaze from his twisted expression. Pleased with his catch, Kandorq licks his lips, and the lack of oxygen clouds Atae's vision, kicking her adrenaline into overdrive. Kandorq's red eyes pierce her wild fuchsia, and Atae explodes.

With the agility of a feral animal, Atae flings every extremity in all directions. Her body wriggles in complete disorder with her arms flailing, legs kicking, and nails scratching. Surprised, Kandorq struggles to keep his grip on the wild youngling. He steps toward the side of the mountain and slams her into the rock face, releasing his suffocating grip. Atae slides to the ground as the stone and rock crumble from her impact. At first, sweet air is her entire world, but Atae's senses return just in time for Kandorq to grab her a second time.

This time he grabs her just under the chin so as not to intrude on her ability to breathe. He presses her against the remaining rock face and pins her under his massive body.

"I love it when they struggle." He watches the muscles in Atae's face twist in a turbulent wash of fear and confusion, and he chuckles. He leans in to trace his lips across her skin along the side of her face. Atae grimaces at his touch and can't help the small whimper that escapes. Kandorq drags his hot tongue from her chin, up her cheek, and to her temple. His fowl breath makes Atae gag as she struggles to get away, and he groans in ecstasy.

"I love that look. You all have the same look," Kandorq whispers. He grins with a strange flicker behind his eyes. An experienced woman would identify it as pleasure, but Atae can only recognize the sadistic nature that forces a feeling of violation to wash over her.

"I want you to remember my face." He groans into her ear, forcing his hot breath down her neck, and she chokes at the smell. "I never want you to forget what I'm going to do and that I'm the one that did it. All because you were too weak to stop me."

Fear and panic threaten to override her once again. She tries to breathe and fight against her instinct, but the tidal wave of adrenaline has her heart in overdrive. A white haze coats the inside of her mind, and numbness settles over everything. A whisper drowns out the world.

Be still.

Atae embraces the numbness and lies motionless against her attacker. Kandorq places his tongue on the side of her chin that he has yet to taste. Atae cowers in the safety of her mind until she remembers his words regarding the others.

How many other younglings has he hurt?

Images of his previous victims, broken and hurting, carve through Atae's mind and spark a small flame of anger. As Kandorq's tongue creeps across her cheek, her fury blazes higher and scorches away the numbing silver haze.

How dare he threaten to hurt me? To even touch me. Father would not stand for this. I am not weak. I am Kaji.

Hoping to enjoy another show of despair and fear, Kandorq leans his head away from Atae to admire his prize. He frowns in disappointment at her blank and emotionless stare but isn't surprised. Sometimes it happens with the weak ones. At least he can enjoy the rest of her. He shrugs and leans in to press his cracking, black lips to her soft, pink ones. Atae grasps the black horns on either side of his face with her thumbs pointed inward. Pleased that she still has some fire left in her, he dismisses Atae's meager protests. When a small grin swells from Atae's lips, Kandorq stops to stare at her hands above him, and his red eyes grow wide with realization. In an instant of fear and panic, his eyes flicker back to Atae's face. Her calm, satisfied expression is the last thing Kandorq sees before she presses her thumbs into his eyes. Kandorq abandons his plans for Atae as his entire focus shifts to stopping her from gauging his eyes out.

He pulls away, trying to escape, but her solid grip on his horns pulls her along with him. She continues to press her thumbs into his eyes, and Kandorq screams. Thrashing and clawing at her hands, he falls backward onto the ground. Atae refuses to let go and falls with him, landing on top of him. With her knees on his chest, Atae thrusts her entire thumb into his eye sockets until Kandorq's eyes burst with a sickening pop. Satisfied, Atae releases him and jumps away from his flailing body.

A black, viscous substance seeps from his eye sockets as he howls in pain, and bloody tears flow down his cheeks. For a few moments, Atae watches Kandorq scratch at his face and roll around on the dirt and rocks, enjoying his screams of pain and curses, until she remembers his companion. Salyn may hear him and decide to investigate. Atae scampers away from Kandorq and, without a glance back, leaps down the cliff.

She lands on her feet in the clearing below and transfers the force from the fall into a roll. Not caring about a trail or noise, Atae runs at top speed. Her only goal is to get as far as possible as quickly as she can. Atae doesn't want to stop until she reaches her home or at least the town, but her body won't comply.

Her lungs burning and chest heaving, Atae stops a quarter of the way down the mountain. Frustrated, she growls at her poor performance. Now, when it counts, her body fails her. Gasping, she places her hands on her hips and struggles to stay upright. She wipes the sweat from her forehead to prevent it from dripping into her eyes. Atae can't remember the last time she had this much trouble breathing.

Branches and leaves block the moonlight, but Atae can make out several large tree trunks within arm's reach. The brush covering the ground is small enough to maneuver, so Atae, still panting, places her hand on a nearby tree trunk and smiles. Jassell trees are the best trees to hide her. She reaches for the lowest branch and hauls herself up. Determined to reach the highest branch strong enough to support her, Atae stops just below the forest canopy.

Atae stretches out on the branch and catches her breath. Her skin melds into the dark gray bark, and her hair disappears into the blue leaves. Atae tries to stay alert for any sign of Salyn, but as the adrenaline ebbs from her system, the exhaustion takes hold. Atae fights against her body's need for rest and snaps a hand at her visor. She drafts a quick message to her father, alerting him of the two trespassers, and sends it. The small hybrid hopes Solum is nearby their scheduled training grounds, because she's certain Salyn followed her into the woods.

Atae doesn't hear or see anything, but she knows someone is out there. She peers down into the forest, struggling to see past the branches and into the darkness. For a long time, nothing happens, then she notices a small figure that is darker than the rest of the night. It moves through the brush, and Atae marvels at the female's ability to sneak through such terrain nearly undetected. A sharp pain swells behind Atae's eyes as she struggles to see the dark shadow.

Atae rubs at her eyes until the pain subsides, and when she drops her hand away, Atae's vision is much clearer. Along with everything around her, Salyn somehow glows with a dim shimmer. In the night, the silent female's small light is a beacon of life that Atae can see through the branches from across the forest. She snorts at Salyn's naïve attempt to light her path. At the sound, the silent figure jerks her head up, and her emerald eyes meet with fuchsia.

Salyn's eyes are slit and framed by a pale, slim face. Thin, brown hair swirls around her feminine features but falls short of her shoulders. Salyn's petite stature and coloration scream at Atae.

Setunn.

Confirming Atae's assessment, Salyn peels back her lips to reveal sharp canines and hisses. In the next instant, she flings her right arm toward Atae. Even with Salyn standing on the ground and well out of arm's reach, Atae flinches back against the tree's trunk, and something small strikes the bark a finger's width from her face. When a sharp pain stabs at the back of her eyes, Atae shakes her head and blinks several times. After a moment, the pain passes, and Atae searches for Salyn. No longer glowing, the deadly hunter blends into the night.

Frustrated, Atae examines the object embedded in the tree's trunk. It is difficult to identify the weapon in the dark, so Atae dips her face as close as possible. It is a straight and incredibly sharp projectile with a thin liquid dripping from the end. Atae sniffs at it, and her eyes widen in recognition. The Setunn threw her venomous claws at Atae. The hybrid has never heard of this technique and wonders whether Deh or Jeqi can do it.

No way. If Jeqi could do this, I would definitely know.

Before Atae can ponder anymore about the impressive ability, she detects an almost inaudible whistling. On instinct, Atae ducks, and another venomous claw whizzes past her head. She inspects the direction from which the claw came and spots Salyn propped on a branch in a nearby tree. Her emerald eyes reflect the moonlight, but the rest of her form remains hidden in the shadows. As she prepares to launch another claw, Atae has no time to marvel at Salyn's ability to climb that high without making any noise. Instead, Atae slips from her branch and grabs a lower one. She swings from branch to branch until she is low enough to jump to the ground.

As she cringes from the impact, Atae's body convulses from exhaustion. She falls to one knee and uses one arm to keep from falling face-first to the ground. Every muscle in her body contracts at the same time, and Atae cries out. An instant later, the pain stops, and her muscles relax. With sweat beading across her forehead, Atae drags herself to her feet and staggers forward. Leaning from tree to tree, stumbling over bushes, and panting, Atae knows the Setunn is watching and toying with her prey.

With each painful step, Atae anticipates a strike from above, but nothing comes, and she totters into a small clearing without incident. The light from both moons illuminates the green grass, numerous wildflower patches, and the little spring at the far edge. She recognizes the meadow from previous visits. In the past, she enjoyed lying in the wildflowers and basking under Sul and Solis. In recent seasons, Atae spent her time here on homework and endless technique drills. She was determined to beat Solum and earn her trip to the Gridiron. Atae snorts as she realizes the pointlessness of her training. It's been no help to her today.

Confident that Salyn will follow, Atae stumbles to the nearest patch of wildflowers, slipping to her knees. Atae can feel the dew seeping into her pants and cooling her feverish skin. The surrounding flowers sway in the wind as she spots a Blousq flower. It's her favorite type. Atae grasps just under the petals and plucks it from the soil, careful not to catch the thorns.

"How did you do it?" Salyn asks. She strolls up next to the hybrid with a piercing gaze that spears Atae with fear and uncertainty. With her throat still sore from Kandorq's rough treatment, Atae responds in a brittle voice.

"Do what?"

"Kandorq will never see again. How did such a weakling manage to bring down a beast like him?"

"I am not weak," Atae whispers.

"After watching you stumble through the brush like injured prey, I'd have to disagree. Perhaps someday you could've been a strong warrior, but now we will never know," says Salyn. She bends down to Atae's eye level with the corners of her small mouth turned up.

She can see the amusement playing on the Setunn's lips, but Atae stares back with a blank face. Salyn snorts at the weakling's silence and flicks her hand. Atae flinches when the Setunn's claws tear into her outstretched forearm, and she struggles to keep her grip on the Blousq flower. An instant later, Atae's arm swells, and the skin around the wound darkens a deep purple.

"Tell me, youngling," Salyn says. "How do you want to die? By poison or blade?"

Salyn motions to the hilt holstered to her hip, but Atae glances back at her injured arm to find the purple rot spreading across her bicep. When Atae's eyes return to Salyn and fall on the hilt, the Setunn speaks with a vicious grin.

"Don't worry. I'll leave your beautiful face unmarred."

Atae meets Salyn's emerald eyes before bringing the Blousq flower petals to her lips and blowing as hard as she can. Caught by Atae's breath, thousands of poisonous, pink pollen slip from the petals and bluster into Salyn's face and eyes.

Surprised, the Setunn hisses, sits back, and wipes at her face, breathing in the poisonous pollen. When the Setunn can see again, she sets her sights on Atae, who remains in the same position. Salyn growls at the small smirk tugging at Atae's lips and stands to unsheathe her blade. Stopping with her hilt in hand, she cringes before her entire body freezes. Atae's smirk broadens into a satisfied smile at Salyn's temporary paralysis.

Atae drops the Blousq flower and struggles to her feet. She stumbles to Salyn and snags the energy blade from the Setunn's stiff hand. Atae holds the unfamiliar hilt, testing the balance and appreciating the shape of the weapon. Atae slips the deadly sword to Salyn's neck, and the Setunn's cheek twitches, a sure sign that the poison is wearing off. As Atae presses the blade into her skin, Salyn claws at the end of the sword with a spasmodic hand.

"Don't worry. I will leave your beautiful face unmarred," Atae says. Then, without breaking eye contact, she slices into Salyn's protesting fingers and deep into her throat. Blood gushes from the wound, splashing Atae and pouring down the Setunn. Atae steps away from Salyn as the warrior gurgles and grips at her throat. Atae watches the fear and anger in Salyn's eyes fade and empty. The corpse falls to the ground in a heap, and Atae stares at what remains of Salyn until her own body gives way.

I'm sorry, Father. I wasn't strong enough. Please, don't be ashamed of me.

Atae doesn't know if it is exhaustion or the poison, but she falls to her knees. Her body convulses again as all her muscles contract at the same time. Atae screams. She screams as loud as her throat and lungs allow. She screams forever. Fueled by the pain, the frustration, the fear, and the sorrow, she yells until her throat gives out. She cries until her mind and body shut down, and she falls into the sweet relief of darkness.

CHAPTER 10

Atae stands in the center of an infinite void, a desolate vacuum that leaves her blind and deaf. She is alone in the darkness but for the fear that claws at her spine. The cold tendrils reach around to her chest and tear at her heart, her lungs burning as she gulps for breath. When emerald eyes shine in the depths of the darkness, the suffocating fear almost overwhelms Atae.

Gasping through the adrenaline-fueled anxiety, Atae waits for Salyn to step forward from the darkness and strike her down. Moments drag on into forever, but the Setunn's unmoving gaze watches with a predatorial gleam. Atae closes her eyes and wraps her arms around herself, trying to avoid the unbearable weight of Salyn's gaze. She takes slow, deep breaths to slow her heart rate. A warrior is always steady, always strong, and never afraid. When she's calm enough, Atae opens her eyes and speaks to the fixated onlooker.

"Hello." She forms the words, but no sound escapes her lips; instead, a deafening silence presses in on her. She cannot hear the sound of her breathing, not the thumping of her heart, nor even her thoughts. The darkness sucks out everything like a black hole.

Frustration seeps into Atae as she fights the silence and the darkness. Unwilling to submit to the emptiness, her frustration and fear swirl into a concoction of anger. Fury at her own weakness surges through her veins. Rage at this place bombards her body. Resentment at the unwavering emerald eyes floods her mind. Atae screams into the darkness only to have her voice swallowed by the silence.

"What is this place?"

Again, Salyn does not respond. Instead, she continues to watch and wait for the perfect moment to strike.

"Screw you!"

Atae launches toward Salyn but slams into something hard. Blinded by the pitch black, Atae trails her hands across the solid form. It is made of flesh, but it's hard and scarred. Atae sniffs the air and smells a familiar rot. She gasps and backpedals as fast as her feet will allow. She hopes the creature did not notice her but knows it is too late. As if to accentuate her fears, a low chuckle emanates from the darkness.

"Hmm. I can smell your fear. Delicious."

Atae trembles as the sharp sense of vulnerability and helplessness returns and steals the air from her lungs. Kandorq's sadistic laugh echoes from everywhere and never stops. Collapsing under the weight of her fear, Atae falls to her knees and wraps her arms around her chest. She screams with all her might, with all her fear and anger. She screams for ages until her lungs burn, and her throat swells with soreness. When she stops, everything is silent.

Atae stands and searches the darkness for Kandorq but finds only the emerald eyes. Then she hears him groan, and his pale face steps out from the blackness like a phantom, his red eyes piercing her with the same perverse violation.

"I want you to remember my face."

"No," Atae screams at him, but nothing comes out. She runs from him, but no matter how fast nor how far she runs, he still whispers into her ear.

"I never want you to forget what I'm going to do…"

Her running turns frantic when Atae feels his hot tongue on her cheek. She swings her clenched fists in a panic but hits only air.

"…and that I'm the one that did it."

"No. You did nothing to me. I stopped you." Again, only silence echoes from her cries.

"All because you were too weak to stop me."

"I'm not weak," Atae screams, sitting up in bed.

"Shh. It's okay, love," Deh says, rushing to Atae's side. "You're safe."

Jeqi's mother lays a damp cloth on Atae's forehead, allowing the youngling to lean the back of her head against the headboard. Atae stares at the light-colored Setunn and sighs with relief. Ensuring that she isn't still trapped in the dream-void, Atae glances around the unfamiliar room, surprised by its elegance. Beautiful furniture adorns the spacious bedroom, lavished with gold trim and silk cloth. Atae lies against the soft pillows and puffy comforter, not caring that her sweat soaks through her sheets. She closes her eyes for a few moments and enjoys the feel of the cold, damp cloth on her forehead.

When nausea rolls over her, Atae drapes her head over the side of the bed, and Deh jumps up to retrieve a metal bucket from the connected bathroom. Atae hangs her head in the bucket and waits for her nausea to pass. After several moments, Atae lays back down and swallows hard. She closes her eyes and exhales a heavy breath.

"What happened?"

"We were hoping you could tell us," Deh says. She rests the damp cloth back on Atae's forehead before motioning to Solum, asleep in a chair across the room. "Your father found you in that clearing half-dead from Setunn poisoning. He brought you here and sent for me right away. This is the first that he has slept in several days."

"Days? I've been unconscious for days?"

Deh nods. Atae stares at her father's large frame, crumpled into an awkward sleeping position in the chair, and Deh smiles at the adoration and hero worship evident in the youngling's eyes. When Atae notices Deh's smile, she blushes and lies back down.

"How am I not dead?"

"You would be if Advisor Solum had not found you when he did. Setunn poison is not the fastest-acting poison, but it will certainly get the job done. I've always feared Jeqi would lose her temper one day during training, so I have kept a salve on hand since her poison sacks developed," Deh says. She removes the cloth from Atae's head and walks to the bathroom.

"Poison sacks?" Atae asks. The blonde exits the bathroom, tilting her head.

"What, dear?"

"Never mind." Atae shakes her head, but the movement forces her to reach for the bucket once again. This time a clenching pain in her abdomen empties her stomach. Afterward, Atae lies back, and Deh places a newly rinsed cloth on her forehead.

"How long does this last?" Atae asks. Deh's eyebrows knit in concern as she brushes the sweat-soaked hair from Atae's eyes.

"The doctor says the poison has already left your system. Something else is causing your fever."

"What?"

"We can talk more later. You need to rest so that your body can heal." Deh pulls the sheets higher over Atae and tucks her into bed.

"But, Deh." Atae sits up to argue, but the Setunn shushes her and points to Solum.

"Do not wake your father. He needs to sleep, too."

Relenting, Atae lies back against her soft pillow and snuggles under the blanket.

"Deh," she says. "Can you throw your claws? I've never seen Jeqi do it, but can you?"

"No. That is a technique that takes many seasons to learn, and I have no taste for killing."

Deh watches Atae nod her head once and close her eyes. The small hybrid trembles under the sheets, whimpering, so Deh climbs into bed with Atae and wraps her arms around her. Without saying a word, Deh embraces the youngling and does her best to soothe her.

"I'm not weak," Atae whispers.

"Far from it."

"He wanted to hurt me and...and..."

"Shh. I know, but he can't now."

"I didn't let him."

"Good girl. Good girl."

As Atae falls asleep, Deh glances at Solum, who stares at her from his chair. His dark features blazing with anger, Solum doesn't say a word as he storms from the room. Deh watches the royal advisor leave then cries tears of pain and sorrow. The tears that Solum is too proud to shed.

CHAPTER 11

The royal palace in Capital City was designed to be the most majestic in the empire. The arches and windows work together to capture and manipulate the light from each sun to create beautiful works of art throughout the palace. But there is one hall deep within the maze of walls that sunlight will never reach. Even artificial light struggles against the shadows.

In the gloom, the walls bleed with crimson jewels and depict the tortured souls of prisoners. History's vilest criminals are strapped onto metal slabs as they cry for mercy. Kaji warriors cut into their flesh and strip the meat from their bones. One prisoner twists in infinite agony as his face is peeled. Another lies motionless as all his appendages are carved away bit by bit until only his torso and head remain. His silent tears and pained expression reveal that, even as a bloody stump, the prisoner lives. On and on, the images of unimaginable torture continue until the dark hall ends at a large door.

Ignoring the gruesome scenery, Queen Sula leans against one wall. She watches the hologram from her visual visor with a distasteful frown. Frack's deep-seated eyes stare back at the queen with his square jaw tight with aggression. His loud voice bellows from the image.

"Two weeks ago, we were attacked on our own soil, and Queen Sula does nothing but hide in her palace. She should be on the warpath and planning retaliation."

"Now, now," Skiska says. The hologram shifts to include her round face and forced smile. "We don't know if this was truly an attack against the empire. It seems to be an isolated incident. None of our enemies have claimed ownership of the attack."

"Yet!"

"We don't really know what happened on that mountain." Skiska eyes Frack with a familiar, scolding gaze, but he refuses to relent.

"Because they won't tell us. We do know that an unidentified spacecraft entered our orbit and, somehow, gained clearance to land in the middle of a forest that's nowhere near a docking station. A Setunn and a Gortox worked together to attack a Kajian youngling. We know that she escaped their custody, and the unidentified spacecraft fled. But we don't know how many of the assailants escaped or even how they slipped our defenses. The youngling's condition and location are also still unknown."

"She is probably receiving medical care," Skiska adds. She sighs when Frack continues.

"With today's technology, no wound takes longer than a week to heal. I'm telling you, Queen Sula Ru-Kai is hiding something from us all. Since the fall of our beloved King Uta, when Queen Sula seized the throne-"

"She is holding the throne until the only Ru-Kai heir can claim it for himself."

"And what if he never does? What if the Kaji choose not to follow him? He is the only Ru-Kai heir, but that doesn't mean the people will follow him."

"Of course, not," Skiska says. "The Kaji do not bow to the Ru-Kai name. We bow to a lineage of ruling warriors with a proven record. We have followed the Ru-Kai for generations, and they have never failed us."

"But we've always had several heirs from which to choose. Never have we been forced to accept an heir simply because of his bloodline," Frack says.

"And we won't start now. But we do owe Prince Truin a chance to prove himself."

"With so many crests vying for the throne, I think he'll have a hard time convincing the Kaji to follow him. The Gridiron can only do so much for him."

"Very true, Frack," Skiska says. "Well, what do you think viewers? As always, our channel is open to comments and opinions. We'll see you next time on the Skiska and Frack channel."

I'll give you an opinion that you can shove up your ass.

Sula waves her hand through the hologram and glances at the closed door at the end of the dark hallway. When nothing happens, she sighs and signals for her visor to activate the Skiska and Frack channel again. She opens the statistic for the channel and raises an eyebrow.

Somehow these fools have convinced 80% of the empire to subscribe to their channel.

Queen Sula flicks and twists her fingers until a list of comments appears, and she selects the highest voted one. The commentary opens to a hologram of a hybrid with pink hair, black eyes, and tan skin. The commenter's handle is PinkKaji. The young adult grins and speaks with a high-pitched voice.

"Queen Sula has revolutionized the empire and led us to prosperity through peace and tranquility."

Sula raises an eyebrow at the perky and optimistic perception of her accomplishments. Reading a written reply to PinkKaji's sunny comment, Sula laughs.

"How did this get the most votes? Your naivety is an embarrassment to your people. I wish there were a war we could ship you off to, so you could harden up from the realities of life. I hope all of your generation isn't as soft as you. Otherwise, we are all doomed. Anyway, Queen Sula didn't care about peace and tranquility. She cared about stabilizing our economy after the war ended."

"A war that she ended by surrendering," another commenter, BigBeast, adds to the thread. Below, CrzyPple voices her opinion.

"No, she didn't. I know we all hate to admit it, but we were losing the war. How many generations of warriors lost armies after armies fighting the Camille? How many Kaji lives were sacrificed? How many Kajian planets were destroyed? For what? Our pride? We don't even know why the war started. Queen Sula saved us from another generation of fighting."

Several angry commenters respond with the various reasons for their roles in the war. All of which refer to some nefarious Camille attack. Then, CrzyPple returns.

"I know the Camille did some horrible things, and they should be punished. But how many dead Camille did you see during the war? That's right. None. We don't even know what they look like. They have galaxies of slaves to throw at us, and, after centuries of fighting, we never even scratched their surface. I'm tired of being cannon fodder."

"I just don't like that we surrendered. And you know that's what happened because they never released the details of the 'treaty.' If there even is a treaty," commenter YutFap adds, but CrzyPPle has a quick response.

"Oh, I'm sorry. Do you have level ultra-clearance that allows you access to top secret information? Anyone with a brain would know that surrendering would include occupation. I haven't seen any Camille soldiers forcing Kaji from their homes, so I'm guessing we aren't being occupied."

Over time, the comments morph into offensive language and absurd conspiracies. Sula chuckles at one commenter's suggestion that the entire hybrid population consists of Camille spies meant to occupy the empire and tear it down from the inside. When a noise echoes from the dark door, Queen Sula wipes away her hologram and eyes the door without moving from the wall.

After a few moments, the metallic noises grow louder and then stop. The door slides open, and Solum steps out. Seeing his queen waiting, Solum pauses a couple of steps into the hall. The heavy metal door slides shut behind him, and he stares at Sula with a calm mask. Blood and other thick fluids coat Solum's hands and arms. Sula glances at the foul-smelling mess on his uniform then to his ebony eyes, noting the dark circles underneath.

"You've ignored my last two summonses. Given the condition of your offspring, I have chosen to forgive you. I've come to you instead." She flashes an irritated smile. "There are things we must discuss that cannot be postponed any longer."

Solum takes a deep breath then continues down the hall. Biting back the discourteous words that come to mind, Sula watches her packmate. He doesn't meet her gaze; instead, he stares beyond Sula, even proceeds to walk past her without acknowledging her presence. Surprised at his audacity, Queen Sula spins around to face the warrior.

"How dare you?"

Solum stops. Refusing to face the raging royal at his back, he angles his face to the side so that Sula can see a fraction of his masked expression. Lips pressed together, she glares at him with furious amber eyes.

"I am your queen, and you will face me when I speak."

"I wasn't there, Sula," Solum whispers. With her temper flaring and blood rushing, Sula almost misses it, but his words reach her ears and calm her fury. She remembers similar regrets when Uta died, and she sighs for her friend.

"She hasn't died, Solum. You can't mourn the loss of your daughter when she is still fighting for survival."

A condescending chuckle echoes from Solum as he faces his queen. She stands straighter and studies him with wary eyes. Solum drops his political mask, no longer wishing to maintain the control that keeps him from violating every code he holds sacred. Instead, he reveals his hatred and vile contempt for his queen. Sula recoils and holds her hands up as though they could shelter her from his animosity.

"I'm not mourning. Atae will recover. She is strong. She is Kaji," Solum says. "I haven't obeyed your summons because seeing you makes me want to forget all about my honor and commit atrocities."

With a frown, Sula stares are her closest friend. She studies his dark features and angry scowl, then shrugs at him. Solum is a passionate warrior and possesses great skill and insight, but they have been packmates for a long time. The last time he was this angry, Solum had just caught his lover in bed with Uta. She smiles at the memory and crosses her arms over her chest to meet Solum's gaze with an arched eyebrow.

"It's been a long time since you've been this angry with me, Solum. I believe last time involved Uta and me in the royal bed-chamber."

Solum blinks at the comment and the memories it conjures. He was expecting a fight, a reprimand, or some nasty retort, not a walk down memory lane. A blush floods his dark skin as his anger morphs into embarrassment.

"That was a long time ago." He tries to wrangle control of his flustered mind, but Sula slinks closer to him with an inviting smile.

"I know, but I haven't seen you this angry in so long. It reminds me of…before."

"Before?"

"Before…Uta and Roga," Sula says. She lays a hand on his chest and peers up into his dark eyes. Solum remembers their relationship before Uta and Roga. It was a passionate, all-consuming affair. An affair that burned bright and hot but ended in an explosion of betrayal and pain. Solum narrows his eyes at his queen and swats her hand away from his chest. Biting back an amused chuckle, Sula smiles at the warrior's rejection but doesn't move away.

"Why are you angry with me, Solum?"

"I wasn't there." His angry tone cracks under the weight of his guilt. "I wasn't there because I couldn't find the ship. I was supposed to be there training with Atae, but I was still here looking for that damn ship. I didn't leave to meet her until I received her message. Despite what you said, I never truly believed she could be in any danger. But I was wrong. If I'd left here on time, she-"

"And if you'd left any later, she'd be dead," Sula says. "You raised her to be strong. She is Kaji."

"You knew about the ship. You knew it wasn't a rumor? How? How did you know about the hole in our security?"

"Did you find a hole?" Sula asks. Solum glares at her, but she doesn't flinch from his anger. She stands firm against it and waits for his response.

"No," he says. "But there must be one. How else could the ship have landed on our planet and escaped without detection?"

"Of course." Twisting from him, Sula averts her gaze, and Solum spots the lie stretching across her face before she hides it behind her royal mask. He snarls at her.

"You knew. You knew about the security threat and did nothing. You allowed an enemy to trespass into our home. You allowed an enemy to attack my offspring."

"Do you think I wanted this?" Sula snaps her head around to face him. "You think I wanted her harmed?"

"I don't care what you wanted. I only care about what happened because of you."

"You wouldn't even have her if it weren't for me. She'd be dead along with Roga if I had not-"

"Don't you ever mention my mate to me again." The veins along Solum's arms and neck bulge with rage as he clenches his fists. "If you were anyone else, Sula..."

Queen Sula steps back from her packmate and reigns in her temper. The snarl slips from her lips as she raises her head, and her mask falls into place. Only her eyes reveal the cold, calculating anger simmering underneath. She straightens into a regal posture that emits an aura of superiority. Determined to get the information for which she came, Sula narrows her eyes at Solum.

"Was she the target?" she asks.

"No."

"Who or what was the target?"

"I don't know."

"Was the Gortox a faithful servant?"

"No," Solum says. Sula releases a silent breath at the news.

"Why did they attack her?"

Solum hesitates before answering, "Wrong place at the wrong time."

"Just a coincidence?"

"Just a coincidence," he says.

"How many escaped?"

"Just one."

She clenches her jaw at his clipped answers but hides her frustration. "What do we know about him?"

"Just that he is a mercenary. And that his name is Lisbon," Solum says. Sula dips her head, then asks a final question.

"How is she?"

"She has healed from her attack, but something else has taken hold."

"Not an illness. Kaji are not susceptible to viruses."

"But she is not only Kaji," Solum says. Sula's brow knits together, and she nods.

"You have a point. Still, are there other theories?"

"One other." He sighs. "This could be her shifting phase. That could explain her current condition and her resistance to the poison."

"Have you seen her shift?"

"Not yet," Solum says. Sula steps closer with an eager expression.

"Coach her. Talk her through it, and help her control it."

"I could be wrong. She could just be sick."

"Or," Queen Sula slips her hand around Solum's arm to lead him down the hall toward Atae's room. "Her body could be ripping itself apart and reassembling on a molecular level. Don't you remember puberty?"

The corner's of Solum's mouth quirks up, and she releases his arm. Sula smiles at him before walking away. Watching her leave, Solum realizes his anger no longer claws at him. Once again, he is amazed by his queen's ability to subdue her enemy without a single threatening move. He chuckles as she reaches the corner. At the last minute, Sula spins to face him.

"Oh, what about the other one? I trust she is still safe?"

"Of course. I spoke with her guardian after the attack. She is exactly where we left her."

"Good. I have a feeling we will need her soon," Sula says, then rounds the corner.

CHAPTER 12

Atae jolts awake as her body convulses, and she curls into a ball with an agonizing groan. As her unused muscles contract all at once, Atae gasps and writhes in the grand bed. Then her body calms, and her muscles relax. Heart still pounding, Atae refuses to move from her fetal position of safety. She just breathes and listens to the drumming in her chest. Atae sits back against the soft pillows and enjoys the cold air on her hot skin.

As she wipes the sweat and hair from her eyes, the youngling notices a mark on her arm. With a small smile, Atae examines her first real battle scar, two thin, black streaks that stretch across the length of her forearm. The hybrid flexes her arm and twists her wrist to each side to feel for any discomfort. She finds it sore from disuse but not painful. She considers the best way to show off her new scar to Jeqi and her other classmates. Atae guesses that she is the first of them to be wounded in a life or death battle. She runs a finger over the rough texture of her healed skin and remembers the unpleasant feelings of helplessness.

Maybe I won't show it off.

Atae's body stiffens, and she flails back into the pillows. She cries out as the convulsions return, and Solum barges through the bedroom door. At first, he searches for an intruder then realizes his daughter is alone and under threat of a different enemy. Solum jumps onto the bed next to Atae and places his rough hands on both sides of her face.

"Focus Atae," he says. "Force all your pain into your eyes."

Unable to think past the agony, Atae does not understand, so she closes her eyes and waits for the pain to subside. Instead, it worsens, and

Atae cries out again. A silver fog slips from the crevices of Atae's soul and drapes her mind. The glinting particles stab at her brain as they search for something.

"Atae, open your eyes. Look at me. Ignore the pain and focus on me," Solum says.

With her jaw clenched, Atae cracks open her eyes and looks to her father for help. She peers into his eyes and sees the inner turmoil that swirls in his dark gaze. She does not understand until his round pupils elongate, and Solum stares back at her with his battle beast eyes. If not for the debilitating pain, Atae would have jerked away from her father in surprise.

"Focus, Atae." Solum speaks with a gravelly voice before the rest of his shift takes hold. His daughter doesn't understand, but she wills the pain down and heaves it away. She forces the pain out of her body through her eyes. A strange, feral growl whispers from the fog within Atae's mind, and her arms and legs stop hurting. For just a moment, she can breathe easy as all her muscles relax. But when the white fog continues its search through Atae's mind, her facial muscles tighten again.

The muscles of her face contract past their breaking point, and Atae hears her cheekbones crack. Her jaw muscles pull at her already clenched mouth, and several teeth snap, filling her mouth with blood and drowning her scream. Panic blossoms deep within her chest as the fog claws at Atae's mind, but before it can overwhelm her, a sharp pain stabs at her forehead. A cracking noise drowns out everything but the pain, and Atae's skull splits apart under her skin. Unable to find what it needs, the fog recedes into the darkness of Atae's soul, leaving her exhausted, unconscious, and whole.

Later, Atae awakens with a start as a familiar nightmare haunts her consciousness. She shakes her head, and the cruel chuckle fades from her mind with a shiver. Heart pounding, Atae whips her head around to search for threats. The light peeking through the large window illuminates every corner of the room, and she marvels at its elegance. A huffing noise draws her attention to a battle beast lying next to her over the bedspread. The animal, covered in silver fur, stares at Atae then bumps its wet, broad nose against her face. A hot slobbery tongue sweeps across her cheek, and Atae giggles. After a couple of licks, she pushes the beast away.

"Stop it. Father, stop it," Atae says. He licks her once more for good measure, eliciting another giggle.

Solum lays his huge, fur-covered head on her small lap, and she pets his face, enjoying the rare display of affection. He tilts his eye up to Atae and offers a low whine. She smiles at his concern.

"I'm fine. Honest," she says. To be certain, Atae touches her cheek and forehead. Her worried expression melts into confusion after she inspects her perfectly normal face.

Was it just a dream? Atae wonders as she looks at Solum with suspicion.

"When did you take your second form?"

Ignoring her protests, Solum attacks Atae with his slobbery tongue again then jumps down to the marble floor. He strides around the large bed to Atae's side. Covered in silver fur, his four legs are like massive tree trunks, but despite his muscular frame, he glides around the room. A thick, hairy tail, long enough to touch Solum's nose, follows behind the beast. The hulking creature sits on his rump and stares at Atae.

Since Solum rarely spends time in his second form around Atae, she marvels at her father and revels in the chance to see his battle beast so close. Atae notes every blade-like talon on the warrior as she does with every battle beast she comes across. Knowing that every Kaji sports four beast blades in addition to the four talons on each paw, Atae notes two of the beast's razor blades on each front leg. They stretch from the wrist to the elbow. The forearm blades are used in combat for defending against belly attacks. The second pair of blades is located at the tip of his tail. The larger tail blade extends past the tip, and the smaller one looks more like a horn, sitting below its larger companion. They are both useful for flailing at opponents.

Atae sighs and runs her hand through her thick hair, then pauses as she realizes how long it has grown. Her short pixie cut is now falling past her ears.

"How long have I been..."

Atae glances at her father, but his only response is an impatient snort and a demanding shake of his head.

"Right. You can't speak."

Atae throws the sheets to the side and swings her legs over the bottom of the bed to stand. Solum growls at her, and she realizes why. Her unused legs complain as she demands too much from them too fast. Atae stretches to work out tension in her unused muscles, then she grips the side of the bed and forces her body to stand. Her muscles rebel against the sudden strain, but she is determined to reach her goal. Atae sets her gaze on the bathroom a few steps away, clenching her jaw and balling her fists. She places one foot in front of the other, and Solum watches in silence. When she reaches the bathroom door, she pauses and glances at her father. Her fuchsia gaze meets the black abyss of Solum's eyes. In his beast form, it is difficult to tell where his coal eyes end and his dark skin begins. Like his first form, the rough silver fur coating his entire body contrasts with his dark complexion. For an instant, Atae draws strength from his dark gaze.

She catches her breath as sweat beads on her forehead, then Atae pushes the door open and walks into the lavish bathroom. Even in her exhausted state, she cannot help but stare in awe at the splendor before her. Exquisitely detailed images of a forest decorate the walls. It's so convincing that, for a moment, Atae worries that she stepped back into the wilds. At the far end of the room, a large pool, carved out of the wall and floor, swirls with frothing bubbles of soap. A small waterfall cascades from the ceiling into the pool to churn the bubbles and small pink leaves throughout the water. Atae removes the thin clothes draped across her body and steps into the warm water.

Once in the pool, Atae snatches a pink leaf and sniffs it, recognizing the scent of the Kisl plant. During her eighth season, Atae learned from Feku about plants with unique characteristics, including healing herbs like Kisl. It is the main ingredient of many topical, pain-relieving medications. Atae rubs the plant between her thumb and forefinger, letting the numbing sensation that spreads over her fingertips confirm her suspicions. She releases the medicinal plant into the water and eyes several more churning about the pool. Realizing her legs have already loosened and no longer ache, Atae reclines into the small lake of relaxation and sinks deeper into the water. Her aches and pains fade across the rest of her body, and Atae sighs in relief.

The stonework surrounding the pool and descending into the water reminds Atae of a spring that she and Jeqi enjoyed numerous times. Atae closes her eyes and leans against the stone, enjoying the sounds of the bathroom. She basks in her memories of Jeqi and their hidden spring. She envisions the field surrounding the spring and how they would train together, talk about battle strategies, and help each other with assignments. Then, an unwelcome memory invades her mind, and Atae remembers her last visit to that field. In a flash, she feels the emerald gaze upon her and the certainty that death will swoop down at any moment. A wave of helplessness and fear overwhelms Atae, and her eyes snap open. She jerks forward and splashes in the water as she searches the room for intruders.

Panic-stricken eyes dart from one corner to another until the moving door attracts Atae's attention. Solum slips in, scanning the room for threats. After a moment, he snorts and trots to the edge of the pool. Solum flops onto the ground with his back to Atae and guards the door. Atae blinks at her father before realizing that she is no longer anxious or afraid.

I am not afraid. I am Kaji. I am strong, like Father.

Relaxing under Solum's protection, Atae smiles and dips under the water. When she resurfaces, her dark hair glistens with blue as it lays slick against her smoky skin, and her fuchsia eyes open to land on the illustration across the wall. Atae swims closer and glides her fingers along it, surprised that every riveting detail is hand etched. The colors glisten like liquid jewels to create a magnificent work of art. Atae marvels at the intricate work and gasps when she realizes the sparkling colors are, in fact, precious jewels. Solum lifts his head to glance at his daughter.

She meets his eyes and asks, "Do you see this?"

Solum glances at the wall and huffs, unimpressed. Rolling his eyes, he sets his head back down. Confused at his lack of interest, Atae runs her fingers across the wall again.

"Where are we?"

After marveling a little while longer, Solum interrupts Atae with a snort. He huffs at her again, and she almost smiles at the clear command to hurry up. If he could speak, her father would claim that he did not have all day for her to waste admiring a wall. Not long after, Atae, clean and relaxed, steps from the bathroom.

Wrapped in a drying cloth, Atae searches through the many elegant and sophisticated outfits in the closet until she finds one of her uniforms. The black bodysuit with short sleeves and pants has the silver logo of Sula Academy across the chest. Atae considers her school uniform appropriate for any occasion. She notices her hair in the mirror and sighs before attempting to detangle the mess with her fingers. Uncertain as to what to do next, Atae shrugs at Solum, lounging on the bed.

"Well, what now?"

Solum hops down and hustles through the main bedroom door, pausing for it to slide open automatically. Atae follows him into a large hallway and is, once again, amazed by the decor. She places her fingers on the wall across from her room and enjoys the touch of precious jewels. Stepping back, she stares at the illustration of a bloody battle. A Kajian male stands in the epicenter of death and carnage as hundreds of fellow

Kaji lie dying or dead alongside thousands of enemy corpses. The Kajian standing in the center of it all is injured, but still, he faces the onslaught. He commands his army and defends his people. Atae swells with pride at the depiction of Kaji honor.

Solum interrupts her thoughts with a low growl. Accepting his command to follow, Atae nods to her father. He leads her down a maze of halls as Atae fawns over the majestic scenes playing out around her. Soon, they reach a heavy, metal door that slides open, and Atae follows Solum into the royal training area.

CHAPTER 13

Atae follows behind Solum and peers around the room. She expects another eloquent and elaborate space that's bathed in jewels. Instead, she finds an outside training arena that's twice as large as her favorite clearing near Mount Tuki. The building behind her extends all around the training area with several access points. Stone hills erupt from the ground and extend above the roof of the buildings. Several warriors climb up and around the mountains and try to drag each other down. In various sections, three-inch steel columns impale the ground and stand almost as tall as the mountains. Some parts encompass only a few beams, while others have hundreds within a small area. She watches a battle beast hone his agility by darting between them at high speeds, cringing when he slips and slams into the solid steel. Atae also eyes several Kaji training on equipment that's grouped in different sections around the arena.

As they walk deeper into the training area, Atae twists around in awe of the enormity of the grounds. She doesn't notice a familiar youngling walking toward her or the two battle beasts at his side. Her tired muscles spasm, and she stumbles forward to land on her knees. With her hands in the dirt, Atae cringes at her weakness and ignores the taunting whispers that crowd her mind. She raises her head only to come face to face with two battle beasts.

She gasps and crawls backward away from the two deadly creatures baring their teeth. Accustomed to the temperament of most battle beasts, Atae doesn't feel threatened by the massive creatures' aggressive displays. Instead, she's entranced by the lighter beast's familiar silver gaze.

It's him, the heir from the market. He was with that rude youngling.

Atae stares until a familiar voice grates across her nerves, and she notices the rude youngling from the market standing between the two battle beasts.

"On your knees, again? Ready to worship me now?" he says. His amber eyes glimmer with taunting amusement as he tilts his head to the side and runs his hands through his wet, red, and white hair. The young male glistens with sweat from his bare arms, and a drenched towel hangs over his shoulder to dampen his shirt. Atae stares up at him from her knees and recognizes the smug expression plastered across his dark face. She growls at the brute with an annoyed roll of her eyes.

"You, I know you."

"Of course, you do," he says, then glances at Solum. "I see you've finally decided to come out and play."

"You were in the market the other day. You were very rude," Atae says. She climbs to her feet as the battle beasts, including Solum, bare their teeth at her. She frowns at their response, but the young male holds up a hand to stop them. The two beasts at his side sit at his command and glare at her. She glances at Solum, but he stares at her with unreadable eyes. The young male steps closer to Atae and peers at her with a hard expression.

"You will address me by my title." He speaks with power and intimidation, but Atae doesn't like bullies.

"Your title? Are you so important that everyone on this planet should know you by sight?"

"Yes. Along with everyone else in the empire."

Atae falters at the youngling's declaration, tilting her head to stare at him in disbelief. "Are you so arrogant that you honestly believe the empire revolves around you?"

He chuckles at her remark. With an amused smile, he steps closer and searches her face for a sign of insincerity. She frowns at him and leans away from his violation of her space.

"What are you doing?"

"You really don't know who I am."

"Why would I?" Atae pushes him away. Again, the two battle beasts jump to their feet and bare down on Atae with threatening snarls. Solum, still scrutinizing her, remains at Atae's side. She crosses her arms and shrugs at the threatening beasts.

"You know you're pretty arrogant for someone who needs his packmates to protect him," she says.

"They aren't my pack. And I don't need them to protect me. They just don't tolerate disrespect."

"Then why are they hanging out with you?"

The brute blinks at the question and frowns in confusion. Intrigued by the blue-haired hybrid, he steps to Atae's right and circles her. The two beasts fall behind him, still watching her like trapped prey. Atae doesn't move but to keep him in her line of sight.

"What do you mean?" He asks.

"You've been nothing but disrespectful. You've failed to introduce yourself and failed to address my father by his title," she says. "You've insulted me during our only two interactions. Then, you throw a childish fit when I don't use a title you failed to declare. I get the feeling you throw a lot of fits. What I can't figure out is why no one has beaten this nasty habit out of you."

"Are you offering to do it?"

The young brute stops at Atae's back, and she whips around to answer his challenge. Solum lunges at her and pins her to the ground with two massive paws. She cries out from the weight of him on her chest, and she struggles to push him away. But he is too big, and she is too weak.

"Father, what are you doing? I can take this arrogant brute."

She yelps from under Solum's shaggy coat when he sits on her. With her arms pinned, it doesn't take long for her to fall still from exhaustion. Atae stares at the cloudless sky as she catches her breath from the exertion, and she snarls when the male hybrid leans over her with a wicked smile.

"You may not know my title, but I know yours."

"I don't have a title." She grits her teeth as the presumptuous youngling kneels close and whispers in a taunting tone.

"Atae, the daughter of Royal Advisor Solum Learska. You were ranked second in your class at Sula Academy. But due to a recent injury by rogue trespassers, you've dropped to eighth. How far will you let your ranking slip before you return to class?"

"You disrespectful brat. I don't know who you think you are, but one day, very soon, I'm going to stomp you into the ground."

The young brute throws his head back and laughs. "Once you're fully recovered, feel free to challenge me anytime. I don't want my victory over you marred by your injuries. I'm going to truly enjoy stomping you back into your rightful place under my boot."

Enjoying Atae's angry growls, the young male glances at Solum with a nod.

"I'm assuming you're here for Dr. Pwen." When Solum nods, the amber-eyed youngling continues. "I'm not finished with today's session, so you'll have to meet with him in the med tent instead of the med wing."

"See you soon, Blue," the brute says to Atae before walking away.

Solum waits for the youngling and his companions to leave before releasing Atae. She rolls to her knees and watches the male hybrid walk away, noticing several Kaji that scramble to clear his path. Atae wonders at the youngling's strength and how much she'll enjoy fighting him.

Solum snorts to draw Atae's attention to a rotund hybrid walking toward them from around a partition along the arena wall. Atae raises her eyebrows at Dr. Pwen's extra set of arms and eyes. His primary pair of arms seem more robust than the second, which extend from his elbow joints with limited mobility. The doctor's central pair of eyes, located in the eye sockets at the front of his face, lock onto Atae. The second pair, positioned on the outer sides of his skull, survey the area around him. Dr. Pwen's bald head and bushy white mustache accentuate the roundness and his plump face. Despite his strange physique, Dr. Pwen's wide grin draws a smile from Atae.

"I see you are doing much better than when I last visited you, Atae," Dr. Pwen says.

"Um, you visited me?" She would definitely remember meeting him before today.

"I guess you wouldn't remember me. You were unconscious at the time," he says. When Dr. Pwen laughs, his plump belly jiggles, his arms wave in the air, and all four brown eyes glitter with amusement. Knowing such personalities in Kaji culture are rare, Atae is taken aback by the doctor's bubbly charm.

"I cared for you after your incident," Dr. Pwen says with a wink.

"Uh, thanks," Atae says. She frowns when the doctor motions toward the pest that challenged her.

"I must say, you certainly know how to make an impression. Warn me before your next visit, and I will transfer to the Southern palace," Dr. Pwen says.

"Do you think it'll be a great battle?"

"Most definitely."

He coaxes Atae to follow him to his medical area, but she glances at Solum for instruction. The royal advisor glares at his daughter, unhappy with her recent behavior, but lifts his head as a gesture to follow the good doctor. When all three Kaji reach the partition, Atae glances at the male youngling sparring across the room.

"Is he as strong as he thinks he is?"

"All Kaji warriors think they are stronger than they actually are. That is why we are always breaking new ground, always getting stronger. Mentality plays a large part in any battle." The doctor pats on an exam table with one of his smaller arms and waits for Atae to sit.

"A warrior's honor gives him strength," Atae says and sits on the table. Solum slinks past the partition and lies in the corner of the medical area to watch Dr. Pwen. Feeling calmer with him watching over her, Atae smiles at her father before tugging at a nearby curtain.

"So, you would not want to watch our battle?" Atae peeks from around the curtain to watch her new rival battle with his elder. He attacks the front defenses over and over again, never attempting to flank.

He truly is a brute.

"Oh, no. I am a specialist, not a warrior."

"I know many specialists, and none of them miss a good show of battle."

"Ah, but how many are doctors?" Dr. Pwen asks. Two hands flicker in the air as he scours his visor for Atae's medical records. Atae watches him search through his files as she considers his question.

"Uh, none, I guess. Doctors don't like violence?"

"It's hard to enjoy a battle when all you can think about is what damage each strike causes to the body," he says. After finding the correct file, Dr. Pwen performs his exam on Atae, assessing her eyes, ears, throat, reflexes, and healed wounds

Ignoring the examination process, Atae watches the youngling across the training grounds battle with the same opponent. Atae has yet to see the youngling dodge or glance an attack; instead, he insists on blocking or taking it full force.

Only a brute would attack the same way every time and expect different results. Atae snorts with amusement.

Then, he does something different, sidestepping a punch meant for his face. Expecting the hybrid to block as he had every time before, the older combatant hesitates in surprise before advancing with a spin kick to the abdomen. The youngling glances off the attack and uses his opponent's hesitation to spin close, hitting home with a neck chop. The stunned warrior doesn't feel the final blow to the back of his head that renders him unconscious.

Interesting.

Atae can't hide the impressed amusement on her face as she watches the older Kajian crumble to the floor. Two other Kaji shuffle over to help their fallen comrade, while a third one steps into fighting stance and continues with the sparring session. Without pausing, the young hybrid continues the battle unfazed by the fresh opponent.

After finishing his exam, Dr. Pwen clears his throat. "How long have you been up and about?"

"Long enough to bathe, then walk here from my room," Atae says. She watches the new opponent bounce from one foot to the other, dodge attacks, and counter with fast jabs.

What's your strategy against this new smaller, quicker opponent?

"Any soreness or muscle spasms?" Dr. Pwen asks. When Atae hesitates to answer, he pulls the curtain closed with one of his larger arms and demands her full attention. She crosses her arms and pouts.

"No, not since bathing."

"What about convulsions?"

"No, not since…" Atae tries to answer but stops when she remembers her last convulsion. She touches her face and jaw. No damage of any kind. Confused, she stares at Solum. She can still remember the pain of her jaw breaking and the sound of her teeth cracking. It must have been a dream because her face is perfectly fine.

"I don't remember the last convulsion," she says. "I had a lot of dreams and…I'm not sure what really happened."

"So, you don't remember much of the incident?"

"It happened really fast. There are some things I remember perfectly and others…" Atae averts her gaze to hide her shame. "Deh said something other than the poison was making me sick."

"Aw, yes. That's correct." Dr. Pwen searches through his notes. "Your temperature was several degrees higher than normal. You were delusional and suffering from convulsions."

"How much of that was due to the poison?" Atae cringes at the thought of being so weak and vulnerable.

"With Setunn poisoning, you can expect muscle spasms that lead to convulsions and death within a few minutes. Nasty stuff."

"Then, how am I still alive?"

"Honestly, I have no idea. With the time it took for Solum to find you then Deh to administer the salve, you should be dead."

"How long has it been?"

"About two weeks," he says. Atae sighs in frustration, and Dr. Pwen frowns in sympathy for her. "It's difficult to determine the cause of your illness because of your unknown origins."

Atae nods at Dr. Pwen's words and glances at Solum. Since Solum is purebred Kaji, Atae assumed at a young age that her mother was not purebred. Solum refuses to say much about his late life-mate, only that she died honorably. In Atae's earliest seasons, Solum squashed any questions about Roga with harsh reprimands for being emotional and weak. Atae only learned her mother's name because an old, drunk war buddy stopped by their home when Atae was younger. He was looking for a good time and was disappointed to find Solum with a youngling.

Atae still remembers the confusion clouding his drunken stare as he pointed at her. He kept asking Solum from where she came. He didn't remember ever seeing Roga with child, and Atae certainly didn't look Kaji. He left sporting a broken nose, three shattered fingers, and a clear understanding to mind his own business. Then Solum told his daughter that even the strongest warriors could falter under the influence of drink and that she would be a fool to listen to his ramblings. Always eager to please her father, the young Atae nodded her head and never gave the drunk another thought. Later, when she inquired about Roga, her father would not tell her or anyone else with which species she shared her genes. He would state that Atae was Kaji and that was all that mattered. Atae accepted the answer in earlier seasons, but as she spends more time with Jeqi and Deh, Atae can't help but wonder about her mother. Dr. Pwen's heavy sigh pulls her from her musings.

"I began to think you were entering your shifting phase, but you proved me wrong, once again," he says.

"Why would you think that? Hybrids don't have a second form," Atae says tartly.

"That's true in most cases. Less than one percent of hybrids have a second form, and it's always a variation of their first form rather than a true battle beast."

"Then why did you think I would shift?"

"Because it's far more likely than you having a natural defense against Setunn poison," Dr. Pwen says. "If you were poisoned during your shifting phase, your body's natural immune system would already be in fighting mode. It could explain how you survived."

"So, I could have a second form?" Excitement dances across Atae's face until Dr. Pwen shakes his head.

"No, your fever broke without you shifting. The only logical reason for your survival is that your unknown origins have a natural resistance to Setunn poison."

"But what if I shifted in my sleep and didn't know it? If no one knew?"

"During your last convulsion, Solum attempted to coach you through the shift. Instead, you passed out, and your fever broke while you were unconscious. You did not shift," Dr. Pwen says. He sets a small, comforting hand on her shoulder, but she shrugs it away and touches her jaw, remembering the pain of her dream.

"But you don't know my origins. You don't know for sure."

"I do," he says. "Seventeen seasons have passed, and you have not shifted once. I am absolutely certain about this. You do not have a second form and will never shift."

Solum places his head on her lap and licks her hands comfortingly. She stares down at him as an unexpected sadness settles in her chest.

Why should I be sad? I've always known that I couldn't shift. Nothing has changed.

Lost in thought, Atae strokes Solum's fur for a few moments of silence, then she smiles.

"It's okay, Father," she says. "I don't need a second form to be strong. I am Kaji."

CHAPTER 14

After Dr. Pwen deems her healthy and advises only light training until her strength returns, Atae immediately challenges Solum to a match. With better things to do, the battle beast puffs at her and walks away. Not wanting to challenge her new rival until she is at full strength, Atae says good-bye to the doctor and exits the training area.

Atae strolls down the magnificent hallways and admires the jeweled depiction of her people's historical moments, following the timeline of her people's ascension to power in their solar system. After she explores several diverging corridors, Atae stumbles upon a striking delineation of the royal bloodline. Her fuchsia eyes follow the beginning of the grand and honorable bloodline with the merging of the Ru-Ghi and Fu-Kai families. Every third season youngling knows the story of the noble Ru-Ghi warrior that conquered the Fu-Kai princess' heart and throne.

Atae's chest swells with pride for her people as she follows the imperial branches of the Ru-Kai lineage. Each generation mates with a new bloodline to add strength to the robust family heritage. Every Kajian knows that it is not the blood of a warrior that makes him or her an influential leader; it is the solid ideals and motives of the warrior. While the lineage is essential for traditional reasons, it is the upbringing and lessons taught to the ruler-to-be that keeps the Ru-Kai family in power.

When each Ru-Kai heir reaches sixteen seasons, he or she is thrust into the Gridiron. Merely surviving is unacceptable for the Kaji; instead, the royal heir must conquer it. Only then will he or she be allowed to return with followers and eventually reign over the Kaji. Allies and

KELLY A NIX

companions gained in the Gridiron are trained alongside the heir. This tradition allows the royal bloodline to stay dedicated to the Ru-Kai promise of protection and strength to the Kaji.

Atae marvels at the detailed pedigree etched into the long hallway. She passes several extravagant doors as well as attentive Kaji guards posted at each entrance. Each guard eyes the youngling, who is so engrossed in the meticulous historic artwork that she fails to notice her surroundings. Atae stops when she finds the Kajian name that makes her warrior's heart sing with pride. The sight of Queen Sula Ru-Kai's mark etched into the wall for all eternity strengthens Atae's hero-worship.

The hybrids of the most recent generation have a strong dedication to Queen Sula because of her support. She implemented programs designed to nurture non-warrior specialists through youngling training, such as Sula Academy & Research Facility. Younglings that participate in such establishments have more avenues and opportunities to bring honor to their families. Atae understands Queen Sula's role in her education because she would never have bested Solum without the Sula Academy's teachings. A stray thought creeps into her mind, reminding Atae of her failure in the wilds of Mount Tuki, and she grimaces at the stab of shame that penetrates deep within her chest. Sighing, she heaves the memories away.

Atae touches the grove symbolizing Queen Sula's position in the royal lineage and follows it to the next generation. As the only offspring of Queen Sula and King Uta, Prince Truin's grove is short and ends the entire pedigree. Atae glances at the previous generations of Ru-Kai. Each offered multiple offspring to ensure that one Ru-Kai heir would conquer the Gridiron and reign supreme. Less skilled Ru-Kai heirs fade from the family tree as they do from history. Concern strikes Atae as she realizes that if Prince Truin perishes in the Gridiron, the Ru-Kai bloodline perishes with him. Centuries of rule brought to an end by one warrior's inadequate skills. Atae gasps at this realization, and a wave of protectiveness for the royal family surges through her. There must be a way for her to help.

Atae decided early in her career at Sula Academy that she would be a warrior, but she hasn't yet chosen her specialty. Like many Kaji her age do, she planned to let the Gridiron decide her warrior specialization. She frowns at the wall of Ru-Kai rulers, and anger fuels her determination. Atae chooses, at this moment, to dedicate her life to the Ru-Kai family as a warrior for the royal heir. Protecting and serving the future leader of the Kaji Empire is one of the most honorable positions. Atae knows she will need to work hard to prove her worth.

Her imagination grows wild as she envisions single-handedly saving the royal heir from certain death. Atae smiles at her musings and again touches the prince Truin's groove. When her finger grazes an unfamiliar mark, Atae frowns at it. Intrigued, she notices the same symbol next to Queen Sula's slot. Unsure of the symbol's meaning, Atae searches the wall for an explanation, scanning every section of the hall around the two names. Engrossed in her search, she almost misses the slightest thump of a footfall behind her. Almost.

Atae freezes, her arm extended and fingers pressed to the wall, as she listens. When she doesn't hear anything, Atae wonders if her mind is playing tricks on her, then she hears the unmistakable sound of someone breathing. Atae's heart thrums with adrenaline and fear as she realizes that Kandorq is behind her. Somehow, someway, he's found her. He's returned to finish the job, and she is too weak to stop him. Atae imagines Salyn standing behind Kandorq with a cruel smile, waiting for the hybrid to face them.

"Youngling," a stern, female voice calls. Atae jumps and spins to face Kandorq with her teeth bared and fists clenched. Her frantic fuchsia eyes do not meet hungry red or wicked emerald, but warm amber. Atae releases the breath she didn't know she was holding, and relief washes over her. Then, she steps back from the empowering presence of the elder female standing before her. Atae notices the guards following the queen, and her eyes widen in realization. She snaps her right fist to the small of her back and the left across her chest. Queen Sula raises one eyebrow at the mistake, and Atae cringes, switching her hands so that the right fist lays across her chest and the left at her back.

"I believe I have startled you," Queen Sula says. She chuckles, and Atae blushes but remains silent. Sula eyes the silent youngling with a curious gleam.

"Why are you in the Royal Hall?" the queen asks.

For the first time since starting her wandering tour, Atae scans her surroundings and notices the extravagant entrances and numerous guards stationed at each door. Atae blushes again. How can she explain without sounding foolish that a future warrior wandered through unknown halls and ignored her surroundings because she was distracted by artwork?

"I asked you a question, youngling."

"I...uh...I don't know where I am, my queen."

"You are on Planet Kaji, of course."

Atae gawks at the queen before noticing the amusement dancing on Sula's dark lips. Atae smiles at the light teasing and presses a hand to the magnificent wall.

"I was…I wasn't paying attention to where I was going. This place is so beautiful."

"I agree. When I am here, I walk the halls and draw strength from the Kaji and their accomplishments," Queen Sula says. She glances down the hall, and her long braid sways down her back.

"Really? Wow. I…uh…I understand," Atae says.

"This is truly my favorite palace. I come here often."

"Palace? This is a royal palace?" Across from Atae, Queen Sula raises an eyebrow at the youngling.

"You didn't know this to be a palace?"

"I awoke from an illness." Atae grimaces at the confession. "My father, Royal Advisor Solum, he brought me here."

"And Solum allows you to roam free without any explanation?"

"No. When I awoke, he was in his beast form. He couldn't explain everything, but he did lead me to the doctor." Atae will always jump to her father's defense.

"And the doctor's report?" Queen Sula asks.

"He cleared me."

"I suppose it will be a while before you are at full strength again."

Atae nods, and the shame of her weakness reignites, forcing her gaze away from the queen. She glances at the royal lineage on the wall and considers her newly adopted and lofty goal. Her eyes land on the unfamiliar mark again, and she bites her lip.

"Your Majesty?"

"Yes, Atae?" The queen laughs at Atae's surprised expression. "I consider Solum one of my most trusted friends. Do you not think I would know of you and your…condition?"

When Atae blushes again, Queen Sula says, "Ask your question."

"I…uh…" Atae glances at the wall as she decides whether her curiosity outweighs her sense of pride. She doesn't want the ruler of the Kaji Empire to think her weak *and* uneducated. Frowning, Atae decides to ask and points to the unfamiliar symbol. "This mark. I've never seen it before."

Sula glances at the mark and huffs. She answers in a tone that suggests if it were not un-queenly, Queen Sula would roll her eyes.

"That, dear youngling, is the mark of royal impurity. The symbol was created just for me. It indicates that I descend from a line that is not pure Kaji."

"You're a hybrid?"

"My grandmother was a half-breed. I forget what species. But even the fraction of alien blood running in my veins makes me an impurity in the royal bloodline. It's actually quite scandalous." Sula wiggles her silver eyebrows, and Atae smiles at the queen's mischievous tone.

"Come, youngling, you will join me for the evening meal."

With that, Queen Sula walks past Atae expecting the hybrid to follow. Excited about the prospect of spending more time with her ruler, Atae falls in line. From behind, Atae admires the queen's ability to project strength with every deliberate movement. Queen Sula's pace is brisk and confident. She nods her head to passing advisors, respecting their titles, but not stopping to ensure that they pay their respects to her. Atae has a feeling that every servant, advisor, and guard they pass will show their respect whether the queen stays to witness it or not.

"Atae, tell me of your training," Queen Sula says, her long braid swinging behind her.

"Solum and I train every day. I am honored to have such a skilled instructor."

"You are attending Sula Academy & Research Facility, yes?"

"This is my final season. We just started weapons training," Atae says. Queen Sula smiles at the hint of excitement in the youngling's voice.

"Oh? What is your weapon of choice? I'm partial to throwing knives," Sula says.

"Well, I don't know yet. I held my first hilt the day of the...the attack," Atae says. Queen Sula halts and twists to study Atae with an appraising eye.

"Do you realize you are part of the first graduating class to attend Sula Academy from start to finish?"

"Uh, yea-yes. I think someone mentioned that before."

Sula watches her a moment longer without commenting then continues down the maze of palace halls.

"I am second in my class. Or, I was," Atae says.

"Only second?"

"Yes. My packmate, Jeqi. She is a fierce fighter and hard to defeat."

"Well, you'll simply have to surpass her." The queen's confidence in Atae makes her swell with pride and determination.

"I will, my queen."

Sula smiles at the youngling's response. The guards stationed at the entrance open two large ornate doors to reveal a marvelous dining hall. The marble walls depict glorious battles with conquered planets, and gold cloth, streaming from the high ceiling to the marble floor, frame each image. A large stone table, big enough to accommodate twenty Kaji, stretches the length of the room. Solum, no longer in his beast form, sits alone at the table, impatient for the queen's arrival.

"I apologize for the wait, Advisor Solum. I seem to have found something that belongs to you," Queen Sula says. She flashes him a charming smile, and Solum stands to greet her.

"My queen." Solum nods at his daughter. "Atae."

"Enough formalities, my friend. They bore me to tears." Sula waves her hand at him and sits at a less prestigious seat across from Solum instead of one of the royal chairs at the end of the long table.

"Tell me, Solum. Any news of my son's progress?" Sula asks. She signals to the servants to serve dinner, and Atae sits next to Solum, eager to learn of her ruler-to-be.

"He is skilled for a youngling of his season. There is certainly no doubt that he is his father's son," Solum says. Sula smiles at the compliment but falters when her royal advisor continues.

"But he has much to learn if he wishes to conquer the Gridiron."

"What do you mean?"

"For one thing, he lacks humility."

"Humility is not needed to lead an empire. If anything, insecurities can cause doubt in one's abilities," Sula says.

"Atae, why is humility important?" Solum asks. Atae swallows her mouthful of food before answering.

"Uh...Well, a lack of humility leads to overconfidence and underestimating one's enemy. That can be deadly," Atae says. She stares at her food as her thoughts lead to the overconfident Setunn she recently killed. Feeling Solum's eyes on her, Atae lifts her head with a forced smile.

"Besides, no one wants to follow an arrogant brute," she says.

"A what?" Sula asks. Atae realizes her mistake and snaps her apologetic gaze to the queen. Solum watches with a raised eyebrow as his daughter treads through her first royal minefield.

"Oh. Not the prince, of course. I was commenting on another youngling I met today."

Sula narrows her eyes at Atae but accepts her explanation. When the queen turns back to Solum, Atae exhales in relief and decides to eat quickly before she can make another stupid remark.

"So, you doubt his leadership skills not his combat skills," Sula says.

"A ruler must inspire his people to fight for him. Prince Truin is too egotistical to inspire anyone but himself," Solum says. "Atae, pride?"

Prepared this time, Atae recites the answer with confidence. "A leader takes more pride in his people than in himself."

"And what does that mean?" Sula asks. Atae thinks for a moment as she stares at her food.

"It means drawing more strength from your people's achievements than from your own. So that when you walk the halls of this palace, the murals fill you with more pride than remembering your grandest battle," Atae says.

Solum smirks at the idolization shining in his daughter's eyes for the queen. Sula has that effect on her people. Sula leans back in her chair with a smile.

"You have taught her well, Solum," she says. "Tell me, Atae. Will you specialize?"

"I will be a warrior of the empire."

Sula frowns at the predictable response. Every Kaji youngling wants to be a warrior for the empire.

"Do you wish to fight in grand battles and conquer planets in the name of our people?" she asks sarcastically. Solum narrows his eyes at his queen's attitude toward his offspring.

"Atae will allow the Gridiron to determine her warrior specialty."

"Actually, Father. I have decided on my warrior specialty," Atae says. "I wish to protect and serve the Ru-Kai bloodline. I want to ensure Prince Truin's success in the Gridiron and as our leader. I will be a warrior for the royal heir."

"Many royal warriors are chosen during the prince's time in the Gridiron," Sula says.

"Jeqi and I are already planning to enter the Gridiron with him."

"And what of the tournament?" Solum asks.

"What about it?"

"You are planning to participate, correct?"

"Yes, of course," Atae says. Then, she remembers her time loss. "It hasn't started yet, has it?"

"No. It starts in a couple of days," Solum says.

"Good," Sula says. "Because if you fail to win the Sula Academy Tournament, you certainly won't be of any use to my son in the Gridiron."

"I understand. Do you know when he plans to enter?" Atae asks.

"My son will hold his pledging ceremony in a few days. He will announce his plans for the Gridiron at that time."

Atae nods and contemplates the road ahead of her that's paved with blood, sweat, and pain. A twinge of doubt slips into her mind, and she wonders if she is strong enough.

All because you were too weak to stop me.

Atae snarls and clenches her fists.

No, I am not weak.

"I will be ready," she says. Solum sighs in exasperation and proceeds to knock the wind from her sails.

"You do not have a second form," he says. "You do not have any native weapons. You are naturally at a severe disadvantage, and you wish to jump in unprepared. You will make a fine royal warrior, indeed." Solum uses sarcasm to mask the concern for his child's safety and the consequences of her rash decision. Atae glares at her father. She brims with anger and determination as she lifts both of her clenched fists.

"These are my weapons." She points to her head. "This is my greatest weapon."

"It's difficult to strategize when you are scared and weak. Impossible when your body is flooded with adrenaline and panic," Sula says.

"I know what it is to be hunted. I know what it is to fight something bigger and stronger. I know fear and panic," Atae says. Remembering her recent battle, she shakes her head to regain her train of thought. "I will be smaller and weaker than anything I come across in the Gridiron, so I will need to be smarter and faster. I will never underestimate my enemy. I have learned firsthand the price for underestimating a weak and frightened prey."

"I may be a master strategist," Solum says with unabashed pride. "But, I cannot teach you speed."

"I can," Sula says. She shrugs with a playful head tilt, and Atae's eyes widen in surprise

"What?"

"Solum is a force to be reckoned with in any battle. However, he is slower than a squished Gru-Po," Sula says. Atae almost giggles at the image of a slime beast the size of a small youngling outrunning her father.

"I am considered one of the fastest Kajian females alive. As I'm sure you know, I am very skilled in battle. My son does not wish to learn from me. Perhaps, you do."

"I would be honored, my queen!"

"Are you sure you can spare the time, Sula? I know how demanding ruling an empire can be," Solum says. He stares at the queen, wary of his old friend's antics. Recognizing the barb, Sula narrows her eyes at Solum.

"I am Queen of the Kaji Empire. I can do whatever I wish whenever I wish. If I want to take a six-month hiatus, I will." Sula says, then whispers to Atae. "Besides, I'll just tell everyone that I am giving my son the best chance at success in the Gridiron."

"But who will run the empire?" Atae asks.

"My advisors, of course. I have hundreds of them, and it's about time they earned their keep."

"Very well, Atae. Tomorrow will be our last training session, and you will begin lessons with Sula after the tournament. That way, I can spend more time refining Prince Truin's skills, and the queen can do the same with you," Solum says.

"Awesome. Jeqi will be so jealous."

Sula wrinkles her nose at the offending squeals of joy and rolls her eyes at the youngling's excitement.

"Jeqi will join you in your sessions with Sula," Solum says.

"What? I didn't agree to that. Who is this Jeqi?" Sula asks. She sets her heated gaze on Solum, but he stands firm.

"She is Atae's hybrid packmate."

"Do you think Deh will let Jeqi train outside of Sula Academy?" Atae asks her father.

"Of course, no one would dare turn down a personal invite from the queen," Solum says.

"Ha. You're assuming that I will do this for you, but why should I? I do not know this youngling. Why should I care if she participates? Why should I train her?"

"Because Jeqi is at the top of her class, and Atae will need a strong pack. I also know you want Atae to have every advantage she can before she gallops into the Gridiron to protect your son," Solum says. His dark, narrowed eyes dare Sula to argue. She growls but relents. No, the queen would not want anything to happen to the fuchsia-eyed youngling.

"Fine, but you will not be distracted from training my son. Developing his skills as a warrior and a leader is imperative."

"Of course, my queen. So that we waste no time, Atae and I will live in the palace until the younglings enter the Gridiron."

Sula nods in agreement, and Atae smiles at the idea of staying in the beautiful palace for so long. Thoughts of exploration between training sessions invade her mind, and Atae remembers her mesmerizing walk through the palace halls. She also remembers her traumatized reaction to Queen Sula sneaking up on her. Exploring alone may not be a good idea.

"And Jeqi? Can she stay in the palace too?" Atae asks. She offers a meek smile to her queen, not wanting to push her luck. Sula watches Atae with her perceptive gaze

"Why?"

With her eyes expressing the turmoil she fears to voice, Atae stares at her queen in silence.

"Strategy, of course," Solum says. He glances at his daughter then continues. "The more time Atae and Jeqi spend together, the more in sync they will become. Pack unity will be an important aspect of their success."

Sula listens to Solum's words but watches Atae as though looking for the real reason for the request. After a moment or two, Sula agrees to let Jeqi stay in the palace until the Gridiron. Then she directs the conversation to empire affairs, and Atae is allowed to eat in peace.

Atae contemplates her situation as she finishes her meal. Her mind wavers between the determination to succeed and the fear of failure. Atae's fear of inadequacy continues to plague her through the end of the meal when everyone bids farewell and leaves for their private chambers.

Nightmares of Kandorq and the anxiety of being hunted intrude on Atae's sleep. She tosses and turns in her bed as she gouges out invisible eyes and slashes at attacking specters. Struggling to see the path, Atae dashes through the dark forest in a frantic attempt to escape the huntress. She falls to her knees and rubs at her eyes when a familiar burning sensation overwhelms her. Soon, they are upon her. Kandorq laughs at her weakness and licks his lips while Salyn watches from behind him. Her green slit eyes bare down on the hybrid, and both tormentors enjoy the smell of Atae's fear.

As his cruel laugh echoes through the trees, Kandorq reaches for Atae, and she jumps away from him. She backs against a tree, clinging to the large trunk behind her. Salyn appears at Atae's side and hisses at her. The youngling tries to escape, but leafy vines somehow entrap her arms and legs to bind her against the tree. Atae struggles as Kandorq and Salyn laugh. Unable to break the vines, Atae claws at them. She hopes to cut her way through, but her fingernails are no match. Still, she keeps scratching and tearing with all her might at the vines. Atae doesn't pause when her fingertips slice open, and her nail beds tear away. The never-ending laughter plagues her mind, driving her to the brink of madness. Finally, she rips free of the vines and lashes out at the Setunn. In a flash, Atae sees Salyn's eyes drowning in fear and anger as she bleeds out again.

Atae awakens with a start. She squints her eyes at the bright moon flooding the room through her balcony. Dripping with sweat, Atae wipes her forehead and cringes at her sharp headache. She closes her eyes and leans against the cool pillows, willing the pain away. A twist of silver fog glints in Atae's mind as it's shoved back into the darkness, unnoticed. The pain subsides, and Atae opens her eyes. Grateful for the cloudy night, she sighs in relief at the darkened room, then pulls at the sweat-soaked sheets. Atae cringes at her sore fingertips and stops to stare at them in the darkness.

Running her thumbs across her fingertips, Atae finds perfectly healthy fingers. Remembering the pain from her dream, Atae wonders about the phantom stinging that still triggers her nerve endings. She cringes again when she peels dead skin from her fingertips. Grimacing, Atae stops rubbing her skin off and returns her attention to the wet bedsheets.

As she pulls the top layer off, the sheet comes away in pieces. Somehow, the hybrid shredded the bedding during her nightmarish struggle. Shrugging it off, Atae tosses the torn sections to the floor. In the darkness, she doesn't notice the multiple tufts of dark blue fur hidden in the shreds of cloth. Crawling onto the now bare, but dry, bed, Atae falls into a dreamless sleep.

CHAPTER 15

"I can't believe it. How did you do it?" Jeqi asks. "How did you manage to score both of us private sessions with the queen?"

"Honestly? I have no idea," Atae says. She chuckles as they push their way through the entrance of Sula Academy. "I thought I was a rambling buffoon. At one point, Queen Sula thought I had insulted her son. You know, the prince."

"Well, if anyone were oblivious enough to do it, it would be you."

"Thanks," Atae scowls at her packmate's good-natured teasing. Jeqi smiles back but pulls Atae up short when they reach the door to their classroom.

"So how are you doing? Really?"

"I'm fine. See, I trimmed my hair and everything," Atae says. She twirls her head around to show off her freshened pixie cut but stops when she catches Jeqi's no-nonsense glare. "I'm almost 100 percent again. Just a little soreness here and there, definitely nothing I can't handle. I'm just ready to get back to normal."

"Well, you picked a great time to come back. Today is our last day of training. It's just supposed to be some review work and details about tomorrow."

"Tomorrow?"

"Round one of the tournament and one step closer to the Gridiron." Jeqi grins and tugs her packmate into their assigned classroom, which bursts with younglings. Atae knows that she should be as excited as Jeqi at the prospect of battle, but something unsettling bubbles up from deep inside and knocks the wind from her lungs. She ignores the anxiety clawing at the back of her mind and takes as deep a breath as she can manage. Jeqi frowns at her friend's odd response but doesn't comment. Instead, she pulls Atae through the crowd of younglings.

It only takes a step or two to realize that the classroom is not set up for review as Jeqi expected. Instead, Feku prepped it for combat training. All the holographic stations are gone, and the windows are covered. The younglings gather in their respective social groups throughout the bare room. Many of them stare at Atae, and others point and whisper. Atae stands straight with her head held high and glares at any onlookers until Seva calls to them.

As the two hybrids walk toward Seva and Debil, Atae notices Seva's remarkable improvement. Last time Atae saw her, Seva looked as though she would fall over from exhaustion. Today, her dark skin glows, and her ebony eyes shine with interest as she watches Atae. The movement of Seva's head when she speaks sends her cropped, red hair fluttering.

"Debil and I want to know about your attackers."

"Yea, who were they, and where did they come from?" Debil asks. Atae notices that Debil, too, seems much better. She notes her radiant caramel skin and short red hair with white tips. As they wait for Atae's response, she notices that Seva stands a finger or two taller than Debil. The blue-haired hybrid opens her mouth to speak, then remembers that she doesn't have an answer.

"Uh...I don't know."

"You don't know? You mean they couldn't figure it out?" Debil asks.

"No. I mean, I didn't ask."

"What do you mean 'you didn't ask'? Don't you care about who or why you were attacked?" Seva says. Atae shrugs with a sheepish grin.

"Well, I kind of figured it was just the wrong place at the wrong time. I mean Ka-" Atae stumbles over the name as a cold shiver runs over her back and sucks the breath from her lungs. Shaking it off, she continues.

"One of them mentioned a ship nearby and a third companion. Maybe their captain. But I never saw him."

"You mean that unidentified ship was them?" Seva asks.

"What? What ship?"

"The ship that landed a day or so before you were attacked. How can you not remember?" Debil says.

Atae frowns at Debil's accusing tone and opens her mouth to tell all the reasons that she doesn't remember an inconsequential conversation from days before she almost died. But Elder Warrior Feku strolls into the room, and all socializing careens to a halt.

Feku stops in the center of the room to inspect his crop of young warriors. This is his last opportunity to bestow upon them the wisdom and strength they will need to survive in this harsh universe. Feku strains under the weight of his responsibility, but he does not falter. He takes several moments to scan the classroom and meet the gaze of every student, recognizing the strength and skills they've developed over the last twelve seasons. A sense of pride pools in his chest as his pupils watch him, eager for the long-awaited challenge. When Feku's gaze falls to Atae, the small pool swells into a waterfall. She glances at her teacher but avoids meeting his gaze. He can read the shame burning on Atae's cheeks, but he doesn't understand why. Twisting his lips into a frown, Feku dismisses the hybrid's odd behavior and addresses the class.

"During the last couple of weeks, the last of the purebreds in this class have finally completed their shifting phases. Congratulations, you now have the same ability as every other Kaji warrior in the universe."

Atae shoots Jeqi a questioning glance, and the blonde nods her head to Debil and Seva. Both purebred females grin at the announcement, and Atae realizes that they must have gained the ability during her absence.

"Everyone, split into three groups according to your ability, battle beasts, partial shifters, and non-shifters," Feku says. He points at different areas of the room for each group to gather. Jeqi follows Atae to the non-shifting area, and almost half of the class, the hybrids, join them. Marqee and Sloan pass by Atae and Jeqi on their way to join with the other purebreds in the battle beast group, and Sloan bumps Atae's shoulders with a fake surprised expression.

"Thought you were dead."

"Sorry to disappoint," Atae says.

"You might as well be. You're five points behind."

"For now."

Atae and Sloan part as quickly as they met but continue to glare at each other from across the room. Jeqi observes the small interaction with annoyance but doesn't say anything.

After everyone finds their assigned group, all eyes shift to Jent, who stands alone in the section reserved for partial shifters. The Kip hybrid rubs his arms and fidgets under the scrutiny of his classmates. Atae notices Jent's desperate glances to the group of battle beasts like he's hoping for support from his packmate. But Tuk refuses to meet Jent's eyes and pretends not to notice his friend's plight. Atae wonders how their pack will hold up in the tournament. She can't help but feel appreciative of Jeqi; at least they value each other as friends. Atae wonders if Jent and Tuk's pack is by agreement rather than a real pack bond, but her thoughts are fleeting as Feku continues.

"How many of you have seen a battle beast shift?" The moment he finishes his question, half the class signals with their visual visor. Forgetting that she'd activated her visor before arriving, Atae blinks away the sudden onslaught of holographic light emitting from the group. Since Atae has never seen a battle beast shift before, her visor remains dark. Glancing at Jeqi, she notes that her packmate has not seen one either. Feku surveys the younglings and nods as though he expected as much.

"What drives a Kaji to shift?" Feku asks. Then he motions to Debil.

"Emotions can force a shift."

"Emotions...hmm. By your logic, you would shift every time your mood changes. So will we be forced to deal with your jealous battle beast next time Sloan pays too much attention to Atae?"

The entire class thunders into a cascade of laughter. Jeqi glances at Sloan and smiles at his attempts to cover his blush with a flippant twist of his mouth. His eyes flutter with a dismissive roll as they search for any place to land but on Atae.

"Why would she be jealous of Sloan and me fighting all the time?" Atae asks her packmate. Jeqi hides her amusement and fights the urge to shake her head at her friend's naivety. Oblivious, Atae watches Debil blush and stare at the ground.

"If all it took were emotions to trigger a shift, you'd be a blushing battle beast by now," Feku says. "Care to guess again?"

Debil shakes her head and steps back into the crowd of students, hoping to disappear. The classroom once again lights up with visual visors as younglings vie for a chance to earn recognition and points. Sloan, crossing his arms over his chest, steps out of the group of purebred Kaji to stand next to Debil. He peers over his shoulder at her, and Debil's heart rate jumps as she swallows. When Sloan peels his gaze away from her to address Feku, his lean stature and confident swagger attract everyone's attention.

"Calling it an emotion is like calling a star hot," Sloan says. He glances at Debil again then drops his voice into a deep drawl. "It's so much more."

"Really. If not emotion, what would you call it?" Feku's stern tone makes it clear that he is not in the mood for Sloan's games.

"Need, I would call it a need," Sloan says.

"What kind of need?"

"A need to hunt or fight, even procreate." Sloan waggles his eyebrows, then his face calms, and his tone grows serious. "It's the need to…survive."

"Survival," Feku repeats as he addresses all the younglings around him. "That's what you're learning here. You're learning to fight, to think, to survive. And not just the Gridiron but life, too."

Feku waits for that to sink in, then waves his hand. "Sloan, lead the group in their shifts to battle beasts."

Sloan nods to the elder warrior then saunters to the front of his group with a smug grin. All of the purebred Kaji look to their temporary Alpha for inspiration as Sloan closes his eyes. The proud smirk on his lip calms, and the suggestive arch of his brow falls. Even from across the room, Atae notices how odd it is to see her rival's face so placid. Usually, he twists his face into whatever annoying expression he knows will aggravate her the most. Underneath her distaste for the young male, Atae admits that this calm Sloan is almost appealing.

Concentrating, Sloan tenses his entire body, and everyone in class watches and waits. After a few dull moments, grumbling escapes the crowd in hushed whispers. Sloan opens his eyes, licks his lips, and glances at Elder Warrior Feku, who continues to watch in silence. Sloan deepens his frown to hide his embarrassment, and his eyes dart around the classroom for inspiration. When they land on Atae, Sloan pauses.

Atae revels in Sloan's apparent inability to shift on command. She nearly laughs when his frantic gaze jumps around the room. She knows he's hoping someone will save him from this embarrassment. His dark eyes fall on her, and Atae's grin grows. But her smug smile falters as Sloan's gaze roams from her fuchsia eyes. She feels him sizing her up as though they are in a match. When he meets her glare again, his orbs of coal stare unblinking as a single spark lights a ring of fire in his eyes. An instant later, across a room of adolescent Kaji, Atae peers into the red eyes of a battle beast.

Refusing to let Sloan unnerve her, Atae doesn't look away. She watches him cringe and struggle as every muscle in his body contracts at once. Atae flinches at the sounds of Sloan's bones snapping and his moans of agony. As flesh and bone break down and reform, Sloan pitches forward onto his hands and knees without breaking eye contact with Atae. She cringes and watches his dark skin stretch around new formations, like a snout, and thicken into the battle beast's tough hide. As silver fur sprouts from his dark skin, Sloan's body absorbs his Sula Academy uniform.

Atae holds her breath as Sloan's convulsions slow, and a thin, red line burns around Sloan's elongated pupil. His blazing red eyes pierce Atae as he steps toward her with a snarl. At first, she falls back a step from the threat then catches the mistake. Atae presses forward with her own silent snarl. His shift nearly complete, Sloan attempts to retaliate with another dominant advancement, but the last change in his anatomy is so sudden and painful that he drops his gaze and all but yelps in surprise. Sloan's blades slice through new tissue and muscle as they erupt from his forearms and tail. Moments later, Sloan stands before the class as a complete battle beast.

Sloan barks at the group behind him, and the other purebred Kaji follow his command to shift. Their temporary leader, or alpha, had given them the order to change; therefore, pack mentality dictates the shift as necessary for survival. None of the younglings have trouble following Sloan's lead, and Atae frowns at the massive pack surrounding him. She hates the idea of following him. She considers death as a viable alternative if ever forced to make a choice.

"Sloan has proven how important it is to harness the urges, or needs, that force a shift," Feku says. His commanding voice drags everyone's attention from the group of battle beasts. Atae crosses her arms over her chest and glares daggers at Sloan when his class score increases by five points. With a ten-point lead, Sloan snubs Atae's threats with a puff and flips his slobbery beast head away from her.

"You were all able to shift without hesitation because the Alpha of your pack, no matter how temporary, commanded it. Kaji descended from pack animals, and, whether we like it or not, packs play a large role in our society. Someone give me an example," Feku says.

All the visual visors in the room light up, including, much to Atae's surprise, the battle beasts'. Even more surprising, the elder warrior signals for Seva, Debil's packmate, to answer. Bewildered, Atae glances at Jeqi with a questioning look, wondering how he expects Seva to answer in her battle beast form. When in their second form, the Kaji communicate with body language because their vocal cords are not sophisticated enough to form words. Jeqi purses her lips in annoyance and motions for Atae to pay attention. Seva's bladed tail swirls and twists above her head for a moment. When she stops, a message lights up on everyone's visors:

'The warriors chosen from the Gridiron to be royal companions are part of the prince's pack. They usually spend their lives serving the royal family in some capacity or another.'

Atae pouts at her ignorance. Of course, the battle beasts still have access to their visors. A stray thought as to why Solum didn't use his the day she awoke from the attack crosses her mind, but she assumes he didn't because they communicate fine without it. Besides, it gave her father an excuse not to discuss topics he wanted to avoid.

Like the attack.

Jeqi's snickers pull Atae from her thoughts, and the blue hybrid responds with a not-so-gentle elbow nudge to her packmate's ribs.

"That's right, Seva." Feku increases her score by two points. "But does that mean they have a pack bond?"

'Of course, you can't have a pack without a pack bond.'

"Who agrees with Seva? Who thinks that a pack cannot exist without a pack bond?" Feku asks. The majority of the class signals with their visual visors. Atae is surprised to see so many of her packmates agreeing with Seva but doesn't let it sway her opinion. Noticing her dissent, Feku motions to the hybrid.

"Atae, what do you think?"

"You can have a pack without a pack bond."

'No, you can't. It's not a pack if there isn't a bond. That's why they call it a pack bond.'

As Atae reads Seva's response, she can hear the sarcasm and condescension. Atae bares her teeth as she places one hand on her hip and glares at Seva, ignoring the bladed tail whipping behind the annoyed battle beast.

"They call it a pack bond because there has to be a pack for there to be a pack bond, not the other way around."

"Do you have support for your argument?" Feku asks Atae. Seva growls and snaps her teeth, eager to retaliate, and Atae huffs, unimpressed. She turns her back to Seva, insulting the purebred female, before responding to Feku's question.

"Yeah. Them." Atae waves her arm at the group of adolescent battle beasts. "You said so yourself. They are pack following an alpha that you designated, yet they are not bonded to each other simply because you gave them someone to follow. As soon as you, or anyone else, knocks Sloan off his pedestal, this temporary pack will break apart into the original, smaller packs. Into real packs with real pack bonds."

"And what do you think a real pack bond is, Atae?"

"It's…" she says but struggles to put words to the bond that she shares with Jeqi. "It's…loyalty and trust. It's knowing that there is someone that will always have your back. Someone you can depend on no matter what. It's like family, but…better."

"Well, that's one way to describe it," Feku says. He all but rolls his eyes at the sentimental description. "I suppose it's worth two points."

Atae smiles as the gap between Sloan and herself diminishes bit by bit but refuses to meet Jeqi's eyes after her embarrassing explanation. Jeqi wraps her tail around her waist for safekeeping then teases her packmate.

"Well, this is awkward."

"Shut up."

"Now, how many of you have seen a partial shift?"

This time, no one signals with their visor, and Feku watches everyone turn toward Jent.

CHAPTER 16

Jent stands alone separate from everyone in the section for partial shifters. His black and gray feathers ruffle in agitation as he tilts his head in an avian-like motion. The battle beasts to his left pace and leer at Jent with slobbery growls. Jent's golden slit eyes, almost bulging from their sockets, dart around the room until they stop on Feku.

"I…I can't. I'm sorry, Elder Warrior, but I can't," Jent says.

"Why?" Feku asks. He crosses his arms and stares at the Kip hybrid. Jent's eyes widen as he realizes the elder warrior's thinning patience, so he takes a deep breath to calm his anxiety.

"I can't do it on command yet. I've tried," he says.

"Do you know what it's like for them?" Feku motions to the group of battle beasts. "They are young Kaji. Too young to maintain complete control of their inner beasts."

Inner beasts? Atae frowns at the term. *What's an inner beast?*

"As they mature, the Kaji's instinctual beast mind and the rational mind will combine. Until then, they are constantly at odds. Look at Debil, Jent."

Every youngling not in battle beast form watches Debil. She paces back and forth, staring at Jent and drooling. She nips at the other Kaji that come near to warn them off.

"Right now, her beast mind is telling her that you are prey because she can smell your fear and anxiety. The only thing stopping her from ripping you to shreds is her rational mind arguing that you are not prey but Kaji. Do you understand?"

Not trusting his voice at the moment, Jent nods his head.

"So what can you do to prove to her inner beast that you are, in fact, Kaji instead of prey?" Feku asks.

Jent closes his eyes and focuses all his thoughts and efforts on shifting. When nothing happens, he opens his eyes and searches for help. His eyes dart across the room until he finds Tuk, hiding deep within the pack of battle beasts. Tuk's initial response to his packmate's silent pleas is a non-committal huff and an aggravated shake of his head. When Jent doesn't take the hint, Tuk grumbles and jogs to his packmate. Tuk stops in front of Jent and glares at him. Jent, unsure of Tuk's plan, watches and waits for something to happen. After a moment or two, Jent relaxes, realizing that Tuk is there for moral support rather than an actual fix to the problem at hand. The idea of Tuk being supportive is foreign to Jent, but he finds it reassuring. Maybe if he concentrates really hard, Jent can shift on command. No one would consider him prey then.

Tuk releases a loud bark that forces everyone in the room to jump in surprise. Jent, at the apex of the sound, nearly jumps out of his skin. The pain that rips through his body convinces Jent that he did, in fact, shed some skin. Instead, claws slice from his fingertips and the ruffled feathers on his forearms, shoulders, and neck clamp down into melded armor. Jent shields his face with his newly armored arms, but when Tuk doesn't attack, he lowers them. Jent notices the changes to his hands and arms and smiles. He punches Tuk in the shoulder and admonishes the battle beast's tactics, but thanks him for the results. Tuk sits on his rump with his chest puffed out, head held high, and quite proud of himself.

Atae, along with all the other younglings, gawks at Jent in awe. Partial shifters are rare; in fact, many Kaji can go their whole lives without meeting one. Atae finds Jent's physical shift unnerving and fights the urge to look away, but she marvels at his change in demeanor. His confidence hardens along with his feathers. He now stands before his admiring classmates with pride and a little showmanship as he lets curious younglings feel his new armor. Atae can't help but envy Jent. He may not be a battle beast, but at least he can shift.

"Now that everyone has seen a partial shift, can anyone else do it?" Feku asks. When no one volunteers, he continues. "What about the battle beasts? Have any of you ever tried to shift only a part of your body? Maybe just a forearm blade or a patch of thick fur?"

This time, when no one responds, Elder Warrior Feku opts to remain silent and watch his students process the new information. Sloan is the first to speak up.

'I thought partial shifts for purebred Kaji were a myth?'

"No, it's real," Jeqi says. The entire class, including Atae, stares at her. "Continue," Feku says.

"It's a legend, not a myth," she says. When everyone continues to stare at her, Jeqi sighs. Then, in the cold, analytical voice she uses every time she addresses the class, Jeqi explains.

"There were a few legendary Kaji throughout history that mastered the ability to control their shift enough to stop it at any point. Usually, this entails forcing the beast blades to shift first, then stopping there. Don't get your hopes up, though, because every one of these legendary warriors was a Ru-Kai ruler."

"Very good, Jeqi." Feku adds five points to her score. "Now everyone, take a look around. Consider how many of your classmates can shift and how many cannot."

The younglings glance around the room, tallying which of their classmates might be a threat in the tournament. Atae eyes Sloan and Marqee, and they both bare their teeth.

"Almost half of you are at a distinct disadvantage in the tournament, not to mention the Gridiron. The Sula Academy Tournament has a low mortality rate. It won't kill you," Feku pauses to tilt his head and shrugs. "At least, it shouldn't. I've taught you everything I can over the last twelve seasons, watched you grow stronger, smarter, and faster. I've watched you build your packs and learn to trust each other. But outside this classroom, you don't get to choose your battalions or your co-workers. And you won't get to in the tournament, either."

Atae glances at Jeqi with a worried brow, and she returns the look with a tight-lipped frown. Other hybrids murmur between their packmates, and the battle beasts pace in agitation.

"What do you mean, Elder Warrior? Are you going to break up our packs?" Trinka, the green-haired hybrid, asks.

"The first three rounds of the tournament require packs of four. You will fail or succeed as a pack. No one member of each pack can advance without the other three. The fourth and final round will be on an individual basis. For the most part, I respected your existing pack bonds when selecting your new packmates, but some of you won't be happy. And I don't care. I don't want to hear any whining. Make one complaint to me, and I will pull your entire pack from the roster."

As he finishes, Feku flips his hands around to grab at his personal hologram controls. With a flick of his fingers, every visor in the classroom lights up with an incoming message that lists the pack assignments. Atae scans her name and sighs with relief to find Jeqi part of her pack. She smiles at the blonde hybrid, but Jeqi doesn't notice. Instead, she studies her own hologram and bites her lip. Concerned, Atae rechecks the message. When her eyes fall on the two names that will complete their pack of four, Atae falls still. She shuts her eyes with an angry snarl.

"No. No way."

"Atae, calm down."

"No. I am not working with them."

"Shh." Jeqi pulls her away from the group to a corner of the room. The reactions around the room vary, but no one seems outraged by surprise reorganization.

"You have to calm down, Atae. If Feku hears you complaining, he'll kick us out of the tournament," Jeqi says.

"Who cares? Why do we need to compete anyway? The only reason to do this stupid tournament is if we were planning to enter the Gridiron with Sula Academy, but we're not. We're entering with Prince Truin, so why do I have to work with him?"

"Shut up." Jeqi watches the crowd behind Atae for signs that someone overheard her outburst. The other students are intermingling and joining up with their new packmates. Jeqi can't see the two purebreds that are tallied to join her pack and hopes they will give her enough time to calm Atae.

"You've kept up your part of the deal, Atae. You get to choose when you want to compete in the Gridiron, but I don't. Not yet. I have to graduate at the top of my class. That was *my* deal with my mother. If I don't compete in the tournament, my ranking will drop, then I won't be allowed to compete with Sula Academy or Prince Truin. So I need you to pull yourself together and suck it up."

Atae glares at her packmate and clenches her teeth, but Jeqi doesn't back down, meeting Atae's emblazoned, fuchsia gaze with her own icy blue. After a few moments, Atae relents, closing her eyes and sighing in resignation.

"Fine."

Jeqi smiles and nods her head in gratitude. She opens her mouth to speak but stops when her gaze shifts to something behind Atae. Jeqi's eyes widen, and she pales. Before Atae can ask what's wrong, she hears a heavy footfall behind her, and a tall figure casts a shadow over the two hybrids.

Atae freezes as memories flood her mind. In an instant, she can feel Kandorq grabbing her from behind. His massive hand snatches her neck to pinch off life-sustaining air, and insane fear swallows Atae's mind and all rational thoughts.

"Atae," says a deep voice at her back that ignites Atae's reflexes into crackling lightning. Twirling around to face Kandorq, she crouches into a defensive fighting stance and snarls like a wild animal. Atae glares at the red-eyed beast and dares him to try to touch her, to hurt her. Clenching her jaw, she bites back a threatening growl at the imposing figure, but it isn't Kandorq. Instead, Atae finds a frowning elder warrior.

"What are you doing?" Feku asks.

Atae straightens from her fighting stance and rubs her arms, looking anywhere but at her teacher. Noticing the soreness from clenching her jaw too hard, she swallows and rubs her throat.

"Atae, answer me," Feku says.

"I...uh..." Atae's throat burns, and her voice twists into a gravelly grunt. She's unsure how to explain her bizarre actions and blushes when she notices all her classmates staring with hushed murmurs.

"I thought you were someone else," she whispers.

"Someone else? Someone bigger and stronger than you?"

Atae sets her jaw, trying hard not to over clench it and hurt herself again, but she doesn't like the elder warrior's question. Still, she answers.

"Yes, Elder Warrior."

"And what were you going to do, Atae? Fight me, bare-handed?"

"It's worked for me in the past," she says. But Atae doesn't like the all too familiar gleam in the elder warrior's eyes. The predatorial glimmer reminds her of Salyn, but it isn't quite the same. She doesn't understand why, but instead of unnerving her, Feku's gaze calms Atae. She's surprised to see him grin at her.

"So, I've heard. I believe that's worth twenty points, don't you?"

Atae blinks at the sudden compliment. Stunned, she gapes at Feku in disbelief, along with the rest of the class. His hunter's glare doesn't shift from Atae, and she knows he is searching for something from her. Something all predators chase after, weakness. His smirk widens, and Atae wonders what he's found.

"Well, let's not bet on that in the tournament or the Gridiron." He pulls out a hilt and hands it to Atae. Too surprised to argue, she takes it and runs her fingers over the smooth metal. Returning her soft gaze to her teacher, Atae smiles.

"Thank you," she whispers.

"Take good care of it, Atae." He flashes her a satisfied smile. "You should look to your newest packmates for help. Private tutoring is essential for you to catch up on the techniques you missed during your recovery."

"Tutoring?"

"Yes, that's one of the reasons I've partnered you two with Sloan and Marqee. With Sloan's help, you might learn to wield that hilt with decent skill."

Atae glances past Elder Warrior Feku to find Sloan and Marqee pushing their way through the crowd of students. They both stand in their first form, frowning at her. Atae returns the resigned expression to her new packmates then nods at Feku.

After the elder warrior leaves to speak with other students, Jeqi whispers to Atae.

"What is wrong with you? Why did you act like you were going to attack him?"

"Don't worry about it," Atae says. She smirks at the opportunity to return Jeqi's multiple brush-offs. But the blonde isn't so easily distracted.

"I'm serious. What was that?"

"It's nothing. I've got it under control."

"No, you don't, Atae."

"What would you know about it?" Atae snaps.

"I know that you are not okay. Something is wrong with you, and you think I don't know or that I'm going to ignore it. What kind of packmate do you think I am?" Jeqi whispers to Atae. The puffy tail wrapped around her waist accentuates Jeqi's frustration. Atae glances toward the two male purebreds strolling toward them and relents.

"Fine, you're right. We can talk, but not here. Not now."

"Where? When?"

"Tomorrow, before the tournament starts. You can meet me at the palace, and I can help you and Deh move in," Atae says. Jeqi nods and, much to Atae's relief, drops the topic. Sloan and Marqee greet the two hybrids with absolutely zero enthusiasm.

"This could be worse," Marqee says.

"Yeah?" Atae asks. "How's that?"

"We could be stuck with just you. At least, we get Jeqi too. She's almost worth putting up with you," Sloan says.

"Are you saying I'm worthless?"

"He's saying you've fallen behind," Marqee says. "We won't have time to train together because we have to get you caught up on your swordsmanship. If you don't catch up, you'll be a liability."

"I hate you both," Atae says.

"Ditto."

Feku clears his throat to reclaim the class's attention. He says, "Now that you've all had a chance to acclimate to my latest announcement, it's time to learn about the tournament. As I'm sure you've already heard, the Sula Academy Tournament is different each season. But one thing always remains the same. You must advance past each round to represent the academy in the Gridiron. As I said before, this season's tournament will consist of four rounds. You will advance through the first three rounds in packs of four, but you are on your own during the fourth round. Round one is a good old-fashioned brawl with a few twists. Half the arena will be in complete darkness with the second half lighted as normal. Fifty packs will enter, but only forty will advance. As soon as ten teams are defeated, the round ends."

Atae glances at Sloan and Marqee to find them whispering to each other. When Sloan glances up from his packmate, Atae flashes him a questioning expression, and he returns an overly sarcastic smile. As expected, Atae huffs in annoyance but returns her attention to Feku.

"Round two will be very different from the first. Strategy will be most important since it will involve an evolving maze. The maze will have forty control panels. Half of your pack will work the controls to clear a path for their two maze runners. The first thirty packs to complete the maze will advance."

Jeqi glances at Atae, who nods at her packmate. Jeqi is skilled in the art of strategy, so there's no doubt that she will work the controls while Atae runs the maze. But Jeqi can't help but frown at the idea of separating from Atae. They are pack and should remain at each other's sides in a battle.

"For round three," Feku says, "each team will capture flags and defend their base. The twenty packs that last the longest will advance."

"That one doesn't sound difficult," Atae says to Jeqi, but Sloan overhears.

"It's always harder than you expect," he whispers into her ear. Atae elbows him, and he huffs, feigning pain at her rejection. She rolls her eyes at Sloan as Feku continues.

"Now, round four will be the most entertaining. For me, anyway. Eighty of you will enter, but only fifty will win and earn the honor to represent Sula Academy in the Gridiron. The goal of round four is simple: Exit through the assigned gate. To access it, you must obtain one of fifty keys hidden throughout the arena. Find the key and exit through the giant gate to win. Any questions?"

Atae, Jeqi, Sloan, and Marqee stare at each other with the same wary expressions.

"Well, this should prove interesting," Sloan says.

CHAPTER 17

"Well, I guess we're all going to die," Sloan says. He smacks Atae in the arm with the flat side of his energy blade. She growls and swings her two-handed sword toward the annoying purebred. He swats away her feeble attack and sneers.

"You can't even manage to hold your hilt correctly," he says. "Did you even listen to my instructions?"

"Nope," Atae says. She lunges with her sword tip pointed at Sloan's mid-section. "You're arrogant and annoying, and I find your voice unpleasant."

Sloan blocks her strike with an effortless swing then twists his blade at the perfect angle to jerk the hilt from Atae's hands. Surprised, she hesitates, and Sloan slips in close to pin his sword against her neck. Atae grabs at his arm, but it's too late. She freezes as Sloan peers down at her over his blade. He stands close enough that his breath brushes her cheek, and she tightens her grip on his arm, forcing him to press his body against hers to maintain control over her.

"Do you think that maybe, just maybe, it might be possible that despite my arrogance and annoying voice, I might still be the best damn blade-master at Sula Academy?"

"No, Jeqi is the best."

"How would you know? Have you even seen her wield a hilt?"

"Nope, but she's Jeqi, and she's the best at everything. At least, that's what our class ranking claims," Atae says. She flashes a defiant smile that falters when Sloan frowns at her, and the light from his energy blade casts an odd shadow over his face.

"Believe me when I say this, Atae," he says. "You must learn to hold your own with a hilt, or we will lose the tournament. And there go our chances in the Gridiron. Whether you like it or not, I am your best bet."

"Well, then we are screwed because you are a terrible teacher."

Sloan deactivates his sword and steps away with a frustrated sigh. "Maybe you're just a terrible student."

Atae scoffs at the insult as she picks up her hilt. With a zing, the two-handed blade erupts from the hilt, and she holds it in both hands like a large baton. "I can do this. With or without your help."

"Not with a blade that size. You need something smaller."

"Why? I'll be fighting battle beasts and warriors twice my size. I need something big and powerful."

"It doesn't have to be big to be powerful. You're not big, but you're powerful," Sloan says. He reaches for her hilt, but Atae hesitates before releasing it to him. After adjusting the settings on the small device, Sloan returns the hilt to Atae, and she activates it. With another zing, a small blade, no longer than her forearm, springs to life, and the hybrid sneers at it.

"What am I supposed to do with this? It's tiny."

"So are you."

Atae snarls at the purebred, and he backs away with his hands held high in placation. "I have to go, but you should try it out tonight. You'll be surprised by the power it holds within its tiny, tiny form."

Sloan chuckles as he leaves Atae in the royal training area. She heaves an exasperated sigh and glances down at the weapon in her hand, then she eyes the dedicated warriors bustling around her. The hybrid is amazed at the number of warriors in the palace, some of whom are no older than Atae. After deactivating her hilt and placing it in her holster, she strolls through the training area to admire the expensive conditioning equipment lined against one wall. She dodges overzealous sparring matches and smiles at their ferocity. As she reaches a corner located on the opposite side of the training area, Atae stops to watch a sparring match between two female warriors. She marvels at their speed and agility and hopes one day to be faster than they are.

As Sul's heat against her skin dulls and its red light dims, Atae traipses through the crowd of warriors. This time, she travels on the opposite side of the small mountain that's centered in the training area. As the crowd thins, Atae finds herself squeezed between the steel poles impaling the ground. Deciding to have some fun, she rushes through the agility course.

Atae darts between the poles with ease at first, but the deeper she runs into the course, the closer the poles gather. When she attempts to quicken her pace, the jerky speed between the small gaps forces Atae to slam against the steel beams. Still, she keeps going until she escapes at the end of the course near the entrance of the training area, just in time for the automatic lights to switch on.

"Poor Blue," a familiar voice says. "It looks like you still need time to recover fully. Or is that the best you can do?"

Atae cringes as the amber-eyed brute chuckles. Rubbing her sore shoulder, she eyes the repugnant male and his two companions. With a tight-lipped frown, she wonders which of her recent visitors she despises more. At least tolerating Sloan has a purpose. She can't think of any reason not to wipe the floor with this unnamed brute. Except Solum will be here soon, and she wants to be fresh for their first session since the attack.

"Too scared to answer? Did you figure out my title? No, if you did, you'd be bowing," the male hybrid says.

Atae laughs at the absurdity of his claim, and the two battle beasts at his side growl. She glances down at them and jerks a dismissive hand. They don't impress her, not even the silver-eyed heir.

"I have more important things to worry about than you and your pack."

"As I've told you before, they aren't my pack. But you're right. I hear you and your tiny blade have a tournament to lose tomorrow."

How does he know about my tiny blade?

"What did you say?" she asks. The arrogant brat rests one hand on his hip and huffs at Atae.

"Don't tell me that you think you can actually win. I mean, maybe your pack will drag you through the first three rounds, but the fourth round? You don't have a chance."

"Argh. What is your problem?" Atae throws her hands up, and the entire training area careens to a halt as everyone stops to watch her berate the other youngling. "Why is it every time that I've laid eyes on you, you insist on insulting me? Do you treat everyone this way, or am I special somehow? If so, I don't see how your pack puts up with your arrogant, self-righteous attitude."

"They aren't my pack."

"So you've said. Personally, if they aren't your pack, I don't know why they follow you. It certainly isn't for your pleasant company."

The ill-mannered male jumps in Atae's face and growls, and she glares back at him as he speaks.

"I am the strongest youngling on this planet. One day, I will be the empire's greatest warrior."

If not for her anger and hatred toward the disrespectful brat, Atae might believe him. She's seen the immense respect other warriors give him, but it doesn't matter.

"I don't care how strong you are or how strong you grow. You will never be a great warrior."

"Ha. That doesn't even make sense. But what would you expect from a weak youngling like you," he says.

"A warrior is nothing without a pack to watch his back. And what pack would take a self-righteous, overconfident prick like you? Some warrior you'll be when you're too busy watching your own back from the enemies you've pissed off," she says.

"I need no one."

"Pathetic."

"Enough." Solum's words, although not loud, echo across the silent training area. As though someone flipped a switch, everyone in the near vicinity returns to their activities. But Solum's sudden appearance isn't enough to tame the two younglings' tempers. They continue to glare at each other in silence.

"I said enough, Atae."

Atae steps away from the brute but refuses to break eye contact, and her father snarls at her.

"You will learn to hold your tongue around our prince, or I will cut it out," he says.

Atae spins around to face her father, showing her back to the other youngling and dismissing him as a threat. He huffs at the infuriating tactic, much to Atae's delight.

"The prince? Where?" she asks.

When Solum nods his head at her rival, Atae's heart stops. Prince Truin watches with a mountain of satisfaction as the obstinate little hybrid realizes her mistakes. He motions toward the two battle beast guards at his side.

"I told you, they aren't my pack," he says. "You should start bowing."

Atae jerks straighter and snaps her right fist over her chest and the left at the small of her back. Her fuchsia eyes meet his amber for an instant before she averts her gaze to drown in her shame.

"Prince Truin, I apologize. I did not..." She's at a loss for words. How can Atae explain her complete lack of respect toward the youngling to whom she wishes to dedicate her life?

"You did not what? Know that a prince has a higher status than even a royal advisor's daughter? That much is obvious." Prince Truin says. "Solum, you've failed drastically at educating your daughter on palace politics."

"I can see that now, sire."

"Let me know when you finish with my guards."

Prince Truin bids farewell to the older warrior and walks away without a glance toward Atae. Cheeks flushed, Atae wishes she could disappear. She rubs her face with her hands and wills the embarrassment to retreat from her mind and chest. How could she let this happen?

...a self-righteous, overconfident prick...

How could she speak in such a manner to Prince Truin?

You disrespectful little shit...

Atae can see her dream of serving as a royal guard swirl away into the abyss of her failure and shame. She peers at Solum with pleading eyes, but he scoffs at her behavior. Nope, she got herself into this mess, and he'll leave her to drown in it. Sighing, Atae accepts the harsh reality of failure and sinks into a self-pitying hunch. Noticing the sudden change in Atae's stance, Solum growls at the youngling.

"Pathetic. One setback, and you are ready to accept defeat?" he says. Atae meets her father's gaze with pleading eyes.

"I...uh...I don't know what to do."

"Are you injured?"

"What?"

"Are you physically incapable of fighting? Are you injured?" Solum asks.

"No, of course not."

"Then you train and fight. Then train some more and fight again."

"But he hates me. He won't want me to be part of his guard," she says. Solum shakes his head at his daughter's naiveté.

"You think Prince Truin will choose his royal guard? The Gridiron will choose many, but Queen Sula will play a heavy hand as well."

"Prince Truin doesn't even get a say?"

"Maybe, a small say." Solum shrugs his broad shoulders, and Atae is, once again, empowered. Excitement and determination flood through her veins, and she cannot help the smile that spreads across her face.

Amazed at how much a pep talk can inspire her, Solum smirks at his daughter then signals to two battle beasts behind him.

"Let's begin. Schinn, at attention. Trikk, at ease."

Schinn, the white battle beast with gray and black streaks, steps to up Solum's right ride. He stands firm with all four feet planted, head held high, glaring straight forward, and tail swishing behind him. Trikk, more black than gray, sits to Solum's left and stares at Atae. Her eyes widen when Trikk sniffs the air and licks his lips. The cold hunger in his obsidian gaze unnerves her, but she does not move.

"Advantages?"

Solum's question pulls Atae from her thoughts, and she glances from Solum to Schinn. Familiar with Solum's teaching methods, Atae steps up to the presented battle beast and walks around him. She studies his body, the blades, and his stance. After making a full circle, she stops to the right of Schinn's neck and stares at his thick fur. Without hesitation, she sticks her hand into the ruff at his throat. Schinn snaps his head around to bite off the offending appendage, but Atae realizes her mistake in time to jump out of harm's way.

"I'm sorry," Atae says. "It helps if I can touch."

Schinn's silver eyes burrow deep into Atae, and he lifts his lips to bare his teeth. Remembering Feku's advice earlier in the day about a Kaji's inner beast, Atae straightens and speaks in a stern tone.

"May. I. Touch."

The two younglings glare at each other for a moment longer until Schinn relents. He returns his head to the attentive stance and stares forward, so Atae relaxes with a silent sigh. Eyeing the back of his head for a response, she slips her hand onto the ruff of Schinn's neck. Seeing his lack of response, she digs deeper into the thick coat. The coarse hair is hard to navigate, and she struggles to find the hide below.

"The fur is a defense in its own right. A blade would need to penetrate pretty deep before reaching the hide," Atae says.

"And a projectile?" Solum asks.

Atae imagines the rudimentary weapons many technologically challenged species use, particularly a handheld cannon that launches metal projectiles meant to tear through the body. The damage dealt against lesser creatures is enough to kill. Atae frowns as she envisions a shell penetrating the course coat then impacting the hide below.

"No, the fur would not stop it, but it would slow it down enough that the hide would not be significantly damaged," Atae says.

"Unless at point-blank range." Solum nods. "The damage from a powerful projectile at close proximity would damage the hide and any underlying muscles. What else?"

Atae nods and walks around Schinn again to analyzes his physique then stops at the tail.

"Royal Guard Schinn, I would like to touch you again." After hearing his rumble of approval, Atae sets her hand on his fur-covered tail with two blades erupting from the end. Muscles ripple across the entire length of the extremity, and Atae is amazed by the tail's reach. With the beast standing eye level, Atae knows Schinn could drop her with a single pounce.

"The large body mass adds power to attacks, and the tail's reach is tremendous. The blades alone could slice into the toughest hides, but with that much power behind each strike, bones will break," Atae says. She sighs with a small, bittersweet smile. Solum notices her appreciation for the great beast and her resentment of never being able to experience the powerful form herself.

"Disadvantages?" Solum asks. Atae glances at Schinn but doesn't bother to examine him again.

"There aren't any. He is fast, powerful, and deadly."

"Well," Solum crosses his arms and glares at his daughter, "If they are so unbeatable, I should just let them eat you now."

"What?" Atae asks, sure she had misheard him.

"You should start running."

Atae's eyes widen at her father's words. He cannot be serious. No, her father would never... Nevertheless, there it is. His empty, coal-black eyes reveal his disappointment in her. Cold tendrils of panic trace down her spine as she struggles for breath. As the fear-laced adrenaline strikes her body in one fell swoop, she bolts away.

She darts across the training area between other warriors, ignoring their shouts of protest. Only two things register in her frantic mind. Find an escape route, and do not let the sounds of chasing battle beasts get any closer. She hears their claws scraping at the stone floor and their jaws snapping at her heels. In her panic, Atae ran in the opposite direction of the exit, so now she must find another escape. When one beast manages to slice into her leg with a taunting nip, Atae launches onto one of the training machines against the walls.

Adrenaline keeps the pain from her wound at bay, and Atae continues to jump from machine to machine, staying just out of reach of the two snapping beasts. When she runs out of equipment to climb, Atae hurls herself onto a stone mountain erupting from the ground in the center of the training area. Schinn and Trikk follow suit up the stone hill as best as they can, but the terrain is difficult to climb with paws. As Atae's lead grows, she reaches the other side of the mountain to find the steel poles stretching from the floor and above the palace walls.

Atae leaps from the top of the three-story mountain into the forest of poles. Grasping the nearest one with both hands, she uses her momentum to swing her legs around to another pole. The steel forest is dense here, so she's able to sway from pole to pole. When Schinn and Trikk catch up, she is far too high for them to reach her. They growl and snap at her in frustration as she holds a pole in each hand and presses her feet against a third and fourth rod. She pulls herself to the top of the steel columns to find tipped blades. Unable to get any higher, Atae flattens herself at the precipice. She maintains as much distance as possible between her and the royal guards.

"Now, you've managed to tree yourself," Solum yells to his daughter as he stands outside the steel forest. "Though, I doubt you'll die of starvation. Your muscles will weaken first, and you will plummet just in time for a late-night snack."

Atae grimaces at her father's imagery. Searching for another escape route, her eyes dart across the gathering crowd of warriors, but Solum puts a stop to that.

"No one will help you. If you are eaten, it'll be because you are too weak to stop it," he says.

All because you were too weak to stop me.

Atae closes her eyes and shakes her head, willing the voice to be quiet and the ruthless emerald eyes to disappear.

"I am not weak," Atae whispers. Her anxiety twists into anger that burns throughout her body. "I will not let you hurt me."

The silver fog returns and seeps into the crevices of her mind, somehow fueling her blaze of fury. The rage sears down her spine and spreads to her muscles, and she gasps at the incinerating pain in her arms and legs. When she opens her eyes, she loosens the vice-like grip on each steel pole, revealing deformations in the metal. Loosening her hold allows Atae to slide her hands lower than her feet so that her head points toward the ground.

Bending her knees, Atae watches the beasts below her. Her fury does not burn into her muscles anymore, but the adrenaline keeps them loose and her mind sharp. She waits for an opening, any opening, then she finds it. Schinn and Trikk lift their snouts and necks to look up at her, but when they look to each other or anywhere at ground level, she falls out of eyesight. They cannot even see her in peripheral because that would require lifting their heads.

I am not weak. Atae cringes as a silver tendril tugs at a crevice in her mind, and her legs tighten, almost causing her to lose her grip and fall. As suddenly as it began, the pain stops, and Atae focuses on the task at hand. She waits a moment or two, and when the time is right, she launches off the steel poles with surprising force. Her leg muscles catapult her like an over-coiled spring, and she dives headfirst towards Trikk. In midair, Atae spins her body and tucks her feet underneath her just in time to land on the unsuspecting beast's head. Atae hears a crunch as Trikk's skull slams into the ground. She smashes him a second time when she propels off him and flips backward away from Schinn. Atae lands next to Trikk's now limp tail and stares at the growling Schinn.

I am Kaji.

Infuriated by his fallen comrade, Schinn lunges for Atae, but she dodges his chomping jaws and rolls away. He whips his bladed tail around, aiming for her head, only to strike the ground when she leaps out of reach. Frustrated with the agile hybrid, Schinn hurls toward Atae with murderous intentions. She ducks underneath the attack and unsheathes her tiny blade. In the same instant that Schinn sails over Atae, she stabs the knife into his sensitive belly, using his momentum to pull Schinn's body across the energy blade. As he lands in a crumpled heap, Schinn's intestines spill onto the cold stone floor.

Adrenaline making her cold and powerful, Atae stares at Schinn and Trikk, then she shifts her heated glare to her father and smirks. Atae leaves the training area as several doctors rush to aid the fallen warriors, and Solum watches each warrior in her path move out of her way. Atae doesn't notice any of them as she walks back to her room. Instead, she replays the fight in her head and ignores the tight muscles that flex with each step.

As she reaches her room and sprawls face up on her bed, Atae reaches one conclusion. She has never moved that fast before. It's impossible. She should be slow and weak after her hiatus from training, not faster.

And stronger. Atae remembers the bent metal under her grip.

As the adrenaline ebbs from her body, and her heartbeat slows to an average pace, Atae sighs and closes her eyes. The silver fog lifts from her mind and whisks away into the safety of Atae's soul, leaving the blue-haired youngling feeling empty and alone.

Atae cries out as all the muscles in her extremities tighten at once. After a moment, they relax, and Atae is left gasping for air. She stands up to check her arms and legs for soreness, but they feel fine. Yet something is different. Atae doesn't feel the power and strength from moments before; instead, she feels tired and weak. Frustrated and confused, Atae groans and plops into bed.

CHAPTER 18

"So when you said you would come and help us move, you really meant you'd bring servants to do all the work for us," Jeqi says to Atae.

They stroll through the palace halls and admire the marvelous depictions of Kaji history. Distracted by a particularly gruesome battle between the Kaji and the Gortox dated only a generation before, Atae does not immediately respond. After they pass the bloody scene, Atae swivels her attention back to her friend.

"Actually, I followed them here. I wasn't sure where they were putting you. I walked all around the palace looking for someone that knew, just to be escorted to the room right next to mine. By that time, the servants had arrived, and I wasn't much help," Atae says. She flashes a sheepish grin at her packmate, and Jeqi smiles as they wander down the hall and around a corner.

"Didn't it occur to you to ask someone yesterday before you went to bed? You know, prepare for the next day."

"No. Last night...I was tired." Atae clenches her jaw at the thought of her father practically feeding her to the battle beasts. Then she releases her jaw and sighs. Atae is too tired from last night's restless sleep to stay angry with her father.

They round another corner into a hall with no outlet, and Jeqi asks, "No training this morning?"

"No," Atae runs her gray fingers along the etched crevices of the wall as they walk. "Last night was my last session with Father. After the tournament, we'll start training with Queen Sula."

They stop in front of a small glass balcony at the end of a hall. Wrapping her tail around her waist, Jeqi sits on a nearby bench and watches Atae walk past her to the clear glass. She smiles at the view of the city beyond the royal garden. Vines and colorful flowers reach above the garden and creep around the windows of the balcony. Only partially risen above the horizon, Solis' red beams crawl across the city and stretch toward the hidden garden. Jeqi's calculating blue eyes rove over Atae, and she frowns.

"You're tired," she says. Atae stiffens, and her eyes bounce across the gardens, looking anywhere but at Jeqi.

"Yes."

"Why?"

"Bad dreams. Nightmares…" Atae says. Solis' light shines through the clear glass and bathes Atae in warmth as her mind grapples with the icy shards of her reoccurring nightmares.

"Atae," Jeqi whispers. The familiar kindness and unhindered concern in her voice draws Atae out of her daydream. She peers at Jeqi over one shoulder, almost expecting to find Deh's loving eyes and patient smile. Jeqi's concerned gaze is so much like her mother's that memories of Deh holding and soothing her echo through Atae's mind and drown out her fear.

"Tell me what happened," Jeqi says. Atae sighs and sits on the bench next to her packmate. She stares out into the city and watches the people move about their daily lives.

"You know what happened. Everyone does."

"No, we don't. We know Solum found you dying along with two trespassers. But no one really knows what happened. You haven't told anyone," Jeqi says.

"I froze," Atae whispers.

"In battle? You froze in the middle of the battle?"

"There was no battle!" Atae jumps to her feet and crosses her arms over her chest to glare out the window. "I didn't fight anyone. I heard him coming, and I hid."

Jeqi remains silent as her friend pauses. Atae closes her eyes and forces her thoughts past the nightmares and onto the real memories of that night. After a moment, she opens her eyes again and stares at the sunrise, unseeing, as she relives the worst night of her life.

"I heard him coming, and I hid. I couldn't hear her, but I knew she was there. Then, she wasn't, and it was just him and me. There was a moment when I could have run. He was too slow. I could have gotten away without him ever catching me. But I didn't…I froze. And when he grabbed me, I…I panicked." Tears glimmer in Atae's eyes, and she's glad that Jeqi can't see them.

"Seasons of training, and I panicked," she says through clenched teeth. "It wasn't until I got mad that I thought clearly. I knew he wasn't going to kill me. That's not what he wanted from me."

Kandorq's haunting words whisper through Atae's mind, and she struggles not to shiver at the memory of his fowl breath against her cheek. Atae shakes her head then stares into Jeqi's cool blue eyes, envying her stoic demeanor.

"He wanted me to remember him and what he was going to do. He thought that I was too weak to stop him. But I am not weak. I stopped him. When I saw the opening, I took it. I didn't hesitate. I didn't freeze that time. I gouged out his eyes, and I ran. I knew that she would hear his screaming and that she would come. I ran as fast and as far as I could." Lost in her memory, Atae shifts back to the window and fidgets with the hilt sheathed against her thigh.

"I ran until I couldn't anymore. I really did. I should have been able to make it to town easily, but I didn't. I couldn't. I run everywhere. I run during training every day. But when I really needed to run, I couldn't. I couldn't do it, even to save my life. So I climbed a tree. I hid and hoped she wouldn't find me, but she did. She was tracking me. All I could see were her eyes. She did something to light her path. I remember thinking that was stupid because then I could see all around her. Then she threw her nails at me," Atae says. She glances at Jeqi, who raises both eyes brows in surprise.

"She threw her nails at me and started climbing a nearby tree," Atae says. "All the while, glaring at me with those evil eyes. I jumped then, jumped down, and hurt myself. I could barely walk. Everything hurt. I knew she was following me, stalking me. She could have killed me then, and I couldn't have stopped her. But she liked to play with her prey. She liked watching me suffer. I found a clearing with Blousq flowers, and I stopped. I couldn't have walked any further if I wanted to. I had a plan, though." Atae crosses her arms again as she stares down at her feet.

"I didn't think it would work, but I wasn't going to just lay there and let her win. She strolled into the clearing with this amused look on her face. She wanted to know how I had done it, how I had killed him. When she cut into my arm, she was going to let me decide how she would kill me. She thought I was weak, too. I proved her wrong. When she breathed in the flower's poison, I didn't hesitate. I used her own blade to slice her throat. And then I passed out," Atae says. She looks up at her packmate with swirling fuchsia eyes, imploring her to understand.

"There was no battle, Jeqi. I was too weak to fight them. All the training I've done, and it meant nothing. I froze. I choked. I'm not going to let that happen again. I am strong. I am Kaji."

"You didn't choke, Atae." Jeqi jumps to her feet and snatches Atae's hand. "You were sick."

"The Setunn didn't poison me until I was in the clearing. I choked before then."

"Not poison. Illness. You were sick," Jeqi says. Atae snorts and pulls her hand free, but Jeqi grabs her shoulder. "Atae, don't you remember falling asleep in the clearing before class? You were tired for days before that. Your injuries weren't healing at your normal pace, and you were more susceptible to pain than normal. I was certain you were starting your shifting phase."

"My shifting phase? I'm a hybrid. The chances of me shifting are extremely small. Why would you think that?"

"Your behavior mostly," Jeqi says. "You always seemed to be winded or tired, and you were healing so slowly. I knew something was wrong. I did some research, and as unlikely as it was for a hybrid to start shifting, it was less likely that you were ill due to other means. Besides, Debil and Seva, even Jent, started shifting around that time. It's common for younglings that remain in proximity to each other to trigger each other's shifting phases. It's a domino effect. When one starts, another of the same age follows, and then another."

"I thought it was just packmates that begin shifting together. I didn't know non-pack could be affected."

"Didn't you notice when Sloan, Marqee, and all the other older younglings shifted last season? It wasn't just one pack at a time. They all started individually," Jeqi says. Her tail unravels from her waist and bounces along her ankles.

"Oh…" Atae ponders her packmate's words then smiles at her. "I remember that. I guess I just didn't notice the pattern."

"I'm not surprised. You would never notice anything that important."

"What's that supposed to mean?"

"It means that it never occurs to you to ask about the events that unfold around you. You either don't notice or don't care to know. That's dangerous, Atae." Jeqi presses her lips together and huffs at her packmate. Atae blinks then frowns at the blonde.

"It's not that I don't care. It's just that I'm focused on other things, like beating Father or training for the Gridiron. Now apparently, I have to master blade-wielding. I can't change what's happening around me. I can only change what I do and what happens to me and mine. You're going to depend on me in the Gridiron, just like I'm going to depend on you. I have to be ready. I won't let you down," Atae says. Her eyes blaze with a fiery determination, and Jeqi pauses in surprise at Atae's resolve.

"Atae, you are the best fighter at Sula Academy. You should be confident in your ability to defend yourself and yours. Why aren't you?"

"I'm not scared. I'm not afraid of anything. I am strong. I am Kaji." Atae spins back around to the window and wraps her arms around her chest with a heavy sigh. Jeqi recognizes her packmate's attempt to shut her out, so the blonde reaches for Atae with a soothing voice.

"I didn't say you were afraid. I said you lack confidence, which is very unlike you. Atae, please, tell me what's wrong?"

Atae doesn't respond but continues to stare out over the garden below. She watches the small trees and bushes rustle in the morning breeze, then Atae is back in that dark forest. The hybrid squeezes her eyes shut and hopes to feel Solis' morning heat through the clear window. Instead, she feels Kandorq's rotten breath creeping down her neck and Salyn's emerald gaze watching her. Atae balls her hands into fists and clenches so tight that her nails cut into her palms. Then Kandorq grabs her neck from behind as his tongue scraps across her face.

"Atae…" A voice breaks through the terrifying fog engulfing her mind, and a steady hand grabs Atae's tense shoulder.

"Don't touch me!" Atae spins around to face Kandorq with her fists raised. "I am not weak. I am strong. I am Kaji."

Jeqi gasps and steps away from Atae. Reality crashes hard into Atae's mind, and she lowers her fists. Reigning in her anxiety, Atae takes a deep breath and speaks in a controlled, monotonous voice.

"And I'm not afraid. And I don't lack confidence. You were wrong, Jeqi. I didn't shift. I can't. I choked, that's all. Don't worry. I won't let it happen again."

Atae strides past Jeqi to leave her behind but stops when the blonde calls out.

"They were mercenaries."

"What?"

"Spies, really. They were sent to gather information about us. The Kaji," Jeqi says. She scrutinizes Atae's response, trying to pinpoint the real problem under her bravado. Atae frowns at the odd piece of information and scrunches her nose.

"How do you know that?"

"I ask questions, Atae. You may not want to because you think you can't change anything, but information can be just as powerful as raw strength in certain situations."

"But who did you ask? How would they know?"

"My mother told me about the trespassers before your attack and warned me to be on the lookout. They slipped by all of our planetary security measures, and no one knew who they were or why they were here. But when you were attacked, we found out. Mother told me that the trespassers were mercenaries sent to gather information, but we still don't know who sent them or what information they stole. The captain of the group took off with their ship when he realized his comrades disappeared. From what mother says, we still don't know how he got through our security," Jeqi says.

She steps closer to her friend and offers a small smile with a shrug. Atae takes a moment to absorb the information about her attackers but frowns when a thought occurs to her.

"The captain..." she says. "Lipson, I think. Yes, that's what he called him. If Lipson got away, how did they find all this out?"

"The big one, the one you blinded-"

"Kandorq," Atae whispers as a shiver runs down her back.

"Yes...him," Jeqi says. She falls silent when she sees Atae's reaction, and her tail wraps securely around her waist. Noticing the blonde's hesitation, Atae tries to mask her anxiety, but Jeqi can see the swirling anguish in those rose-colored eyes.

"What about him?" Atae asks.

"He's still alive, Atae."

Atae stumbles as though Jeqi's words were a strike against her chest. The air in her lungs disappears, and her mind shuts down. She is back on that horrific mountain with Kandorq's foul breath against her face, his red eyes ablaze with sickness, and his cracked lips curved with anticipation. His deep, rough voice echoes through her mind.

"Atae..."

"Atae, listen to me." Jeqi's gentle voice and soft hands encompassing Atae's face pulls her back from the abyss. "Breathe, Atae. He is not here.

Kandorq is locked away under the palace. He can't hurt you. So breathe. Control yourself."

Atae counts her breaths and focuses on slowing her racing heart. When her body relaxes, Atae steps away from her packmate, and Jeqi lets her.

"Why is he still alive?" Atae asks. She clenches her fists again and winces when her nails dig deeper than before. Jeqi notices her pain and glances at Atae's clenched fists, hanging by her sides. When blood drips, Jeqi reaches for her friend's hands, but Atae steps away, jerking her fists and splattering blood across the walls around them.

"Tell me, Jeqi!"

"For information. As you said, the captain, Lipson, got away." Jeqi reaches out to help the blue hybrid, and Atae relents. The blonde grabs her hands, and Atae winces as Jeqi examines the self-inflicted injuries.

"Besides, I think Advisor Solum enjoys making Kandorq scream. These are deep, Atae. They're deeper than your nails are long. How did you do this?" Jeqi asks. She sighs in relief when Atae's skin knits together, confirming that she's healing normally again.

"What do you mean?" Atae asks. She's more concerned about Solum than Jeqi's questions. But when Jeqi traces her packmate's fingertips, Atae flinches and pulls away.

"Ow." Atae glares at her friend then inspects her fingertips. Ignoring the clotting blood on her palms, Atae notices soreness in all her fingers as she rubs dead skin off the tips.

"Has that happen before?" Jeqi asks. Atae glances at her, considering the question. She remembers a restless night with sore fingertips, but she shrugs it off and returns her attention to where it belongs.

"What did you mean about Solum making Kandorq scream?"

"Well," Jeqi sighs, "According to Mother, Advisor Solum visited Kandorq every day that you were unconscious. He tortured him. Solum wanted answers, but Kandorq never gave in. He never told him anything, just screamed. Then you woke up and told Mother what Kandorq...what he wanted. And Solum heard you. Mother said that when your father left your room that night, he didn't come back until morning. That night, the entire palace heard Kandorq screams, and he told Solum everything he knew, which wasn't much. Apparently, he's more muscle than brain."

Struggling with this new knowledge, Atae swivels away from Jeqi. She covers her face with her hands and fights the overwhelming shame that threatens to wash over her. Solum knows. Her father knows what Kandorq tried to do. What she almost let him do to her. As the tidal wave of guilt and humiliation threatens to pull her under, Atae's anger bubbles up from within the depths, and she latches onto it. She clings to the life preserver of hate as it pulls her above the debilitating waves of shame. Embracing the strength of her fury, Atae drops her hands from her face and spins back to glare at Jeqi.

"Good. Kandorq deserves it and much more."

"Atae-"

"We should leave. The tournament will start soon."

Jeqi watches with concern as her friend walks away. She knows that Atae is struggling within, but she doesn't understand why. Jeqi has always admired Atae for her strong will and determination to overcome any obstacle in her path. It's what makes Atae such a valuable ally. Jeqi knows that her packmate's confidence has cracked, and soon it will crumble under the pressure that Atae places on herself. It can't be just the attack that has Atae so shaken, but something else. Jeqi follows Atae, deciding to stay close until she figures out how to help her friend.

CHAPTER 19

Atae sighs as Deh fusses over her daughter. Atae has often envied Jeqi's relationship with her mother, but not today. Instead, she grumbles at Deh's overprotective behavior and shuffles away to give them the illusion of privacy. Atae glances at the giant arena wall before them and watches her classmates slip into the massive entrance. She was surprised to learn that the field in which she trained with Solum would host all four rounds of the tournament. Where grass and weeds once stood high above her head, now stands a massive domed arena built from structured energy. Atae places her hand against the wall, expecting to feel the rough stone it mimics. Instead, her fingertips glide across the smooth sensation of placid water. She pushes against the barrier to break the surface as she would with a pool of water, but the energy field stands firm. She rubs her palm back and forth and smiles when the energy ripples like surface water.

"Are you done?" Jeqi asks.

"Are you?" Atae drops her hand to glance over Jeqi's shoulder at Deh's retreating form. The elder Setunn shuffles over to a small group of waiting parents, each displaying a varying degree of pride and worry for their offspring.

"Let's go," Jeqi says.

Atae follows her packmate to the simple archway designed to resemble white, stone blocks but stops when she realizes a translucent energy field stretches across the entrance. Jeqi doesn't notice her friend's hesitation at first and crosses through the barrier with several other classmates.

"Whoa." Atae watches the energy shimmer around Jeqi and smiles. Once inside, the blue-eyed hybrid notices her packmate's absence and spins around to find Atae, dumbstruck.

"What are you doing? Come on," Jeqi says. She catches sight of something behind Atae and snaps her mouth shut. Jeqi's eyes grow wide, and she straightens her posture. Atae wonders at the odd change in the blonde's demeanor, then a familiar tendril of fear laces up her spine at the thought of what lurks at her back. At the sound of a familiar voice, the taut tension throughout her body twists into a different kind of misery.

"It's an energy field, Blue," Prince Truin says. He flashes a mocking smile as he steps up behind Atae along with Queen Sula. "You act as though you've never seen one. It's only the most mass-produced technology in the Kaji Empire. In fact, our entire post-war economy was built around the manufacturing and selling of this nifty little product. Yet you've never seen one. Why am I not surprised?"

Jeqi, of course, recognizes the royal family and salutes them with the traditional right fist to the chest and left at her back. Her eyes dart from Queen Sula to Prince Truin, with her tail straight as a rod.

"Your Majesty. Your Highness. I am honored to meet you both," she says.

Atae is not as excited to see the prince as Jeqi. The memory of their previous encounter haunts Atae, and the shame from her insults washes over her. She salutes the royal but refuses to meet his gaze.

"Queen Sula. Prince Truin. It is good to see you both again."

Jeqi gawks at her packmate, and Atae realizes that Jeqi doesn't know about her previous encounters with the future king of Kaji. She grimaces at the idea of informing Jeqi of her mistake. Prince Truin's smile sours at the blue hybrid's placating response.

"I see you have found your place. Tell me, how's it possible that you've never seen an energy field?"

"I've seen one," Atae says. "I've just never touched or interacted with one, I guess."

"That's really not surprising given Solum's aversion to them," Queen Sula says, and Atae gapes at her. "Oh, he'd never admit it. Nowadays, energy fields are used in every application imaginable from construction to cooking. Yet I'd wager that you don't have any type of energy construct in your home."

"You're right. We don't."

"As I said, he'd never admit it, but Solum prefers to avoid them if he can. I think it stems from a certain bad experience in his youth. Maybe, one day I'll recall the tale. It's quite entertaining." Queen Sula winks at the younger hybrids.

"I would like that." Atae can't help but smile back at the charismatic leader while Prince Truin huffs at his mother's antics.

"By the way, Atae, you are looking well," Sula says. "The palace is fluttering with tales of your escapades last night. I expect the same today."

Atae's smile falls and twists in confusion. She's uncertain if the queen is referring to her fight with Prince Truin or his royal guards.

"Yes, I heard what you did to my guards. They are still recuperating in recovering tanks. Schinn will have a new scar where you sliced him open. It serves them right for taking it easy on you, though. I would have eaten you alive," Prince Truin says. He bares his teeth at Atae, and she struggles to prevent her eyes from rolling to the back of her head. Jeqi, on the other hand, steps back in shock from the prince's threat. Atae glares at him but says nothing; instead, she hangs her head and sighs.

"Of course, my prince. I am here to serve."

"Even if it is to serve as my meal?"

Atae refuses to look at the young royal, afraid she might lose her temper again. It seems Truin can press her buttons faster than Sloan. Staring anywhere but at him, Atae's gaze falls to Queen Sula, who peers back at her in disappointment.

"Hmph. It seems you've already cowed her, my son. And here I thought you were Solum's daughter." Queen Sula peers at Atae with a raised eyebrow, daring the young hybrid to prove her wrong. Perhaps the queen expects to see Atae standing up to the prince. The blue hybrid feels stuck between a rock and a hard place; anger the prince or disappoint the queen. Well, Atae has always been gifted at aggravating others. Why not put it to good use?

"With your guards injured, do you have any remaining pack to protect you? I don't see anyone. What will you do if you come across a warrior that won't pull their punches?" Atae asks the prince. Jeqi gapes at Atae in horror and moves to silence her, but Queen Sula stops the blonde with a wave of her hand. Prince Truin jumps into Atae's face with a threatening snarl.

"I don't need anyone to protect me. The royal guard is for tradition only. I am the strongest youngling on the planet. I am stronger than many of the warriors leading our armies."

"How can you be sure about that? I mean, you only fight loyal servants of the empire. Their honor binds them to protect you, not hurt you. Have you ever been seriously injured in a fight, Prince Truin?"

"Of course not, I am a mighty warrior. I have never lost a battle."

"Do you always feel the urge to announce your greatness to those around you? It seems to me that if you were truly great, you wouldn't have to keep reminding us." Atae's words strike the prince like a slap to his face, and he growls, but she continues unfazed. "The fact that you do makes me think that you know."

"Know what?" Prince Truin asks through bared teeth.

"That every fight that you worked so hard to win, every fight that you bled and sweat over, struggled to breathe, and urged your body not give in so that you could win and beat your opponent…They were all lies because your opponent would never have hurt you. Every warrior you've ever fought is bound by his or her honor to protect you, even from themselves. You will never truly know if you are the strongest Kaji because no loyal Kaji will ever truly test you," Atae says. Her cold, fuchsia eyes pierce his glowing amber. With only a hint between them, the seething prince can't hide the sudden elongation of his pupil.

Prince Truin spins away from the blue hybrid and takes several deep breaths to calm his fiery temper and stop the shift. After a moment, he swivels back to Atae with his normal eyes, his calm royal demeanor washing over him, and all traces of his explosive temper gone.

"I look forward to our fight, Blue. Be prepared," he says icily. Then he bids goodbye to his mother and stomps through the arena entrance and disappears.

"Magnificent. You truly are Solum's heir," the queen says. She chuckles while Jeqi tries to reign in her panic. Horrified that her packmate just secured their positions as palace servants, Jeqi presses her hands against her cheeks and gawks at Atae.

"What did you just do?"

Jeqi surges toward her pack, attempting to grab Atae's shoulders, but the blonde's hands slam into the solid, translucent energy field instead. Realizing the entrance is one-way, Atae is grateful for the barrier to allow her packmate time to calm down. She ignores Jeqi's anguish as she addresses her queen.

"Did you want me to argue with him?"

"Oh, yes." Queen Sula's amusement sparkles in her amber eyes. "It's important for a future king to have a companion that will test his temper and isn't afraid to stand up to him. He must learn to earn respect instead of just demanding it like an arrogant brute."

Atae's cheeks redden with embarrassment as she realizes the queen remembers her remark at dinner.

"Yeah, until we get sentenced to kitchen duty for the rest of our lives," Jeqi says. She drowns in anxiety as her agitated tail lashes out around her, then she pales when Queen Sula narrows her eyes at the youngling. The queen stares at Jeqi long enough for the young female to squirm, then Sula smirks.

"Don't worry, my pupils. He may be the prince, but I am the queen. Consider all his threats of reprimand idle at best. Now threats of bodily harm are up to you to stop."

"Forgive me, my queen," Jeqi says. "I, uh…we greatly appreciate your support. But is there a reason for your visit? I only ask because the tournament will begin soon."

"Yes, of course. With all the sparks flying, I almost forgot. I came to wish you two luck. You both must perform exceptionally well. I can't very well take you under my tutelage if you lose the tournament."

"Don't worry, my queen. We won't fail you," Atae says.

"Good, I shall be off to my viewing box. I don't want to miss anything."

"You're staying to watch? You and the prince?" Jeqi asks. "I didn't know there would be a live audience."

"Don't worry. It's just the two of us. I always insist on watching in-person when I am planetside. And I can do that because I'm the queen."

Queen Sula chuckles at her own remark and waves goodbye to the younglings as she crosses the entrance to disappear after her son. Atae smiles at Queen Sula's behavior. A stray thought whisks through her mind that perhaps the queen enjoys antagonizing her son and that she is using Atae to fuel her amusement. But that would be absurd. Queen Sula is the ruler of the Kaji Empire and would never resort to such petty antics.

"She's not really what I imagined," Jeqi says.

"Right? She's better." Both younglings giggle from opposite sides of the energy field.

"Come on. We need to get into position." Jeqi waves at Atae to follow her. The blue-haired hybrid nods her head and holds her breath as she steps through the field.

"Ow." Atae's visor studs tear free of her earlobes and fall to the ground on the outside of the energy field.

"You're not allowed to bring your visor. Or anything else for that matter. Only your hilt. Did you even read the rules?"

"There are rules?" Atae massages her earlobes, and Jeqi sighs as she leads them through the crowd of younglings to their assigned position. The tournament arena is far more extensive than anything Atae could've imagined. The royal palace could fit inside the massive field. The walls, masquerading as stone, stand five stories high, and an energy field fluctuates above them to create a dome. Large boulders and jagged stones jut out of the ground, and a large pool of water cuts the arena in half. So the only way to reach the opposite end of the field is to cross a fragile-looking bridge. Not trusting its dark complexion, Atae and Jeqi eye the calm water.

"What do you think of that?" Atae asks.

"Nothing good."

As the two females cross the massive arena, they pass dozens of small, translucent energy domes that house fellow competitors. Groups, no more than four, stand inside their energy constructs, waiting for the tournament to begin or for their fellow packmates to join them. Atae doesn't notice the silver orbs residing at the top of each energy field, but Jeqi takes note and bites her lip. When they reach their assigned dome, Marqee waits inside, and he nods in greeting when they cross the energy field. Two of the three metals orbs docked to their mound detach and drop down to join the group.

One small, round ball buzzes around her head, and Atae sneers at it. "What is that thing?"

"It's a camera," Jeqi says. She swats at the second orb humming past her ear, and Marqee shrugs, seemingly unbothered by his camera.

"Every competitor has one assigned to follow them throughout the tournament," he says. "Just destroy it when everything starts."

"We won't get into trouble?" Jeqi asks.

"Maybe a point or two. It's not like you can't afford it."

"I think it's worth it. This thing is freaking me out. Why are they recording us? It's weird."

"Spectators can use their visors to watch the competitors they want without the distraction of the others," Marqee says. He smiles at Jeqi, flashing his adorable dimples, and the blonde bites her lip to stop her impending grin. Atae doesn't notice her packmates odd response, nor her blushing cheeks.

"There are spectators? Why are there spectators?" she asks.

"Because that's just how it works, Atae," Jeqi snaps. "The Sula Academy Tournament is the second most-viewed production every season. Our performance here will help determine our odds in the Gridiron."

"Yeah, if we're lucky, we'll get our own fan club," Marqee says.

"Doesn't Sloan already have one? I can't imagine why."

"Where is Sloan?" Jeqi asks.

"We still have time. He'll be here," Marqee says. Atae twists her mouth and jams a hand to hip before raising an eyebrow at the dimpled purebred.

"How can you be so certain?"

"Because he knows me," Sloan shouts from several domes away with Debil wrapped around him. Arms slip from his neck and slide down is dark, muscular arms to grab his hands and his attention. Turning back to the purebred female, Sloan says something that pulls a cascade of giggles from Debil, and Atae is thankful to be out of earshot. He slips from Debil's grasp and sends her a faux pouting expression as he joins his pack under the dome.

"Did you miss me?" Upon his arrival, their last camera activates and buzzes overhead.

"About as much as I'm going to miss these cameras," Atae says. "Where have you been?"

"I ran into an old friend. Tell me, how is it possible that you've never seen an energy field?"

"You've never seen an-"

"I've seen one. I've seen dozens of them. I've just never used one before today."

It doesn't occur to Atae to wonder how Sloan knows of her inept experience with energy fields. Instead, she stews in her embarrassment.

"Wow, these are really annoying," Sloan admits and snatches his camera from the air. He smiles at its amusing struggle to escape his grasp until it lashes out with a crackling shock that reverberates up Sloan's arm.

"Ouch." He drops the nasty ball, and it returns to its mission. "Oh, you are so going to die as soon as this round starts."

"You realize that you're threatening a machine," Atae says.

"A machine that's going to die."

Atae bites her cheek to hide her amused smile, but Sloan catches it with a wink. Before Atae can salvage her reputation with a snide remark, an alarm blares, and their translucent dome glows green. The majority of the other energy field follow suit, but a few flare red. The remaining younglings rush to their assigned vaults. Once their packs are complete, their energy construct changes from red to green. It only takes a moment for every dome to signal green, but it doesn't last long. In harmony, all the fields deactivate with loud cackles that echo across the arena.

Atae, Jeqi, Marqee, and Sloan gather close as they walk across the field and inspect the competition. Their cameras buzz all around them, and Atae swats at one that skims her ear.

"How am I supposed to concentrate with these things flying around?"

"Like this," Sloan says. He unsheathes his hilt, and his broadsword springs to life. With a few swings of his blade, metal scraps and electronic parts crash to the ground. All four cameras meet their deaths within moments.

"I told you I'd kill them."

"I'm pretty sure that we're going to get into trouble for that," Atae says. Sloan shrugs at her with a crooked smile and sheathes his hilt, while Atae hides another amused smile by glancing around the field. Jeqi motions toward several packs.

"Offensively, those are the ones we should target."

"Fine by me," Sloan says. "Just waiting for the signal."

As if on cue, a massive hologram assembles over the pool in the center of the arena, and everyone pauses to watch.

"Welcome, everyone, to the twelfth seasonal Sula Academy Tournament." Skiska's voice booms across the arena, and her round face beams. "I don't know about you, but I'm very excited to see how this turns out."

"As is the rest of the empire. Almost 60 percent of the entire viewing public is tuned in today." Frack's square head assembles next to his co-host. "This season's class of younglings marks the first group to attend all twelve seasons of training that Sula Academy offers."

"So, they should be the best of the best."

"Should be," Frack says. "I'll believe it when I see it."

"Well, let's get started, shall we?"

"Everyone knows the tournament rules, but we'll remind you. All of our competitors have been stripped of their visors and anything else deemed helpful," Frack says. Atae strokes her empty earlobes with a begrudging frown.

"Only one weapon is allowed. Most competitors chose a ranged or bladed hilt," Skiska says. Jeqi touches her holstered hilt and glances at each of her allies, sporting weapons of their own.

"Everyone must enter the arena in their first form. After that, all's fair," Frack says. Atae glances around the field to confirm and pauses when she notices Debil and Seva watching them. She waves at the two purebreds, but Debil glares at her from across the arena.

"She's going to be a problem," Sloan whispers at Atae's back. The blue hybrid stares up at him.

"What did I do to her?"

Sloan chuckles at Atae's question and shrugs in answer.

"Now, the rules for round one," Frack says. "This is an all-out brawl. For every competitor that yields to another, the winning competitor wins ten points. Once a competitor yields, he or she can no longer fight. If you continue to fight, your entire pack will be disqualified. Falling unconscious, dying, sustaining a crippling injury, or a verbal surrender constitutes yielding."

"As always, leaving the arena disqualifies your entire pack," Skiska says. "Fifty packs of four will compete, but only forty packs will advance to round two. When ten complete packs yield, the round ends."

"Don't forget, only half the arena is lighted."

"Oh, that's right. That should make things more interesting." With Skiska's words, an energy field bursts into life and splits the arena in half over the giant pool. From a distance, Atae can tell that the energy construct is not dangerous but meant to control the light on either side of the arena.

"It gives the purebreds on the dark side a great advantage if they can shift fast enough to put their night vision to use," Frack says.

"Which side are we on?" Jeqi asks no one in particular, but Marqee answers.

"We'll find out soon enough."

"I think that about sums up the rules for round one," Skiska says. "Should we get started?"

"Yes, enough rules. Let the tournament begin!"

With that, the lights around Atae's pack darken as their side of the arena falls into a pitch-black fog.

CHAPTER 20

"Of course, we get stuck on the wrong side," Marqee says. From his voice, Atae can tell he is a few paces behind her.

"Jeqi," she says.

"I'm here," Jeqi answers from Atae's left. The darkness is thick and heavy against her chest, but Atae commands her lungs to breathe steady and deep. She reaches for her packmate and grips Jeqi's shoulder. The blonde stays close, using her Setunn night vision to watch the battlefield around them.

"You didn't expect this to be easy, did you?" Sloan chuckles at Marqee's side. "We can't see a thing. We need to shift."

"Wait," Jeqi says. "Follow me."

Atae, still holding Jeqi's arm, reaches back with her free hand to grab an arm behind her. Startled, Marqee pulls away at first, then he recovers and snatches Atae's hand. He does the same for Sloan. Jeqi guides her pack to the protection of a nearby boulder. When they all have a secure hold on the stone, she glances around.

"I'll be back."

"Where are you going?" Atae asks.

When no one answers, the darkness grows much heavier, causing her lungs to tighten, so Atae presses her face against the stone. The rough texture keeps her grounded and beats back the phantom laugh whispering through her mind.

I am not weak. I am strong. I am Kaji.

"She's gone. Sloan, you shift first," Marqee says. "I'll watch your back."

"Both of you should shift now," Atae says over her shoulder. With the side of her face pressed against the rock, Atae watches other younglings activate their hilts in the distance. She shakes her head at the stupidity. Now, the handful of energy blades dancing in the darkness are targets for aggressive younglings hoping to win points.

"Do you think we're going to trust you to protect us? You can't see anything," Sloan says. If it weren't for the darkness, Atae knows she'd see a snide expression plastered on the older Kaji. Instead, she watches a nearby energy blade clatter to the ground and disperse into the darkness.

"Neither of us can see right now. Both of you need to shift as quickly as possible, and you need to trust Jeqi and me to do whatever it takes to survive this round. If that means protecting you two idiots for a few moments, then so be it."

"Hurry up," Jeqi says from Atae's side, making her jump. "Those around us are almost finished shifting. We'll be ripe for the picking soon."

"Fine," Sloan says, his voice already gravelly from the change.

"Where did you go?" Atae asks.

"I scouted the area and took advantage of a few exposed purebreds and some idiots with hilts."

"How many did you get?"

"Six."

"Well, I'm impressed." Atae attempts a strained chuckle then grows serious. "Tell me what you see."

"We are surrounded by battle beasts," Jeqi says. Atae nods at the sounds of nearby beasts crawling to their feet. She listens to a fight break out to the left of their little pack and another to the right. A scream echoes across the field, but Atae can't determine how far the victim stands.

"We need to get to the lighted side," Atae says. Another scream echoes across the field, and this time, she watches the light from a hilt fall in the distance.

"We don't have long."

As the screams close in on Atae and her pack, a familiar tendril of fear laces up her spine and taunts her with the voice of nightmares. The sensation of Salyn watching her from under the dark cloak slips into the back of her mind. She pushes against the weight of the abyss surrounding her and darts her eyes around the darkness. She searches shapes or figures until a sharp pain stabs into her skull as a familiar silver wisp invades

Atae's mind and tugs at a mental switch. Pressure builds behind her eyes, and she grabs at her head in pain. When discomfort subsides a moment later, Atae opens her eyes to an illuminated arena. She watches battle beasts tear down the remaining hilts glowing in the distance as she whispers to Jeqi.

"Is it over? Why did they turn the lights back on?"

"What are you talking about?" Jeqi says. She scopes out their tiny perimeter around the boulder for threats. Atae's brow furrows as she notes the strange shadows and the shifting darkness. When she focuses on one particular warrior, the area around him brightens, but anything beyond the warrior's near vicinity darkens. Only when she focuses on the arena as a whole does everything brighten. With sudden realization, Atae gasps, causing Jeqi to spin around. Upon seeing Atae, the blonde gapes.

"Atae, your eyes are-"

Before Jeqi can finish her thought, Atae grabs her by the shoulder and pushes her to the side. Jeqi stumbles to her knees to the right of Atae just as a battle beast lands between them. Seva had planned to pick Jeqi off while her back was turned, but, thanks to Atae's quick reflexes, she missed. Now, the battle beast swings her snarling jaws toward Atae and growls at the helpless hybrid. Atae sidesteps to Seva's left and away from the still vulnerable Marqee and Sloan. The beast follows her prey with her bladed tail thrashing above.

Back on her feet and behind Seva, Jeqi unsheathes her claws and hisses, but Atae motions for her to fall back. Someone needs to protect Marqee and Sloan. She can't spare a glance at their progress but hopes it won't be too much longer.

Just a few more moments.

Seva's massive jaws snap and snarl at Atae, and she steps back. Atae searches her brain for any plan or idea on how to hurt her opponent without drawing her hilt and attracting more enemies. When Atae spots Debil stalking her from behind, she worries at her chances of escaping this predicament. Tournament participants are counseled to exercise restraint and avoid any severe injuries. A broken bone here or there, maybe a light mauling, but nothing life-threatening. Still, accidents happen on occasion, and Atae suspects that she might be on the receiving end of an accident today.

Might as well. She unsheathes her hilt. Brandishing the small energy blade fills her with a swell of confidence, and she smiles at the circling battle beasts.

Debil spins around to whip her bladed tail against Atae's small frame. She tries to block the strike with her hilt, but the strength of the blow knocks it from her hand. As the beasts circle in for the final blow, the confidence that filled Atae swirls away. Once again, fear surrounds her, and she struggles to breathe. The silver particles that coat her mind tug at another switch, and something sharp slices through Atae's arms. Unprepared for the sudden pain, Atae falls to her knees, cradling her arms to her chest, and Seva uses the distraction to attack. At the moment that Seva pounces, Atae throws her arms up as a shield against the battle beast's jaws.

Seva yelps when her mouth falls upon two razor-sharp blades instead of vulnerable flesh. Atae's eyes widen as Seva falls back, shaking her head and whining at the sudden injury. Debil growls on behalf of her packmate and snarls at Atae. This time aiming for the hybrid's unprotected back, Debil swings her bladed tail again. Still on her knees with her forearms shielding her face, Atae spins toward the incoming blade. Sparks dance through the night as Debil's tail blade bounces off Atae's forearms. Undeterred, Debil swings her tail around for another blow, and Atae braces for impact until Marqee slams into Debil. Sloan tackles Seva before she has a chance to rescue her packmate.

Jeqi runs to Atae's side but stops an arm's length away. Ignoring the tussling beasts all around her, Atae stares at the blades erupting from her forearms. Similar to the daggers on a battle beast's front legs, the thick, sharp edges curve the length of her arm.

Impossible. It can't be real. I'm hallucinating.

As the blades recede, the real pain of muscle and tissue splitting apart pushes all doubt from her mind. When her forearms are completely smooth again, Atae stares up at Jeqi, who gapes in return.

"Your eyes...your arms..."

"My hilt," Atae says, pulling Jeqi from her stupor. "I need to find my hilt."

"Don't worry. I got it." Jeqi hands it to her with a nod and glances around the darkness. Sloan and Marqee jog to their side with slobbery but triumphant expressions. Atae searches for Debil and Seva, hoping to find their unconscious bodies. Instead, she spots them scampering off toward the other end of the arena.

"You let them go? Why?" Atae throws her hands into the air, and Sloan huffs at her. He tilts his head as his red beast eyes watch Atae. Hoping he doesn't catch the change that Jeqi found, Atae refuses to meet his gaze. She doesn't know for sure what's going on, but she definitely doesn't want Sloan to know.

"We should head for the bright side. It'll be easier to fight the hybrids that gather there than the battle beasts here," Jeqi says.

Sloan and Marqee sprint toward the light barrier that separates the two halves of the arena, and Atae and Jeqi follow suit. A few strides in, Sloan snaps at a hybrid classmate that gets too close. He bites down on one leg and pulls the younger Kajian to the ground, dragging him like a toy. When Sloan drops his victim in the dirt, the male hybrid tumbles into a crumpled heap ahead of Atae and still tries to climb to his feet. Atae admires her classmate's determination and strength but doesn't hesitate to slam her fist into his jaw as she sprints past. The whiplash from the attack knocks her classmate unconscious, and Atae can't help but wonder if she or Sloan wins the ten points. Either way, they take down two more younglings on their way to the light barrier.

Weaving between the battling younglings throughout the arena, Jeqi uses her hilt to hamstring unsuspecting victims. She dodges a wild tail blade and slips underneath to slice at a passing battle beast's hind legs. When he snaps at her with his powerful jaws, Jeqi leaps from her run to slam her knee into the side of his head, stunning him. With a final elbow jab to the forehead, the beast crumbles into unconsciousness.

Meanwhile, Marqee defends his little pack against one or two lone battle beasts that attack on separate occasions. He deals with the first attacker, who's already injured, with a quick and crippling tail strike to her ribs. When they reach the edge of the pool, Tuk barks, dodges Marqee's tail blade, then tackles him to the ground. With Sloan's mouth full of hybrids and Jeqi slicing into her latest victim, Atae jumps to Marqee's rescue.

She digs her small energy blade into Tuk's side and smiles when he recoils away from her and Marqee. Tuk swings his tail blade around, aiming for Atae. This time, she holds firm to her hilt and deflects the attack, but she can't stop his jaws from crunching down on her arm. She screams, and Marqee, back on his feet, snatches Tuk by the neck with his powerful bite. Marqee yanks on the battle beast and digs at him with his clawed paws until Tuk yelps and releases Atae. A moment later, Tuk falls to the ground in another unconscious heap.

Atae stumbles to the edge of the water, cradling her arm, and waits for her pack to join. Jeqi climbs over the body of her latest triumph to reach the shore and tears a strip of cloth from her pant leg. Sloan joins them as Jeqi tightens the makeshift bandage around Atae's bleeding wound.

"Your arm is broken, but this should help with the bleeding," Jeqi says.

"Figured that was the case," Atae says. She watches the tranquil water and ignores the warm blood dripping from her fingertips. A couple of bubbles interrupt the glass surface, and she frowns. "Anyone think we should swim it?"

As expected, Sloan and Marqee back away from the shore and growl in warning.

"I agree," Jeqi says. "Maybe the bridge is a safer bet."

"Has anyone tried to cross it, yet?" Atae stares at the small planks stretching across the pool. Barely wide enough for a battle beast to walk and no railing, she wouldn't call it a bridge.

"I don't think so," Jeqi says.

"Maybe there's a reason for that." Atae glances at Jeqi with a shrug. Sloan snorts at her hesitation then darts across the planks. When he reaches the other side and barks at his packmates, Atae grumbles, and Jeqi smiles.

"If he can do it-"

"Yeah, I get it."

Atae sprints after Sloan with Jeqi at her back. Halfway across the bridge, Atae breaches the light barrier, and light floods her senses. The pain from her scorched corneas doesn't slow her down, but the sudden onslaught of sharp knives and pressure behind her eyes comes close. She stumbles to the shore, falling to her knees, and rubs at her closed eyes until the pain dissipates. When she opens them again, Sloan stands at eye level, staring at her with his red, beast eyes. Much to Atae's surprise, he steps closer and sniffs her face with his wet nose. Sloan has never shown any type of concern for her. Why is today different?

Jeqi screams, and Atae spins around toward the bridge. Moments before, a giant tentacle erupted from the calm water and wrapped around Jeqi's leg mid-step. The slick, green limb oozes a foul-smelling slime that burns Jeqi's skin. She screams in pain as her flesh boils, and she slams face-first into the wooden planks. The tentacle pulls Jeqi across the bridge toward the water, but she latches onto the opposite edge with a vice-like grip.

"Jeqi!" Atae runs to her friend's aid as Jeqi claws at the beast with her free hand, but the ooze just eats away at her fingers and nails. Marqee bites at the creature but drops his prey in a yelp of pain. Gagging on the acidic ooze, he stumbles into the water on the opposite side of the bridge. Atae grabs Jeqi and pulls against the slimy limb, but the blonde hybrid screams. Atae kneels at her packmate's side and tugs on the tentacle with her uninjured arm, ignoring her own burning skin. Atae will not let her packmate die. She will not fail her.

The creature lashes out at Atae with the end of another long tentacle and strikes her in the face. She cries out in pain and wipes at the ooze burning at her face and ear. Sloan slices into the offending extremity with his tail blade, and it flops into the water. Two more erupt from the pool and attack the battle beast, but Sloan dodges away from the bridge to draw the creature away. The attacking tentacles follow him, but the third remains wrapped around Jeqi's leg.

When the creature tugs at Jeqi and drags its prey closer to the dangerous water, Atae ignores her own pain and doubles her efforts to free her friend. Without warning, a familiar sense of helplessness envelops Atae, squeezing against her lungs, as she flails against the tentacle with both hands. For a moment, as her skin boils from her fingers and her nails rip away, Atae remembers Kandorq's hand on her throat and her futile attempts to pry it free. She can feel the insane panic darkening her mind and electrifying her body to act without reason. Amid the black madness, a silver tendril slips from the crevices of Atae's mind and tugs at a hidden neuron.

But Atae ignores everything. She ignores the insanity building in her mind and the pain of her fingertips splitting open. She needs to destroy the tentacle that threatens her packmate. When the creature loosens its hold, Atae doesn't notice. She keeps ripping at the tentacle's oozing skin, happy to tear away chunks of tissue. She doesn't stop until the creature whips its injured extremity away, leaving a screaming Jeqi behind. The beast's blood stains the wooden bridge as the tentacle retreats into its pond, and Atae watches her thick claws recede into her bloody and burned fingers.

Claws. I have claws, too?

Oblivious to the silver swirl of mist that slips from her mind, Atae smiles at her newly discovered weapon and the damage it inflicted. Jeqi's groan pulls Atae from her musings, and she hurries to help her injured packmate. Atae uses her uninjured arm to sling one of Jeqi's arms around her shoulder and pulls the blonde to her feet.

"What were you saying about the bridge?" Atae asks.

"Shut up."

As Atae helps Jeqi to the shore, a soaking wet Marqee waits with a large gash melted from his jaw. He whines in concern and shuffles next to Jeqi to help carry her weight.

"Your face looks like my leg," Jeqi says. Marqee sniffs at the muscle sloughing from her leg to reveal the white bone beneath. Sloan trots over to join them, brandishing his own injuries. His tail suffers several burns along its length, and he sports a noticeable limp.

"Are we having fun yet?" Atae asks him, and he barks a confirmation. "Marqee, stay here with her. Sloan and I can take down a few stragglers."

"We need to stay together," Jeqi says. "Separated, we're vulnerable."

"We're vulnerable now. If an entire pack attacks us, someone's going down."

"And how does separating improve our odds?" Jeqi cringes when Marqee grazes her injured leg as he dashes off after a limping hybrid that dared to swing his hilt at Sloan's back. Dozens of younglings battle around them, and Atae scans the vicinity.

"We've already taken down, what? Fifteen competitors? The round ends after forty fall, so we have to be close. Sloan and I can speed things up by picking off the stragglers."

"We've only taken down fourteen, including that one," Jeqi says. She motions toward Marqee as he returns unscathed. "And it's not about the numbers. It's about the packs. A hundred of us could fall, but as long as one member from each pack remains, all 50 packs are still in play."

"Well, then, how many packs still stand?"

"How should I know?"

As if in answer, the light barrier in the center of the arena disperses, and the giant hologram returns with Skiska's and Frack's large heads floating above the pond.

"Congratulations. If you are still standing, your pack has advanced to round two," Frack says.

"Well, that was good timing," Atae says. Most of her classmates breathe a sigh of relief and stop fighting, but several battle beasts continue with their skirmishes. Blood covers the arena, and scores of younglings litter the floor. Most of them are unconscious, but a handful cry out in pain as medical attendants rush in from the entrance to aid their fallen charges. When one reaches her pack, Jeqi shoos the medic away.

"Call us a transport. We're going to the palace for medical treatment. The medical wing here is going to be swamped with injuries."

CHAPTER 21

"Let me see them," Jeqi says after Atae describes her new claws.

Jeqi and Atae relax on white metallic lounge chairs amid the chaotic palace medical wing. A dome, protruding from her chair, encases Jeqi's injured leg, and inside the dome, blue healing gel soaks into her cells to stimulate rapid regeneration of injured tissue, muscle, and bones. Separate vaults on Atae's armrests enclose her burned hands and her broken arm. She twitches her nose and cheek due to a tingling sensation from the healing gel slathered across her injured face. The slime smells odd, and she fights the urge to brush it away with her shoulder.

"How come they didn't just put me in one of these recovery chairs after my attack? Or the tanks?" Atae asks. Busy medical specialists hurry all-around to tend the injured warriors in the royal medical wing. Atae and Jeqi lie at the end of a long row of recovery chairs with an equally long row of Kaji-sized containers behind them. Severely injured warriors submerge their entire bodies in healing gel within the large, spherical pods to reduce healing time. Recovery chairs and tanks are essential equipment for medical centers, and the palace medical wing has dozens. Atae and Jeqi claimed the chairs at one end of the medical office for more privacy. Jeqi's fluffy tail curls in her lap as the blonde raises an eyebrow at her packmate.

"How do you know they didn't? You were unconscious the whole time," Jeqi says.

"Hmph. Did they?"

"Not that I know of. Besides, your injury was superficial. It was the illness that incapacitated you. Which, apparently, was due to you starting

157

your shifting phase." Jeqi unsheathes her Setunn claws and flicks her fingers at Atae. "Now, show me your claws."

"What does that feel like?"

"What?"

"Your claws? Does it hurt when you call on them?"

"No." Jeqi stifles a snicker. "Of course, not. It's like flexing a muscle. Why? Did it hurt you?"

"Yes, it felt like the blades cut their way out of my arms," Atae says. She inspects her uninjured arm, wiggling her fingers inside the healing dome on her hand. "Everything happened so fast. It's hard to remember how it happened. But the pain, the pain made it real."

"What about your eyes? They were different."

"I think they shifted, too. I could see through the dark. It was amazing."

"Did that hurt, too? Or did they just adjust to the dark?"

"No, it felt like my head was going to split open," Atae says. She remembers the horrible pain behind her eyes. The last time she felt something like that was in the forest hiding from Salyn. Atae gasps at the realization. She forces her mind to relive that night, holding back the barrage of fear and guilt with a steel wall. Atae remembers hiding in the tree and knowing the Setunn was hunting her. The headache had come on fast and hard, but when it was gone, Atae could see Salyn as clear as day. As the truth settles into her chest, Atae shakes the horrid memories away with a heavy sigh.

How could I be this stupid?

"This wasn't the first time I shifted," Atae says.

Jeqi gapes at her packmate. "And you didn't tell me? This morning you said you couldn't shift. You lied to me?"

"No, I just realized it," Atae says. "Salyn, the Setunn that attacked me, I thought she turned on a light so she could see."

"Setunn have night vision." Jeqi presses her lips together and glowers at Atae as she scrambles to explain.

"I know, but it was the only thing that made sense. It never occurred to me that my eyes had shifted."

"Mother said that the doctor and Solum thought you could shift after your attack, but when they tried to make you, nothing happened. If you could shift then, why didn't it work?"

"I don't know," Atae says. She recalls her father attempt to help her shift. The memory of her teeth snapping from the pressure of her clenched jaw makes Atae run her tongue over the back of her teeth. She fights the urge to run her fingers over her lips since healing domes still encompass both of Atae's hands. She leans back into the chair and sighs at her confusing memories of fever and fear.

"I just don't know."

"Come on, Atae. Show me your claws." Jeqi wiggles in her chair against the healing domes holding her in place as she implores her friend. Jeqi growls when Atae doesn't respond, too distracted by her rampaging thoughts. The blonde opens her mouth to snap but pauses due to the unsettling sensation of the tendons in her leg reattaching to the newly healed bone. When the strange feeling passes, Jeqi repeats her command to Atae. The fuchsia-eyed hybrid jumps at Jeqi's tone, then glances around the medical wing.

"Do you think this is a good place to try that? What if someone sees? What if Sloan and Marqee see?"

"So what if they do? You can shift, Atae. This is big."

"I know, but-"

"But what?" Jeqi knits her brows at the anxiety plaguing her packmate.

"If we tell anyone or someone else finds out, they will tell my father," Atae says.

"Why is that a bad thing?"

"He'll want me to master this new…skill right away. Don't you get it? Solum will pull me from the tournament. I can't do that to you. I won't fail you."

"Atae, that won't be failing me," Jeqi says. "I'm the only one who has to compete in the tournament. If Solum pulls you from the roster, it won't disqualify me, or Sloan and Marqee."

"But you'll suffer a loss. The first three rounds are designed for packs of four. Without me, you'll be at a disadvantage."

"I don't like this." Jeqi shakes her head. "I think you should tell Solum. You're going to need help with this."

"Just wait, okay? Give me a few days to think about it. Round two, at least."

Chewing on her lip, Jeqi stares at Atae, then glances down at the healing domes repairing her injuries. Jeqi suffered a lot of damage in just one round. If Atae weren't there, Jeqi would be at the bottom of that pond. The truth is that they do need Atae, but it isn't fair to her. Atae deserves proper training on how to control her new shifting ability. She needs it.

"What if you go feral?" Jeqi asks. Atae snorts and scrunches her nose.

"Come on, Jeqi. Those are just stories."

"No, it's real. It happens all the time in the overpopulated Gridirons."

"Overpopulated? What do you mean?" Atae asks. She makes a funny face trying to scratch her gel covered nose without disrupting the domes on her arm or hands.

"Each Gridiron is designed to provide the same amount of food, but some have more participants than others. On occasion, the food supply isn't big enough to support a large surge of entries—what are you doing?"

"My nose itches." Eyes crossed, Atae wrinkles her nose, and Jeqi laughs at the odd twists to Atae's face. She has mercy on her packmate and scratches Atae's nose.

"Thank you," Atae says. "That was driving me crazy. So what does an overpopulated Gridiron have to do with me going feral?"

"That's how I know that it's real. Starving purebreds lose control of their battle beasts and go feral in the GirdIron. It doesn't often happen because it's usually not overpopulated. But it does happen, Atae. What if it happens to you?"

"If I ever start to feel out of control, I promise to tell you. But so far, I haven't felt anything like that. It's just the same old me."

"Except now you're hiding claws and blades."

"And night vision." Both younglings smile at each other, and Jeqi nods.

"Fine. We won't let anyone know. At least, for now. Round two will be held in a week. We will discuss this again afterward."

"Fine by me," Atae says.

"So, let's see your claws."

"No, I told you. I don't want anyone to see. Especially Sloan and Marqee."

"First, they are on the other side of the medical wing. You made sure they were placed as far from us as possible, remember? Second, they're going to find out eventually if they haven't already."

"No, they won't," Atae says.

"Okay, fine. Just show me already. No one is paying attention to us. Besides, it's just your claws. No one will notice," Jeqi says. She holds up her hand and unsheathes her thin claws for demonstration. When none of the medical specialists or warriors notice, she sheaths them again.

"Okay, let's do this." Atae removes her hand from the healing dome and stares at it. Clenching the muscles in her arm, she bites her lip and narrows her eyes in concentration. Blue gel slips down her wrist and arm, but otherwise, nothing happens. So Atae waves her hand around as if the force of her swing will pull the claws out. When that doesn't work, she curses and swivels back to Jeqi.

"It's not working. You said it was like flexing a muscle," Atae says.

"For me, it is. It also doesn't hurt when I do it. Obviously, it's different for you."

"What do you mean?"

"Well, think about what triggered the shifts before. Maybe, it's an emotion," Jeqi says. Atae considers her friend's words and tries to describe what she felt during their struggle against the water beast. Atae remembers the concern for her packmate and the fear of not being able to save her. She also remembers something silver.

Jeqi jolts Atae from her thoughts with a slap across the uninjured side of her face. The loud smack draws several eyes from around the room. Furious, Atae swats the air around the blonde with a vicious growl. Atae struggles against the healing domes that hold her in place while Jeqi smirks on the opposite side of her friend's free hand and just out of reach for retaliation.

"What was that for?"

"I'm trying to make you angry."

"Well, congratulations. I'm going to kill you!"

"I guess anger just isn't enough to force your shift. Maybe Feku is right," Jeqi says. Atae pauses in her struggle for revenge long enough to ask a question.

"Right about what?"

"Maybe emotion doesn't drive your ability to shift. Maybe it's need, like when purebred Kaji shift into battle beasts. You are Kaji."

"Of course, I am." Atae glowers at her packmate, but a stray, unwelcome thought burns through Atae's mind. Perhaps it isn't need that triggers her shift, but fear. Atae's eyes fall away from her friend as shame stings her face.

"Well, don't you look lovely," Sloan says. He pokes his head between their chairs and motions to the blue gel slathered across Atae's cheek. "Will it leave a scar?"

"What are you doing spying on us? And why does everything that comes out of your mouth have to be sarcasm?" Atae huffs.

"Why do you assume that was sarcasm?" He waggles his eyebrows, and, as expected, Atae rolls her eyes with a snort. He laughs and steps out from around the chairs to join Marqee and face the hybrids.

"And I wasn't spying. Your life just isn't exciting enough for me to eavesdrop. I was actually visiting a friend in one of the tanks." Sloan points to the recovery tanks behind Atae and Jeqi. "Apparently, some blue-haired hybrid cut him in half with her hilt. Don't worry. He'll be completely healed by the end of the day. But I'm quite impressed."

Atae smiles at the compliment but can't help the retort. "Remember that next time you feel the urge to annoy me."

"Enough," Jeqi says. Her admonishing glare bounces from Atae to Sloan before she cringes at another odd sensation from her healing leg.

"Are you okay?" Marqee asks around his healing mask.

"I'm fine. The medical officer said we'll be completely healed by midday. What about you two?" Jeqi's eyebrows knit together as she assesses the substantial damage to Marqee's face. Sloan slips a hand onto Marqee's shoulder and shakes his head with a sigh.

"Unfortunately, they couldn't help my ugly friend here. They say he'll be permanently disfigured. Forever stuck with his hideous face."

Atae's eyes widen, gaping at the dimpled purebred, but the healing mask hides his expression. "It's not going to heal?"

"Oh, no," Sloan says. "It's going to heal fine. He's just stuck with his normal face forever."

Atae plops back against her lounge chair in exasperation as Jeqi giggles, and Marqee punches Sloan in the arm. Atae isn't sure whether she's angrier at herself for falling for the stupid joke or him for making it.

Him, definitely him.

"Weren't you injured, Sloan?" she asks.

"Yeah, I dislocated my shoulder. Nothing serious. Just a quick pop, and I'm good to go."

"I thought I saw your tail burned, too." Marqee furrows his brow in faux confusion "But you don't have a tail in this form. What happened to your injuries?"

"Nothing, I'm a fast healer." Sloan shrugs.

"Uh, huh." Marqee chuckles. "So, your ass isn't slathered with gel under that uniform?"

Never one to pass up a challenge, Sloan grins at his packmate and says, "I'm happy to pull down my pants and show you."

"Don't you dare," Atae says. Sloan twists his mouth into a playful pout as all four younglings laugh. Then Jeqi pulls them back to reality.

"Do you guys know how we placed? I haven't had a chance to find my visor. I'd like to know who won this round."

"Uh, about that," Marqee says. He swivels to Sloan with an expectant head tilt.

"Well, the good news is that we took down the most competitors," Sloan says.

"That's great. That means we won. How do they award the points? Do we all get an equal share, or are we awarded for the number we individually took down?" Atae says.

"As a group, we earn ten points for each person we takedown. So, if we took down fourteen competitors total, then we each earned 140 points," Jeqi says.

"Whoa, that's a lot of points."

"Except, we didn't get 140 points," Sloan says. "Well, we did, but…"

"But we were penalized twenty-five points for each camera that this idiot destroyed," Marqee says. He points a thumb at his packmate, and Jeqi gasps.

"What?"

"Jeqi, it's okay. I'm sure you are still in the lead. Right, guys?" Atae says.

"Uh, yeah, but only by a few points. Debil and Seva's pack took down ten, so they kind of shot up in the rankings." Marqee frowns, glancing at Sloan, as Jeqi hyperventilates in her chair.

"Breathe, Jeqi. I need you to breathe," Atae says. She whips around to glare at Sloan. "Why didn't you take them down when you had the chance? Now we have to deal with them during the next round."

"What's the big deal? You're still in the lead, Jeqi. Personally, I'm more bummed that we placed tenth in the tournament than I am that your class ranking almost dropped." Sloan shrugs, and Atae sneers at him.

"It's important that she graduates first in her class. She certainly doesn't deserve to lose it because of something as stupid as destroying cameras."

"Fine. Next time I won't touch the cameras. Happy?" Sloan says.

"It's fine, Sloan. It was for the best. The cameras would have caused issues anyway," Jeqi says. In a semi-calm manner, she glances at Atae. It takes a moment for the blue-haired hybrid to catch on, but her anger deflates when she realizes the major favor Sloan did for her. The cameras would have recorded her shifts, and Solum would've pulled her from the roster. She's going to have to figure out how to control this thing before round two.

"Well, once you're healed, we should meet for another session with your hilt. You were terrible with it today. I think you've actually gotten worse," Sloan says.

"What? How would you know? I barely had a chance to use it."

"Exactly, it took you forever to use it on that water beast thing. Why were you scratching at it? It's not like you have claws, Atae."

"Whatever." Atae pouts at the jab and bites her tongue. He has a good point. Why hadn't she used her hilt to free Jeqi? Thinking back, Atae only remembers the cold grip of panic that clouded her mind. She certainly won't admit to Sloan that she made a mistake and let her fear overwhelm her. One day, she's going to shut him up for good, but not today. Today, she needs to work on controlling her new ability.

"How about tomorrow morning?" she says.

"Tomorrow morning is Prince Truin's pledging ceremony," Marqee says.

"So?"

"So we have to go," Jeqi says. "Didn't Solum tell you?"

"No, why would we have to go? I've never gone to any palace function," Atae says.

"We know," Sloan says with a snicker. "But now your Queen Sula's protégées. So you have to go to certain events like this one."

"What do you mean, 'you know'? And how do you know about that?"

"Atae, you are oblivious to everything. Can't you pay attention to anything?" Jeqi says.

Sloan and Marqee laugh at Jeqi's outburst and Atae's confusion before bidding them goodbye. Atae promises to meet Sloan in one of the palace training rooms before he leaves. Then, she sulks in her chair while Jeqi fumes. Although she's not sure why the blonde hybrid is angry, Atae knows it's best to wait for Jeqi to calm down before broaching the topic of her shifting ability again. It isn't long before Jeqi agrees to help her packmate, but she has no idea where to start.

CHAPTER 22

Atae runs through the dark forest to escape the voice that haunts her. The vines and branches reach out to tug at her arms and scrape her flesh, but she breaks free in a near panic. Atae can feel the glowing emerald eyes stalking her and growing ever closer. She stumbles on a root, and a blade whistles by her ear, startling the terrified youngling.

Atae continues deeper into the abyss and glances skyward for a hint of direction, but to no avail. The sky is as dark as the cold emptiness of space and lighted only by the two red moons that glare into Atae's soul. She blinks as Kandorq's blood-red eyes stare back at her. He smiles a sick and twisted grin that's filled with perverse desires. Atae backpedals away from the evil creature, but, quick as lightning, he snatches her throat and squeezes the breath from her. She claws at his hand, but Kandorq's grasp is rock solid.

"Too weak to stop me." Kandorq's deep voice snakes around Atae's body and slithers through the crevices of her mind. She digs her nails into Kandorq's flesh, trying to pry his hand off her windpipe, but he chuckles, unfazed. Atae rips chunks of skin and muscle from his hand. She is not weak. She will not let him touch her. She will not let him hurt her.

"No!" Atae awakens in her bed as her scream drowns out Kandorq's twisted laughter. Her eyes dart around, startled to find her palace bedroom rather than the pitch-black forest. Her night vision swings from the lavish furniture to the puffy bedding all around her as she shifts her focus. She sighs, realizing it was only another dream, another horrible nightmare that she must struggle to forget. An odd sensation pulls her from her thoughts, and she glances down to find thick, warm blood dripping down her heaving chest and soaking into her nightclothes.

What have I done? Atae touches the ruined flesh of her neck then applies pressure to stop the bleeding. She jumps at the sound of knocking at her bedroom door, followed by Solum's concerned voice.

"Atae, I heard you call out. Are you okay?"

Solum doesn't wait for an answer and rushes to open the door. Atae darts to her bathroom and locks the door.

"I am fine, Father. Please go back to bed." Atae stands in the center of the dark bathroom, staring at the door and pressing a hand against her neck. She hopes that Solum takes her at her word and leaves.

"There is blood in your bed. You are injured," Solum says. Atae groans, realizing that her father isn't leaving, and checks her wound in the mirror. Atae inspects the superficial injury, noting how quickly it's clotting, and sighs.

"It's nothing. Please, go."

"Atae, I will break down this door if you do not come out, right now."

Atae peers down at her claws, still extended, then to her elongated pupils in the mirror.

He can't see me like this. Atae closes her eyes, ignoring the swirling silver haze draped over her mind. She exhales to calm her racing heart, but Solum's voice interrupts.

"Atae!" Solum slams his fist into the door, and she jumps.

Shift. Come on, shift back. Atae flails her hands in the air and clenches her eyes shut, but nothing changes. Why is it a problem now? Her body seemed to shift back on its own before.

"That's it. I'm coming in," Solum says. Atae shuffles away from the door, cringing at the chaos about to ensue, but Deh's surprisingly stern voice thrums from inside the youngling's bedroom.

"No, you will not."

Atae wonders when Deh joined Solum in her bedroom. Both the adults' rooms were on either side of Atae's bedroom, which gave them the prime opportunity to check in on her. Atae wonders if this was intentional and wouldn't put it past her overbearing father and a concerned Deh. Atae learned a long time ago that Solum and Deh have different parenting techniques, but Solum doesn't mind calling on Deh when he needs a female's parenting touch. Of which, Atae is grateful because there are certain situations in which only Deh could assist her.

This is one of those times. Atae sighs when Deh agrees.

"Solum, leave her to me. I will speak with her," Deh says. Then, she whispers something that Atae can't make out through the door. Solum huffs at the quiet suggestion but relents.

"Fine."

Atae notices the edge in her father's voice and smiles at the obvious ploy to hide his concern. With the realization that Deh has come to her rescue, Atae calms, and the churning silver particles in her mind recede into the darkness. Her body reverts to her standard form. Hissing from the intense headache and the pain of her fingers splitting open, the youngling almost misses Deh's soothing voice.

"Atae, may I come in?"

"Is Jeqi with you?" Atae asks between breaths. She presses a clawless hand on her wounds and uses her other to activate the bathroom light.

"No, dear," Deh says. Atae can hear the smile in her voice. "I am afraid that she has inherited her father's ability to sleep through the sounds of war. They are both sleeping soundly."

Atae isn't sure if she's happy or disappointed that Jeqi isn't waiting on the other side of the door. With only a slight hesitation, Atae unlocks the door and steps back, allowing Deh to slip into the bathroom with a warning glace to Solum. The threatening glare that dares the concerned father to cross her sends chills down Atae's spine. Perhaps it is Deh's iron will that Jeqi's father, a known warrior in the king's army, finds attractive. Everything else about Deh screams non-Kaji, from her bright blue eyes and tan skin to her soft blonde hair and short stature. This female is warm and comforting and exactly what Atae craves at the moment.

"Oh, Atae." Deh's concerned eyes find the youngling's blood-soaked hands and chest. "Let me see."

Atae sits on the counter next to the deep bath and drops her hand from the wound. Deh steps close to inspect the wound, while her unkempt blonde hair whispers behind her. Atae smells Deh's sweet, familiar aroma and smiles until she feels a soft push against her shins hanging off the counter. Atae glances down to find Deh's blonde tail whipping back and forth, and she gulps at the telltale signs of an agitated Setunn.

"How did this happen, dear." Deh's soothing voice and concerned eyes contradict her pressed lips and lashing tail.

"I...um..." Atae stutters, unsure what to say. Deh's eyes shift from a swirl of concern to an icy fierceness that startles Atae. She's so distracted by the sudden change, Atae doesn't notice Deh's hand on her shoulder.

"Who did this to you, Atae?"

Deh's hand tightens on Atae's shoulder, and the hybrid's mouth falls open in shock. She'd heard that Setunn were protective of their offspring, but she never imagined Deh could look so terrifying.

"It was a dream."

"What?" Deh's blonde tail hesitates in its furious swishing. Atae's cheeks flame with embarrassment, and she closes her eyes, wishing she were back in that dark forest.

"I...I had a bad dream," she whispers.

"What?" Solum asks from outside the bathroom door. Deh leans away from Atae to close her eyes and purse her lips.

"She had a nightmare. Now go away."

"A nightmare?" Solum says. "What sort of nightmare?"

Atae groans at her father's probing and rubs her hands over her face. She just wants them both to go away.

"Tell us what your dream was about while I clean your wound, then we will leave you be," Deh says loud enough for Solum to hear. Accepting her father's silence as agreement, the youngling nods and stares at the mural on the bathroom wall as Deh cleans her wound with the water from the sink and a bathroom cloth. Atae admires the beautiful craftsmanship of the intricate carving. The bright and glittering forest around them looks nothing like the terrifying darkness of her dream.

"She was stalking me again. Like she does every night. I can't do anything but run from her. I know that at any moment she can strike me down, but still, I run. And then he shows up and grabs me like he does every night. I can't move or fight. I can't even breathe. I just panic like I do *every* night," Atae says. Tears gleam in her eyes, but she refuses to let them fall. "In my dream, I clawed at his hand on my throat, trying to escape. I guess I scratched my throat in real life."

"These scratches are deep," Deh says. "A little a deeper, and we would not be having this conversation."

Atae avoids Deh's probing gaze so as not to reveal anything regarding her new shifting ability. She hears Solum rustling on the other side of the door and wonders about his thoughts on Deh's words. Does he wonder how she could cut herself so deeply, or is he only concerned for his offspring?

"Don't worry. They will heal fine and completely before the prince's pledging ceremony tomorrow." Deh smirks, misinterpreting Atae's worried glances at the bathroom door. Atae smiles, feigning relief.

"Atae," Deh says. She tugs at the youngling's chin to force her to meet her gaze. "You are a youngling. You should never have had to face the dangers that you did. But you survived them. I am grateful that you are still here."

Deh's words are meant to comfort her, but shame and guilt surge within Atae. She should have performed better, shifting phase or not. Kandorq should never have touched her, and Salyn should never have found her. Atae lifts the corners of her mouth to hide her inner turmoil from Deh. The hybrid's feeble attempt does not fool the experienced mother, but unable to do more, Deh relents. She pulls Atae close in a comforting embrace and touches the youngling's tender face with her soft tail. After a moment, Deh releases her daughter's packmate and leaves her alone in the bathroom.

As soon as Deh opens the door, Solum slips in on four furry feet. His battle beast eyes watch his daughter with a concerned gleam, and she smiles at his familiar form. She climbs off the counter and greets him on the floor, rubbing his thick white coat. Atae giggles when Solum licks her face then lays on the cold tile floor with him wrapped around her. It's been a long time since Solum comforted her like this. He's always more affectionate in his second form, and she doesn't mind.

Atae remembers several nights when Solum snuggled with her as a child. She'd woken from nightmares and called out to him, so he nestled in with her as a battle beast and licked her face to make her giggle. His warmth and strength comforted her, and she felt protected from the monsters of her imagination.

Now, Atae clings to the familiar protection, basking in the peace of mind her father offers. She stares up at the glittering forest around her and imagines the comforting sounds of her familiar home and training grounds. Soon, she slips into a soundless slumber with Solum's dark battle beast eyes watching over her.

CHAPTER 23

Solum growls as he reads another disappointing report. He stands from his workstation and swivels to the holographic star map behind him to study it. Solum's office is small and bare, lacking any of the comforts and luxuries found within the rest of the palace. After Atae's attack, he commandeered the private room and disposed of all distractions to undertake a mission that is now proving impossible. Solum swipes his hand across the hologram, and a region of the Kaji Empire disappears from the star map. One sector searched top to bottom with no results; the remaining ten enlarge to fill the holographic space.

Where could the mercenary be? Where is he going? Where did he come from? What did he come for? How did he get through our defenses? Solum frowns at the numerous questions plaguing him but shelves them all when a knock pulls his dark eyes away from the star map.

"Come in," Solum calls as he faces the door in front of his workstation. Feku steps into the modest office and salutes the royal advisor with the traditional clenched right hand to his chest.

"Advisor Solum."

"Feku, my packmate, how are you?"

"I am well. It's been too long since we last spoke. Especially, since I see your young whelp every day." Feku smirks as he sets both hands on his hips. Solum smiles and joins the other warrior on the opposite side of his workstation.

"I agree. And you are doing well with Atae. Every day, I see improvement. She's far smarter and a much better fighter than I was at her age. I suspect you're the one to thank for Atae's sudden change in tactic. One day she is a solid rock of defense, and the next, she won't stand still long enough for me to land a blow. Should I blame you for my loss a few weeks back?"

"I may have suggested a few techniques that I knew would throw you off your game. You should have expected as much. Atae will be a force to be reckoned with in battle. She is small, but her strength is in her quick mind and agility."

"True," Solum says. "But she has more power in each strike than any youngling her size has a right to."

"She's too much like her mother," Feku says. He pauses mid-nod when he notices Solum's reaction. The royal advisor's proud smile and jovial dark eyes harden into an impenetrable mask, hiding the pain and grief that surges through him at the reminder of his long-gone mate.

"Atae is why I am here." Feku changes the subject. "Have you caught the leader of the mercenaries that attacked her?"

"No," Solum says. He grunts at his failure and motions for Feku to follow him to the star map. "I just received a report that Sector One is clear of any signs of the vessel our captive described. And we still have no idea how he slipped our defenses undetected, twice."

"It must be some type of new technology. This could be dangerous. Where did he get it? Who else has it?" Feku voices the concerns that plague Solum.

"We won't know until we find him. And I'll be the one that pries the information from his broken body." Solum clenches his fists with an eagerness to get his hands on this worthless mercenary. He wants information on the dangerous, new tech as it could change the Kaji Empire's defense strategies. But, more importantly, Solum needs to know what the escaped mercenary was after and who sent him. Fears buzz through his mind, and he bats them away, unwilling to give them substance.

Were they looking for her? No, they wouldn't have harmed Atae if that were the case. We know that He has scouts out looking for her or evidence of her whereabouts. Was the mercenary one of His agents? The Gortox isn't a Believer, but that doesn't mean the missing captain wasn't one. Where the hell is he?

"The Barrier was activated the moment we found out that he'd escaped Planet Kaji." Solum deactivates the star map hologram. "He cannot escape our borders without passing through one of the ports, and we are searching every vessel. The traders are not happy, but we have confiscated millions of valuable and illegal items. So everyone thinks it's a standard crackdown on inspections."

"That's a solid strategy." Feku nods, unwilling to voice what they both know. The empire cannot keep the Barrier up forever due to the resources it consumes, and with the mercenary's new technology, it may not matter. Feku redirects the conversation back to the purpose of his visit.

"What is your strategy for Atae? I hear she'll enter the Gridiron with the rest of her class."

"Well, she's recently decided to enter with Prince Truin in hopes of being chosen as a royal companion. She wants to be his royal guard," Solum says. He leans against the desk of his workstation, quirking the corners of his mouth. Feku smiles with similar mirth.

"That's a noble quest. She has the talent and the drive."

Both warriors chuckle at the idea of Atae following in her mother's footsteps, but Solum frowns when his fond memories sour. They always do when thinking of Roga.

"Last I knew, she was going to let the Gridiron determine her fate. Let the scoring system tell her where she would succeed in life. What changed her mind?" Feku asks. Solum squashes the pain from his past to focus on the gifts of today.

"I'm not certain," he says, "but I suspect it was the queen. Sula has the unique ability to inspire her warriors, and I fear Atae has fallen into her web. Atae has been swept away by the honor and glory of protecting the royal heir. She hasn't considered the harshness or the duties that come with the position."

"Like, what if the royal heir isn't a Ru-Kai anymore?"

"So you've heard the rumors too. The crests are stirring, and thoughts of circumventing the throne are circling," Solum says. He grips the desk on either side of his hips and stares at his packmate. Solum does an excellent job of hiding his anger and disappointment in the Crests of Kaji. There were once twelve, but now there are only eleven family lines that have existed since the dawn of Kaji: Fu-Kai, Ru-Ghi, Levia, Lu-Stugh, Helphia, Delva, Fesqov, Qreskia, Renfrosq, Seston and Menkad.

There are, of course, other family bloodlines, such as the royal Ru-Kai crest, but none have deeper roots in the Kaji family tree. Each Crest of Kaji has sat on the throne and ruled the Kaji Empire for as long as they were able to hold power. The Ru-Kai line, a descendant of the Ru-Ghi and Fu-Kai families, has held the throne for centuries longer than any crest. Yet even the most loyal warriors must have a worthy leader, and some crests doubt Prince Truin.

"I doubt anyone is conspiring to take the throne, but this is the first time that the Kaji has had only one heir. King Uta was a fine king, but he died young. He left an heir only by chance and died before holding his son. There are usually several heirs to fight for the throne by proving themselves in the Gridiron. Do you remember the last time the eldest heir was chosen? Now, we have but one choice, and what happens if he is killed or bested in the Gridiron? There isn't another heir to take his place. The Kaji will not settle for an unworthy king, even if he carries the Ru-Kai name," Feku says. Solum twists his mouth into a snarl and flings one hand through the air.

"I know all this. Prince Truin has the potential. I've seen it. But he also suffers from the cockiness of youth. I honestly don't know what will happen. I suspect that Queen Sula has a plan though. His pledging ceremony is today, and she has demanded that every heir of the crests attend. Sula plays the politics of power very well, much better than Uta ever did."

Solum's voice softens as he reminisces about his dead packmate. Feku smiles and remembers how it was when they were all young and stupid.

"Sula was once Uta's royal guard, wasn't she?" he asks.

"Yes, he named her lead royal guard too. Of course, it was all a ploy to spend more time with her. Even then, she was obstinate. Sula wouldn't let him get away with anything, and he admired her for it."

"Ru-Kai males seem to be attracted to stubborn females. I hear that Prince Truin and Atae met recently, and there was some chemistry. The way I hear it, all he talks about is defeating her in combat," Feku says. He lifts his eyebrows at the royal advisor, but Solum straightens and scowls at the idea of his daughter having a romantic interest in anyone.

"That is ridiculous. Atae is too young to consider such things. Besides, the prince despises her. She insulted him on numerous occasions before she realized that he was the prince. He merely wants to put her in her place."

"And if I know Atae, he will have a hard time of it. And she may be too young for romance, but he is male. We are never too young."

Feku bellows with laughter, and Solum can't help but smirk.

"I'm beginning to remember why we haven't spoken in so long," Solum says.

"Okay, okay. It's good catching up with you, old friend, but the truth of my visit is about Atae."

"What about her?"

"I'm concerned that she is turning sour."

"What? Why would you say that?"

"She is jumpy and unpredictable since her return," Feku says. They both know that he means since her attack. "She seems fine when she's active and has something to focus her thoughts and energy on, but when her mind wanders, I fear it goes to dangerous places. She thinks no one notices, and maybe no one else does. But I do."

"Have you noticed a change in her fighting style?" Solum asks. He crosses his arms and frowns for fear of Feku's answer.

"I haven't seen her fight. I was hoping to see her in the tournament, but..."

"But Sloan ruined any chance of that," Solum says. He raises an eyebrow at the mention of Atae's rival. "I was surprised to hear you'd teamed them together. Atae did nothing but complain about it over dinner. I'll admit that I've often fueled that fire by using her rivalry with Marqee and Sloan as motivation during training. But partnering them seems-"

"Risky, I know," Feku says. "But if they can learn to work together, the four of them will be unstoppable."

"Is that what you think?" Solum asks. He narrows his eyes, and Feku rushes to defend his decision.

"Marqee is a solid fighter, and he's smart."

"And Sloan?"

"Sloan is the best blade handler in the class."

"He's a wild card, Feku. When they were younger, I used to wonder why Sloan's family chose to send him to Sula Academy rather than private tutors with his siblings. I assumed it was the typical crest politics and in keeping with appearances. Then I ran into him the other day. It was the first time I'd spoken to him since he learned to shift."

"You saw it?"

"I couldn't miss it. Anyone familiar with the signs would recognize it immediately. Do you think Sloan's family knew when they sent him away, or were they just lucky?" Solum says. He wrinkles his nose with obvious disdain for Kaji that would turn their backs on family. Feku shakes his head with a sad sigh.

"It's impossible to detect a ferog before they enter their shifting phase, but don't think his father didn't celebrate his good fortune. A ferog entering the Gridiron is suicide, but I doubt Sloan's family will give him a choice."

"You're concerned about Atae's performance, yet you weigh her down with this liability. There's nothing she can do for him."

"No, but he can help her. She needs him." Feku implores his packmate to listen, and Solum sighs.

"Best in the class? I gather he's trained with his grandfather."

"No more than Atae's trained with you."

"I'm not the leading blade master in Sector 3."

"All the more reason for Sloan to tutor her. She's fallen behind, Solum. She's missed weeks of intense blade training."

"Yes, yes. I understand." Solum throws his hands up in resignation. "Let's just hope it doesn't blow up in your face. Atae's had enough to deal with. Something is definitely off. I've had one session with her, and it was...interesting. She panicked and had to pull herself together mid-fight. Still, she took down two battle beasts, and her group dispatched the most competitors in round one."

"But she panicked first? She never panicked before," Feku says.

"Before that...disgusting beast..." Solum's fury returns with a vengeance, and he snarls at the thought of that grotesque creature in the royal dungeon placing one finger on his daughter.

"I know of no other youngling that could have done what she did. She should be proud that she was strong enough to kill a full-grown Setunn and cripple a Gortox. Instead, she seems afraid and insecure. I'm at a loss on what to do for her, Solum."

"She doesn't feel safe anymore." Solum's anger bleeds from his body as guilt floods his mind and heart. It was his job to keep her safe, and he failed. While he was trying to track down the intruders, they found his offspring. Solum frowns at his inadequacies then cringes when Feku speaks.

"Something has to be done. The tournament is one thing, but if she panics in the Gridiron, even for a moment, it could cost her. I don't know how to fix this, but there has to be a way."

"I will think on it, Feku," Solum says. He nods in agreement as he sits at his workstation. "Is there anything else?"

"No, my friend. That is enough for one day." Feku grimaces then leaves his packmate to struggle for an answer.

Solum stares at the report still open on his workstation as he ponders his daughter's predicament. She was too young to face death, to face Kandorq. She is afraid of him, but why? He can't hurt her anymore. Except in her dreams. Solum's frown deepens as he remembers last night's terrors. Atae awoke screaming and was too ashamed to tell him why. If Deh had not been there, Solum worries that he would never have known the depth of her anxiety.

But why is she ashamed? Is it shame? Or is it guilt? Why either one? She should be proud to have fought off the dangers that she battled, yet she does not feel safe anymore. Well, she feels safe when Solum is with her as a battle beast. Atae did not stir once from her sleep after he curled around her last night. He did not leave her side until she woke late this morning and began readying for the pledging ceremony that commences at mid-day. But Solum cannot be with Atae at all times. Is she afraid without him, now? Why is she not confident in her ability to protect herself?

"I know fear and panic."

Atae wasn't expecting nor prepared for Kandorq and Salyn. She didn't know what to do at first and must have panicked.

"I have learned firsthand the price for underestimating a weak and frightened prey."

Atae doesn't think she protected herself but that her enemies underestimated her.

"I know what it is to be hunted. I know what it is to fight something bigger and stronger."

This feeling of inadequacy haunts her still, even in her dreams.

"She is turning sour. How do I stop this?"

Solum considers the few sour warriors he's encountered over the seasons. They were unpredictable, suicidal, and controlled by fear. What honor they had left was tied to their closest packmate. Once that was severed, they were left to rot in their fear. No, he can't let that happen to Atae, not his child.

Solum struggles to remember a young warrior in Roga's first pack that turned sour after their time in the Gridiron. A giant arachnid took one of his eyes before he managed to kill the disgusting creature. After that, the warrior was terrified of any arachnid, small or large. Roga had no patience for fear and weakness. She was determined to rid her pack of a worthless warrior, one way or another. Roga took the warrior to a planet scheduled for purging whose primary species was a non-sentient arachnid. She told the young warrior to purge the world, and only after every arachnid was destroyed could he return home.

The warrior panicked and refused the order. He was too afraid to set foot on the planet's surface, so Roga kicked him off her ship and left him stranded. Returning a month later to check on his progress, Roga found the warrior sitting at a campfire eating a roasted arachnid limb. Solum remembers Roga describing the emptiness in her packmate's eyes and how much it haunted her even then. But the young warrior's eyes weren't empty for long, because they filled with fiery loathing when they found Roga. He didn't say a word to her as they left the desolate planet behind. In fact, the young warrior never spoke to Roga ever again, abandoning his pack in search of another. Later, Roga told Solum that she didn't regret her decision because that youngling had earned great success in the king's army. She predicted that he would be the king's general one day, and that was worth sacrificing their relationship.

Solum smiles as he remembers the strength and honor of his lost mate. He yearns to feel the unwavering passion that she exuded in life and the tender submission that she reserved only for him. Solum's smile fades, once again, as his memories melt into guilt and regret. His breath catches as Solum remembers their last words to each other. She wanted a child, and he did not. They were at the peak of their careers, and she was leaving for another difficult mission. Solum argued that a child would complicate things, and he did not want a youngling to disrupt their lives. Roga was furious with him, but also hurt and betrayed. She left questioning their future together. If only he had relented to her pleas. If only he had held her instead of pushing her away. If only he had stopped her from walking out the door.

If only…

As the guilt and regret intensify, a phantom pressure seizes Solum's chest, and he cannot breathe. The crushing weight of never again seeing his mate's smile drains the life from him. Solum would give nearly anything to watch Roga bite her lip in concentration one more time or to snicker at some prank she planned. He struggles to force his lungs to expand, not to give up, and to continue living beyond this pain and loss. But without Roga, what's the point? She was supposed to be here with him to stand by his side. She was supposed to help raise their child. Now, he must raise Atae alone.

His lungs expand, and Solum inhales as he remembers holding Atae for the first time. Countless times the blue-haired youngling unwittingly pulled Solum from the brink of darkness. He cared for her as an infant and never allowed anyone to help. Every smile or innocent garble lightened his mind and heart and pushed back the dark haze that engulfed him after Roga's death. Even today, when Solum's thoughts drift to darker memories, it is Atae that reminds him to keep fighting. Roga was meant to be his strength through life. When he lost her, Solum struggled from hour to hour. Facing a world without his mate was more frightening than facing a planet of enemy warriors. But the first time he held Atae and claimed her as his own, Solum gained new strength.

Now, whether she realizes it or not, his daughter needs his help. If she is turning sour, her future will be short and dishonored. Roga sacrificed her relationship with a packmate to save his future. Could Solum do the same? Could he bear his daughter's hatred in exchange for her future? Solum swipes his hand through his holographic workstation. With a couple of finger twitches, an image of the king's general, Mendor, appears. His one eye stares into Solum's soul, and Solum decides that he would sacrifice anything and everything for his child.

CHAPTER 24

"Why are we doing this?" Atae whines as she follows Jeqi down the hall toward the throne room. "I look ridiculous."

Atae tugs at the royal garb that hugs her small frame. A deep gray with red trim and black embroidery, the bodysuit is the most extravagant outfit Atae's ever worn. The only thing she likes about the ensemble is the coin-sized medallion pinned to one shoulder with a decorative chain. One side of the coin boasts the Sula Academy logo, and the other brandishes the Ru-Kai crest.

When the servants fastened the medallion to her garb, Atae was amazed by the intricate artwork and its similarity to the palace walls. The winged battle beast of the crest is fierce and protective, and the sword and shield of the logo are bittersweet. The medallion is the perfect symbol for her past and future training, and she hopes to keep it after the pledging ceremony.

"You should be honored to wear the royal garb," Jeqi says. Her tail sways behind her.

"I am honored. This outfit just isn't me. It's too fancy. I'm going to fall on my face."

"Probably."

As they reach the main entrance to the throne room, Jeqi smiles and greets the guards stationed on either side of the door. The two younglings step inside and stop at the head of a white staircase with stone railing. The mid-day stars, Solis and Cerule, shine through the giant glass wall, casting a beautiful gleam across the walls depicting the Ru-Kai's ascension to power. The high ceilings add to the elegance of the throne room. Atae leans against the white railing while both hybrids admire the splendid architecture. Recovering quicker than Atae, Jeqi tugs on her packmate to ascend the grand staircase and into the central area of the hall, where the royal guests gather. Someone with a pretentious voice announces Atae and Jeqi's arrival with their names and status as the queen's protégées. To Atae's horror, everyone waiting in the busy throne room pauses to glance at the new arrivals.

Nervous, Atae misses a step and stumbles into Jeqi. The blonde stops short of tumbling down the remaining steps by grabbing the banister with one hand and reaching to steady Atae with the other. A loud chuckle cascades through the crowd before everyone returns to their conversations. Once on the main floor, Jeqi glares at Atae with fury and rosy-cheeked embarrassment. Without saying a word, the Setunn storms off, leaving Atae alone in a sea of royal guests.

"Don't worry. We all stumble the first time," a deep, melodious voice says behind Atae. She swivels to greet the unfamiliar voice and freezes at the sight of the young male. His chocolate skin is smooth against his chiseled cheeks and strong chin, and his thick, white hair sways above his shoulders. Still, it's the young purebred's intense, silver gaze that captures Atae. His dark lips curve into a polite smile, and something inside Atae's chest flutters.

Colorful eyes indicate an impure Kajian bloodline, as does a male with chromatic hair. Female Kaji sport red roots that fade to white tips; anything else implies the same impurity. The majority of purebred Kaji have coal-black eyes, but a few pure bloodlines carry the silver-eyed gene. Only the Crests of Kaji can produce younglings, or heirs, with silver eyes, and within the latest generation, only half of the heirs boast this exceptional trait. It is so rare that Atae is taken aback at the sight of this handsome youngling.

After a moment of silence, he ducks his head and whispers, "Are you okay?"

"I'm sorry." Atae's eyes widen, and her cheeks flame. "I've never met an heir, certainly not one with silver eyes. At least not in this form. They are beautiful."

"And I've never seen pink eyes," he says. He lifts Atae's face with a gentle hand on her chin. Calloused from training, his fingers are rough against her soft skin, and Atae shivers at the strength she imagines he must possess. When her abashed eyes meet his steady gaze again, he smiles.

"And they are just as beautiful."

Atae's eyes widen as her whole face flares red from his compliment. The silver heir rubs his thumb across her cheek then pulls his hand free. Atae sucks in a breath that she hadn't realized she was holding. No one had ever complimented her appearance before. Her strength and technique, yes, but never her looks. Atae had never thought of herself as attractive nor unattractive. She's unsure what to think of this young male and blurts out the only thing that comes to mind.

"They are fuchsia, not pink." Realizing the childishness of her argument, Atae grimaces.

"Fuchsia? I'm afraid I'm not familiar with that color."

"It's just another word for pink."

"Well, fuchsia does seem more warrior-like than pink," he says. Amusement sparkles in his silver eyes, and Atae smiles at her new companion. Her eyes fall to a medallion fastened to the chest of his formal attire, and she reaches out to touch it, flipping it over to see both sides. It has the Ru-Kai crest on one side and an unfamiliar sigil on the other.

"You serve the royal crest, but you are not a Ru-Kai heir," Atae says.

"You don't recognize the crest?"

"Uh, no. I don't follow politics."

"I'm an heir to the Fu-Kai crest. I am honored to serve as Prince Truin's royal guard."

Atae freezes with her arm still between them, and her eyes widen with realization. Just above the medallion on his bare chest, a scar descends below his bodysuit, and Atae is certain it extends the length of his torso. She knows this because she gave him the scar only a couple of days ago. With great care and deliberate movement, Atae pulls her arm back to her side and meets the silver heir's analyzing gaze. Feeling duped, she presses her lips together and lashes out at the royal guard.

"Schinn, I take it. How many hours did you spend in a healing tank after our last encounter?"

"Just long enough to enjoy you and your little friend's visit," he says. Schinn flashes a half-smile at the hybrid, and she balks.

"What do you mean?"

"I mean, sitting in the tank just behind your recovery chairs allowed me to overhear some interesting facts about you. Facts that you don't want anyone else to know," Schinn says. Atae glances around the crowded room and tugs him close to prevent eavesdropping.

"What do you want?" Atae asks. "You know what, I don't care. If you tell anyone, you'll get far worse than a gutted belly."

"Don't worry. I'm not here to blackmail you. I'm here to offer my help," he says. Schinn snickers when Atae's nose crinkles and her mouth twists into an absurd scowl.

"What?"

"You need someone to guide you. Learning to control your shift is hard, even with a family to support you. Alone, it is nearly impossible." When a couple nearby glances at the two younglings, Schinn grabs Atae and drags her to the window overlooking the royal garden. "I want to teach you to control your shift."

"Why? Why do you want to help me?" Atae shrugs off Schinn's arm.

"It's not about helping you," he says. "It's about helping Prince Truin. You are a good fighter, and it would be advantageous for you to be one of his protectors. No matter how strong he is, the prince will need all the help he can get in the Gridiron."

Schinn glances around the room to ensure none of the guests are getting too close and spots Solum. When the battle-hardened warrior swivels toward them, Schinn grimaces.

"How do you know that I'm entering with him?" Atae asks.

"Meet me in Training Room Four tomorrow at midday," Schinn says. Then he slips from Atae to disappear into the crowd before she can stop him. Annoyed by Schinn's sudden departure, Atae doesn't notice Solum's arrival and jumps when he places a hand on her shoulder. She twirls around to face a threat with her fists raised before realizing that, once again, she has overreacted. She closes her eyes to calm her racing heart and convince her mind that Kandorq is locked away forever. Atae opens her eyes to Solum's stern frown. If she looked closer, Atae could have seen the worry that his frown concealed; instead, Atae looks away, ashamed of her panicked response.

"Come," Solum says. Atae follows him to stand next to the throne where Jeqi awaits. Apparently forgiving Atae's earlier mistakes, Jeqi smiles at her packmate, and the blue hybrid grins in return. The blonde's eyes dance across the crowd as she waits.

"Queen Sula and Prince Truin will arrive soon," Jeqi says.

"Do you both understand what this ceremony is for?" Solum asks. He watches the guests as though he were surrounded by enemies, and Atae frowns at her father's odd behavior. She doesn't understand why he would treat the queen's royal subjects with suspicion.

"Prince Truin is announcing his intention to enter the Gridiron," Atae says.

"Yes, but there is more to it. You need to understand the prince's position." Solum glances at the two naïve younglings then back to the ever-growing crowd around them. "Prince Truin is the only Ru-Kai heir, so what happens if he dies or proves unworthy in the Gridiron?"

"He won't. I'll make sure of it."

Solum studies his daughter's fierce determination and almost believes her, but he understands the cruel unpredictability of life. Solum knows how one decision can change the lives of millions for better or worse. One small stroke of fate's mighty scythe can rip the center of your universe from your life forever, leaving in its wake nothing but an empty husk.

"You may be able to keep our prince alive, but you cannot prove his worth for him. He must do it and without refute. There must be no doubt in anyone's mind that he will make a worthy king. Anything less, and he will lose his right to the throne," he says.

"What? Of course, he is worthy. He is our prince. He is heir to the Ru-Kai crest. Who else would rule?" Atae says. She frowns, appalled by the mere notion that her prince might be unfit. She ignores the rogue thoughts that whisper through her mind about the *arrogant brute* or the *disrespectful brat* that she met before Prince Truin revealed himself.

"Anyone who conquers the Royal Brawl," Solum says. Upon seeing Atae's confusion, he asks. "Do you know what a Royal Brawl is?"

"No."

"Yes," Jeqi says. Solum motions for her to explain.

"If a Kaji warrior wishes to challenge the ruling monarch for the throne and right to rule, they must declare their intentions before the royal court. The royal family must then host the Royal Brawl within one month. It's supposed to be very exciting and draws more attention than the Gridiron. It's a tournament that consists of several rounds. The challenger must triumph over the king's chosen defenders during each round. There are multiple defenders in some rounds. If the challenger survives long enough, he must defeat the king in the final round. Only extraordinary warriors ever attempt the feat because each round is to the death."

"Whoa. How come I've never heard of it?"

"There hasn't been a ruler to challenge." Jeqi shrugs. "At least not in our lifetime. Queen Sula is only a regent until the next ruler is chosen."

"Have you seen a Royal Brawl?" Atae asks her father.

"I defended King Uta's honor once or twice." Solum smirks at his daughter's reverent gaze.

"Wow," Atae says. Then, she frowns. "King Uta died before Prince Truin was born, right? Why didn't anyone try to claim the throne then?"

"Queen Sula is well-respected by our people. She has proven her ability to rule on many occasions, so the Kaji would never have supported a usurper. Remember Atae and Jeqi that no matter who claims the throne, the Kaji decide who will lead them. They will never follow a warrior that they consider unworthy."

"But how do they know if the warrior is worthy?" Atae asks.

"How do you determine the worth of a warrior?" Solum glances at her before darting his eyes back to the throng when a surge of whispers cascades through the crowd.

"I fight them."

"And if you can't fight them?"

Solum recognizes the catalyst for the sudden buzz and faces the main entrance.

"I watch them fight," Atae says. Then, her eyes widen in realization. "That's how the Kaji determine who is worthy of leading. They watch the Gridiron."

Jeqi elbows her packmate to hush as the throne room falls into a suffocating silence moments before the doors open and reveal the royal family. Queen Sula enters first and stops at the top of the staircase to survey the room. She notes which crests sent their heirs as she instructed. She smirks after confirming that all the Crests of Kaji are present with their heirs. No Kaji would dare defy her. Now, she must solidify her son's rule.

Donning an elegant red ensemble with full shoulder pads and long sleeves, Queen Sula descends the grand staircase. A silver coin emblazoned with the Ru-Kai crest sits in the center of Sula's chest with extravagant black and silver embroidery spiraling outward across the entire bodysuit. In the royal attire, Jeqi and Atae appear young and awkward, but Queen Sula exudes power and poise. Her red outfit drapes over her curves, accentuating her toned legs and powerful arms.

Pulling strength from the image of her son's crest rising to power, Queen Sula ignores the crowd and sets her amber gaze on the illustration above her throne. When she steps off the stairwell, she lowers her gaze to the parting group and glides to her throne, sitting with a hard and stoic expression. Atae admires the queen's elegance as the mid-day light shines across her face and sets her chocolate skin to glow, and her coarse hair flares out like a red and white halo.

Atae follows Queen Sula's gaze across the throne room to find Prince Truin gripping the banister as he surveys his subjects. Atae wonders about his thoughts because his face is as stoic and unreadable as the queen's impenetrable mask. Truin wears a similar red garb, fit for a young Kaji prince, which compliments his short red and white hair. Atae feels his amber gaze on her before it shifts to the rest of the royal guests. She watches her prince descend the stairs with grace as his two royal guards, Schinn and Trikk, follow suit. Atae can't help but compare the older royal guards to Prince Truin as they follow him into the parting crowd.

Schinn's masculine frame is well-formed and matured compared to the younger prince, and his silver eyes and hair prove a pure bloodline that Prince Truin cannot claim. With his short white hair and black eyes, even Trikk, the eldest of the three, looks more Kaji than the prince. The older younglings have larger frames with broad shoulders and more muscle than the younger hybrid, but Atae suspects her prince will surpass their size and strength given time to mature. She surges with pride at the thought of Prince Truin proving to the doubting Kaji that he is a strong and worthy warrior.

But is he a leader?

The intruding thought twists Atae's pride as she watches Prince Truin take his throne next to his mother. His guards stand at attention behind him in silent support as they watch the guests in the same fashion as Solum. Atae glances at her father and wonders if he is acting as the queen's guard. Atae's thoughts are pulled back to the royal family as Queen Sula speaks deep and loud for all attendees to hear.

"Welcome, my guests. I am pleased to see you all. My son has an important announcement."

With a signal from his mother, Prince Truin steps from his throne with a nervous lurch, and Atae cringes for the young royal. He ignores the whispers that cascade through the crowd and raises his head with a willful fierceness.

"Seventeen seasons ago, my mother, Queen Sula, ironed out a treaty with the Camille Empire that put an end to a galactic war that spanned generations. Peace is a wonderful thing, but it leads to complacency and weakness. Fearing for her people's future, Queen Sula established the Sula Academy & Research Facility. She hoped to keep future generations from losing the strength and honor for which our elders had given their lives." The older warriors in the crowd nod their heads in agreement at Prince Truin's words.

"And when the treaty is finally broken, we will be prepared," Prince Truin says. His mischievous grin instigates a cascade of muffled chuckles, but everyone falls silent when Queen Sula clears her throat. Truin glances at his mother and frowns in submission.

"But it has survived this long and, who knows, maybe it will last another seventeen seasons," he says. The crowd mumbles at the unnerving thought of returning to war against the Camille, and Atae can taste the tension in the air.

"Sula Academy has been training younglings for twelve seasons," Prince Truin says. "And as we have all seen, they are a force to be reckoned with in the Gridiron. This season's class of younglings will be the first to have attended Sula Academy from beginning to end. This class will be the best of the best and will prove Queen Sula's strength as a warrior and a leader. In six months, they will compete in the Gridiron, and it promises to be very exciting. In fact, if they perform as well as we all have come to expect from Sula Academy, the Ru-Kai crest promises to establish an academy on every home planet in the empire." As the crowd murmurs with excitement, Atae notices Prince Truin's smug expression. She has to fight the urge to roll her eyes at the pompous youngling.

"To make things even more exciting, I have decided to compete in the Gridiron with Sula Academy," Truin says, trying to echo his mother's grave, commanding voice. The crowd bursts into a loud commotion of disbelief, causing Atae to step back in surprise. Of course, the prince wants to compete with the strongest of warriors.

What do the Crests of Kaji expect from their prince?

"Forgive my boldness, Your Highness, but I...we all fear for your safety. You are our only prince," an older Kaji with scars on one cheek says with honest concern. The crowd parts around him, so Prince Truin and Queen Sula can peer at him unhindered. Sula opens her mouth to respond, but her son is quicker.

"I will prove to the Kaji that I will be a worthy king, or I will die trying." Prince Truin speaks with such conviction that Atae stands taller with pride for him.

"But who will lead us then? With no king to challenge, there can be no Royal Brawl. You are the last of the Ru-Kai crest, and Queen Sula cannot rule as regent forever. Who will take the throne if you perish?" a silver-eyed Kaji with braids asks as he pushes his way to the front of the crowd with his daughter. Atae doesn't hear concern for their prince in the elder warrior's voice, but curiosity. Ambition seeps from his half-hidden grin as he places a hand on his daughter's shoulder.

The daughter stands firm with strong shoulders and muscled arms crossed over her powerful chest. Thick shoulder-length hair frames a sharp face. The youngling's tall height distorts her age, but Atae guesses that she is less than a season from maturity. Prince Truin glares at the youngling, hiding his seething hatred under a mask of indifference. Surprised to see such loathing from the prince, Atae suspects that the two heirs have a history.

"I foresaw the anxiety my son's decision would cause our people," Queen Sula says. She stands from her throne and demands attention from everyone. Prince Truin is the only one that refuses to face his mother. Knowing what the queen plans to say, he grimaces as she speaks.

"The Kaji should never pause for the uncertainty of the future. So I declare this, here and now, for all of the Kaji to hear. If my son, Prince Truin, is slain in the Gridiron, whosoever defeats him shall win his right to the throne of the Kaji Empire."

As the crowd roars with disbelief, outrage, and excitement, the tall heir peers at Prince Truin with her father's ambition shining bright in her small, silver eyes.

CHAPTER 25

"What? Is she allowed to do that?" Atae asks her packmate. The entire throne room roars with excitement around them, and the blonde glances at Atae with a shrug.

"She is the queen," Jeqi says.

"My queen, are you allowed to do this? It has never been done," the scarred warrior asks. Atae nods her head, glad to hear someone voice her question.

"I am Sula Ru-Kai, Queen of the Kaji Empire, the strongest galactic empire in existence." Her cold, threatening voice that echoes throughout the throne room like a promise of death. Her molten amber eyes scour the room for any who would challenge her claim to the Kajian throne. Finding none, Queen Sula shifts her battle-hardened gaze to the large window behind the crowd and speaks with conviction as she envisions the countless souls that look to her for leadership.

"The Kaji have lived and died by my word for decades, and today is no different." She returns her gaze to the Crests of Kaji. "My word is law. Any citizen who wishes to discuss the matter may do so with the Kajian council. They are fully aware of and support my decision."

"But why?" the same scarred warrior asks. "He will be the target of every ambitious Kaji in the Gridiron. You are throwing him to the battle beasts."

"I am no scrap of meat to be thrown to wild animals. I will not be beaten," Prince Truin says.

Queen Sula glares at her son's youthful arrogance then returns her gaze to the chattering crowd. She clears her throat, and the throng of Kaji quiet.

"As a mother, I have done all I can to teach my son to be an honorable warrior. I have provided him with the best advisors and instructors our empire has to offer. I have spent his entire life trying to teach him the ways of our people and the true meaning of strength and honor." Queen Sula sets her hard gaze on her son, and he frowns at her in return. "As queen, I cannot allow an un-fit warrior, Ru-Kai or not, to claim the throne. If Prince Truin has failed to absorb what has been laid before him, he does not deserve his birthright. Any warrior who cannot protect what he claims as his own shall not keep it long."

"I can and will protect my birthright. I am the Ru-Kai heir and the future King of the Kaji Empire."

"But what pack do you have to protect you, my prince?" The scarred warrior asks. He searches for a straw of hope for his prince's survival. It's no secret that Truin lacks a genuine pack since his attitude drives away most potential packmates. Those loyal to the Ru-Kai crest can be called upon and labeled packmates in duty only. Prince Truin doesn't have a true pack bond with any warrior he calls pack.

"I don't need a pack to protect me," he says. Truin's amber eyes are as molten as his mother's when he dares any of the heirs to oppose his declaration of strength and ability. The ambitious youngling with silver eyes chuckles and draws every eye in the room as a wave of tense silence threatens to smother them all. The youngling's voice is smooth and silky as it slips from her dark smirking lips.

"You mean there isn't a warrior that will follow you. No one will stand next to you in battle or die for you. Your crest, maybe. Your mother, definitely. But not for you."

Prince Truin glares at the taller youngling with a fury Atae has never seen from her prince. What's worse is the thread of fear she sees in his eyes as he glances back at Atae. The silver heir managed to stab Prince Truin in the open wound that Atae had sliced into existence only recently. Doubt knocks the wind from the young prince as he steps back away from the crowd. The throng of Kaji smells blood and surges with whispers.

No, they can't doubt him. Not now. He hasn't even entered the Gridiron. Atae's eyes dart across the faces in the crowds as they twist in disapproval of her prince. *Of course, Prince Truin has warriors that will stand with him. He will not be alone.*

"He has me," Atae says loud enough for a few nearby guests to hear. When the crowd shifts in unison to meet her, Atae recognizes her mistake. Wide-eyed, she peeks at Solum for help, but Atae's father shakes his head and clenches his jaw at her outburst. Refusing to rescue Atae from the consequences of her actions, Solum pinches his dark lips together and stares at her. Realizing that her father has abandoned her to the mercy of politicians, Atae takes a deep breath and glances at Prince Truin. Her deep fuchsia eyes meet his swirling amber, and certainty washes over her.

"I will stand with Prince Truin. I will ensure his survival, or I will die with him."

Solum wipes his hand over his face, exasperated by her foolishness. Yet, the crowd loves it. Excited cheers echo from the guests until Jeqi steps forward from Solum's side.

"I promise the same," Jeqi says. Despite her stoic mask, the puffed tail around her waist warns Atae of her packmate's fury. Jeqi hates rash decisions, and the blue hybrid just made a massive one in front of all the Crests of Kaji. Atae slips a comforting hand onto Jeqi's shoulder, but after an icy glare, she yanks it back for fear of losing it.

"As do I," says a deep voice that interrupts chattering throng. It's a voice that Atae would recognize anywhere. The crowd parts to reveal Sloan, garbed in formal attire with a crest plastered on his medallion. Unfamiliar with the emblem, Atae cannot determine with which family it belongs, but she notes that the ambitious female with silver eyes wears the same crest. Atae stares at her rival in awe and confusion.

Sloan is an heir to one of the Crests of Kaji? How did I not know this?

Atae glances at Jeqi, but her scorned packmate is of no help. The blonde sneers at Atae and refuses to acknowledge the surprising turn of events. When Atae swivels back to Sloan, she finds him sporting a smug smile, and his eyes dance with that familiar mischievous glint. Pouting, Atae glowers at him as she crosses her arms over her chest.

"Well," Sula says. "It seems my son has plenty of support. Anyone daring to challenge Prince Truin in the Gridiron will have a hard time getting past his pack."

Queen Sula narrows her eyes at the silver-eyed youngling who dared to challenge her son. The bold heir lowers her gaze and hunches her shoulders in submission to her queen's higher status. Sula surveys the remaining heirs with pressed lips before lifting a dismissive hand.

"Now, it seems there is nothing left to discuss. Everyone should reach out to their communication networks tonight. By morning, I expect every citizen in our empire to know what transpired here today. Now be gone. I have better things to do than play hostess."

Eager to spread the exciting news, the crowd surges out the door leaving behind only a handful of warriors. Queen Sula steps away from the dwindling group and disappears behind several hanging drapes. Atae zeros in on Sloan with a furious stride and leaves a miffed Jeqi behind to sulk. Prince Truin reaches Sloan before Atae, however, and demands his own answers.

"What do you think you are doing, Sloan?"

"Saving your butt. You were drowning up there. You're welcome."

"You've played our hand. Now, everyone knows where your allegiance falls, including your sister," Prince Truin says. He points an accusing finger at Sloan, who snorts in return. Atae glances from one heir to the other with a furrowed brow.

"What are you talking about? You have a sister?" she asks.

"Please, Royce knows exactly where my loyalties lie, and it isn't with her. She's shadier than our father. Smarter, too," Sloan says.

"Yes, but she is dangerously charismatic. I hate charismatic people. Like you," Prince Truin says.

"You're just jealous because you have no people skills."

"Wait, you both know each other? How?" Atae says.

The male younglings finally decide to acknowledge the baffled hybrid. Prince Truin glares at her as though she were too simple to understand the basic principles of life, and Sloan chuckles with smug satisfaction.

"Of course, we know each other," Prince Truin says. "As the prince, it is my duty to know every heir to the Crests of Kaji."

"Unlike some commoners, who can't even recognize their own prince," Sloan says. Atae narrows her eyes at the two younglings ganging up on her. She props one hand on her hip and points a finger at Sloan.

"An heir, huh? Then, where are your private tutors? Why are you attending Sula Academy?"

Atae watches Sloan flinch at the barb and grind his teeth. When he glowers at her in silence, Atae grins as a realization slides over her. She's found a way to get under his skin.

"Oh, I get it. That silver-eyed youngling is Royce, your sister." Atae slips in closer to Sloan and flashes a smug smile. "You're a black-eyed mark on the silver-eyed lineage. Rejected by your own family. That must sting a bit."

Sloan closes the gap between them and growls at Atae. His dark gaze burns under his thick eyebrows, and a snarl twists his lips.

"You know nothing, so shut your mouth."

Atae sees something feral flash across Sloan's eyes, and she steps back, frightened by the familiar predatorial gaze. With the scent of Atae's fear permeating his nostrils, Sloan's eyes elongate and flare into a deep red. Atae no longer sees Sloan's red, beast eyes, but instead, she finds Kandorq's twisted, red orbs glaring into her soul.

"Solum!" Prince Truin calls for help as he struggles to subdue a shifting Sloan. Atae hyperventilates as the throne room disappears, and the never-ending dark forest returns. Shadows dance around her as the suffocating darkness of the abyss weighs down her body and mind. Atae falls to her knees, fear tracing up her spine, and a familiar taunting whisper brushes against her ear.

Too weak to stop me.

"No, I am strong. I am Kaji," Atae whispers. Kandorq's chuckle envelopes her in a paralyzing blanket of fear. Weary of this struggle, Atae wonders if she should give in to the insanity.

What's the point in fighting? He always returns.

Enough. A thin whisper spears Atae's mind, and she jolts at the intrusion. A tendril of silver fog escapes from a hidden crevice in her mind, and Atae stares at it in wonder.

"Atae, move!"

Solum's voice breaks through her dark haze, and she lurches back to the reality of the throne room. A completely shifted Sloan snarls and snaps at Solum and Prince Truin as they venture near the battle beast. They distract Sloan, drawing him closer to Schinn and Trikk. With his back to Atae, Sloan growls and lashes out at the offending Kaji. He howls at Solum and Prince Truin as they maneuver closer for an attack.

Relieved that Sloan seems to have forgotten her, Atae jumps to her feet and creeps backward, away from the furious beast. Her eyes dart across the room in search of a nearby exit then settle on the main entrance. The giant door at the top of the elegant stairway is halfway between her and the guards.

Maybe, if I move very slowly and quietly…

Before the blue hybrid has a chance to find out, a firm hand grips her right arm, and Atae squeals in surprise. Jeqi slaps a hand over her packmate's mouth to muffle the sound. Still as night, they both watch the battle beast for any indication that he'd heard. When only an ear flickers in their direction, Jeqi releases Atae's mouth and pulls her back toward the wall behind the thrones. As they reach the large drapes framing the Ru-Kai's crest, Jeqi disappears behind them.

Atae lifts the drape and reveals a hidden pathway. She glances back to find Sloan leering at her with his red beast eyes. She ducks into the small hallway before he has a chance to chase after her. The wall slides shut behind her and leaves a howling battle beast on the other side.

CHAPTER 26

For a moment, Atae just leans against the wall. She closes her eyes and enjoys the cold brick against her hot skin. Atae listens to Solum's muffled voice directing guards to subdue the furious battle beast, and she smiles at the sounds of Sloan flailing about on the other side of the wall.

"What are you smiling about? This is your fault," Jeqi says. Her accusation blusters through Atae's musings, and the blue hybrid opens her eyes.

Jeqi stands shrouded in darkness and floating particles of dust that were stirred up from their bustling entrance. Her blue Setunn eyes reflect the small beams of light that escape from the throne room through crevices in the sliding wall. Atae drops her gaze from Jeqi's eerie appearance and fights the memories of similar but emerald eyes.

"It's not my fault that Sloan can't control his anger," Atae says. She pushes past Jeqi and eyes the dark, narrow pathway that's covered in dust and recently disturbed cobwebs. Atae remembers the queen disappearing behind the drapes and wonders where this path leads. With her tail thrashing at her back, Jeqi huffs at Atae.

"His anger? His anger didn't trigger his shift. It was your fear."

"That's not true. Sloan started shifting when I angered him. I saw his eyes." Atae glances over her shoulder at Jeqi. "Did you notice they changed color? I've never seen a battle beast with red eyes. Why do they change color?"

"Probably the same reason he has black eyes while most of his lineage has silver. Genetics."

Atae nods, satisfied with the answer, then stumbles down the dark hall, using a hand on the wall to guide her. Atae frowns as she struggles to see through the gloom. A few tiny beams of light slice through the dark hall, but accomplish little against the shadow. Atae pauses to close her eyes and concentrate on shifting her eyes, but nothing happens. She sighs in frustration and continues down her blind path. When she hears a chortle from her packmate, Atae frowns but bites her tongue.

I don't need her help to navigate a stupid tunnel.

Then her foot catches on an uneven stone, and Atae crashes to the floor. She lies in the dirt and cobwebs, listening to Jeqi's muffled laughter. She considers the best way to salvage her pride and dignity as the blonde watches her with a satisfied and, somewhat, taunting smile.

Maybe, I do need her help.

"I swear it's true," a muffled male voice says, followed by a light female voice.

"There is no way. Queen Sula would never do that."

Atae lifts her head at the intrusion of unfamiliar voices. Jeqi steps around her comrade to investigate one of the tiny beams of light that shines through a small hole in the grimy stone wall.

"Maybe I should enter the Gridiron and defeat the prince," the male voice says.

"It's two servants in the kitchen. They're alone," Jeqi whispers.

"Then, you'd be king," the female says. Atae cringes at the servant's high-pitched giggle, but the male seems to enjoy the sound.

"And you'd be my queen," he says.

Jeqi's eyes widen when the female giggles again. The hybrid spins away from the two lovers and blushes.

"Oh, uh," she says. "We should keep moving."

Jeqi shuffles away from the wall, expecting her packmate to follow. Instead, Atae glances at the tiny hole in confusion.

"Why? What are they doing?" she asks. "If they're plotting against Prince Truin, we should find out as much as we can."

"I don't think they are plotting anything." She bites back a chuckle when Atae peeks through the hole for confirmation.

"Nope, definitely not." Atae hurries away from the peep show, and in her haste, she bumps against a hidden switch on the far wall. The two hybrids watch in horror as a section of the kitchen's stone wall slides open between them. Thankfully, decorative curtains hide the sudden gap, but the noise captures the servants' attention.

"Did you hear something?" asks the female.

"Just the thumping of my heart, my dear," the male says.

"What did you do? What did you touch?" Jeqi asks. She darts across the far wall, searching for the switch to close the hidden door, and Atae rushes to help her.

"I don't know," she says with a curse. "We can't let them find us. They'll think we're peepers."

"You think?" Jeqi says. She squeaks in triumph when she finds the switch and activates the door.

"There it is, again. I'm telling you I heard something."

"It's probably just some rodents. I often hear them running along the walls. I'm certain the palace is overrun with them. Now, where were we?"

The two hybrids hustle along as the muffled sounds of passion grow louder. Atae struggles along the dark path, and amused by her blind stumbling, Jeqi follows a few steps behind. Catching the chuckle from her packmate as she trips down a few unseen steps, Atae huffs.

"You know, you could lead the way. You're the one with night vision."

"I don't think so. I'm enjoying myself too much. Besides, you owe me."

"I told you. Sloan's shifting was not my fault. Argh." Atae stumbles to her knees against several ascending steps, and Jeqi glides past her.

"That's not what I meant, but yes, it was," Jeqi says. She doesn't hide her amusement as she stops to wait for Atae to recover. Atae remains on the ground, leaning against the steps, and stares up at the blonde.

"How is it my fault that he can't control his anger? A warrior is always clear-headed and doesn't let frivolous emotions, like anger, cloud his judgment. He knows that."

"His anger pushed his change to the edge, but it was your fear that released it."

"My fear? But he was already shifting. And I wasn't afraid of him."

"You could have fooled me." Jeqi frowns at her friend. "One moment, you were arguing with him like you always do, and the next, you're scrambling away, like frightened prey. A lot of young Kaji have trouble controlling their shifts at times. Even Prince Truin had trouble yesterday when you angered him, but Sloan kept his shift in check until you became prey. What happened to you? I could smell your fear from across the room. Everyone could."

Shame washes over Atae as she remembers the way Sloan's eyes shifted to red and the icy fear that raced down her spine. She wasn't afraid of Sloan. Atae knows that, but she was…is afraid of Kandorq. In that instant,

Atae's mind saw Kandorq's sick, red eyes glowing with a predator's need to hunt. And Atae reacted just like prey. Scared, weak prey.

"I wasn't afraid of Sloan." Atae sighs and climbs to her feet, wiping the dirt and cobwebs from her royal attire. When Jeqi tries to argue, Atae cuts her off. "I'm not afraid of Sloan or other battle beasts. I'm afraid of Kandorq and that damn Setunn."

"I don't understand. What do they have to do with this?"

"It's hard to explain," Atae stares down the dark path. "Maybe, it's like this hall. I'm just struggling to get through to the other side, where I know there is an end to it. I know that, with time, I'll get there. I know that when I do, it'll be lighted, and I won't be alone. I won't be scared anymore. It'll be like it was before, maybe even better. And to get there, I have to keep moving, but these damn steps and cracks keep pulling me down."

Atae peeks at Jeqi, imploring her to understand, but she knows it isn't possible. Atae wraps her arms around herself, squeezing tightly, as she whispers through the blackness and reveals the fear that plagues her mind.

"These memories or flashbacks, whatever you want to call them, it's like I'm there, like I never left. Like this is a dream, and I keep waking up in that forest with him breathing down my neck and her stalking me. I just want it to stop, to end. I know it will eventually. I know that if I hold on long enough, I'll heal. I'll be back to normal. I just have to keep fighting."

Jeqi watches her friend grapple with an internal enemy as Atae's gray uniform, smudged with dirt and cobwebs, clings to her thin form. A stale breeze twirls the short, blue locks that frame the small hybrid's frowning face. Her fuchsia eyes swirl with fear and shame, but Jeqi also sees just a hint of hope in Atae's gaze. Hope that Jeqi can save her from the monsters in the dark. Looking at Atae now, most would see a scared youngling clinging to herself and unfit to wear the royal attire she dons. Jeqi sees a young female with the potential to influence the universe if only she could find her way out of this dark place.

Jeqi slips a hand over Atae's upper arm and guides her through the dark path. She leads the blue hybrid up the steps and around the obstacles. After a few steps, Atae grabs Jeqi's hand and clings to it, grateful for her packmate's help. The blonde's soft, silver tail wraps around Atae's clinging arm, and she finds comfort in the loving embrace. They walk in silence until they see a light, shining at the far end of the path. Jeqi glances back at Atae with a teasing smile.

"You still owe me."

"What do you mean?"

"In the throne room, and in front of all the heirs, you opened your big mouth."

"Oh, yeah. I guess I did kind of pledge our lives to the prince," Atae says. She recollects Jeqi's fury and Solum's bafflement. "But weren't you already planning to help Prince Truin in the Gridiron?"

"Of course I was. I just wasn't planning on telling everyone where I stand on the matter. It's called strategy."

"Oh, we should probably talk about that."

"Obviously," Jeqi says. She grumbles at her packmate's oblivious nature.

"Hey, how can you expect me to know these types of things? I'm a warrior, not a politician."

"Shh." Jeqi pauses to listen to a soft song echoing down the passageway. Neither hybrid understands the lyrics, but the sad voice reverberates into their souls. Atae sneaks closer to the source of the familiar voice only to have Jeqi grab her arm.

"Stop, it's the queen."

"I know." Atae tugs her arm free. Both girls tread forward until the voice is right outside the wall. Luckily, several small beams of light reveal holes for the younglings to peer into the room.

Atae first spots the white, stone coffin carved into a warrior's likeness, and then she notices the chamber walls, covered in jeweled depictions of the warrior's life from birth to death. One, in particular, catches Atae's eye. It's an image of the warrior fighting and losing to a horde of Gortox while a green-eyed, Kajian female escapes the battle. Atae remembers the story of a mighty warrior who fought off ten of the massive and grotesque creatures but later died of his wounds.

King Uta.

Atae's eyes widen as they fall upon her mourning queen. Solis' and Cerule's light flickers through the crystal ceiling and glistens off the disturbed dust particles that float around Queen Sula. She stands at the foot of her mate's tomb with a hand grazing the edge. Her eyes are downcast to his muscular form, carved into the coffin. Dirty and covered in cobwebs from the hidden path, Sula's red and white hair hangs lifeless around her angular face. The red bodysuit that once hugged her strong form now bunches around her hunched body.

She doesn't move from her slumped position when Solum slips into the crypt. The royal advisor grimaces at his intrusion and bows his head at his late king's stone depiction.

"Why are you here? Why do you disturb me?" Sula asks. She scrunches her face, almost pleading for Solum to go away. He doesn't answer but waits in silence for his queen. Atae watches her with a furrowed brow. How can this be the same warrior that stood defiant and strong in front of her people just a short while ago?

Why does she seem so defeated?

The moment the thought crosses Atae's mind, Queen Sula lifts a longing gaze from her mate and settles a hardened stare onto Solum.

Not defeated then, just resting. Atae admonishes herself for ever doubting her queen, even for a moment.

Solum refuses to glance around the crypt at the images of his friend's life, especially avoiding the green-eyed female in the last scene. Instead, he watches his queen slide to the head of King Uta's tomb and run her hand over the carved depiction with nimble fingers. She caresses the side of his face and manages a tight smile at the memory of her lost mate.

"He was a strong warrior. He was courageous and stubborn and convinced of his own greatness. So much like our son. I know Truin will be a great warrior and leader one day. Not today, but someday. If he survives long enough." Her voice cracks as she says the last few words. The fear of losing her child swirls in her amber eyes, and Solum can relate. But he knows who to blame for their current predicament.

"You've just ensured that he won't," Solum says. Sula gathers her senses and ignores the blush of embarrassment across her cheeks. Showing such weakness in front of anyone, even Solum, was a mistake. He watches her glare at him from across the room, but he refuses to back down.

"You've turned his Gridiron into a Royal Brawl. Now, it's not just the crests that we have to worry about usurping the throne. It's every citizen of the empire."

"Yes."

"The chances of him surviving are nil, never mind proving himself."

"Yes."

"Yes, what?" Solum growls and surges toward her with his arms thrashing out with each word. "Was it your intention to kill off your only son and the last remaining Ru-Kai? Another crest wiped out of existence? Is that what you want?"

"Enough," she says. "I've ensured that whoever survives my son's Gridiron will be the strongest warriors the Kaji have ever produced."

"And if your son isn't one of them?"

Queen Sula flinches away from Solum as though struck by his words. With her back to him, she raises a fist above her head, and it shakes from the emotions raging against her control. As though coming to terms with the consequences of her decision, Queen Sula lowers her unsteady hand onto her mate's tomb and speaks in a firm tone.

"Then he is not fit to rule."

"You're sending him into certain death and condemning him when he can't change fate," Solum says.

"The Kaji don't believe in fate. We aren't the Setunn," Queen Sula says. She flashes a melancholy grin. "We don't believe in an afterlife, either. Yet, I still pray to Uta when I need guidance."

"Did you pray to him when you decided to kill his child?"

"Watch your tongue, Solum. I am still your queen."

"For now. What happens when your son dies in the Gridiron? If the Ru-Kai aren't fit to rule, who is?"

"Whoever is strong enough to…to defeat him."

"To kill him, you mean?"

"Yes," Sula grimaces, "to kill him."

"And Atae? What of her in your plans? Are you willing to sacrifice my daughter as well?" Solum steps back to distance himself from the impending answer, and Sula snarls.

"Careful, Solum. You're treading on thin ice."

"She's chosen to stand by Prince Truin's side in his Gridiron. Because of you, it will be a massacre. And knowing her, she'll be running to the front line. How does your master plan work if she's dead?"

"She has to be strong." Sula slams both fists into the tomb. "They all have to be strong. Stronger than we are. Smarter than we are. They can't make the same mistakes."

"What do you mean, Sula? What are you not telling me?" Solum asks. He searches her gaze from across the room, but she reveals nothing to him. Sula lifts her hands from the stonework and smooths her outfit as she regains her composure.

"I am your queen, Solum. There are many things I keep from you. But understand this. I will always choose the Kaji. There is nothing I won't sacrifice for my people."

Solum stares at her as his loyalties collide. The surge of pride that swells within his chest at her proclamation is overwhelming. Every ruler should be this dedicated to their people. But at the same time, the pit in his stomach turns acidic. What kind of parent would sacrifice their offspring?

"What about Truin? And Atae?"

"That's your task, of course. Don't you remember?"

The cold stare from his queen reminds him of the night she called him to the throne room. The secrets she shared with him and the plans they devised; he remembers every detail. He remembers the task she set upon him. But how can he accomplish anything against these odds?

"I can't save Prince Truin from this, and I've given my word that Atae could choose her Gridiron."

"Now, I guess you have a choice too. Your honor or your daughter's life?" She doesn't bother hiding her humorless smile as she crosses her arms over her chest. He grinds his teeth at her dig but doesn't take the bait.

"Neither. I choose to make sure Atae survives this shit storm you've created. I will do everything in my power to prepare her. I expect you to take her training with you seriously."

"Of course, as long as you do the same with my son," Sula says with a reassuring nod. "For your sake, I hope she gives you a reason to deny her entry. Your daughter's quite impulsive, so maybe something will come up in the next six months. Maybe she'll lose the tournament. Then it's a moot point."

Solum shakes his head, unable to find humor in her comment. "No, she's far too skilled to lose. The tournament is just a formality."

Queen Sula watches him salute her and turn to leave. She's already returning her gaze to the king's tomb and contemplating her recent decisions when Solum spins back to face her.

"You're taking a big gamble here, Sula."

"I know," she says. "But the Kaji will be better for it. And so will our younglings."

With a frustrated sigh, Solum storms out of the tomb. His mind reverberates with one haunting thought:

"If they survive."

Atae watches her father leave and struggles with the emotions battling within her. She doesn't understand how Solum can be so confident of her failure in the Gridiron.

At least he has more faith in me for the tournament.

Jeqi tugs her along the path toward the exit and away from King Uta's tomb. As soon as they are far enough to avoid detection, Jeqi glances over her shoulder to Atae.

"You have to figure out how to control your shift before round two," she says. "If the cameras catch you shifting, it'll be the perfect excuse to pull you from the tournament and the Gridiron. We have to compete with Prince Truin, or we won't be chosen as royal companions."

"More importantly, Prince Truin won't have anyone to protect him if we aren't there," Atae says.

"Right. Any ideas on how to master your new skill?"

Atae considers the question as she follows Jeqi toward the light at the end of the path. It doesn't take long to remember her recent run-in with Schinn.

"About that…"

CHAPTER 27

"I told you this wouldn't work," Atae says. She sidesteps Jeqi's latest attack and falls into a squared defensive stance. She holds her arms up to guard her face and chest, watching Jeqi for offensive signs. The blonde hesitates only an instant before rounding her strike toward Atae's new position with a feinted backhand to her face, followed by a real jab to the ribs.

"Why not? If you shift, you could easily beat me." Jeqi says. Her blows glance off Atae's forearm then an elbow. The Setunn hybrid follows up with a sidekick to her opponent's unguarded midsection, knocking the wind from Atae's lungs.

"Ugh!"

Furious for letting the attack breach her defenses, the blue hybrid growls at Jeqi's smug expression and bouncing stance. The blonde waves her hands to taunt her packmate into attacking. Atae grinds her teeth, switches into an offensive position, and braces her legs for a charge. In the instant it takes for Atae to decide on her plan of attack and reposition, a sharp pain spears her arms and legs like an electric shock then disperses. Taught to block out superficial pain in the heat of battle, Atae barely registers the sharp pinch. She launches at Jeqi with a vicious roar as the muscles in her legs propel her body with such force and speed that Jeqi is caught off guard. The momentum of Atae's attack, combined with the powerful punch, sends Jeqi flying backward onto her rear with a crushed nose.

"Because I don't need to shift to beat you," Atae says. She flashes a smug grin as she stands victorious over her packmate. Jeqi peers up at her attacker over a swollen nose and places her hands to the bleeding spout.

"Argh. Was that really necessary? Why do I bother helping you?" Jeqi climbs to her feet, still cradling her nose. "You said Schinn would meet us here to help you shift. Instead, I stand here bleeding. Again. Can we ever do something together that doesn't involve one us bleeding, preferably me?"

"We are Kaji," Atae shrugs. "It's what we do."

Jeqi sighs then glances cross-eyed at her nose. Grimacing, she places both hands on either side of the bloody stump and clamps down on it. She jerks the angled portion of her nose to the correct alignment without so much as a groan. Jeqi blinks away the tears of pain, refusing to let them fall. Both younglings remember Feku's lesson on tears. Watering eyes are a normal part of nose injuries, but a true warrior does not indulge them.

Jeqi wipes the clotting blood from her re-aligned nose onto her black uniform and frowns at Atae. During another painful blade session that ended with Atae bleeding and Sloan bruised, Jeqi interrupted to pull Atae away for their meeting with Schinn. Refusing to reveal the real reason for their departure, the hybrids bid farewell and, in Atae's case, good riddance to Marqee and Sloan for the day. But only after agreeing to another session tomorrow. When the two younglings arrived in Training Room Four, Schinn was not there. Apparently, he was running late or decided not to show. To pass the time, Atae and Jeqi decided to spar in an attempt to force Atae's shift, but that was proving fruitless.

When Jeqi notices Atae rubbing at her arms and stretching her legs, she asks, "Are you okay?"

"I should be asking you that."

"You do, and I'll break your nose. What are you doing?"

"I'm just stretching. I guess I should have done more before our spar because my muscles are sore. They are loosening up, though," Atae says.

The training room is simple, with hard metal walls draped with mirrors and hard, white floors. Training equipment lines the walls in front of the mirrors, but the center of the room is uncluttered and big enough for several sparring matches without them interfering with each other. The training room is marked private and occupied, so Atae and Jeqi spar alone until Schinn arrives.

The heir walks through the sliding door without looking up as he tugs on white gloves over his dark hands. The gloves and matching boots trim his blue bodysuit and make Jeqi raise an eyebrow at the male's color coordination.

"You didn't say he was a silver heir," Jeqi says. When Atae doesn't answer, Jeqi glances back to find the blue-haired female blushing bright red. "You've got to be kidding me."

Jeqi crosses her arms and sighs as her tail flickers in agitation. Schinn stops a few arm-lengths away and smiles at the younger females.

"Sorry that I'm late. Sloan wasn't easy to subdue yesterday, and I had to spend some time in a tank," Schinn says.

"You don't want any scars to mar your pretty face?" Jeqi says with a plastered smile.

"I think of scars as memories. I'd prefer to keep only the pleasant ones," Schinn says. He glances at Atae and rubs a hand over his chest. Jeqi scoffs at the flirtatious remark that refers to the scar Atae gave him. When she glances at Atae, Jeqi frowns when she finds her packmate blushing even more.

"Are you here to help or play games?" Jeqi asks Schinn. "Because I warn you, I am in no mood to play."

"I can see that," Schinn raises an eyebrow at Jeqi's broken nose. "Don't worry. My intentions are pure…for now. I've come to teach Atae to control her shifting ability."

"How?"

"Well, the first thing you have to understand is what triggers a shift-"

"Need. We know," Jeqi says.

"We recently covered this at Sula Academy," Atae says.

"Okay, the next thing is to understand your beast."

"My beast? But I don't have a beast," Atae glances between Schinn and Jeqi with confusion. "I only have blades and night vision."

"And claws," Jeqi says. She wraps her tail around her waist and studies her packmate. Atae filled her in on the self-inflicted damage from the other night, and Jeqi doesn't like the idea of her friend hurting herself, even by accident. She hopes Schinn can offer some legitimate insight, and he isn't wasting their time as a ploy to spend more time with the naïve hybrid.

"I don't mean your physical beast. I mean your mental beast," Schinn says. "It's like having a wild animal inside you. It only has basic instincts to guide it, but it usually fights you for control. Some say we are born with this second identity, but it remains dormant until we shift because that's when we need it."

"Why do we need it?" Atae asks.

"When you shift, your body activates muscles and nerves that were previously inactive. Your mind suddenly has to interpret signals from new sources, and it doesn't know what to do with them. To make matters worse, not all the muscles and nerves that were active since birth are active after the shift. So the mind has trouble adapting to the body's changes."

"I don't understand." Atae frowns at Schinn's explanation and shakes her head, while realization dawns on Jeqi's face.

"It's a coping mechanism."

"A what?" Atae asks. She's relieved that Jeqi understands. Jeqi always manages to simplify complex theories for Atae.

"The 'beast' is a second identity that the mind creates to understand and translate the shifted body," Jeqi says in a fascinated tone. "With a beast body comes a beast mind to control it."

"That's a good way to put it," Schinn says. "Do you understand, Atae?"

"I get what you're saying. But I've never felt anything like that."

"Hmm," Schinn places a hand to his chin. "How many times have you shifted?"

"Well," Atae says. "I'm pretty sure the first time was on Mount Tuki when I was attacked."

"Pretty sure? You either shifted, or you didn't."

"If it were that simple, we wouldn't need you," Jeqi says.

"My eyes shifted. I'm certain of it."

"Just your eyes? What about the blades and claws?" Schinn asks.

"No, just my eyes."

"Then don't count that as a successful shift," Schinn says. "It's common for Kaji younglings to start a shift and revert back before completing it. This can occur several times before the shifting phase is complete. The shifting phase begins when the first shifting attempt occurs and ends with the first completed shift. During that time, hormones drive emotions through peaks and valleys. That is why most Kaji pull their young out of society long enough to teach them control."

"Huh, I guess someone didn't spend enough time with Sloan during his shifting phase," Atae says with a sly glance at her packmate. Schinn frowns at the comment and shakes his head.

"Sloan possesses great control over his shift. It's his beast that he struggles to control."

"What do you mean?" Jeqi asks.

"Yeah, he didn't seem too in control in the throne room," Atae says.

"Sloan is a rare type of Kaji. He's a submissive warrior with a dominant beast." Schinn says. Both Jeqi and Atae burst into laughter, and Schinn steps away from them in surprise.

"That is the stupidest thing that I've ever heard," Atae says.

"Have you met Sloan? He is one of the most dominant males at Sula," Jeqi says.

"Exactly. I spend most of my time at Sula fighting him for the top score. Below Jeqi, of course."

"It's not that simple," Schinn says. "After your first complete shift, sometimes even during unsuccessful shifts, your beast appears. For most, it's like riding back seat to your own body. It's very unsettling, but once you shift back, so does your mind. And you retake control. Your beast never leaves after that. Eventually, your beast half melds with your rational half, but until then, your beast is a passenger in your mind."

"Dual identities," Jeqi says.

"Yeah, I get it. It's like what Elder Warrior Feku said a few days ago about a constant battle for control." Atae glances at Jeqi. "I just thought he meant that it only happens in battle beast form."

"The battle is more intense in beast form, and some control is relinquished to the beast mind but never all of it," Schinn says.

"Otherwise, they go feral," Jeqi says.

"Whoa."

"In our first form, Kaji still feel the presence of the beast mind, but it can't take control. The beast mind is wired to control a beast's body and lacks the rationale to adapt to our first form. I would guess that Sloan's beast has some effect on his personality. Without his beast as a constant companion, I wager Sloan would be very different," Schinn says. He shrugs with a half-smile at Atae.

"Hmm. That would explain it," Jeqi says.

"Explain what?" Atae asks.

"Sloan's been different since last season when he learned to shift."

"What are you talking about? Sloan's always been annoyingly sarcastic. Although...his aggression has increased since last season."

"Among other things." An amused grin slips across Jeqi's lips, and Atae furrows her brow.

"Like what?"

"Well, he's been more..." Jeqi searches for the right word to describe Sloan's recent effect on the opposite sex. It doesn't take much. A flirtatious flutter of his eyes, a suggestively arched eyebrow, or a small teasing smirk sends every female in sight blushing bright red. Well, almost every female.

"Been more what?" Atae asks.

"Um…Charming," Jeqi says as though testing the word. Upon hearing it aloud, she nods, satisfied with her choice. Atae, on the other hand, wrinkles her nose and twists her mouth into a sneer.

"Charming?"

"Charming? Huh," Schinn says. "Interesting."

"So you don't think he's attractive at all?" Jeqi asks Atae. The blue hybrid crosses her arms over here chest and glowers at her packmate.

"Ugh, no. He's Sloan. Aggravatingly sarcastic and annoyingly strong Sloan."

"Okay." Jeqi raises an eyebrow at her friend's denial. Meanwhile, Schinn tries to direct the conversation back on track.

"Well, as we were-"

"Wait. Do you?" Atae asks Jeqi.

"Find Sloan attractive? Of course." Jeqi says. As though her confession is run-of-the-mill gossip, the blonde shifts her attention back to Schinn with the intent to continue their initial discussion.

"Wha-" Atae's first attempt to respond is silenced by her shock, and she only accomplishes odd gurgling noises. When Jeqi glances back to her with a confused frown, she tries again.

"Really? Why haven't you said something?"

"I said he's attractive, Atae. I didn't say I wanted to make him mine." Jeqi shrugs at her gaping packmate. "You're one of the only females I know who doesn't find him attractive."

How can they be so blind? He's just so…Sloan. Atae shivers in disgust at the thought.

"That's probably due to his beast's strong presence," Schinn says. He flashes an uncomfortable smile and hopes to drive the conversation back to a more productive topic. "I'm grateful that my beast likes to watch quietly until there is the possibility of battle."

"Really?" Atae forgets about Sloan and slips close enough to peer into Schinn's silver eyes. "What is it doing now?"

Schinn returns Atae's curious gaze, and one corner of his mouth quirks upward. Without thinking, he pushes a stray strand of her short, blue hair from her forehead. When his fingers graze her skin, a flutter rises from Atae's stomach and dances in her chest to the rhythm of her racing heart.

"He's purring," Schinn says. Atae blushes and steps back after realizing how close they stand. Jeqi snorts and juts her hip out.

"How do you know all this? And why are you interested in helping us?"

"Because," Schinn glances from Atae to Jeqi, "my family specializes in shifting phases. That is why I was designated as Prince Truin's guard. I was assigned when he began his shifting phase, and I helped guide him through it. I have studied and trained all my life to serve the Ru-Kai family in this capacity. After doing so, I asked to stay on as his guard."

"Oh," Jeqi says. She flashes a tight-lipped smile. Atae glances from Jeqi to Schinn and swallows hard.

"Well, I've still never felt anything like a beast mind or dual identity."

"Okay, when did you first shift completely?" Schinn asks.

"You mean like with my eyes, claws, and blades all at the same time?" When Schinn nods, Atae shrugs. "I haven't."

"What do you mean? You said you'd shifted before."

"I have, but not everything at once. My eyes and claws, and even my blades have shifted by themselves. I've shifted eyes and blades together then my eyes and claws but never all three."

"But it all started over a month ago during your attack?" Schinn asks. Atae nods in confirmation. "That's interesting."

"Also," Atae says. "They don't feel like incomplete shifts. They don't even feel like the same shift. I mean, my eyes shift completely and separately from my blades and claws. And my blades shift separately from everything else. The same for my claws."

"Fascinating."

"What?" Atae and Jeqi ask together.

"Most Kaji, even partial shifters, can only shift everything at once. Only incredible Kaji, with immense control, can pick and choose which body parts to shift. It sounds like you have that unique ability."

"Like one of the legendary warriors?" Jeqi asks, and Atae beams.

"No way!"

"Don't get too excited. This complicates things," Schinn says. He shoves his hands out in front of him to illustrate his point, and Atae's excitement drains away.

"What do you mean?"

"This means you may not have a beast mind," he says.

"Isn't that a good thing? I mean, the way you describe them, they kind of sound like a hindrance more than anything," Atae says.

"Then I didn't do it right." Schinn stops to think for a moment then tries again. "The beast mind understands how to use your night vision and your weapons."

"So do I," Atae says.

"Really?" Schinn grabs the hybrid's arm, holding it up between them. "Unsheathe your claws."

When nothing happens, he raises both eyebrows and drops her arm.

"I see your point. But that's what you're supposed to teach me," Atae says.

"I can't," Schinn says. He snags Atae's arm again, this time, raising it to eye level. Running his knuckles across her palm, he splays her fingertips between them. Atae's eyes dart from their intertwined hands to Schinn's intense, silver gaze as her heart races and invisible wings flutter in her stomach. She finds it difficult to concentrate on his next words until Jeqi snorts, and Atae refocuses with a sheepish expression.

"You have nerves in your fingertips that your mind doesn't understand. Without the beast mind, your mind may never be able to translate the electrical signals from the nerves in your fingers, or your eyes, or even your forearms," Schinn says. "Without a beast mind, I don't know how to help you."

"What? That doesn't make sense." Atae snatches her arm away from Schinn. She stares at him as confusion clouds her eyes and anger twists her face into a scowl. How dare he give up without even trying?

"Atae." Jeqi motions to something behind Schinn, but Atae ignores her.

"You're wrong,' Atae says to Schinn, forcing him back a step. "It's not possible for my mind to not be able to control my own body."

Schinn blinks in surprise at her sudden animosity, but Jeqi distracts them before he can respond.

"Atae," she says.

"Oh no." Atae gazes beyond Schinn to find Solum walking into earshot of their conversation. The silver heir glances back then twirls to greet the royal advisor.

"Advisor Solum, it's a pleasure to see you again," he says.

"Schinn," Solum acknowledges the royal guard then glances at the hybrids. "Atae. Jeqi. Come with me."

Advisor Solum swivels away from the three younglings and strides back the way he came. Atae and Jeqi jump to follow with apologetic glances to Schinn. As they reach the door, Atae glances back to meet Schinn's silver gaze one last time only to find him strolling away toward the back of the training room. The blue hybrid frowns and crosses her arms as she follows behind Solum and Jeqi.

CHAPTER 28

"What were you discussing with Schinn?" Solum asks. He leads the two hybrids through the palace halls as Atae tries to answer.

"Uh..."

"Strategy for the Gridiron," Jeqi says.

"Good. Try not to let the whole palace in on it, Atae," Solum says. He glances over his shoulder at her with a raised eyebrow.

"Eventually, I'd like to hear your ideas so that we can devise a solid plan. But today we have another issue to resolve," Solum says as they turn a corner.

"What issue?" Atae asks. She glances at the unfamiliar hall, grimacing at the gruesome images etched into the stone walls. The carvings depict captured enemies, tortured in various ways, and their horrific pain-induced screams.

"Your behavior in the throne room yesterday was inexcusable. It cannot happen again," Solum says.

"I'm sorry that I spoke up. I should have kept my mouth shut, but they were starting to doubt the prince. I couldn't let them turn against him," Atae says. She jogs to catch up to Solum and plead her case at his side.

"I'm not talking about your big mouth. I blame myself for not teaching you about court politics," Solum says. "I'm talking about your behavior when Sloan shifted."

Atae's eyes widen at the mention of her shameful reaction to Sloan in front of Prince Truin. Of course, Solum witnessed her failure too.

What about Schinn? Did he see it? He didn't mention it. Maybe he was being polite.

"I...I..." Atae tries to find the words to explain her miserable performance in the face of fear. Does Solum think she is afraid of battle beasts? Surely not. She has proven herself numerous times against multiple battle beasts. Why would Sloan scare her? But what other explanation could he find? Solum would assume she feared Sloan, not the phantom creature that haunts her dreams.

"I'm sorry," Atae says. Avoiding the disappointment and shame she expects to see in her father's eyes, Atae slows her pace to fall behind. As Jeqi passes her friend, the blonde reaches out with her tail and tugs on her Atae's arm. She leads the blue-haired youngling down the hall a few steps behind Solum. The soft touch of Jeqi's furry tail comforts Atae and reminds her of their recent trek down the dark path to King Uta's tomb.

"What do you plan to do?" Jeqi asks Advisor Solum. They round another corner, and a large high-security door comes into view.

"I have decided on a way, or a training exercise, to rid Atae of this unfounded fear of that beast."

"Really?" Atae twists her face into a frown, crestfallen by her father's abhorrence of her apparent fear of battle beasts. It was one battle. Sure, it was a horrific mistake that would have gotten her killed in the Gridiron, but usually, he just lectures her to do better. As far as Solum knows, the throne room was the first incident of her showing any type of fear for a battle beast, right?

"Let me guess, it's going to involve one of us bleeding," Jeqi says. She cradles her nose as they reach the high-security door. Solum smirks and presses his thumb against the security pad until the door beeps and slides open.

"We are Kaji," he says.

Solum wipes the blood from his thumb, and Atae's eyebrows rise at the high-security clearance. The royal advisor leads the two younglings through the door and into the navigation room, a small, barren room with no windows. The smooth walls reflect the single light source in the center of the ceiling. To the right of the three Kaji, Solum accesses a small control panel using his visual visor. He selects a few options, and the control panel beeps in confirmation. Then the door slides shut behind them with a tone of finality.

The entire room quivers, and the two younglings grab each other for support. As the navigation room descends below the palace grounds, they relax and watch the wall above the control panel flicker into a viewing screen. At first, the three Kaji only see dirt and the structural workings of the palace as they leave it behind, then the soil and rocks give way to a massive cavern. Jeqi and Atae step closer to peer down as they descend upon a maze of metal cubes and energy fields. Jeqi wraps her tail around her waist for safekeeping and regards Solum.

"This is the palace dungeon." When Solum nods in confirmation, Jeqi continues. "This is where all the most dangerous criminals are housed."

"And prisoners of war are held and...interrogated," Atae says. She remembers the carvings on the walls at the entrance and watches the compound as it draws closer. She wonders if Solum brought Sloan here to calm down and shift back to his original form.

Is that the exercise? A second chance to face a battle beast? Maybe a criminal? That would be cool.

"So what are we doing here?" Jeqi asks

The navigation room slows to a stop at the bottom of the cavern and maneuvers between other cubes. Atae watches as large and small cubes fly by at incredible speeds. Curious, Jeqi uses her visor to access the control panel.

"Fear is a pit, and it grows deeper and darker the longer you dwell in it. Shine a light on it, and you'll find it's just a hole to be climbed," Solum says.

Jeqi and Atae glance at each other, then at Solum. Before either has a chance to question the older warrior, the navigation room jolts to a stop. Jeqi grabs Atae to keep from toppling over as the momentum pushes her to one end of the room. Solum steps around them to activate the control panel, again. The younglings watch the viewing screen above Solum as it displays the outside of a nearby large, metal cube. Upon Solum's command, the room shifts closer to the hub until it bumps against it. The viewing screen flickers to reveal the inside of the cube. But it's dark inside and appears empty.

"Father, what's going on?" Atae asks.

Jeqi tries to peer through the darkness, but her night vision doesn't work through video. Solum slips both hands onto his daughter's shoulders and meets her gaze with a furrowed brow.

"Atae, I need you to understand that your mind and fear can make simple obstacles into treacherous feats," he says. His intense, black eyes burrow into Atae's soul, and she drops her gaze as shame crawls into her chest.

"I'm sorry about the way I responded to Sloan's battle beast. I won't let it happen again. I was just surprised."

Solum studies Atae while she struggles with her inner doubts, and he nods his head with a deep, resonating sigh. The royal advisor straightens to submit another command to the control panel. With a beep, the wall next to the viewing screen slides open into the dark cell. A fowl stench escapes the dark room, and Jeqi backs away from it, covering her nose. She reassesses the control panel, hoping to determine the contents of the cell without suffering the stench of it. Curious to see her father's plan in action, Atae wrinkles her nose, but steps closer. She swivels away from the open door to face her father when he speaks to her in a grim voice.

"You're in a pit. And it's time for you to pull on the strength I know you possess. You have to stand firm against your fears and climb out," he says.

Atae frowns and sighs. *I can't believe Father actually believes I'm afraid of battle beasts.*

"You are going into that cell, and you are not coming out until you are no longer afraid of that beast," Solum says. "I don't care if you have to kill him to make it happen."

"Really?" Atae's eyes widen in surprise. Is she allowed to kill some random criminal? The thought of doing so creates a knot in her stomach, so Atae decides that won't be necessary.

"Atae, no," Jeqi snaps her eyes up from the control panel. "That's Kandorq's cell."

Motivated by sheer terror, Atae lunges away from the open door. She's certain that the creature from her nightmares will reach out and pull her into the dark abyss. Solum snatches Atae by her uniform and drags her back to the open door. Jeqi lurches into their path and hisses, startling Solum. He hesitates long enough for Atae to pry at his grip and bite his arm. He growls in frustration and swings Atae like a club against Jeqi. The hybrids crash against each other, slamming Jeqi into the metal wall, while Solum holds tight to Atae. The blonde crumbles to the floor with a painful cry. Undeterred, Atae continues to bite and scratch at Solum's arm and hand until he smashes her back into the viewing screen and pins her against the shattered mess.

"Stop. You will do this, or I will leave you in that cell to rot," he says

Atae is back in the forest and trapped against the rock face. Tears well in her pleading eyes.

"Please, don't do this," she says. Solum flinches from his daughter's cries, and upon his hesitation, Atae believes he's going to release her. A wave of relief washes over her, only to freeze into an icy chill as Solum steels his resolve.

"You are strong. You are Kaji," he says. Then with a quick lurch, Solum tosses her into the dark cell. She skids across the floor until she crashes into the far wall of the cell. Atae jumps to her feet and dashes for the open cell door, but it slides shut as Solum watches his daughter scramble in fear, and Jeqi screams at his back.

"What have you done?" Jeqi runs to the control panel and commands the door to open. When nothing happens, she swirls to him, and he slides to the floor with his back against the closed door. A tingling numbness washes over him as he processes the last few moments.

What have I done?

Atae begged him not to do it, and still, she beseeches. Solum cringes at his daughter's sobbing and banging through the door. His body jolts from the reverberating metal of each strike, and he clings to the painful feeling.

"Open it," Jeqi demands. But Solum just stares at the wall across from him as Atae continues to hammer on the door. She begs and sobs to be let in, and he hangs his head in his palms. When his hands find moisture on his cheeks, Solum wipes the tears from his eyes and stares at his fingers in horror.

I'm crying? When did that happen?

Solum remembers the last time he allowed tears to wet his face. It was when he lost Roga. A familiar pain attacks Solum, and he forgets how to breathe. Jeqi twists her face into a scowl at the royal advisor, and she shakes her fists him.

"Do you hear her? That's your daughter, begging for you to help her."

Still, Solum says nothing. He drops his hands and presses the back of his head against the metal door. He grimaces as though in pain but doesn't move from the door. Furious, Jeqi kicks and punches at the royal advisor with as much strength as she can muster. At first, Solum lets her assault him; he deserves punishment. But after a few painful strikes, he grabs one arm in mid-attack and pushes her down to the floor. She struggles to pull away but stops when she notices the tears streaking down his face.

"Why are you doing this?" she asks. Her stormy blue eyes of rage and fear glower over her bruised nose and into his black abyss of pain and loss.

"I'm helping her," he whispers.

Atae's banging and pleading stops, and an eerie silence falls. Jeqi stares up at the door, terrified of what the silence means. Hoping for peace, Solum embraces the deafening silence until the attempts to escape renew with more fear and panic than before. Solum groans, and Jeqi struggles out of his grip.

"You call this help? Throwing her to that creature?" Jeqi says. "If you won't save her, then I will."

CHAPTER 29

Atae slams into the closing door as it latches shut. She bangs on it and pleads to be let out.

"Please don't do this. Please let me out. I promise I'll do anything you want." Tears stream down her cheeks, and blood drips from her raw fists.

"Please, Father. Please, help me. Don't do this." She whispers through the sobs with her face pressed against the door. The irrational fear of something stalking her in the dark cell terrorizes Atae. The dread that at any moment Kandorq will snatch her up from behind threatens to overwhelm her. Her heart races, and the roaring of blood and adrenaline drowns out everything around her. Blinded by darkness and deafened by panic, Atae's fear heightens further, and her rational thought slips away. Insanity settles into the crevices of her mind.

When a shadow moves at the other end of the cell, Atae freezes. Too frightened to look, Atae stares at the door with her back to the impending shadow. She imagines Kandorq striding toward her with his evil, red eyes and anticipatory smirk. She can smell the foul stench of his breath and his thick tongue on her cheek. When she hears his chuckle emanating within her mind, she panics.

"Open the door, please. Please. Don't let this happen. Father, please."

When the rustling noise is upon her, Atae swivels to see an indistinct figure in the darkness reaching toward her. She falls to the ground to avoid his grasp and backpedals until the wall stops her with a hard thud. Through the black void, Atae can only make out Kandorq's large frame, but her imagination fills in the gruesome details.

"I remember you," he whispers through the dark. "I knew you'd come back to me. They always do."

He twists his gruesome mouth into a smile and licks his lips, imagining all kinds of terrible things for Atae as his red eyes roam over the youngling. Atae shivers at the violation and wraps her arms around her upper body. She closes her eyes and shields her face.

"Hmm. I can smell your fear. Delicious."

Terrified, Atae presses one side of her face into the hard wall at her back as he leans down to her and strokes a finger across her cheek. She wishes she could dissolve into the wall to escape the vile creature as his breath, foul and disgusting, whispers against her ear.

"I've been waiting for you."

"Please, please. Help me," Atae says to anyone who will listen.

As the fear-driven irrationality drowns her mind, Atae slips into a mental void that pulls her deeper into delirium. Her chest tightens, and she stops breathing. The darkness swallows her whole, and she no longer has the strength nor the will power to stop it. With the pressure of fear and panic seizing her mind, something deep within Atae breaks with an audible snap that echoes through her soul. Silver fog bursts from the echoes, and Atae is forced to let go.

Enough.

Beast steps forward out of the silver smoke and pushes Atae's quivering presence aside with disgust. Beast opens her fuchsia eyes and drops her arms to grip the floor. She swivels to face the creature that dares to threaten Atae. Beast feels the solid wall at her back and the damp dirt under her palms, but not the fear and vulnerability that plagues Atae. No, Beast is strong and brave, and she knows what to do.

With a thought, Beast's eyes shift to activate her night vision. The dark cell transforms into a grimy, blood-covered box with a small bucket in the corner. Beast sniffs and confirms, smiling when she recognizes the scent of Kandorq's dried blood on the walls. Turning to see the Gortox approach, she frowns in disappointment.

Kandorq isn't bent over her as Atae imagined but still struggling to find her in the dark. He stumbles toward Beast with a single incomplete hand that reaches out in front of him. Someone amputated each finger on the outstretched hand, leaving only twitching nubs. His other hand and lower arm are missing past the elbow. The torturer stitched close the amputations and left them to rot with infection. As Kandorq reaches Beast, she sidesteps him and observes the rest of his status. Infected from lack of care, the sockets that used to contain his eyes now seep black and green goo. Kandorq's tormentor removed his horns, teeth, and tongue, from the look of his gawking mouth. The Gortox gurgles as he stumbles into the wall where Beast stood.

Atae stares at Kandorq through Beast's eyes, and relief washes away her fear and panic. Amused that Atae would be frightened by this pathetic creature, Beast snorts. The noise draws Kandorq's attention, and he lurches in her direction.

"Peh, kah meh," Kandorq pleads as he stumbles closer to her.

Death would end his suffering, Beast says to Atae.

He doesn't deserve mercy, Atae says. She reminds Beast of Kandorq's offenses with memories of his attack. Beast bristles at the images and growls at Kandorq. His face, dark with pain, lightens at the sound and hopes for a quick end, but Beast has another idea. As his outstretched hand comes close, Beast calls her blades forth, ignoring the slicing pain as they erupt from her forearms. With one swift motion, Beast cuts off the Gortox's remaining hand.

Screaming, Kandorq drops back and flails his arm as blood spurts all over the room. When it sprays across her face and neck, Beast revels in his pain and enjoys the feel of enemy blood on her skin. Still screaming his tongue-less ramblings, Kandorq stumbles and falls on his back. Beast jumps on to his chest and smiles at the crunching and snapping of bones under the impact. Beast crouches down over Kandorq's face, pressing into his damaged ribs. She watches him gurgle blood, and Beast smirks in satisfaction as Atae cheers in her mind.

Relishing the sounds of Kandorq drowning in his blood, Beast slips gentle hands over his smooth head. Careful not to touch the seeping remains of his horns, Beast caresses his sweaty cheeks. Soon Kandorq stops struggling and lies back to accept his fate. Atae whispers to him. She knows only Beast can hear her, but she still savors the satisfaction and strength the words give her.

I know you remember my face. It was the last thing you saw. I never want you to forget me. I never want you to forget what I'm going to do and that I'm the one that did it. All because you were too weak to stop me.

Grinning at the irony in Atae's silent words, Beast calls upon her claws. She slips her fingers over Kandorq's bald head and digs her talons into his skull as he struggles and screams. The deeper she penetrates, the more he cries until she hears a loud crack and brain matter squeezes out under her nails. Kandorq's body spasms and lurches, then it falls still.

Beast pulls her claws from the Gortox's skull and smiles as Atae dances across her mind.

I am strong. I am Kaji, Beast says.

After a moment of mute celebration, Beast regards the sealed door, prodding Atae for information on how to escape. Then Kandorq gasps for air, and Beast spins to face the corpse. When she finds it sitting up and watching her, Beast steps to the side, and Kandorq's eyeless sockets follow her. Disappointed that her initial attempt to kill the pathetic creature failed, Beast surges forward and slices Kandorq's head off with one mighty swing. The detached head rolls into a corner facing away from Beast, and she snorts in satisfaction. Atae urges Beast to watch the head to be sure the deed is done, and she complies.

When both are certain of the kill, Beast turns away only to be drawn back by sounds of the skull retching. The decapitated head rolls around to face Beast and meets her gaze with its puss-filled sockets. The skull opens its mouth to speak, but tongue-less, it gags.

What is it? Beast asks.

I don't know. Ask it.

Beast snorts at the ridiculous idea of using Atae's mouth to speak.

Then I'll do it, Atae says.

And leave you to defend us? No

I am perfectly capable of defending us. I've gotten us this far.

No, you were cowering in the corner. Beast sneers at Atae.

Before Atae can respond, the gurgling, bodiless head screeches, and Beast jumps back. Then both Beast and Atae scream as something tears at their mind. Atae can feel claws ripping at her existence and pulling her apart. Beast falls to the ground, shifting back to her first form, as all of her effort and concentration falls onto the mental trespasser.

Unafraid of the intruder, Beast snarls and snaps at it then lunges into its murky darkness. She tears into it and demands that it retreat or be destroyed. When it decides to run, Beast builds a mental wall around their mind. She vows that nothing will intrude on them again without explicit consent. After ensuring that Atae is okay, Beast stands and snarls at the corpse. Daring it to move, Beast glares at the dead creature until an explosion tears her from her triumph.

Jeqi blasts the door open, sending it flying across the cell to cold-weld against the opposite metal wall. Holding a small ranged hilt, Jeqi steps into the cage as light escapes the navigation room and glistens off the dust, fire, and metal bits swirling around her.

"Atae! I'm here."

Upon seeing Jeqi, Beast smiles with pride that her packmate has caused such destruction for the sake of Atae. Seeing her friend covered in blood with a disturbing smile, Jeqi pauses to take in the scene. In a final display, Beast steps over to Kandorq's skull and crushes it with her foot.

It's dead now, Beast says. Atae smiles at her counterpart's confidence but worries about the corpse reanimation and the mental barrage that they survived.

Do not worry. The threat is gone, Beast says.

Jeqi steps forward with her arms out and a questioning frown. "What happened?"

Beast glances up from Kandorq's remains with a smug expression and crosses her arms over her chest. Jeqi spots the corpse and hustles over to survey the damage. She unravels her tail from her waist and pokes at the dead Gortox with the tip.

"You killed him?" she asks. Beast shrugs, and Jeqi slips closer to whisper to her friend. "Did you shift?"

Beast smirks and lifts her hand to demonstrate, but Solum steps out into the cell. As his concerned gaze falls on Beast, she narrows her eyes at him and steps around Jeqi. She faces Solum with a threatening growl and decides to call on her blades.

Stop!

Beast blinks at the plea. She stands firm in a defensive stand, eyeing Solum as he surveys the dimly lit cell.

Why? He is a threat. Beast asks.

He is our father. He is not a threat to us.

He betrayed us. Sire or not, he is a threat.

He knew of Kandorq's weakened condition. Who do you think cut him down, piece by piece? Atae forces Beast to recall Jeqi's words.

"Advisor Solum visited Kandorq every day that you were unconscious, torturing him."

"The entire palace heard Kandorq screaming, and that night he told Solum everything he knew."

Impressed by her sire, Beast grins as Solum finds Kandorq's severed hand and picks it up to examine the cut. Recognizing the suspicion in her father's expression, Atae implores Beast to detach the hilt from the thigh of her uniform. Beast complies, gripping the hunk of metal, and holds it up for examination. She wonders why Atae has it.

I do not need this weapon. I have my own.

Solum doesn't know that, and we need to keep it that way, Atae says. If she could, she'd roll her eyes at Beast's arrogance.

Why? He should know how dangerous I am to deter future betrayal, Beast says. She glares at Solum as he glances with narrowed eyes from the severed hand to Beast. His gaze falls to the hilt in her grip, and as though accepting the silent explanation, Solum drops the bloody hand.

If he finds out about our ability to shift, he will pull us from the Gridiron line up, and Jeqi will be alone. She needs her pack, Atae says.

"You have done well," Solum says. He greets Beast with a hard expression to mask his inner storm of emotion. Beast stares at her sire and wrestles between her desire to attack and Atae's silent pleas to submit to him. Unwilling to back down from his offspring no matter how angry she is with him, Solum stands eye to eye with Atae. With great resentment and muted obscenities toward Atae, Beast lowers her gaze and crosses her arms. She tightens her grip on the hilt with a silent growl.

Before Solum can say another word, Beast grabs Jeqi and pulls her to the navigation room. Solum watches them leave, noting Atae's odd behavior. Beast motions for Jeqi to activate the control panel then sheathes the hilt. Puzzled by her unusual silence, Jeqi eyeballs her packmate before selecting the exit option. She doesn't mind leaving the royal advisor behind. She's content to let him stew over his recent decisions while he waits for the navigation room to return for him. Jeqi wonders if they can lock him in there for a few days as punishment for his behavior, but he probably has some override code to recall the navigation room. When the room jolts to a start, air swirling around them from the missing door, Jeqi spins back to Atae and demands answers.

"What happened? Are you okay?" Jeqi's puffed tail flickers as she struggles to balance her concern and curiosity. When Beast just stares at her as though the answers are apparent, Jeqi steps closer.

"What's wrong with you? Why haven't you said anything?"

Answer her, or let me, Atae says. Beast puffs out loud at the suggestion. *It's my mouth.*

Mine. Beast says, and Atae growls.

"Hello? Are you in there?" Jeqi asks, but Beast ignores her.

This is my body, and you will step aside, Atae says. She summons the strength to fight for control, but Beast hardens her mental defenses against Atae.

When the threat has passed, Beast says.

What threat? Jeqi won't hurt us.

Jeqi slaps Beast across the face with all her might. The blue hybrid falls against the side of the room and cringes from the unexpected display of dominance. After a moment of stunned silence, Beast growls at Jeqi but doesn't retaliate. Instead, she opts to accept Jeqi's authority for the time being.

"Have you gone mad? Is that it? Has fear finally scrambled your brains, and you've lost the ability to speak?" Jeqi taunts Beast but hopes her words are just that as her tail lashes out behind her.

Atae sighs and nudges Beast to tug on both ears. Confused by the absurd idea, Beast does it with some hesitation and without taking her eyes off Jeqi. Taking Beast's lead, the blonde does the same. As Beast's fingers graze her silver studs, her visual visor populates. Startled by the sudden private hologram that scans the room, Beast lashes out at the image, and Jeqi steps back from the random strikes.

"You have lost your mind."

After finding nothing to highlight as points of interaction except Jeqi's active visor, the hologram disappears, leaving a confused and defensive Beast behind. Snarling and swirling around as she tries to fight the offending image, Beast ignores Atae's silent command to send a message to Jeqi. After a few moments, she settles down and complies with Atae's request. Using memories and Atae's instructions, she creates a message.

Jeqi gapes at the painfully slow process. When the blonde is convinced that Atae has lost her mind, a message pops up on her visor.

'I'm not crazy, but I'm pretty sure Beast is.'

CHAPTER 30

"Beast?" Schinn says. He furrows his brow in disbelief as he glances from Jeqi to Atae and back again. Jeqi stands next to Schinn in their private training room and watches Beast survey the room with intense dedication. She walks from one end of the room to the other, sniffing the air. On occasion, she stops to stare at some of the equipment. Unsure what to think of Atae's new counterpart, Jeqi watches Beast, studying her movement, facial expressions, and demeanor, as she has since leaving the navigation room.

"She said she didn't have a beast," Schinn says. He motions toward her, and Jeqi glances at him in with pressed lips.

"Well, now she does." Jeqi looks look cross-eyed at her healing nose. The swelling from the injury makes her sound nasal, and she can tell that the bruising has spread to the tissue under her eyes.

"How do you know?"

"What?"

"How do you know she didn't just go sour or something?" Schinn says. Jeqi snarls at him, and he snaps his head to her in surprise. "I mean, that could be why she isn't talking. Are you certain it's a beast?"

"Yes." Jeqi swivels back to watch Beast lift some workout equipment and sniff it. "Beast is different."

"What do you mean?"

"I've watched her since we left the dungeon," Jeqi says. Beast strolls toward them from the far end of the training room with a confident, smooth stride.

"I've known Atae since our first season at Sula Academy. She is strong and confident, but she's also clumsy and uncertain. She is impulsive and rash." Jeqi rolls her eyes at memories of Atae dragging her into trouble. "But she's also loyal and wickedly impressive in combat."

"Yeah, I've noticed," Schinn says. He rubs the still tender scar over his chest. Jeqi smirks at him. She knows all too well how effective Atae can be in battle, and how completely naïve she is outside it.

"Atae doesn't pay attention to her surroundings if she feels safe, and she has a tendency to zone out during boring conversations," Jeqi says. "Beast is different. Beast is fast and deliberate. She is always assessing her environment. I have yet to catch her off guard. Even her walk is different. I haven't seen her stumble once. It's like she thinks she owns everything around her."

Beast smiles at Jeqi as she approaches. The blonde peers into her packmate's fuchsia gaze and stares at the surprising bout of clarity and confidence, especially given Atae's recent uncertainty and fear. When Beast's smug expression morphs her confidence into arrogance, Jeqi fights the urge to roll her bruised eyes. Beast jerks her hand and flips her fingers through the empty air, and Schinn scrunches his nose in confusion. Realization dawns on his face when his visual visor receives a message from Atae, and Jeqi raises a snide eyebrow at the silver heir. Holographic words that are only visible to Jeqi and Schinn's visors assemble beside Beast, and the blonde's mouth twists into a frown as she reads Atae's words.

'She considers this her territory, but doesn't care for the notion of ownership.'

"I take it ownership is beneath her, like speaking," Jeqi says. Startled, Beast searches the ground at her feet and lifts each foot to peer under it. While Jeqi and Schinn blink at the odd behavior, Beast snaps back to her previous position. She crosses her arms with a sheepish frown.

"Ha. She thought you meant literally. Like she was standing on something," Schinn says. Beast's hard eyes turn to glare at Schinn, and she growls.

'Yeah, but I explained it to her,' Atae says via the visual visor and Beast's indulging hand motions.

Schinn clears his throat, then steps closer to Beast to peer into her eyes. Beast's scowl deepens as the silver heir pushes a stray hair from her forehead. She twists her mouth in disgust and clenches a fist, but restrains from using it. Jeqi wonders at the influence Atae has on her counterpart.

"What's it like in there, Atae?" Schinn asks. Jeqi raises an eyebrow at his ignorance of the struggle she observes in Beast.

'It's like being in the co-pilot seat of a transport vehicle,' Atae says, 'but all your controls are disengaged. It's a great view, but you can't do a damn thing except yell at the pilot.'

"So, you two communicate? What does she say?"

'Weird things. Like, that she doesn't like you because you are submissive. Or that Solum is the enemy, and she can't trust me to protect us.'

"Submissive? I'm not submissive," Schinn says. He steps back from Beast, scrunching his nose in distaste.

"What about me?" Jeqi asks. She narrows her eyes as Beast meets her gaze and dares Atae's counterpart to judge her.

'She thinks you're a great packmate and is quite proud of the destruction you wrought in the dungeon. How did you do that, by the way? There's no way that was a standard ranged hilt.'

"Don't worry about it." Jeqi flashes a crooked smile and flicks her tail playfully. No one needs to know her plans for the Gridiron, especially Atae, with her big mouth. Beast quirks her head in curiosity and smiles at Jeqi's coy response.

"Atae, can you control Beast at all?" Schinn asks. Beast snaps her head around and bares her teeth at him while slipping into a defensive stance.

'She doesn't like that idea at all. She is about to bolt.'

"We aren't trying to hurt you, Beast," Jeqi says. Beast responds with a ridiculing snort, making her thoughts clear on whether Jeqi or Schinn could harm her. Jeqi remembers the patient and loving tone that Deh uses to calm those around her and attempts to mimic it.

"We aren't trying to get rid of you, either. We need you. But we also need Atae. Right now, we have limited access to her."

Beast rises from her defensive stance and frowns in thought. Sensing Beast's unease, Jeqi slips a hand onto her shoulder and speaks in a soft, comforting tone.

"We need to find a way for you and Atae to work together as a normal Kaji warrior would. It may be better for you to be co-pilot. We don't know yet."

Beast narrows her eyes at Schinn then glances back at Jeqi. With a grumble, she relents and nods her head. Jeqi smiles in relief and pulls her hand from Beast's shoulder but doesn't step away. She often struggles to maintain the balance between her two conflicting cultures. It's nice when her mother's soft and submissive culture, which is usually a hindrance, actually helps Jeqi excel. Jeqi decides to stay close, offering Beast her silent support and ensuring that she's nearby if the edgy youngling chooses to do something stupid.

"Great. So," Schinn eyes Beast with a wary frown, "how much control do you have, Atae?"

'I don't have any control over Beast. She considers my advice or demands, but I can't make her do anything.'

"Hmm. But Beast can shift at will?"

'Yeah, it's pretty awesome,' Atae says. Beast blinks, then flashes a smug smile. Schinn grins at her and nods his head.

"Show me."

'She wants to know why.'

Beast scowls at him, and Jeqi tenses at her side. Annoyance flits across Schinn's face, and he takes a deep breath to regain his patience.

"Because I need to observe how the shifting occurs. Is it partial, complete, or something new altogether?"

Beast slips a hand onto her hip and grins at Schinn's aggravation.

'She says the shift gives her many weapons to choose from, and it's none of your business how many or what kind.'

"What? I'm trying to help here."

Beast snorts back.

"How dare you! You pompous-"

"Stop. What is wrong with you two?" Jeqi says. Schinn walks away from the two hybrids to pace at the back of the room.

"Beast obviously has trust issues, and she called me submissive. I am not submissive."

'He's right on both accounts. She thinks Schinn is hiding something,' Atae says. Jeqi swivels to Schinn with a raised eyebrow, and his stride falters.

"That's ridiculous," he says.

Beast shrugs at him then crosses her arms to storm out. Unsure what to do, Jeqi steps forward to stop Beast, but Schinn lunges past her. He lurches toward the blue hybrid with an animalistic snarl, aiming a powerful kick at her head. Moments before it smashes into her skull, Beast dodges with surprising speed. She ducks underneath the attack and elbows Schinn in his gut. He stumbles to his knees and struggles against the upheaval of his stomach's contents. Beast follows him and calls her blades. She grabs Schinn's thick, silver hair and pulls his head back to expose his neck, slipping a forearm blade under his chin. As the razor edge bites into Schinn's skin, Jeqi lunges to stop her packmate from killing him.

Beast jerks away from Schinn, and Jeqi stops at his side. Beast clutches her head, falls to her knees, and screams like a wounded animal. She scratches at her head and, when her claws extend, she digs into her face. Shocked by the blue hybrid's odd behavior, Jeqi runs to Beast's side.

"Beast. Atae. Stop! You're hurting yourself."

Beast continues to scream and tear at her flesh, unhindered. Beast's claws slice into the muscle and fat of her cheeks and peel the flesh from her skull. Blood floods from the wounds and covers her hands and chest.

"Schinn, help me!" Jeqi grabs at Beast's clawed hands, trying to subdue the wild youngling. Schinn watches the crazed Beast in astonishment as he rubs the shallow cut on his neck. Then Beast stops, and Atae lies back against the cold ground, panting and gurgling blood. Jeqi leans over her friend with concern and fear swirling in her crystal blue eyes; Atae opens her pained fuchsia orbs to meet her gaze.

"I did it," Atae says. Somehow, she forms words with her split lips and carved cheeks. "She's pissed, but I did it."

"You did well, Atae," Jeqi says. "But we need to get you to a tank. Right now. So you need to stand up."

"Sure."

With Jeqi and Schinn's help, Atae struggles to her feet and walks toward the exit. As they reach the door and it slides open, Atae tries to speak through blood and drool. She ignores the damaged cheek muscle flapping against her tongue.

"I hope this doesn't leave a scar. It'd be the stupidest scar to explain."

Atae falls unconscious against Jeqi and Schinn, and they rush her to the medical wing. When Atae awakens, it's to Schinn's muffled voice. It carries through Atae's unconscious mind along with Jeqi's familiar tones. She doesn't move or register consciousness.

"I spoke to Dr. Pwen. He said she'll have to spend the night, but she can be released early morning," Schinn says.

"Just in time for our session with Sloan and Marqee. Good," Jeqi says. "Don't tell Solum about this. He can't know about her shifting ability."

"He stopped by when I was speaking with Dr. Pwen."

"What? What did you tell him?"

"That a hilt training session with Sloan got out of hand," Schinn says. "I sent him a visor message to play along, no questions asked."

"You're friends with Sloan?"

"I wouldn't say that, but he owes me one."

They both fall silent for a few moments, and Atae almost slips back into the beautiful embrace of unconsciousness.

"Is this because of her parentage? Can that affect her shifting phase?" Jeqi asks.

"Do you know her parentage?" Schinn asks.

"No," Jeqi says. "Her father won't tell her, and I've tried to figure it out. But she's...too Kaji. She's smaller and has odd coloring. Otherwise, she's Kaji."

"She's definitely not Setunn, Runx, or Kip. Hybrids like that are easy to pinpoint," Schinn says. "You know, with the extra appendages or tails and whatnot."

"I can only assume she descends from a G2 species, but there's only a handful that can interbreed with the Kaji. And all of them could result in her appearance."

"You could always try genetic testing. She may not be a half-breed. Maybe, a dilution of Setunn or something."

"Does it matter? Is that why this happened? Why she lost control and couldn't get it back?"

"I don't know," Schinn says. "I've never seen or heard of something like this before, except in cases of a battle beast going feral."

"But feral beasts can't shift back. They remain in their shifted forms with no rational thought," Jeqi says. "Atae was there and present. We could communicate with her. Feral beasts can't do that. Can they?"

"No, but if she loses control to her beast again, I don't think she'll ever get it back."

Listening, Atae slides her eyes open. She notices the cool touch of healing gel all over her body before registering the odd floating sensation of the recovery tank. The blue gel presses into her eyes and gives everything a blue tint. Foggy from tranquilizers, Atae wonders how she can breathe through the gel that fills her mouth, throat, and lungs. She also doesn't understand why the gel doesn't sting her eyes when she blinks, but those thoughts slip from her mind in the haze.

Atae can see Jeqi speaking with Schinn outside her tank, their voices muffled and hard to understand. It takes a great deal of concentration to make out the words, but she's certain they are talking about hiding her injury from Solum. Or maybe Sloan? That doesn't make sense. She decides that eavesdropping isn't worth the effort, not with the drugs pumping through her system. The recovery tank is a new experience for Atae, and she enjoys it. She feels relaxed and disconnected from the world around her. At least she does until Beast snarls at her like a wild animal.

How dare you! I should shred you to pieces for your betrayal.

Beast's bodiless voice barks from a churning cloud at the back of Atae's mind. The silver mist rages with orange-sienna particles that pulsate with anxiety and hide the slivers of frightened-golden flecks deep within the fog. An angry-red flash lashes out at Atae to accentuate Beast's words.

What did I do? Atae asks. She struggles to concentrate through the medically induced haze.

You took my body. Now they are trying to kill us. Wake up, or you'll drown!

The frightened gold flecks reverberate through Atae's mind to snap her out of the haze. She jolts forward and fights the drowning sensation from being submerged in the blue healing gel. Atae struggles to fight Beast's panicking golden fog as it encompasses her mind. It tries to convince her body that it shouldn't be able to breathe through this foreign matter. Her brain finally registers the odd awareness of the thick substance in her eyes and nose, and Beast's drive to escape bombards Atae's mind. She thrashes about through the gel in an attempt to orient herself and find a way out until she hears a loud thud that resonates through the gel.

Through the blue haze, her eyes fall upon Jeqi's even bluer gaze, and Atae calms. Jeqi's hand presses against the tank's glass, and her no-nonsense glare over a gel smeared nose tells Atae to quiet down. The blue hybrid sighs through the gel even though Beast argues that it isn't possible and that they should be dead by now. She inwardly grumbles at Beast's complaints and outwardly grins at Jeqi's annoyance with her.

Jeqi would never try to drown me, Atae says to Beast. Then she remembers a sparring session that ended with Jeqi holding Atae's face under the running water of a river until she passed out. *At least, not to kill me.*

I don't believe you. They are trying to kill us. We have to get out. Beast says. Instinct drives her to escape the danger she cannot fight. Beast's golden mist of anxiety washes over her counterpart like a wave of cold water, and Atae cringes against it.

Calm down. We are not dying. We are healing.

Atae pushes her feelings of assurance and tranquility at Beast. Atae waves her hand through the blue gel and touches the healing skin on her face. Tissue adhesive holds the skin and muscles in place to accelerate the healing. Atae can feel a difference already. Beast also notices the healed tissue, and her golden fear calms to a distressed orange-sienna. Atae frowns at the sensation of Beast pacing back and forth across her mind within the churning cloud.

The youngling closes her eyes and concentrates on blocking everything out except Beast. She ignores the cooling gel against her skin and muffled voices just outside her tank. Instead, she focuses on Beast's confidence and power within Kandorq's cell. Atae remembers the feeling of Beast's snarl on her lips and the threat of her bared teeth. As the rest of the world falls away, Atae relaxes. Within her mind, she stands in the center of a dark and empty room. A glimmer of light flickers across from her and shines bright enough to illuminate the churning fog that hides Beast. Sienna and gold particles swirl within the mist, along with tiny bursts of red. Atae waits for Beast to step from the fog and face her counterpart; instead, the mist shifts into a large ball then reshapes. As the new shape begins to look familiar, Atae realizes that Beast is the fog.

Now, Atae stands face-to-face with Beast in the empty room. She has the odd sensation of peering into a warped mirror at a disfigured reflection. Beast's slit, fuchsia eyes glower at Atae. The sharp blades erupting from Beast's hanging forearms point away, but the razors on her fingers twitch.

I'm glad I have control. Otherwise, you would have destroyed this tank the moment we woke up, Atae says to Beast. She gapes at the irrational part of her brain, amazed by her counterpart's strong instinctual impulses.

Yes, but I wouldn't have been captured in the first place.

Captured? Jeqi is not an enemy. She is pack. Why don't you understand that?

Jeqi is pack. Schinn is not, Beast says. She lurches toward Atae to stress the importance of her words.

Why do you say that?

He is dishonest. And he attacked us, Beast says.

No, he isn't. And he attacked you to subdue you. And for that, you were going to kill him. Why? Atae says. The memory of fighting with Beast and forcing her to let go of Schinn flashes across Atae's mind. The pain of seizing control and fending off Beast's mental attacks was all-consuming. Atae didn't even register the damage to her face from Beast's attempt to maintain dominance until after she seized control.

He attacked me as an enemy would. I destroy our enemies without hesitation and without mercy, Beast says.

232

So if Jeqi attacked you, would you kill her too?

Yes.

Even if it's just sparring? Atae asks. When Beast furrows her brow in confusion, Atae frowns.

Sparring is practice fighting without attempting to kill your partner. Atae reminds Beast with memories of sparring sessions with Solum and Jeqi. Beast snorts at the idea of fake battle and returns to her anxious pacing.

You can't spar, can you? Just like you can't speak. You can't rationalize that behavior. That's why you don't understand certain things. You aren't capable of understanding. You are all instinct. That's why this tank drives you crazy. Instinct is telling you that we will drown, and you have no rationale to argue with that logic, Atae says. Beast growls but slows her agitated pacing. *I can never give you control again. You'll never give it up. Your instinct to survive is too powerful.*

You cannot shift without me. Beast says. Atae chuckles at the threat.

I've believed some crazy notions in the past. At one point, I believed that I'd never beat Solum, then I did. I once believed that I'd be a victim to a sick creature's whims, but I wasn't. I even believed I would never possess the ability to shift, and we both know that isn't true. But don't think for a moment that I believe you'll never help me shift, Atae says. She crosses her arms and glowers at Beast.

Because if you don't agree to work with me, as a Kajian beast should, I will spend every night sleeping in one of these tanks. I will spend every free moment enjoying the relaxation and weightlessness while you slowly go insane.

Beast stops pacing to stares at Atae with unhindered fear, and Atae smiles. *We are strong. We are Kaji.*

CHAPTER 31

Jeqi waits outside the tournament arena and watches Atae study the busy entrance. Every time a classmate comes too close, Atae freezes as though she's afraid any movement might spur Beast into a violent meltdown.

"Can you do this?" Jeqi asks.

"I can and I will," Atae says through clenched teeth. "I am in control."

With her tail dancing behind her, Jeqi's eyebrows knit together, and she slips a comforting hand onto her packmate's shoulder.

"I'm here. We'll do this together."

Atae nods at her, and they proceed into the arena. Beast, bubbling with an orange-brown anxiety, paces in the back of Atae's mind. The crowd of younglings grows thick as Atae and Jeqi progress further into the arena, and Beast's distress at being surrounded pummels against Atae's consciousness. She clenches both fists and walks, taut with tension, alongside Jeqi.

This time, they find two energy domes at their assigned position. Two sets of visual visors sit on a small energy table in the center of a translucent blue dome; the second dome has a yellow glint and stands empty. Jeqi points to the hollow dome.

"That one's yours," she says.

"What? What do you mean? Where are you going?" Atae asks. Beast watches from within, and Atae shivers at the sensation of her counterpart looking over her shoulder.

"Remember, this round, we have to split up," Jeqi says. "Marqee and I are the strategists. You and Sloan are the runners."

No. We will be alone. Too many enemies. Destroy them all, Beast says

"Okay," Atae says to Jeqi. Then she growls at Beast to calm down. Jeqi offers a small smile to her friend.

"You can do this, Atae. I may not be right by your side, but I'll still be watching and helping you progress."

Atae nods her head and enters the yellow dome while Jeqi steps into the other one. Atae ignores the camera that whirls to life above the dome and watches Jeqi place the visor studs into her earlobes then activate them. The blue-eyed hybrid flashes her packmate the thumbs-up sign and a smile as her assigned camera circles above.

Atae closes her eyes and clenches her fists. She tries to quiet Beast's demands and subdue the onslaught of sienna anxiety and golden panic that threatens to drown her. Breathing grows difficult as her chest tightens. She can feel her claws extending and biting into her palms.

No. Don't, Atae says.

We are surrounded and alone. No pack to protect us, Beast says. She reaches for the mental switch that calls her blades forth.

"Atae."

A deep, familiar voice breaks through her inner turmoil, and Beast hesitates. She rummages through Atae's memories to identify the sound and finds Sloan's sarcastic smirk and dominant antics. She recognizes his strength and skills, and she bristles at Atae's constant struggles against him.

Enemy.

No. He is not an enemy, Atae says. *He's...*

She pauses, uncertain of what to call Sloan. Neither he nor Marqee is pack, are they? Yes. For the purposes of the tournament, they are pack. But true packmates? Absolutely not.

"Atae, are you okay?" Sloan asks.

Ally. He is an ally, Atae says. She opens her eyes to meet Sloan's concerned expression. Beast watches the dark male from behind Atae's gaze and finds red eyes hidden within him. Atae can feel Beast's intrigue and the smirk that flitters across her counterpart's lips.

A powerful ally.

"Atae, answer me," Sloan says. He sets a firm hand on her shoulder. At his touch, Beast's fog blooms crimson, and it bubbles up deep within her to cascade through Atae's body. She gasps out loud as wave after wave of heat crashes into her.

"Don't touch me." She knocks his hand away. "I'm fine."

The command comes out more aggressive than she intends, but pulling herself out of Beast's swirl of alien emotions takes its toll on Atae's patience.

"What's wrong with you?" Marqee asks. He scowls next to his packmate, and Atae stares at him so as to focus on something other than Sloan. Beast silently assesses the shorter youngling and combs through Atae's memories to determine his status as Sloan's packmate, therefore an ally as well.

"Nothing." Atae flashes a fake smile to rein in her frazzled appearance. "Just a last-minute meditation session."

"Right," Marqee says. He sends Sloan a meaningful glance and smacks him on the chest. "Good luck."

Atae watches Marqee join Jeqi in the blue dome and grab the remaining set of visor studs, then the empty energy table dissipates.

"Why are you nervous?" Sloan asks. Atae scoffs at him.

"I'm not."

"Then why were you meditating?"

After watching Marqee and Jeqi exchange words regarding their visors, Atae opts to survey the arena rather than look at Sloan, especially after Beast's carnal reaction. Instead, she asks Beast to assess their competition.

"Why do you care?" Atae asks Sloan. She notes the blue and yellow domes throughout the arena while Beast decides which classmates they should target first.

"I find it's important to know the state of mind of all my packmates. Especially those with which I'm about to partner in a dangerous tournament." He flashes a half-grin at Atae, but it slips when he realizes that she is avoiding his gaze.

"We are not pack. Allies at best," Atae says. She ignores the crimson sparks from Beast. She reminds Beast of her task, and her inner counterpart complies. The glares from Debil and Seva bump them to first on Beast's list, and Atae agrees. She still doesn't understand their problem with her.

"Allies in the tournament, and allies in the Gridiron. Works for me."

"Ha. The Gridiron? The only way I'd work with you is if the prince himself..." Atae curses when she realizes the truth of his words.

"Yep, you want to protect Truin, and so do I. Looks like you're stuck with me." Sloan slips closer to Atae. "You don't have a problem with that, do you?"

"Of course I do, Sloan," Atae says. She inhales through Beast's distracting fog, then she shivers as a delightful sensation glides up Atae's spine and sucks the breath from her lungs. She manages a breathy response.

"You're quite annoying."

Atae points out the pond in the center of the arena to Beast, distracting her with memories of Jeqi's attack. The distraction offers Atae some relief but not much.

"Is that why you won't look at me?" Sloan asks.

With pressed lips, Atae swivels to face him. She meets his gaze and clenches her jaw while Beast basks in Sloan's natural swagger. His crooked smile and confident gaze send her careening into a crimson storm. Atae, on the other hand, isn't impressed. She glowers at Sloan for instigating such a sensual response from her counterpart.

"Just stay out of my way." Atae spins away, but Sloan grabs her arm.

"We need to work together on this, so follow my lead," he says.

A hint of a growl escapes from his lips, prompting both Atae and Beast to meet his gaze. Atae glimpses the determination to win in Sloan's dark eyes, and Beast sees the demand for submission from his inner beast. For the first time, they both agree on one thing. They will not submit.

"Don't play your dominance games with me, Sloan." Atae rips her arm from his grasp. "They won't work."

Surprised that his ploy didn't subdue her, Sloan watches her swirl away from him. He glances at Marqee in the other dome, who observed the entire exchange, but he just shrugs. Jeqi rounds on Marqee, demanding an explanation for their behavior. He throws his hands up in defense, but before he can explain, a warning alarm sounds. And the remaining younglings scramble to their assigned domes. Skiska and Frack appear as giant floating heads above the center of the arena.

"And here we go again, folks. It's time for round two of the Sula Academy Tournament," Frack says in his gruff voice.

"Yes, round one was quite exciting, and it seems the rest of the empire agrees. Almost seventy-five percent of the public tuned into to watch live or recorded sessions. I'm hoping this round will be just as exciting," Skiska says.

"I guarantee that interest in this tournament will double after the pledging ceremony yesterday." Frack sends a telling glance to his co-host. "If you haven't heard, Prince Truin will be competing in the Gridiron with this season's Sula Academy graduates."

"And according to Queen Sula's decree, anyone that defeats her son in battle shall inherit his throne," Skiska says in an overly chipper tone.

"So those of you who win will have a chance to fight alongside our future ruler. Or if you have what it takes, you could become the next ruler of the Kaji Empire," Frack says.

"Well, that's a prize indeed. What are the rules for round two, Frack?"

"This round is going to be tough, and it's all about strategy. Two younglings from each pack will be the strategists, and the remaining two will be the runners."

As Frack explains, translucent energy walls sprout from the ground all around the arena, creating a complex maze. A floor erupts from under Jeqi and Marqee that raises them high into the air, and Beast growls at their distance. She demands action to save their packmate, but Atae points out that the same thing is happening to all the blue domes and their inhabitants. When ceilings assemble above Atae and Sloan to cover the entire labyrinth of halls, the domes drop. Atae watches Jeqi step onto the energy field above them and point to other competitors.

"You're on offense," she says to Marqee. "Make sure Debil and Seva never reach the goal."

"What's the goal?" Marqee asks. He scans the maze while swatting at the nosy camera that circles his head.

"The goal for this round is for each team's runners to reach the center of the maze," Skiska says. A golden light flickers from an energy platform above the pond. "Careful though, there are going to be a lot of traps and surprises along the way."

"Yep," Frack says, "and you'll have to watch out for other runners, too. Keep in mind, only one runner from each team has to reach the goal to advance the entire pack. If both runners are incapacitated, the strategists can jump in to run the maze, but they have to start from the beginning. And that won't be any fun. I can promise you that."

"Runners won't get any points for taking down other runners, but there aren't any penalties for it, either."

"The same goes for strategists versus strategists," Frack says. He wags his finger at the audience, and Skiska smiles at him.

"Yes, but strategists can earn ten points each time they take down a competing runner. Don't forget that your main focus is to get your team to the goal."

"Strategists will use the visors provided to control the maze walls, traps, and other exciting functions. Help your teammates progress, detain your opponents, or take down the competition altogether. It's your choice. Either way, forty packs will compete in this round, but only the first thirty to reach the goal will progress to the next round."

"Well, that should wrap up the rules for this round. I think it's time to see what these younglings can do," Skiska says. The two giant heads in the sky dissipate, and Atae glances at Sloan while Beast fidgets in her sienna haze.

The maze of energy walls and ceilings shifts from a translucent haze to silver metal, and Atae loses sight of Jeqi. Beast churns and emits an orange pulse from her swirling ball.

We're fine, Atae says. *We can do this.*

Atae and Sloan survey their new environment and glance at each other. The empty metal hall that offers only one path to follow, so Atae nods and sprints forward.

"Wait," Sloan says. Then, he sighs and follows after her. Darting down the hall, Atae frowns when Beast blares an orange warning to stop, but the hybrid doesn't comply. A wall materializes in front of her, and she slams into it.

"I bet that hurt," Sloan says. Atae glares at him as she rubs her forehead. Beast snickers from within a green-yellow swirl, and Atae sucks her teeth in annoyance. When Sloan swivels back toward the direction they came, another wall bursts into life to block him, and he sighs. A camera that's stuck on the other side of the wall slips right through the energy field unhindered, much to Atae's disappointment.

Great, the cameras have free rein.

"We're boxed in. We can't go anywhere," Sloan says.

"Really? I hadn't noticed."

Another energy field slides across the bottom of the maze just above the dirt floor. This time, Atae reacts to Beast's orange warning and jumps, so as not to trip over it. Sloan manages to avoid the same debacle as the cube completes its construction.

"Now what?"

As if to answer Sloan's question, the entire cube lurches to the side, and it reminds Atae of the navigation room in the royal prison. There isn't a viewing screen inside this box, so she has no idea if they are moving closer or farther away from their goal. When they come to a sudden stop, Atae topples forward into Sloan, and he stabilizes them against the wall. Beast's yellow-orange excitement swirls with whips of crimson, and Atae cringes before pushing away from her ally.

The wall ahead slides open to reveal a new route with a tall ceiling and several obstacles blocking the path. Several tiles levitate above the ground and shift from one side to another, acting as steps to a dozen ropes hanging from the ceiling. Atae notices that the dangling cords work as swings to the next obstacle, but they vary in size and shape. Beyond the rope-jungle, a section of the wall mimics the rock face of a mountain. The 'mountain face' sits at the top of the wall and continues around a blind corner.

"Are we supposed to complete the obstacles?" Atae asks. "Why don't we just walk around them?"

Sloan frowns, wondering the same thing. Before he can form a response, the wall to his left slides open to reveal two runners. The two hybrids rush past Sloan and Atae toward the obstacle course. Atae grabs the closest one and slams him into the wall, pinning him with her forearm against his neck.

"Go, I'll catch up," she says to Sloan over her shoulder. He hesitates, balking at the order, then follows the second runner. Another orange flash from Beast warns Atae to focus on her enemy, but only serves to distract her further. The runner lands a powerful strike that knocks the wind from her lungs. The larger hybrid breaks Atae's loosened grip and slams his knee into her chin. He stands over her as she scrambles back and struggles to clear her vision after the jarring hit. Beast rages within Atae to attack and destroy this weakling, and Atae has to rein in her counterpart's attempts to call upon their blades.

When his partner screams in agony at the opening of the obstacle course, the runner glances back to investigate. Atae uses the opportunity to kick out his knee and follow up with an uppercut to his exposed neck. Choking from the damage to his throat, he falls back onto his injured knee and topples over. Sloan appears at the runner's side and grabs him by the hair. He drags the injured youngling toward the obstacle course with an eager smile.

"Hey, what are you doing? He's mine," Atae says. She rushes after Sloan until he stops several steps from the edge of the path and glances at Atae with a mischievous bounce of his eyebrows.

"Watch this."

Sloan tosses the runner on to the floor next to his unconscious partner just below the floating tiles. Upon touching the energy floor, the hybrid screams in agony as blue electricity climbs up his body from the floor. He convulses for a moment before falling unconscious, and the power stops flowing. Both Atae and Beast watch, slack-jawed. Then the blue-haired hybrid grins at Sloan.

"Cool."

"Right?" Sloan nods then points toward the tile steps. "Okay, we've got to go."

Without another word, both younglings scramble toward the obstacle course with their cameras in tow. Sloan, a few steps ahead of Atae, reaches the tile steps first and leaps forward. Knowing his ally is close behind, Sloan moves on to the next energy tile as soon as his foot touches the first. But in the same instant his foot comes into contact with the initial levitating step, an inner mechanism triggers, and a cascade of small spikes erupt from the tile. Luckily, Sloan's fast pace protects him from the unexpected trap. He leaps from one tile to the next before any of the triggered spikes can harm him. Atae, on the other hand, is not so lucky.

Atae notices the crippling spikes just as she leaps from the floor, thanks to a warning from Beast. An instant before her foot reaches the energy tile, she twists her body to the right, aiming for the smooth, thin side of the step. Atae throws herself away from the offending spikes and toward the next awaiting step. Realizing she doesn't have enough momentum to land on the next tile, Atae flings out her arms to catch herself. Her desperate fingers reach the stone just as Sloan leaves it behind. She grasps the smooth step with one hand and clings to it as most of her other hand slides off from the momentum of her fall. As the last of her fingers start to slide free, spikes erupt from the top of the energy tile.

Atae screams while an energy spike impales one finger, and others sprout harmlessly around her remaining digits. The barb acts as an anchor and prevents Atae from slipping any further. Hanging from the tile, Atae watches Sloan dive for the ropes in the next obstacle and falter as the cord he clings to gives out. Atae can't help the sudden rush of concern but sighs in relief when Sloan saves himself by grabbing another rope in reach. Sloan swivels back to his ally, and Atae waves him away with her free hand. She urges Sloan to go on as she swats at the floating camera to get out of her way. He hesitates for a moment but then continues toward the mountain wall. Another runner appears behind a sliding wall and leaps into the rope-jungle. The purebred female dangles from her cord with one hand and activates her hilt with the other. She swings it toward Sloan and his ropes.

Trusting Sloan to fend for himself, Atae weaves the fingers of her free hand in between the spikes so that both hands grip the tile. Then, she swings her legs back and forth until she gathers enough momentum to flip herself up and over. Atae summersaults on to the top of the tile, sacrificing one foot to the spikes in exchange for one chance at a stable launchpad. She stifles a cry of pain as several small spikes impale her left foot through her thin footwear. She forgets about the pain when an energy blast from a ranged hilt sears the tip of her ear off.

"Ow!"

She glares over her shoulder at a hybrid runner that sprints toward the tiles after Atae.

Where was my warning, Beast?

I didn't see him, Beast admits. *But I'll kill him for you.*

Atae huffs in annoyance and leaps from her designated launch pad to the next tile. Instead of landing on the protruding spikes, she pushes off from the thin, smooth sides of each step. She moves fast and pushes hard enough to keep her momentum going until she reaches the rope-jungle. Atae leaps from the last tile, throwing both hands out, and snatches the closest rope with her injured hand. The rope tugs at her damaged flesh as Atae holds tight against her weight. The force of her jump swings Atae into the other dangling ropes, but too many are missing thanks to Sloan and the other purebred. None that remain are in reach.

Left with little choice, Atae releases the rope at the height of her swing, falling toward the hard ground below. The angle of her fall pushes her out enough that she manages to grasp another rope. Atae sighs in relief and pauses to assess her next move. She frowns at the brush of green-yellow amusement from Beast, then she snickers at the yelp of pain from the runner behind her landing on the spiked tiles. She also notes the unconscious female runner on the floor, presumably where Sloan knocked her down.

Ignoring the pain in her injured limbs, Atae climbs the rope to the optimal height to swing herself in the direction of the next obstacle. After jumping from one cord to another, catching herself when one gives out under her weight, Atae finally reaches the mountain face obstacle. She swings to the damaged wall, and finding nothing to land on, Atae slams into the hard rock. She scrambles to find a footing and slips downward, scraping against jagged edges until her un-injured hand snags a solid ledge. Atae dangles until her feet find notches in the rockface. She's impressed that the energy wall feels so much like a mountain face.

Sloan cries out in pain, and Beast roars with a deep blue wave of concern. Clenching the rockface with her body, Atae glances up to find

Sloan almost to the top of the wall. His camera zips around him as he clings to the jagged rocks further down the path and past the corner. What Atae can't see is Sloan's outreached hand. It's close to the top ledge and impaled on an energy blade.

"Move, Sloan," Atae says.

"I can't! My hand is stuck."

Sloan growls down to Atae, not bothering to hide his pain. Atae leans over, as much as her unstable footing will allow, and spies the knife spearing Sloan's hand to the wall. Cringing at her ally's predicament, Atae leans back just in time to avoid an energy blade that impales the stone to the right of her head. Atae flinches away from the knife, causing some unstable rock to give way, and she scrambles to keep from falling. Beast floods Atae's mind with golden panic, and she struggles to concentrate through the haze of adrenaline.

Atae flails out for the knife embedded in the wall and finds it to be a stable handhold. Dangling, once again, by one arm, Atae scans the area for the source of the energy blades and sees several more shooting from the opposite wall. A score of knives erupt and slam into the mountain face in an eerily straight line leading to Sloan, but none of them strike him or Atae. She smiles when she recognizes Jeqi's handy work.

Look, Jeqi is watching out for us, Atae says. *I need you to stay calm, Beast. You're making this too hard.*

This is hard for you. Not for me.

Still dangling by one hand from the hilt of the energy blade, Atae takes a deep breath then grabs her wrist with her free hand and shoves both feet against the wall. She pulls with her arms and pushes with her legs, jumping up across the wall to a nearby blade. Atae repeats the process until she is even with Sloan against the wall.

"Are you okay?" She asks.

"Do I look okay?" Sloan struggles not to lose his footing because they both know that if he slips, the blade will not hold him. Instead, it will slice through his remaining hand, and he will fall.

"There is a blade next to your right foot. Step on it. Use it as footing," Atae says.

Sloan nudges his foot around until he finds it. Stepping onto the protruding blade, he gasps as he relieves the pressure from the blade slicing through his hand.

"So, are you going to pull that thing out or what?" Atae says. She surveys the area for any newcomers, and Beast silently assures her that no one will sneak up on her. "If any more blades are triggered, we are sitting ducks."

"Why did they stop?" Sloan asks. Meanwhile, Beast warns of an incoming runner just before she slams into the mountain face. Atae grabs her hilt, ready to defend Sloan from the incoming runner, but an energy blade slices through the air and lands next to the runner's head. Startled, the runner loses her grip and plummets to the floor.

"I think Jeqi is using them to help us out." Atae chuckles at the electrified noises below. For once, she agrees with the mist of green pride emanating from Beast.

"Then, why did she shoot me?" Sloan snarls, and Atae shrugs.

"I don't know. Maybe she has to fight the other strategists for control of the traps. All the more reason why we should move on. Can you pull it out?"

"If I could, I would have already. The blade is not coming out."

"Well, the blade can stay as long as it wants. It's your hand that has to move on. Since the handle is thicker than the blade, you can't pull it through. So that leaves two options."

"I'm not giving up, Atae."

"Then, that leaves one option."

"I know!"

Sloan shakes his head with a furious expression, then sucks in a deep breath. He glares and clenches his jaw.

"I loathe you."

Then, Sloan steps off one knife to dangle from the other. He only hangs for a few moments, but the pain of the blade slicing his hand in half lasts forever for Sloan, and he screams out in agony. Atae can only watch and cringe as her ally suffers a devastating injury then falls. Sloan drops a few feet before he grasps a blade protruding from the wall with his intact hand, and his camera rushes to catch up with his sudden elevation change.

CHAPTER 32

"Are you okay?" Atae says. She stares down at Sloan and swats at her annoying camera.

"Quit asking me that."

Atae laughs at him before evaluating the short path forward then around a left corner. The mountain face lasts a few more steps then fades into a smooth metal wall. The corner obstacle is a large 'tree branch' erupting from the wall at the same height as the mountain face. The problem is getting to the tree branch.

"Follow my lead," Atae says. She jumps to the blade that Sloan had used for footing and uses the energy blades as steppingstones, then she leaps from the mountain wall to the corner obstacle. The giant tree trunk erupting from the perpendicular wall is low enough that Atae lands on it with both feet. Expecting the force of her jump to propel her across the rough bark, Atae gasps when her feet stick like glue to the bark. Instead of skidding to a stop, the momentum forces her body forward, and her feet stay put, effectively pushing Atae headfirst off the tree trunk. At least it would have if her shins didn't stick to the bark as she fell. Once again, Atae finds herself dangling in the air. This time, she's upside down, facing the direction from which she came. As the blood rushes to her head, Atae spots Sloan jumping for the trunk after her.

"Don't land on the tree!"

Sloan twists in midair away from the branch and throws his uninjured hand out to Atae. She snags him, and the momentum of his jump swings them toward the wall behind Atae. Sloan runs up the 'metal' surface and jumps backward onto the tree trunk, pulling the hybrid along with him. Sloan rips Atae up from her knees, ignoring her cries of pain. While most of Atae escapes the sticky tree bark, her skin stays behind, leaving gaping wounds on her shins.

"Ow! How is it that you can rip the skin from my shins but can't manage to pull a stupid knife from a wall?"

"What, you think I lied? That I wanted this?" Sloan holds up his gnarled and bloody extremity, and Atae cringes. His hand is sliced in half from the center of his palm until the split between his second and third fingers.

"Eww, get that thing away from me," Atae says. She stretches to see what awaits them around the corner, ignoring the sensation of sap seeping into the puncture wounds on her left foot. Several bars hang from a sloping ceiling that leads to a standard-sized hall. One unconscious purebred lies under the bars, marking the end of the obstacle. Several runners jump from outside a sliding door, just past the bars, onto the dirt floor without incident. The runners push past each other and away from the obstacle course. Sloan points with his good hand, cradling the injured one against his chest.

"Looks like the dirt is safe to walk on. I guess that's the direction we need to go," he says.

"So far, every obstacle has had some unexpected trap. The tile spikes, the snapping ropes, the wall with no ledges, and now a tree branch with sticky sap. What do you think is going on with those bars?"

"Who knows. Maybe they're just holograms, and we'll plummet to our deaths. Either way, we can't jump with this black sap sticking to us."

"Do you still loathe me?" Atae asks. She grins at him with a playful gleam in her eyes that piques Beast's interest. Sloan shrugs at the hybrid.

"Yes. What's your idea?"

"If I fall, leave me behind."

"Duh," Sloan says. Then he watches Atae pounce off the tree. "Wait, what are you doing?"

When Atae jumps, she does so with enough force to pull her feet from the sap. Naturally, globs of it stick to her shoes. Atae slams into the wall just below the hanging bars and shoves her feet into the wall to run along with it. The sticky sap gives her enough footing to dart across the wall and slip down toward the floor. Moments later, she passes the unconscious runner and lands in the smaller hallway on the safe, dirt floor. She plants her hands against both hips and raises her eyebrows at

Sloan, daring him to catch up. Beast bubbles with amusement until she blasts her counterpart with another orange warning.

Atae swirls around in time to receive a nose crunching blow to the face and another to her gut. She keels over, grabbing at her face and stomach, and Beast howls for Atae to get up and retaliate. As Atae pulls herself to one knee, Beast urges her to block an incoming attack with a forearm blade. Atae refuses to shift, and the struggle with Beast's red wave of anger costs her. The attacking runner slams his fist into Atae's face from the side to further damage her broken nose, and she stumbles to her right along with the momentum of the attack. As she leans forward, holding her nose with one hand, Atae slips the other onto the hilt attached to her thigh.

She activates the small energy blade, and it zings to life. Atae swirls to face her opponent, expecting to find him unarmed, but his long-bladed hilt disappoints her. She falls into an offensive stance that Sloan taught her, then Atae launches at the runner. He blocks the feint to his head and the real attack to his chest by whipping his long blade down in an arch. She sweeps a leg under him, but the runner jumps over her. Before she can regain her footing, he swings his sword down toward Atae's sprawled form. She rolls to the side of his blade and into the nearby wall.

"You are really bad at this," the runner says. He stabs at her prone body as she huddles against the wall. A storm of red and gold rages against Atae's mind as Beast screams at her to destroy the runner. Atae defends against the incessant stabbing with her dagger and flails against Beast's mental attacks.

"Yes, she is," Sloan says. He whacks the runner upside the head with the blunt side of his hilt. The runner falls back from the jarring strike, and Sloan uses the opening to push him into the electrified obstacle course. Ignoring the cries of pain, Sloan offers a hand to Atae.

"That was pathetic."

"I'm only as good as my teacher," Atae says. She ignores Beast's similar assessment of her skills.

"Let's go," Sloan says. He holsters the hilt against his hip, and Atae follows suit.

They both charge down the path, and several runners join in along the way as walls slide open. Atae indulges Beast's urges and elbows a few runners that get too close. She smiles when she smashes against someone's face, ignoring her own bruised and surely broken nose. When Beast flashes another warning, Atae slams on her breaks and puts her arms out to grab Sloan. They both skid to a stop right in front of a materializing energy field. Several other runners aren't so lucky and slide right through it. Most of them just shrug and continue onward until they find another more solid wall a few steps later. One runner tries to backtrack through the first energy field, but it remains solid from that direction.

"It's one-way," Atae says. "But why?"

"Nothing good. Look, they're trapped in there."

Sure enough, a green gas seeps into the small chamber, and the handful of runners panic, searching for an escape. As several fall unconscious, a few smart ones use their uniforms as masks, but that only lasts so long. Lucky for them, the left wall slides open, and the remaining runners stumble out of the gas chamber. Unlucky for Atae and Sloan, the one-way field drops, and the green gas creeps toward them.

"Uh oh."

Atae backpedals along with Sloan, but their progress halts when another wall slides shut behind them. Pinned against the far wall, the two allies shove the bottom half of their faces into the fabric of their uniforms as the gas seeps closer.

What do we do? Atae asks Beast. Her counterpart points out the still open wall to the left of the gas chamber. *Oh, good idea.*

Atae motions toward the gap, but another field slams down between her and the toxic cloud. Atae stumbles back into Sloan, and together, they breathe a sigh of relief. Beast's hackles rise in an orange flurry, and Atae glances around for a threat as an energy floor assembles under them.

"We're trapped in another cube," Sloan says.

The metal box that encases them shoots upward, slamming its occupants into the floor. Atae's stomach lurches along with the box. From the force, she can only assume they are flying high above the arena floor. Pinned to the floor and looking upward, Sloan notices a strap drop from the ceiling of the cube. When the box heaves to a stop, the momentum launches Sloan and Atae into the air. Sloan snags the strap, but Atae isn't so lucky.

Since she was pinned to the floor facedown, she never noticed the strap, and her stomach flipped when the box flung her into the air. Beast, on the other hand, enjoyed the ride and found it quite thrilling. Neither reacts well when the floor slides open to reveal the arena, a dozen stories below. Atae spins in mid-air, frantic to find something to cling to, and finds Sloan's outreached hand. She snatches his injured hand, ignoring the grotesque feeling of exposed bone against her fingers. When her body's weight tugs against Sloan's grip, he cries out in pain but doesn't let go.

"Why are you so heavy?" he says. When he glances down, Sloan's black eyes meet Atae's terrified fuchsia gaze. He realizes that this is the only time, other than in the throne room, that he's ever seen Atae afraid of anything. Her lips tremble as the wind whips her midnight blue hair and stings her eyes. Something sharp pinches into his hand as she tightens her frantic grip, and blood gushes from his wound.

"I won't drop you, Atae. I promise."

She nods at him with wide eyes. When her buzzing camera reminds her that everyone is watching, Atae takes a few deep breaths. After collecting herself, she searches in and around the box to find a way out of this predicament and finds absolutely nothing. Without thinking, she glances down, and a wave of nausea slams into her. Beast only makes it worse with another barrage of panic and fear. She rages against Atae and demands control so that she can save them both.

Shut up. You're going to get us killed, Atae says, but Beast refuses to relent. *How have you survived this long? Let me free. I will save us all.*

After pushing Beast back, Atae scans the ground for an escape route. She notices Jeqi on top of the maze with dozens of other strategists, although several of them lay across the fields, unconscious. Jeqi wails on a larger purebred after dislocating his arm, and Atae huffs at her packmate's distraction.

"Jeqi!"

The blonde glances up at the sound of her name. Paling at the sight of her packmate dangling from that height, Jeqi ends her fight with a whack across her opponent's temple. As the larger strategist collapses, Jeqi faces Sloan and Atae, then lifts both hands toward the hovering cube. Using her visor, she commands the box to return to the maze by swinging her arms downward

Atae sighs in relief when the flooring slides closed below her. She taps her toes on the energy field to test its solidity, then presses her weight against it. Atae releases her iron grip from Sloan's injured hand and draws her hand against her chest. She hopes the copious amount of blood hides her receding claws well enough. Sloan stares at the new holes in his hand and growls at her.

"Ow."

The cube descends at a reasonable rate and then lurches in another direction. Atae twists her mouth into a guilty frown and rips a strip of cloth from her pant leg. She wraps it around Sloan's hand to stop the bleeding. He watches her, tight-lipped, and winces when she ties off the bandage.

"Don't be a baby," Atae says.

She rolls her eyes before releasing his hand and stepping away. He flashes a crooked smile at her when Atae crosses her arms to wait for their box to stop. She refuses to look at him as Beast shivers with crimson sparks. Atae notices that Sloan's presence has a calming effect on her counterpart. Well, not exactly a calming effect, but at least she isn't actively attacking Atae and trying to seize control. The cube finally comes to a jarring halt, and the left wall slides open.

Atae cringes at the bright light from Solis and Cerule shining through the arena's dome ceiling. She steps out of the box and onto an energy deck that leads to a white energy disc floating above the giant pond. Looking around, Atae notices dozens of bridges that circle the center platform, and numerous unconscious Kaji scattered around. A giant pillar of light stands at the core, with one person standing idle at the top.

"That's our goal," Sloan says.

"Obviously," Atae says. "But how do we get there? Walking up to it just seems way too easy."

As though answering her question, a wall slides open at the end of a nearby bridge, and two runners, a hybrid, and a purebred pile out. They catch sight of the endgame and run straight for it. Several of the water beast's tentacles emerge from the pond below and attempt to snag both younglings. The creature catches the hybrid and drags her, kicking and screaming, into the dark pool.

"I saw that coming," Sloan says. Both Atae and Beast snicker.

The purebred runner manages to evade the tentacles and reaches the disc. Stepping onto the white energy activates the pillar's defense system, and several energy blades shoot out from the column at the center of the energy disc. The runner dodges one then two but fails to anticipate the third. It nails her in the shoulder hard, and momentum whirls her around. She tries to recover, but a fourth blade spears her through the leg, and she stumbles to the ground. When she crawls on her stomach toward the pillar, a tentacle erupts from the pool below, still carrying her lost packmate. The water beast tosses the unconscious hybrid at his purebred partner, and they both skid across the energy platform. Atae watches to see if the purebred runner will continue, but the blow from her packmate's body stopped her in her tracks.

Two more runners appear on the opposite side of the platform from Atae and Sloan, while another wall on a nearby bridge opens to a third runner. Glancing at each other, the two allies decide that it's time to move.

"Get behind me," Sloan says. He activates his hilt, and a longsword springs to life. He steps forward and swings the blade into a defensive stance, waiting for Atae to follow his instructions.

"What? Why would I do that?" Beast snarls an agreement.

We are strong. We are Kaji.

Sloan sighs at Atae's protests and glances over his shoulder at her. "Just trust me."

Atae bites her tongue and decides to comply, but only because she owes him due to the fiasco in the box. She activates her hilt and steps in behind him. He darts across the energy bridge, and Atae follows suit. Tentacles explode from below and strike at the advancing younglings. Atae prepares to defend herself from the impending assaults but finds she's not needed. Sloan's fluid movements are graceful and impossible to mimic as far as Atae is concerned. She watches him block every incoming strike and sever several appendages, gaining ground with each movement. They edge their way across the bridge unharmed while Atae watches Sloan's dance of death as though mesmerized, and Beast licks her crimson lips.

Once they reach the white platform, Atae says, "Okay, I admit it. You're really good at that,"

"I told you."

Atae grumbles at Sloan's typical arrogance, while Beast warns her of an incoming attack. A nearby runner advances upon her with his sword drawn, but Atae manages to sidestep the strike. Then Sloan dispatches him with a couple of swings.

"You distract the other runners. I'll get to the pillar," Atae says. Sloan nods and knocks another incoming runner to the ground with an adept swipe to the legs.

Beast flares orange through Atae's mind and floods her body with alarm. Atae twirls to face the danger just in time to deflect an airborne energy blade with her hilt. Beast's hypersensitive hearing picks up an almost silent incoming whistle and indicates that another knife is on its way. In the split moment that it takes Atae to register the sound, she raises her hilt to deflect the second blade.

Without hesitation, Atae jumps away from her current position and runs parallel to the pillar. Beast shifts the muscles in her legs to increase speed and power. The corners of Atae's mouth quirk upward as three blades swish behind her head, one slicing a few hairs. Atae stops in mid-stride just in time for another knife to streak in front of her face. The blue hybrid darts away from the pillar but only for a few strides because the next two blades nick Atae's arm and leg. With another sudden shift in direction, this time heading toward the pillar, Atae deflects an incoming energy blade with her hilt.

As she closes in on her goal, the pillar surprises Atae with a whip of energy. Beast urges her to dodge, but Atae opts to deflect the attack. The whip swirls through the air and cracks across the energy blade of her hilt. Electricity shoots through Atae's entire body, and she screams. Crumbling to the ground, the hybrid struggles to stay conscious. The shock was short but powerful, and Atae can still feel her teeth chattering. Beast warns her to move, so she complies. Another whip strikes the ground where she once crouched. Standing, Atae gathers herself for another assault on the pillar, this time vowing to avoid the energy whips.

Another two runners race ahead, and one takes a strike in the chest. Showing no mercy, Atae follows after the purebred and leaps into the air. Anticipating Atae's attack, the remaining runner watches for her competitor to fly overhead then land ahead of her. The runner cocks her leg and releases a powerful sidekick into Atae's rib cage the instant she lands. At least, it would have been Atae's rib cage if Beast hadn't anticipated the strategic counterattack and instructed Atae to prepare to catch the offending leg on impact.

Instead, the purebred finds herself in a precarious one-legged position. Recognizing the snare, she tugs at her leg. She leans back until her hand touches the ground and then whips her second leg around to strike Atae in the face. The powerful assault causes Atae to release the runner's leg and stumble backward in a stunned haze. Beast urges Atae to focus, but their opponent attacks too fast with a follow-up jab to her gut.

Atae cringes as Beast's orange-brown frustration and red fury slams into her mind with each physical attack that the runner lands. The blue-haired youngling growls before she rushes headfirst into her competitor. The cumbersome attack blindsides the runner, and both younglings tumble to the ground. Atae pins the purebred to the floor with her energy blade pressed to the female's throat. Atae snarls at her enemy with Beast urging her on, and the runner flinches away with both hands fighting against Atae's hilt.

Atae can feel Beast pushing all her weight into the energy blade, but the runner holds firm against it. Beast's bloodlust fueling her rage, Atae slams her free fist into the purebred's ribs over and over again. With each strike, the runner groans in pain but refuses to let Atae's blade slips any closer to her throat.

"Stop," Debil says. Like the flip of a switch, Atae recognizes the runner. She pushes against Beast's bloodthirst until the red fog that saturates her mind ebbs. Fighting the urge to decapitate her enemy, Atae slams her free fist against Debil's temple, and the purebred groans and struggles to stay conscious.

Atae lunges for the nearby pillar and makes contact. When her hand touches the smooth energy field, several brick-like shapes emerge from the column. As she reaches for the lowest stone, Beast reminds Atae of their ally. She spins around and yells for Sloan, pausing at the sight of him.

With his hilt gone and several injured or maimed runners lying on the ground at his feet, Sloan tackles one remaining opponent. Once pinned, Sloan proceeds to beat him into submission. Atae sprints to his side and grabs the purebred's arm mid-swing. He twists around to face her with his other fist raised for an attack but pauses when he finds Atae's fuchsia gaze. The blue hybrid grimaces at the blood splattered across his arms and face, and for the first time, she recognizes the battle raging behind his eyes. Sloan's beast wars against his restraint, and Atae isn't sure who won this battle.

"You're done," Atae says. Beast adds a bestial growl behind her command.

For a moment, she isn't sure if Sloan will comply, then he nods his head and stands. She darts back to the pillar with Sloan in tow, tripping up an incoming runner and dodging a few energy attacks along the way. This time, she doesn't hesitate to climb the column when her touch activates the stone ladder. Sloan grabs at a separate stone path beside her, and they ascend together. They are about halfway up the pillar when a couple of runners decide to use their ranged hilts. An energy disc careens by Atae's head, and she cringes from the heat of the attack. When a second one strikes her abdomen, she screams from the searing pain. Her uniform burns away, and the skin underneath sizzles. Atae's grip on the stones slip, and she tumbles down a few rungs before Sloan manages to grab her flailing arm. She crashes against the protruding brick and groans.

"Why do I keep using my hurt hand to do this?" Sloan winces in pain. Atae ignores her injured side and grabs hold of the stone ladder again.

When Sloan releases her, they both scale the pillar. Atae notices other runners climbing the column now, but she and Sloan lead the pack. Moments later, the two allies reach the top of the pillar and join the one runner that beat them.

"Hey," Jent says.

Atae and Sloan clamber over the ledge, and the pillar flares gold to indicate their arrival before returning to white. Sloan and Atae lie on the cold, imitation stone floor and catch their breath as runner after runner joins them on the pillar. It isn't long before a dozen cameras buzz all around, and Atae cringes from the noise.

I can't decide if you were more of a hindrance or help today, Atae says to Beast. She huffs from within her ever-changing mist. Atae smiles as the excited yellow particles swirl around the green specks and combine to gleam in a calm blue hue.

After several long moments and numerous flashes of gold to indicate new arrivals, Atae sits up and stares at Sloan. He lies with his eyes closed and arms behind his head. She wonders if his beast is this calm, too. When he opens his eyes to meet her gaze, she knows it isn't.

"I've decided," Atae says. Sloan raises an eyebrow. "You can be my ally in the Gridiron."

"I'm honored," Sloan says sarcastically. Atae nods her head and lies back down, swatting at her camera.

"But you're going to have to teach me that sword work."

"What do you think I've been trying to do?"

"And you're still annoying."

CHAPTER 33

"This isn't working," Atae says. She fidgets against the dirt floor of the palace's training arena. Both Cerule and Solis beat down on Atae and Schinn as the two younglings lie side-by-side on their backs and squint up into the sky.

"It takes time and practice."

"We've been here all day," Atae says.

"No, we haven't, but we will be if you don't take this seriously," Schinn says.

Atae sighs in resignation and closes her eyes. Beast simmers within a pale orange cloud of annoyance and watches her counterpart with a wary eye. The young hybrid takes a deep breath to calm her mind and body. She lets every worry, memory, and musing escape her mind, focusing on the feel of her lungs inhaling then exhaling. When each breath becomes the entirety of Atae's world, Beast's constant turmoil of chaotic emotions somehow ebb. The mist of pale orange particulate at the back of Atae's mind swirls into a calm bluish-green cloud, and she experiences serenity for the first time since Beast's arrival. Atae feels as though she's floating in a tranquil lake, and she never wants to leave.

"This is amazing," she whispers to Schinn. He chuckles and tilts his head to watch her. Schinn's breath against her cheek sends an exciting jolt across Atae's skin, and her heart flutters.

"I told you it would work," he says. Atae meets his gaze with a lazy smile. Hovering within her calm, sleepy sphere, Beast ignores her counterpart's conversation.

"How did you learn to meditate like this?" Atae asks.

"It's a tradition for all the heirs in my family to learn coping skills like this so that we can help the royal heir when necessary."

"Truin needed help when he started shifting?" The idea of Prince High-and-Mighty struggling at anything makes Atae smile but also tugs at her gut.

"No, Prince Truin required very little guidance during his shifting phase. In fact, he's displayed an immense amount of control for such a young Kaji. He doesn't confide in me very much, but I'd guess he's nearly merged with his beast."

"Already? I thought that only happens when you reach full maturity. He's too young."

"That's the case for most Kaji, but Prince Truin is not like most Kaji," Schinn says.

"Yeah, I know," Atae says. She watches the lines of his frown dimple his forehead, and she years to run her fingers over his dark skin to smooth away his stern expression. "Do you enjoy serving him? As his protector?"

The question catches Schinn off guard, and he hesitates. When he answers, he stares up into the sky to avoid her rosy gaze.

"I've never thought about it," he says. "A Fu-Kai heir has served as the royal heir's guard since the Ru-Kai took power. It's tradition and a great honor among my family. My mother and father were very pleased."

"Oh, that's good, at least." Atae's eyebrows knit together in confusion, and Schinn glances at her with a defensive sneer.

"It's a well-respected position, Atae."

"I know that." She sets a soothing hand over his chest. "I think it's very noble. I plan to dedicate my life to the royal guard as well."

Schinn slips his fingers over her hand, and he smiles when he notices Atae's pulse jump. He likes the way her fuchsia eyes swirl and her cheeks blush at each innocent touch. Schinn wonders what her skin would feel like against his lips, and the thought of finding the answer thrills him in a way he's never experienced. When Schinn's silver gaze darkens, Atae forgets how to breathe

"I just...I just wondered what made you do it?"

"Do what?" Schinn asks. He smiles at her ramblings.

"Join the guard, of course. I just figured there was a story behind it. Some inspiration or something. But fulfilling parental expectations is good too." Atae flashes a teasing smile, but Schinn doesn't return the expression. Instead, he frowns and brushes Atae's hand away.

"It's not just my parents. I'm an heir to one of the Crests of Kaji. A silver heir," Schinn says, climbing to his feet. "What would you know of family pressure? You're just a hybrid."

Atae sits up, pressing a hand to her chest, and glares at Schinn. A searing pain lances through her heart at his insult, and unsure what to do with the alien emotion, Atae pushes it down. Surely he didn't mean to lash out at her. It was an accident.

"You're right. It's just Father and me, so I don't get it. I don't understand what you must go through with your family." Atae tries to placate him with submissive words that pull Beast from her slumber. For some reason, Atae hates the idea of Schinn being angry with her. She likes him best when he's smiling at her and holding her hand.

Schinn stares at the young hybrid, still sitting on the ground, and cringes at her vulnerable expression. He shouldn't have lashed out at her that way. It isn't her fault. She doesn't know anything about the crests nor the politics surrounding them. All the more reason for her not to be involved.

"I'm sorry. I shouldn't have said that." Schinn extends a hand to help Atae to her feet. "Sometimes I'm an idiot."

"Well, I won't argue with that." Atae lifts the corners of her mouth into a small smile, but she hesitates at the hand Schinn offers. Beast rages within a red storm, demanding blood for his offensive comments, yet Atae chooses to ignore her counterpart and accepts his help. Standing, Schinn pulls Atae close.

"You're very intriguing, Atae," Schinn says. She holds her breath when he pushes a stray hair from her eyes.

"Uh-huh."

Jeqi clears her throat from several steps away, and Schinn jerks back from Atae. The blue hybrid takes a moment to steady herself after the heir's sudden departure, then twirls to glare at Jeqi.

How did she sneak up on us like that? I thought she was training with Marqee today? Atae huffs at her packmate's intrusion, and Beast grins within a green puff.

"Your swordsmanship is really bad. You should be working with Sloan," Jeqi says. Beast whispers a crimson agreement.

"We were meditating," Schinn says.

"Is that what they're calling it now."

"I actually got Beast to calm down," Atae says. "For a moment, anyway."

"Is she causing trouble again?" Schinn asks. When he steps forward in concern, Beast bubbles with pale orange annoyance.

"Yeah, I'd like to see if I can calm her again." Atae tilts her head to Jeqi. "Distract me. How did we rank yesterday in round two?"

Closing her eyes, Atae listens to Jeqi explain their performance, and she watches Beast's churning cloud calm into an innocuous shade of blue-green.

"Well, round two was a lot harder than I thought it would be, but Marqee did a good job taking down competing runners. He's the one that set up that gas chamber. Of course, Seva and Debil's strategist, Rakum, is the one that let them escape. And then he tried to turn it on you guys. Can you believe that?"

Jeqi swivels to Atae with outrage, her tail puffed to twice its size, and the blue hybrid grunts in response. Schinn watches the two hybrids interact with an amused expression.

"That's why I took him down," Jeqi says. "While I was distracted, another strategist tried to take both you and Sloan out with a drop trap. Don't worry. I took out both her runners for that little mistake. We couldn't help you on the energy platform, so Marqee and I just started wailing on any runners we came across."

"What about Seva and Debil?" Atae asks without opening her eyes.

"Oh, Marqee took Seva out early, but Debil managed to slip past him. I saw you slow her down, though. She only barely made it. I think they came in like twenty-fifth or something like that."

"We came in second?"

"Yep, you guys earned us an easy ninety points for that," Jeqi says. "Marqee and I got another eighty."

"Nice. How did Jent beat us?"

"His armor. In his shifted form, those feathers turn into impenetrable armor. Nothing slowed him down. He was pretty amazing."

"That's what happens when you and your beast work together," Schinn says. "You had your moments too. But it seemed like you two were at odds for the most part."

"Yeah, no kidding. I almost beheaded Debil. Beast has to feel and think exactly the opposite of me, so everything I do is a battle to keep her instincts from overpowering me. It's exhausting. And distracting," Atae says.

Beast swirls to life within a pale orange cloud of annoyance that rubs against her counterpart's psyche. Atae closes her eyes and breathes with calming thoughts. Noticing her struggle, Schinn slips his hand into her, giving a supportive squeeze.

"You must maintain control at all times, Atae. We can't ever have a repeat of last week. She's too dangerous."

"I know," Atae says. "But is it supposed to be this hard?"

Schinn notices the slight weariness in her voice; a fatigue that only Kaji with dominant beasts experience. It's a mental exhaustion that squirms into the mind and body due to day after day of constant battle. It's a never-ending struggle for control that only ends one way.

"No," Schinn says. "Your beast is dominant, but so are you."

"So?" Atae allows Beast's annoyance to creep into her voice as she raises an eyebrow at Schinn.

"So she shouldn't be fighting you this much," he says. "You should be working together."

"That's a great idea, Schinn. Why didn't I think of that?" Atae waves her hands in the air with a sneer. "She doesn't want to work with me."

The silver heir steps back, surprised by Atae's response. She's never gotten upset with him before now.

"But why?" Jeqi asks. She slips a hand over her packmate's shoulder again; this time, she implores Atae to listen.

The blue hybrid bites her lip with a furrowed brow. "What do you mean?"

"I mean, why doesn't she want to work with you? You said her instincts drive her to fight or flight when the pack's not around. She wants to survive. Working with you gives her the best chance of survival. So why doesn't she want to work with you?"

Atae considers her friend's words and searches inward for Beast's answer. It's biting and straightforward.

You are weak. You cannot protect us.

Atae clenches her fists and sets her jaw against the fury that scorches through her veins. Her face twists into an angry snarl as she growls.

I am not weak. I am Kaji.

You are not Kaji, Beast says. She slaps Atae with memories of her cowering in Kandorq's cell and falling apart in front of Sloan in the throne room. Worst is the memory of the phantom Kandorq taunting her in her nightmares.

I am Kaji, Beast says. She reminds Atae of her strength when killing Kandorq and fending off his mental attack. With each memory, Atae experiences a faded version of the emotions that dominated the situation.

Her stomach drops as she remembers the panic of cowering in Kandorq's cell and the fear that overwhelmed her at Sloan's feet in the throne room. Then Atae recollects the confidence and power that she felt when standing over Kandorq's crushed head. Her stomach settles, and her chest fills with warmth. Atae's fuchsia gaze drops to the floor as she ponders the truth of Beast's words. Her voice is soft and uncertain when she speaks.

"She thinks I'm weak."

"What? That's ridiculous. Why would she think you're weak?" Jeqi says. She squeezes Atae's shoulder in denial.

"Because I was." Atae yanks from Jeqi's touch, averting her gaze in shame. "When she appeared, it was in Kandorq's cell. I was so…"

Atae darts her eyes over Schinn and grimaces. She's hesitant to reveal such intimate knowledge to…whatever he is to her. But she takes a deep breath and rips the scab from her healing wound.

"I was scared. Terrified. I couldn't fight or move. I couldn't even form a coherent thought. I was…I was broken."

Her tail drooping to the floor, Jeqi cringes as she watches one of the strongest younglings she knows crumble under the weight of her shame. The blue-haired hybrid stands with her back to them and her arms wrapped around her torso.

"I was weak and useless. And that's when she just appeared. She stepped out of the shadows and took control. At that moment, she was everything I wasn't. She was strong and fearless. The fear and panic were just gone. Suddenly, everything was so clear."

"That's why it took so long for her to emerge," Schinn says. He snaps his finger with sudden clarity and the excitement of new understanding. Atae spins to him in confusion, but Jeqi asks first.

"What do you mean?"

"After your ordeal with the Gortox and the Setunn, when did your shifts occur?"

"I don't know. They were pretty random."

"It usually happened when she was fighting," Jeqi says. "When she needed help."

"Or when I was scared," Atae says. She bites her lip as Jeqi glances at her in surprise.

"Exactly." Schinn sports a big grin. "You only shifted when you absolutely needed it. When you were so frightened or lost or angry or, whatever intense emotion you want to call it, that you needed help. So you called your beast."

"I never called Beast. I didn't even know she existed," Atae says.

"No, but your subconscious did it," Jeqi says. "Your mind created Beast the moment you gained the ability to shift, maybe before that. Maybe even at birth. I don't know. But Beast had to exist when you first shifted, otherwise you wouldn't have been able to do it."

"If that's true, why did it take so long for her to manifest?" Atae asks. She plops a hand on her hip and presses her lips together at Jeqi and Schinn. Jeqi smiles at her friend.

"Because you're strong. Not just physically, but mentally too. Your beast couldn't break through until you were mentally weak. Until you were…broken."

Atae stares at Jeqi as she recognizes the truth of her words. Then she nods and slips her gaze away from her blue eyes.

"So that's why she appeared at my worst. Now, she thinks that's my standard condition and that I'm too weak by myself to protect us."

"So you'll just have to prove her wrong," Schinn says.

"How?" Atae asks. She jumps back in surprise when Schinn drops to the ground and sweeps his leg in a wide arch. Then he follows up with a kick to Atae's ribs, and she stumbles backward. She snarls at the silver heir, her anger colliding with Beast's boiling red fury.

"What was that for?"

"I'm trying to help you." Schinn slips into a defensive stance. "Your beast thinks you are weak. Prove her wrong."

Atae grins with understanding and pushes Beast back into the farthest corner of her mind. Atae drops into a familiar fighting stance as Jeqi steps away from the impending battle. Atae ignores the swirl of emotion and color raging against her psyche. All she can see is Schinn and his beautiful silver eyes. Her fist collides with his face, cracking his cheekbone, and she revels in the strength of her attack.

Schinn stumbles back from the unexpected strike but recovers quick enough to block her second punch to his ribs. He didn't plan for Atae's sudden backward twirl nor her elbow colliding with his jaw. Again, he stumbles away from the hybrid, but Atae pursues him. She kicks at his head, but he deflects her foot with both hands. He leaves his left hand across his torso for protection and jabs his right fist into Atae's midsection. Schinn smiles at the crunching noise and her sudden intake of breath. Atae growls, then knees him in the groin.

Schinn yelps in pain but remains upright. He slams his forehead into hers, and Atae stumbles backward, dazed. Schinn grabs her uniform by the collar and sweeps Atae's legs out from under her. She lands hard on her back, and the tall youngling pins her to the ground with a hand to her throat. The hybrid swings her fists at him, but Schinn's longer arms keep his chest and face out of her reach. He clenches her windpipe tighter, and she struggles against his grip for a sliver of air. Angry spittle flies from Atae's mouth as she bares her teeth, but he just stares back with empty eyes. Only a moment longer. Watching her smoky gray skin darken from lack of oxygen, Schinn leans close to her ear and whispers.

"I guess your beast is right. You are weak."

Before Schinn can lean back, Atae takes advantage of his off-balance stance over her. She snatches his shoulders and bucks her hips upward. He tumbles forward over her head, and Atae somersaults with him, pinning him under her body when they come to a stop against the dirt floor. Schinn's strong hands still grip her throat, and he squeezes even harder in a desperate attempt to stop the sudden turn of events. But Atae isn't having any of it. She chops both of her hands into the purebred's shoulders, forcing him to release her throat, and she gulps for air. Schinn screams when her blow snaps both of his clavicles, and his arms fall limp at his sides. He grimaces up at Atae as she pants through a victorious smile.

"I am not weak. I am Kaji."

CHAPTER 34

The next day, Schinn hustles into a private training room to find the large room empty but for Truin, Sloan, and Trikk grappling in the center. He sighs with an annoyed twist to his mouth, crosses his arms, and stops to watch the exciting match. All three heirs exhibit signs of fatigue and minor injuries. Sloan's carefully sculpted face brandishes a shiner and a split lip, while Trikk favors his left side, indicating a rib injury, and blood drips from Prince Truin's bruised jaw. Regardless of the injuries, neither youngling surrenders to his opponents.

Sloan drives a powerful jab at Prince Truin's face in the same instant that Trikk lashes out at his gut. In an impossible maneuver, Truin crouches low to dodge Sloan's attack and block Trikk's punch. Sloan responds by diverting his momentum into a double-fisted slam toward Truin's head. Anticipating the adaption, the youngest heir grabs Trikk and pulls him into the path of Sloan's strike as he rolls away from the colliding younglings. Sloan grimaces in sympathy when his fists slam against the side of Trikk's face, and the royal guard crumbles.

"Oops. That's got to hurt."

Truin jumps to his feet and launches toward his preoccupied friend. Sloan spots the hybrid's movement in his peripheral vision and twirls to block Truin's powerful spin kick with both elbows, leaving his stomach vulnerable. The prince shows no mercy with a follow-up sidekick to Sloan's gut. The older youngling groans but doesn't succumb to the pain. Instead, he growls and takes his revenge with a kick to Truin's head.

Knowing his friend's temper, the prince anticipates the heedless attack and dodges. He dances under Sloan's outreached leg and pops up next to the taller heir's shoulder. Truin relishes the expectant victory as he swings his arm to strike Sloan across the neck and send him into unconsciousness. To the hybrid's surprise, Sloan deflects the attack and slams his foot against Truin's knee. Sloan smiles in satisfaction when the knee buckles with a loud crack, and Truin cries out. He stumbles to the ground and kneels on the only good knee remaining, then Sloan backhands him across the face.

"Looks like I'm winning," Sloan says. He spits blood from his busted lips while one eye swells shut. He stares down at his friend's bruised face and smirks at the blood gushing from Truin's nose.

Snarling, Truin prepares for the inevitable follow-up punch and refuses to falter from his kneeling position. Sure enough, Sloan swings his second arm in a full arch with as much force as he can muster. At the last minute, Truin deflects the attack toward Sloan's torso and leans outside the arc of the swing. Sloan's arm collides with the prince's defensive block enough so that the smaller heir can snatch the outside of Sloan's attacking arm. Holding tight, Truin slams the palm of his free hand into Sloan's elbow and smirks when the joint snaps. As Sloan cries out, Truin pulls him down and into his elbow jab. After a vengeful crunch from his friend's nose, the royal youngling releases him.

"Who's winning now?" Truin says. He snorts and wipes the dripping blood from his face. His exhaustive panting sprays red drops across the white floor, adding to the faint orange stains. From his kneeling position, Truin watches Sloan roll onto his back to stare up at him. The larger youngling tries not to move his injured arm while he rubs the blood from his nose and struggles to catch his breath.

"I'm willing to concede to a tie," Sloan says. He flashes a bloody smile, and Truin chuckles. While the chatty heirs recover from their beatings, Schinn walks over to Trikk and kicks him awake.

"Are you still alive?"

Trikk groans as he regains consciousness. Facedown on the ground, he takes a moment to gather his senses before rolling over to a sitting position. Trikk touches the side of his face that Sloan damaged, assessing the damage.

"Who won?" He asks.

"Not you," Sloan says.

"Thanks to you." Trikk swivels his head around and grimaces from the pain of it. Sloan chuckles at his comrade's discomfort and can't help but jeer him further.

"I bet that hurts."

Trikk glares at him but doesn't bother responding. He learned long ago that feeding into Sloan's games only results in more aggravation.

"It's a tie," Schinn says.

"Again?" Trikk presses his lips together at Prince Truin. "There are no ties in the Gridiron. Only victory or death."

"Well, it's a good thing we aren't in the Gridiron," Sloan says.

Schinn shakes his head and frowns at Sloan before offering a helping hand to his fellow guard. Trikk accepts and climbs to his feet. Moments later, Prince Truin leans against Trikk as he stands on one leg. Sitting up, Sloan twists and pulls at his injured arm until the elbow joint pops back into place. The room echoes with the dark heir's grunts of pain.

"What's the latest on Blue?" Truin asks Schinn. Sloan jerks his head up with interest.

"The other day, we may have had a breakthrough," Schinn says. "But it's still hard to tell whether she's going to keep it together through the Tournament."

"Isn't that the point?" Truin spins to face Sloan. "You said she would be an asset. So far, she's been more trouble than she's worth."

"She and Jeqi are the top fighters at Sula Academy. I might be able to take them one-on-one. But put them together, and there's no competition. And that's before Atae could shift. Once she gets that under control, they'll be unstoppable. You want their help."

"If she can get it under control," Schinn says. "I'm not sure she can, definitely not by next week's round."

"Just get her through the tournament," Sloan says. "Then you'll have six months to work out the kinks before the Gridiron."

"Solum should work with her after the tournament. He'll be able to reach her in ways that I can't."

"No," Truin says. "Mother said that Solum's looking for a reason to pull her from the Gridiron. I'm tempted to let him."

"You should. She's unpredictable." Schinn jerks a hand through the air in front of him. "Atae is far more skilled in combat than I would have ever guessed. But between battles, she's easily distracted and emotional."

"Distracted by you, maybe," Sloan says.

"What of her beast?" Truin asks. He glances at the entrance of the room where Marqee shuffles in to join them. Sloan lifts his uninjured arm as a silent greeting.

"Her beast is a distraction at all times." Schinn shakes his head. "She's getting better, but I'm surprised no one has noticed."

"Is that why she keeps zoning out?" Sloan asks. "Sometimes, even in the middle of a conversation."

"Yes." Schinn nods. "We only have to deal with our beasts' urges and emotions. She has to deal with that, plus conversations with her."

"I take it we are talking about Atae?" Marqee asks as he joins the group. He motions to Sloan's injuries. "Looks like I missed a fun scrap."

"Where have you been?"

"I'll tell you in a moment." Marqee smiles as his dimples crinkle across his cheeks. "Is she getting any better at controlling her shift? She almost took Sloan's hand off the other day."

"A little," Schinn says. "Maybe."

"Well, what's the deal? You said if Atae submitted to Sloan and accepted him as alpha, he would be able to subdue her beast," Marqee says. "When he tried that, she shrugged him off like he was nothing. I've never seen another Kaji not respond to Sloan's beast like that. He's way too scary to ignore."

"Yeah, it just seemed to piss her off and make things worse," Sloan says.

"It's because both she and her Beast are extremely dominant. That was our breakthrough today. Until she can prove to her beast that she is stronger, they are going to keep fighting each other," Schinn says.

"Again, this seems like a lot of work for one little hybrid," Truin says. Schinn throws his hands out toward the prince, imploring him to listen.

"We don't need her. If we let her enter the Gridiron with an uncontrolled beast, we will get her killed. She deserves better than that."

"We're not doing anything that she hasn't asked for. She wants to fight in the tournament and the Gridiron. We're merely helping her do it," Marqee says.

"What she wants isn't necessarily what's good for her," Schinn says. Sloan snatches the silver heir's collar and jerks him close with a growl.

"Atae and Jeqi are the best fighters at Sula Academy and deserve a chance to fight at Prince Truin's side. We need them as much as they need us."

"Even if that chance gets Atae killed?" Schinn asks. He pulls free of the dark heir's grasp and averts his gaze.

"Sloan's right," Marqee says. "We need all the help we can get, and Atae and Jeqi are very good. More importantly, they're loyal to Prince Truin."

"What do you mean?" Truin asks.

"I guess none of you've been on KIC lately," Marqee says. Sloan shrugs and twists his lips into a sneer.

"Why would we? We all have lives."

"Well, let me show you one of the empire's top ten most popular channels as of last week."

Marqee hustles to a small control panel hidden in the wall next to the room entrance. After using his visor to select a few options, the room dims, then a giant hologram forms around the younglings. Truin, Trikk, and Schinn wait in silence for Marqee to rejoin them, while Sloan makes impatient noises and grumbles at his slow packmate. Marqee tries to ignore him but can't help an amused glance as he passes. The hologram displays a list of channels available for selection. The dimpled male searches for a moment then selects the Skiska and Frack channel.

"Ugh, the gossip channel? Just kill me now," Sloan says. Schinn glances at him as though considering his request. Sloan arches a daring eyebrow, and the silver heir swivels back to the materializing hologram.

"This is a clip from yesterday's upload," Marqee says.

Skiska and Frack appear in large boxes for everyone to see. Only their faces and torsos are visible to the camera, and they bicker back and forth without shame. Frack flails his arms about to accentuate his claims, and his wild, silver hair adds to his hyperbole. Next to him, Skiska's calm, round face and short, red hair seem tame. Frack's deep-seated eyes widen with excitement as he finishes his latest rant.

"I'm telling you that the Royal Gridiron will be the most horrific one in Kaji history!"

"I think you might be right about that, Frack," Skiska says.

"The Royal Gridiron?" Schinn asks. Marqee pauses the recording long enough to answer.

"That's what they're calling Truin's Gridiron."

"Well, it makes sense. I mean, your loving mother did turn it into a giant Royal Brawl, complete with defenders and challengers. Too bad, the challengers are going to outnumber the defenders by like a million to one," Sloan says to Truin.

"Well, aren't you a ball of starlight today," Marqee says. "You've been in a bad mood since Atae skipped your sword match in favor of session with Schinn yesterday."

"Pff, like I care," Sloan shrugs. "It's just that she is awful at swordplay, and we were finally making some progress. She's got the memory of an insect. You miss one session, and it's back to square one."

"Don't worry. I'm sure she'll be at today's lesson."

"Good." Sloan turns back to the hologram, ignoring Marqee's amused grin and Schinn's suspicious frown.

"And I think today's guest will also agree," Skiska says when the recorded hologram continues. "Please welcome Royce, an heir to the Levia crest."

Royce's sharp features and shoulder-length, silver, and red hair assembles inside a holographic box separate from Skiska and Frack. Her voice is smooth and slips from her dark lips like music as she offers a charming smile

"Thank you for having me. I've always admired your channel and passion for truth. It's rare in today's society, Sula's society."

"Sula's society? We've heard that term quite a bit recently. Specifically, since Prince Truin's pledging ceremony, at which he announced the Royal Gridiron. What does it mean?" Skiska asks Royce. Frack interrupts with his loud opinion.

"I can tell you what it means. They're talking about this strange peace with the Camille. No one trusts it."

"Well, not quite, Frack. But I like your enthusiasm," Royce says. Her chuckle makes Sloan's skin crawl. "Sula's society refers to this unnatural integration that she's forced upon the Kaji. Yes, our economy has benefited, and our ties to our allies are stronger than ever. But it's at the expense of our society and culture."

"Are you claiming that the Kaji are changing?" Skiska asks.

"Yes, little by little. I believe that if we continue Sula's society as it is now, generation by generation, the Kaji will grow soft and weak. Look at the number of hybrids among my younger brother's class at Sula Academy."

Sloan growls and clenches his fists. His sister tilts her head upward and stares at the audience with her silver gaze on fire.

"For the first time in history, Planet Kaji's latest generation consists of just as many hybrids as purebred Kaji. If something isn't done, you'll see the same thing throughout the empire."

"Exactly. It's not right, I tell you," Frack says. "These hybrids will claim citizenship in the Gridiron and start demanding the Kaji change to accommodate their non-Kaji halves. The Setunn especially. Those religious zealots are already making noises. What happens when the Faithful show up and want to compete for citizenship?"

"Well, that's definitely a frightening thought. But aren't you being a little harsh on the hybrids? If they are strong enough to earn citizenship, don't they deserve a voice?" Skiska says. She eyes Royce with a dubious frown, but the silver heir's charms break down the co-host's defenses.

"Skiska, ever the voice of reason. I was hoping you'd ask that question. The hybrids are inherently weaker than the purebred Kaji. A few have slipped through the Gridiron, not because they are strong, but because we have allowed them to live. We forgot the threat they pose against our society. We allowed them to live as babes, and now they've grown into parasites that slowly destroy the Kajian way of life. My generation must step forward and accept the heavy mantle that our elders failed to bare. We must purge the Gridiron of hybrids. No more will gain citizenship. No more will gain a voice in our empire. Not a drop of tainted Kaji blood, Ru-Kai or not, will walk away unharmed. Only the pure will survive. Together, we can destroy Sula's society and rebuild the empire to its former glory."

Marqee pauses the recording with Royce's face twisted into a maniacal grin. All five younglings gape at the giant hologram while the shock of her words sinks deep.

"My sister..." Sloan says. "That malicious bitch has lost her mind."

"Sane or not, she's gaining a lot of support. You won't be the only target in the Gridiron," Marqee says.

"You mean the Royal Gridiron?" Truin says.

"Shouldn't we speak out against her?" Schinn asks. "Try to garner our own support?"

"No." Trikk speaks for the first time in a while, and everyone stops to listen. "We cannot stop her from speaking. We cannot stop her from gathering supporters. We can only prepare. Because in six months, we must stop her from taking the throne."

"No pressure, though," Sloan says to Truin. The prince snorts at the dark heir and shakes his head. Trikk stares at Truin with a stern expression, and the royal heir stands straighter under his guard's expectant eye.

"You are Ru-Kai. You have the support of an empire if you can prove yourself worthy. Destroying Royce and all of her followers in the Royal Gridiron might just do it."

"If not, it'll be one badass way to die," Sloan says with a crooked smile.

CHAPTER 35

This time when Atae and Jeqi arrive at their assigned position within the tournament arena, Marqee and Sloan are waiting for them. Marqee flashes his dimpled smile at Jeqi, and she returns it with a small blush before looking over the arena. Atae is too distracted by Beast's flight-or-fight urges to notice the exchange. When, what feels like, the millionth wave of adrenaline and anxiety blasts through her psyche, Atae groans and rubs her eyes in frustration. She follows Jeqi up the small dirt ramp that leads to their translucent energy dome, where both Marqee and Sloan wait. As always, the moment they step through the energy field, the cameras activate, and Atae feels like an insect under a magnifying glass.

"You look like you need to meditate some more," Sloan says.

"You know what? I think you're right," Atae says. "I'm going to stand way over there, so you stay here and practice the art of silence."

Atae shuffles over to the edge of the dome, but instead of closing her eyes to meditate, she examines the arena. Thirty energy ramps lead to base camps that carve into the arena walls. Outside the bases, the dirt and gravel floor dips into a giant bowl-like valley with the white energy platform from round two at its epicenter. At the top of a massive pile of rock and dirt, the platform towers above the rest of the arena like a glowing lighthouse. Atae wonders what part the energy disc will play in this round.

Atae asks Beast to assess their competition as each base fills with its assigned pack. She complies, happy to keep an eye on their enemies. With Beast distracted, Atae takes a deep breath and revels in her reprieve from her counterpart's never-ending pressure. She mulls over everything she's learned about Beast over the past several days.

How can I prove to you that I'm strong enough to protect us? she asks.

You cannot because you are not. I am strong. I am Kaji.

I got us through that maze, even when you were trying to get us killed. I'm the reason we made it through.

Lies, Beast says. She slaps Atae's mind with a red whip. *I kept us alive. Jeqi helped more than you.*

What's that supposed to mean?

Without our packmate, you would have failed. We would have died.

Atae snorts at Beast's melodramatic statement. No one died in either round of the tournament. But is she right about Jeqi? Is Atae leaning on the blonde too much? Jeqi has been an excellent packmate since Beast's appearance. Even before that, she was there to comfort Atae in the wake of Kandorq's attack. Jeqi has always been a good friend. But maybe that's the point. Perhaps it's time for Atae to stand on her own, at least long enough for her to show Beast that she can. Atae swivels to watch her makeshift pack and finds them chatting about last night's hilt session between Sloan and Atae.

"I especially liked the part where you disarmed her for like the hundredth time," Marqee says between chuckles. "And she got so mad that she broke your arm, trying to get it back."

"Yeah, I probably shouldn't have held it over her head like that." Sloan shrugs.

"You think?" Atae says. "I'm pretty sure taunting your student is the least effective way to teach."

"Atae, you literally bit off a chunk of his ear," Jeqi says. "I don't think you can blame that on Sloan's teaching method."

All four of them burst into laughter, and even Beast finds it amusing. The warning siren blares to life, and straggling competitors sprint for their assigned bases.

"Here we go again." Atae sighs as her camera zips by her face. Jeqi pats her friend on the back with an encouraging smile.

"We can do this. We are Kaji."

Atae glances at her with a contemplative expression. She opens her mouth to speak but decides against it and just nods. She peers out over the arena in time to see Skiska and Frack's giant holographic heads assemble. Frack throws his arms into the air and announces in a boisterous voice.

"It's time for round three of the Sula Academy Tournament. I must admit that I was pleasantly surprised by our competitors in round two."

"As was I," Skiska says. "They were all rather ruthless toward the end."

"And I expect nothing less from this round, folks. So get ready to see some blood."

"Yes, round three is going to prove far more difficult, I think. It seems each pack has an assigned base on the perimeter of the arena."

With Skiska's words, the domes encircling each base flares green before returning to their translucent hue.

"Yep, and each group must gather as many flags as possible from the energy platform in the center of the arena," Frack says. The white disc hovering over the massive mound of dirt glows bright red for a moment.

"Once a competitor has a flag in their possession," Skiska says, but Frack interrupts.

"And don't try to snag more than one at a time. That's considered cheating, and you'll get a nasty surprise if you do it."

"Good point, Frack. It's important to grab one flag at a time, but feel free to steal from competitors. You won't earn any points this round for incapacitating a competitor, but you can earn a hundred points for each flag you steal from a competing base."

"But you have to get it back to your base," Frack says. "There are two goals for this round. Gather as many flags to your base as possible, and survive the longest."

"That's right. You see, as soon as you get your first flag back to your camp, you have to defend it. And not just from other competitors."

"Nope," Frack says. "It's the hordes that you have to worry about. Once your base is established with your first flag, you have to keep the horde from entering your base. If your base is overrun, then your pack is done."

"Hordes of what?" Marqee asks.

"Nothing good," Jeqi, Atae, and Sloan chant together.

"The twenty packs that last the longest will advance to the next round. For each small member of the horde killed, packs will earn five points plus fifty points for the big ones. Once your pack is overrun, your dome will reactivate. You can retreat to safety until the round ends, or you can continue earning points by fighting the hordes," Skiska says.

"At that point, you can't steal any more flags, but other packs can steal your flags. So you better not leave them unprotected," Frack says.

"Well, I think that's everything you need to know about this round."

"That's right. Let the bloodshed begin!"

As the two giant heads disappear, a sheet of rain falls from the energy dome above, soaking everything within moments. The rain beats against the energy field above their base, and Atae glances at Jeqi. The blonde has always enjoyed the sounds of rainstorms, but with her tail wrapped around her waist, she doesn't look happy about this new obstacle. The base domes remain active while a small jungle takes shape below. Branches and leaves sprout from the ground and cover the valley. Roots crawl up the hillside and latch on to rocks and boulders. Giant logs hide among fallen leaves and bushes. A fog appears and swirls between the camps and the platform, creating an ominous feel. As if the arena is replicating a murky day in the wilds, the rain slows to a drizzle, and the lights dim into a lazy haze.

"It's a jungle made of energy constructs," Jeqi says. "Neat."

Atae agrees with her packmate, but Beast snuffs her nose at the imitation. The blue hybrid smirks at her counterpart and swivels to face her makeshift pack.

"We don't have long. What's the plan?" Atae asks.

Everyone stares at Jeqi, and she huffs.

"Get a flag. Meet back here. We'll reassess after that."

"Sounds good to me," Sloan says.

Everyone faces the arena and waits for the dome to drop. Ready to run at her side, Jeqi slips in next to Atae. Atae grimaces at another wave of anxiety from Beast then makes a decision.

"I need you to stay away from me, Jeqi."

"What?" Jeqi steps back in surprise.

"I need to do this alone. I need to prove that I can do it alone."

"Of course you can do it alone, but you don't have to. That's why we're pack."

"I know. But this...I need to do it alone. To *prove* that I am strong enough," Atae says. She emphasizes the word 'prove' so that Jeqi will understand to whom she is proving her strength. The camera buzzes close to her ear as a reminder of the thin line she walks with Solum looking over her shoulder.

"Okay." Jeqi shrugs with a frown. "I understand. I know you'll do well. With or without me."

Beast's anxiety surges into a flood of golden panic that crashes throughout Atae's mind, and her heart rate picks up from the adrenaline rush. She smiles at her packmate, hiding the storm within. Then the energy fields dissipate, and everyone rushes into the jungle. When the dome drops, Atae gasps at the icy cold rain that pelts against her skin. Sucking in a freezing breath, she steps off the base onto the energy ramp and falls flat on her face. The slick rain makes traction on the smooth energy field nearly impossible. Sloan and Marqee skim past her with a loud cackle from the darker heir. Atae catches a glimpse of Jeqi disappearing into the thick fog and wonders if going it alone was the best choice.

Atae ignores the snickers from her inner counterpart and scrambles back to the solid ground of her base. Once she gathers herself again, Atae runs toward the ramp and leaps. When she lands, her feet slip down the slope, and Atae adjusts to stay upright during the ride. When she hits the slick mud below, her momentum and the steep grade of the hill combine to pull her further than she expects. With a smile, she surfs down the knoll until a rock crosses her path, and she tumbles.

Atae pulls her arms in close and rolls into a ball, but the force of her fall is painful. She scrapes across gravel that digs into her exposed skin. A low-hanging branch whacks her in the face, and her eyes tear up. A root the size of her head reaches up and slams into her knee halfway down the hill. Atae cries out in pain until she rolls to a stop against a large, hollow tree trunk at the bottom of the small valley.

Get up, Beast says. She barrels through Atae's mind with a searing, orange flash, but the hybrid gasps for breath as she stares up into the domed sky. She swats at the camera buzzing in her face, and the dribbling rain pats against the thick mud that's caking against her arms and legs. Deeply embarrassed, Atae wonders what it must be like for her father to watch her clumsy fall, and she envisions him shaking his head in shame. Several younglings run past her, but the large bush growing out of the hollow log hides her prone body well. A sudden, white spark lights off the dim sky, and Atae furrows her brow.

What is that?

When screams explode from the direction of the platform, Atae jumps to her feet. The fog and dim lighting prevent Atae from seeing further than a few steps, but she can hear the panicked screams and other younglings scampering past. She pulls her hilt from its holster and activates it. The light from the small energy blade glints across her mud-covered face, and she grimaces as a large cut on her cheek scabs over.

Ignoring her throbbing knee, Atae marches through the jungle in the rain and mud. She pushes forward until the tail blade of a battle beast swings out of the fog and straight for her head. Atae drops to the ground and rolls to the side under a large bush, expecting the purebred to be on her heels. Instead, she can hear it growling and snapping inside the mist. Beast warns her to run, but Atae waits for the Kajian to step forward. She listens to it crash into the plant life all around and rustle among the leaves and mud. When an alien screech pierces the night, Atae realizes that the battle beast is fighting something else, something big.

She decides to maneuver around the fight without interrupting. Unable to see through the fog, Atae uses the sounds of the scrap to keep her distance. When she's far enough from the noise of snapping and tearing, Atae breathes easy and continues toward the center of the arena. At least, she thinks it's the center. It's tough to determine direction through the thick fog and rain. Atae follows a trampled path through the leaves, pressing deeper into the jungle. It isn't long before she notices a red light maneuvering through the mist.

Atae can hear the light rustling through the hidden bushes before it disappears into the fog. Another one appears a moment later from a different direction, and Atae ducks low to the ground to let it pass her unnoticed. Beast's low-humming anxiety isn't much help in deciphering whether or not the red lights are threats, so Atae opts to slip past them undetected whenever possible. She avoids three more red lights before bumping into a massive wall of mud. Atae glances up to find a red light hovering above her, but still hidden by the fog. She jumps out of the way, and a hybrid with green hair lands in a crouch with a red, glowing rod strapped to her back.

A flag.

The green hybrid darts away and disappears into the fog. Beast grumbles from within a churning brown and gold swarm of particles as Atae spins back to the massive mound of mud. She grabs the nearest branch sticking out from the slick slope and pulls herself up to reach the next foothold. She scrambles up the slippery wall, digging her fingers into the gravel and clay until she reaches the top.

Heaving herself over the edge and onto the white energy platform, Atae rolls to her feet and scans the area for an immediate threat. No one else is on the platform, and the mist stops below the lip of the disk. Atae wipes rain and mud from her face and peers out over the low-lying fog. She spots Jeqi climbing the ramp to their base, and Marqee bursts from the jungle to follow in her footsteps. Beast catches sight of several unconscious Kaji scattered along the platform, and she warns Atae to be cautious.

Another competitor climbs onto the platform and spots Atae. The purebred snarls at her before darting toward a row of white rods protruding from the center of the platform. The flags line a large black circle, and the competitor tugs one rod free. Upon his touch, it glows red, and he uses the attached strap to swing it around to his back. Atae steps forward to grab a flag, and the purebred decides to snag a second. When the second activated rod touches the first, an explosion erupts from the two flags. The blast throws the unconscious and badly marred Kajian over the edge of the platform.

No cheating.

Both Atae and Beast snicker as the blue hybrid swings a flag over her shoulder. Before she has a chance to leap off the platform into the fog, another white spark explodes in the sky. She glances up as the pretty sparks dance through the air then fall into the night. Again, she wonders what it means. Then the black circle at the center of the platform slides open, and the most massive clamox beast Atae has ever seen crawls out.

The massive, fur-covered arachnid towers over Atae with its eight hairy legs and slimy jaws. The creature ducks its boney head to point its long, sharp horn at Atae and charges. The hybrid springs to the side, hoping to outmaneuver the gigantic beast, but its long legs make it far more agile than she anticipates. It twirls to face her and spits a spray of webbing that burns at the skin across her face. She screams and rips it away as Beast blasts her psyche with commands to run from the clamox.

You are too weak to stop it. Let me kill it, or run and cower.

No. I am Kaji. Atae darts toward the giant arachnid with her hilt drawn.

When the creature spits another spray of acidic webbing, Atae dodges to the right and jumps toward an unsuspecting limb. She slices through the appendage as close to the abdomen as she can reach. The clamox screeches as green blood spews from the severed leg. It whips the stump around, coating the platform in the sticky fluid. Another leg slips in the slime, and the creature stumbles, slamming its abdomen into the ground. Atae uses the opening to leap onto the clamox beast's back and drive her blade deep into its lean body. It screams and flails as Atae runs her small sword through the length of the creature.

As she pulls her hilt free of the carcass, Atae steps down into the green pool of blood as it mixes with the light rainfall. She grimaces at the foul smell and swats as her camera buzzes her ear, but she inwardly gloats to her counterpart. Beast ignores Atae's claims to victory and watches the dead creature from within a purple and brown swirl.

Beast flashes orange in warning, and Atae spins back to the dead clamox to find dozens of smaller versions of the creature erupting from the egg sack hidden within its fur. The smaller clamox are the size of Atae's head and much faster. They scuttle toward her and latch onto her legs before she has time to move. Kicking and screaming at them, Atae shuffles backward and over the edge of the platform with her camera zipping after her.

CHAPTER 36

Atae lands hard among the leaves and mud of the jungle floor, and fog swirls around to meet her. Stunned from the impact, she tries to suck air into her lungs, but they refuse to respond. She rolls over to find two clamox smashed under her body and a third crawling across her stomach. She scrapes it off her body, and it tumbles away. As the small creature climbs to its eight long legs, Atae scrambles for her hilt. She finds it lying to her left and snatches it, activating the blade. The clamox launches into the air toward her face only to be met with Atae's energy blade. She spears the arachnid into the mud.

Expecting the remaining horde to follow, Beast growls at Atae to move. When her lungs recover, Atae jumps to her feet and sprints into the fog with her red flag glowing against her back. Atae catches sight of a red light peeking through the mist straight ahead, and she unsheathes her blade, hoping to dispatch the competitor and move along. Breaking through the fog, Atae leaps at the unsuspecting purebred and finds a long energy sword waiting to deflect her attack. Sloan pushes Atae's blade aside with a flick of his wrist and tugs the hilt out of her hand.

"How many times have I told you not to attack at that angle? It sets you up for an easy disarm," he says.

"Sloan? What happened to you?"

A grotesque mixture of green slime and mud drips from the dark heir's face and neck to cover his chest. The drizzle, too light to wash the filth away, makes the sticky mess worse. Sloan flashes a crooked smile, and Atae grimaces at the green between his teeth.

"Did you bite one of them?"

"You're one to talk about biting. Speaking of which, here's this back," Sloan says. Atae takes the hilt from his offered hand and smiles in realization.

"You were the battle beast that fought the first clamox. You almost took my head off with a wild tail strike," she says.

"Yeah, that thing was mean. But the little ones? They are creeping me out. Don't let them bite you."

"I don't plan on it." Beast huffs at her inability to stop the small arachnids so far, and Atae hangs her head. She grimaces at the memory of her hastened retreat that ended in a graceless fall.

Maybe, you're right. Maybe, you could do better.

Finally, you see the truth. Let me free to destroy our enemies, Beast says.

The horde breaks through the fog in a wave of angry hisses. Atae jumps back onto a fallen log and swipes at the arachnids with her hilt. The energy blade cuts through them like butter, and they shrivel up into balls as she hacks away at them. But they keep coming, no matter how many she kills. The living creatures climb over their dead comrades until a pile of corpses lay at Atae's feet. She notices Sloan having similar problems at her side.

When Atae steps back from a particularly aggressive clamox that jumps straight at her face, she stumbles off the log and lands in a thick pool of mud. Staying focused, Atae manages to slice the attacking creature in half mid-flight, but she struggles to keep the remaining horde off her fallen body. One arachnid pierces her leg with its venomous jaws, and she cries out in pain before raking her energy blade through its prone body. Sloan pulls her from under the horde by her uniform and drags her to her feet.

"Come on."

He points at a nearby tree the size of a house. She tries to run after him, but a searing pain lances up her injured leg, and she stumbles. Catching herself on a nearby branch, Atae hobbles after Sloan as she swings her blade at the pursuing horde. The thick fog conceals everything but a few steps ahead, so Atae yelps in surprise when she stumbles on to two younglings lost in the mist. Sloan and Atae dart past their competitors, who jump in surprise.

"Hey," a purebred named Quin calls out, but he changes his tune when the horde converges on them. Atae hopes that her classmates will distract the arachnids long enough for her and Sloan to escape up the tree. Just as Sloan and Atae reach the base of the massive tree, the ground gives way under their feet, and they plummet down a steep bank of mud. Their fall is short, but the muck, gravel, and leaves that they dragged down blocks their path out.

Sloan jumps up and scans the area for threats before knocking some gunk from his uniform. He stands in the center of a sinkhole under the tree and peers up into the sky between the giant roots and dripping rain. The slick mud will make it hard to climb out, but they can do it. Sloan glances down to find Atae sitting on the ground and clutching her injured leg. He rushes to her and rips open her pant leg to assess the wound.

"It's just a bite," Sloan says. "It's going to hurt pretty bad for a little while, but it'll heal quickly. We'll have to wait until then to climb out of here."

"We can't wait," Atae says. She motions toward the sounds of fighting above them. "Those things can easily slip through the cracks. They'll swarm us again, and we'll have nowhere to go."

Atae grimaces as a sharp pain shoots through her leg, and she digs her hands into the mud at her side. With each wave of pain, Beast beats against her confines, spilling her red anger into Atae's psyche. The blue hybrid struggles to keep her counterpart from activating a shift as two cameras circle above them. When she feels the bite of her claws extending into the thick mud, Atae sighs in resignation.

"You have to leave me," Atae whispers, but another burst of white light drowns out her words. Sloan watches the anger and shame twist across her face as the flickering lights streak across the sky. Then the light dissipates, and the shadows hide her expressions from him.

"What?" Sloan asks.

"Another horde is coming. You have to leave me here and go help Jeqi and Marqee protect the base."

"Are you crazy?"

Atae blinks at the question. *Maybe I am.*

"What?" she says.

"I said, are you crazy? I'm not leaving you here. We need your flag points. You're not incapacitated or unconscious. There is no reason to leave you here."

"I'm weak and injured. At this point, I'm just a hindrance."

Sloan laughs and twists away from Atae in exasperation, and she stares at him in disbelief.

"What's wrong with you?" she says. "Why are you being so difficult? I thought you'd jump at a chance to prove once and for all that you're the better warrior."

"I don't need a chance to prove I'm a better warrior, Atae. It's obvious every time you pick up a hilt. I just find it hilarious that now you're worried about being a hindrance." Sloan throws his hands into the air, and Atae glowers at him. As the pain from her leg ebbs, so does Beast's rampage, and Atae sighs in relief.

"What's that supposed to mean?" she asks.

"You've been a thorn in my side since I started at Sula Academy. I am one of six heirs to the Levia crest. I should be at the top of my class with no competition, especially not from hybrids. Instead, I'm constantly fighting for second place with you and can't get near Jeqi's monopoly on first place. Do you know how much flack I get from my family because of you?"

"So? What do I care about your family issues?"

Atae growls as another wave of pain pulsates through her leg. This time, Beast doesn't use the opportunity to press Atae for control. Instead, her red swirl of mist darkens to a solemn purple as she listens to Sloan.

"Exactly," he says. "You don't care. You didn't even know I was an heir until I threw it in your face. The fact that you are one of the strongest younglings I've ever met has been a thorn in my side for seasons."

Sloan crouches and snatches Atae's face in both hands. She wants to stop him, but pulling her hands from the mud would reveal her shift. Instead, she stares as he lowers his gaze to peer into her fuchsia eyes. Rain slips down her face and onto his hands as he snarls at her.

"But not today. Today, you are on my side. For the duration of this tournament, your knack for besting opponents far above your skill level will actually help me. Today, you are anything but a thorn. So there is no way I am letting you give up that easily."

Beast tenses against his proximity to Atae's vulnerable state. The blue-haired hybrid closes her eyes and clenches against her counterpart's attempt to shift. Trying with all her might, she cannot stop her forearm blades from slipping free. As they break her skin, Sloan releases her face and grabs her arms, covering the sharp points with his rough hands. He flinches when the blades bite into his palms, but he doesn't pull away. Surprised, Beast pauses mid-shift.

"You, Atae," Sloan says. "You earned the second-place ranking. You broke Marqee's leg on three separate occasions. You trained with Solum for seasons, and you defeated Solum. You are strong. You are Kaji."

Atae watches the grit and drive surging through Sloan's onyx gaze, and Beast stares into the red eyes of his counterpart. Something from his inner beast persuades Beast to take heed of Sloan's words. With a sigh, Beast takes a step back from Atae's mind, and the hybrid breathes easy. The constant pressure from Beast ebbs, and her presence saunters into a corner to watch. Feeling the tips of her blades recede from his palms, Sloan smirks.

"And on a good day, you can almost defeat me," he says. Atae snorts and pushes him away with normal hands.

"On my worst day, I could stomp you into the ground."

Atae watches Sloan turn away, then wipe his bloody hands on his uniform.

What does he know? Atae frowns, eyeing the camera zipping by her head.

Everything, Beast says.

Searching for an escape route, Sloan inspects the hole they tumbled down. Atae watches him with renewed eyes. She wonders the truth of Beast's words until she notices a small arachnid scuttling between the giant tree roots. Atae jumps to her feet, surprised to find her leg mostly healed, and darts forward to impale the intruder with her hilt. Keeping an eye out for more, Atae calls to Sloan.

"We're running out of time."

"Yeah, yeah. I'm working on it."

Watching the twisting roots for movement, an idea forms in Atae's mind that makes Beast smile with anticipation. Atae jumps and spears one large root, cutting it free from the crumbling mud and debris. She repeats the process two more times before a section of the ceiling caves.

"Hey, I found our way out," Atae says. She stares up into the dim sky and smiles against the onslaught of cold rain.

"Good, because our way in is now serving the horde. Let's go," Sloan says. He rushes past her to climb out of the hole. Atae glances at the mud and leaves that cover their path into the sinkhole, and she frowns at the horde scampering through the cracks and crevices. She grabs Sloan's outreached hand, and he pulls her up and out.

"Any idea which direction our base is in?" Atae asks, and Sloan shrugs.

"Nope."

"Great."

A giant clamox barrels through the thick mist toward Atae and Sloan. They both dart away in different directions, and Atae takes a leg out on her way. The tall creature stumbles under the loss of a limb as green blood spews, but it stays upright and sprays a large glob of acidic web at her. Beast growls at Atae to dodge it; instead, she smiles and jumps right at the webbing, using her hilt to slice it in half. It falls away, and Atae charges toward the giant arachnid. A few steps before reaching the clamox, another one joins the fray. The second massive creature charges at Atae with its horned head positioned low, but she uses a nearby tree branch to jump over the beast's dangerous horns. Atae lands on its hairy abdomen and stabs her blade deep into its flesh.

She hangs on tight as the creature stands tall over the fog and tries to shake her off. Atae uses the opportunity to pinpoint their location in the arena and smiles when she realizes how close they are to home base. When the eggs hidden in the arachnid's fur crack open, Atae cringes and puts the poor creature down with a yank of her sword. The clamox collapses, and Atae rolls away to avoid the new horde. She finds Sloan waiting next to the corpse of the other giant clamox, and he rushes her along.

"Let's go before we're overrun."

"That way." Atae points toward the base. "It's not far."

Using roots and rocks for traction, Sloan follows Atae up the muddy hill. When they reach the energy ramp, Atae scrambles up, and Sloan can't help but laugh at her flailing arms and legs. At the top of the ramp, a dome glows green, and Jeqi and Marqee guard the edge with ranged hilts. They fire energy blasts at a few small clamox that managed to follow Sloan and Atae to the base.

"What took you guys so long?" Marqee asks. He surveys the jungle edge for pursuers, but the rolling fog makes it hard to decipher shadows from threats.

"Oh, we stopped for tea," Sloan says. He cocks a sarcastic eyebrow at Marqee as he slips his flag into an open slot next to the other two.

"And we had some lovely biscuits," Atae says.

She chuckles, and Sloan smiles at her. Marqee pauses in his perimeter check to glance at Atae in surprise. She shrugs and pulls her flag free of the strap.

"Well, I'm so glad that you two were having fun while we've been busy earning points," Marqee says.

"Oh, man. I'm sorry. All we've been doing is killing giant, acid-spitting, horned arachnids," Sloan says.

"You got one of the big ones? Those are worth fifty points," Jeqi says. Her tail twitches around her waist with excitement, but she stays on guard for any incoming threats.

"Four, actually. Because I'm a badass," Atae says. She slips in next to her packmate with a smug grin. Beast scans the fog for threats, while Atae searches the horizon. Sloan unsheathes his hilt, and it zings to life.

"Hey, two of those were my kills."

"Yeah, yeah. Whatever." Atae waves him away then points at one of the other glowing bases. "What's going on over there?"

Four cameras buzz throughout the group as they watch another pack shoot energy blasts at the small shadows in the dark and one massive clamox beast. The base guards panic when the horde swarms from the dead carcass of their downed prey. When the smaller arachnids cross the dome barrier, it falls.

"I guess they lose," Marqee says. "Should we go steal their flags?"

"No," Sloan and Atae answer together.

"Well, I'm convinced. It's not often that you two actually agree on something," Marqee says. He glances up when another white explosion lights the dim sky.

"We need to prepare for the horde," Atae says. "The big ones are mean, but it's the little ones that will overrun us."

"And when you kill the big ones, their babies go homicidal," Sloan says.

"Great, Marqee and I will stay up here and pick off as many as we can from a distance," Jeqi says. She points at Sloan and Atae. "You two stand at the base of the ramp and kill any that make it through."

"Let's do it," Atae says.

She flashes an excited smile, and Beast warns her of the dangers of the horde. She brushes off her counterpart's anxiety with a shrug and slips down the ramp with ease. She activates her hilt and waits for Sloan to join her. They stand there for a while, waiting for the horde to strike, but the ranged hilts pick off what small clusters break through the fog. Several white explosions spark the sky during their wait, and Marqee announces the demise of each dome he watches grow dim.

After a dozen bases fall, a couple of giant clamox burst from the mist and charge toward Atae and Sloan. Jeqi takes the first one down with a couple of well-aimed energy blasts, and Marqee manages to take down the second shortly after. Sloan and Atae steel their resolve in preparation for the hordes to come. Sure enough, the smaller arachnids attack in a swarm of hairy legs.

"Another base down," Marqee calls as he blasts several hissing arachnids into oblivion.

"And another," Jeqi says.

Atae can barely hear them over the onslaught. She swings her blade at the skittering creatures and kicks at their faces. She stomps on their segmented bodies when they get too close and smiles when the brave ones jump at her. She just flicks her hilt, and the attacking arachnid falls to pieces. For the first time in what seems like forever, Atae savors the adrenaline coursing through her veins. Even when a couple of the bugs scamper past her blade, she laughs and dropkicks the clamox back into the fog.

Beast watches from her ball of golden anxiety at first, but then she eases into the fray of battle. When a clamox gets too close, Beast presses a gentle orange warning, and Atae reacts. When another aggressive arachnid leaps into the air toward Atae's face, Beast suggests using her forearm blades but doesn't fight against Atae's decision to use the hilt instead. She watches Atae and Sloan fight back to back against the horde as Jeqi and Marqee guard overhead.

When Jeqi and Marqee take down another two giant clamox, the new hordes collide with the arachnids already swarming. The enormous throng slams into Atae and Sloan and overrun them. Three clamox latch onto Atae's legs before she can stop them. She scrapes them off with her hilt only to have another scamper up her arm and sink its fangs into her shoulder. She cries out and grabs the small arachnid, ripping it away. Atae keeps swinging and kicking at the bugs as they crawl over her face and body, but after a few more bites, she falls to her knees in pain.

As they swarm past her, Atae watches her dome fall. Through the haze of pain and incoming darkness, she can see her packmates falling. Marqee manages to shift and tear into a dozen arachnids before succumbing to the horde. Soaked in green slime, Jeqi claws away chunks of a giant clamox that gets too close until a glob of acidic webbing surprises her. She screams in pain when the throng overcomes her, too. Sloan rages at the top of the ramp, killing everything in sight with a swing of his blade. Atae's attacks are clumsy and basic compared to his elegance and grace. Still on her knees, Atae swings her hilt like a bat and cuts through the clamox as they crawl over her. Beast roars in her mind to keep fighting, and her counterpart's anger and determination empower Atae to keep moving even as an arachnid latches onto her shoulder.

Atae screams and throws her back against the ground to crush the offending creature, but the multitude of arachnids surges. When another searing bite tears into her chest, Atae can't scream due to the weight of the horde on top of her. Through the mass of legs and hairy segments, she glances up to find Sloan faltering. Atae's last sight before falling into the dark arms of unconsciousness is Sloan stumbling to the ground.

CHAPTER 37

Atae awakens with a sudden jolt. Jeqi places a comforting hand on her shoulder and presses her back against the recovery chair. Atae complies, and Beast's swirling orange haze calms to a soft blue. With a sigh, the blue hybrid glances at her blonde packmate, who sits in a separate recovery chair to her right. The two females lie in the center of the palace medical wing.

"How long have I been out?" Atae asks. She checks over her gel-lathered wounds. "These look almost healed."

"I just woke up, too." Jeqi grimaces with her eyes closed as her silver tail sways lazily at her side. "The attendant mentioned that Solum ordered us to be cared for in the palace. I don't think we've been here long."

"Where is Father?" Atae glances around for him. Instead, she finds Sloan unconscious in the chair to her left and Marqee on the other side of Jeqi.

"I don't know. I haven't seen him," Jeqi says.

"Don't worry, Blue. He was here to check up on you and make sure his only daughter is treated with the utmost of care," Prince Truin says. He saunters toward them from the other side of the med wing.

"My prince, it's always a pleasure to see you," Atae says, flashing him a sarcastic smile.

"Atae," Jeqi says. "Please excuse her, Your Highness. She obviously suffered some brain damage in the tournament today."

"Ha." Prince Truin sneers at Atae but doesn't comment. Instead, he grins at Sloan's unconscious form and strolls up to his friend to yank on his nose.

"Wakey, wakey."

Murmuring curses, Sloan groans into consciousness and slaps at the prince's hand. He grasps at his bare chest and smears the healing gel slathered across his dark muscles.

"I hate clamox."

"I think they hate you, too," Prince Truin says.

"Why are you here?" Atae asks. Jeqi punches her in the arm, and she scowls at the blonde. "Ow. What? Why are you hitting me?"

"Can you treat the prince and heir to the Kaji Empire with a little respect before he banishes us to the kitchen?"

"He can't reprimand us," Atae says. She glances at Prince Truin with a smug smile. "Queen Sula said so. We're her protégées, remember?"

"Ah, but there are so many other ways to punish you," Truin says.

"Uh, before this turns into the pissing match of the ages," Sloan says. "Why are you here, Truin?"

"I just wanted to be the one to tell you how you guys ranked in this round." Prince Truin brandishes an evil grin before he activates his visual visor from to read. "Taking down all those giant clamox first earned you guys the most points by far."

Jeqi glances at Atae, and she grins back. Beast ignores the excitement with a roll of her eyes, and Sloan eyes his friend.

"But," he says.

"But you worked them into such a frenzy that they targeted your base way before they decided to take down the majority of the bases. Fifteen bases out-survived you guys."

"Fifteen? That means we barely qualified for the next round," Atae says. Jeqi huffs, and her tail taps the ground in disappointment. Sloan glances at the two hybrids and shrugs.

"But we did qualify, and it sounds like we got a lot of points. Any idea where we rank overall in the tournament?" Sloan says. Prince Truin frowns in concentration as he flicks his wrist and waves his fingers at the hologram.

"Looks like...oh, not too bad. You guys are third overall."

"Yes." Atae pumps her arm in the air.

"I wouldn't get too excited, Blue," Truin says. "You're on your own in the next round. No one there to save you this time."

"I don't need anyone to save me. But if I did, I have a pack. How about you?" Atae sneers at her prince, and Truin grits his teeth.

"I have to admit it. You impressed me today. You almost saved me the trouble of outing you to Solum."

"Truin," Sloan says, but it's too late.

"Out me about what?" Atae asks. She gasps at the cold realization clawing up her spine, and Beast growls at Prince Truin's threat. He stares at the blue hybrid with a twisted smirk.

"Schinn's been begging to reveal your newest ability to Solum since the beginning. He's very concerned about your well-being. But Sloan's been so adamant that you'll eventually be an asset that I decided we'd see what you could do in the tournament. I honestly expected you to lose it and go feral by now. But here you are, keeping it together. As I said, I'm impressed."

Atae stares at Prince Truin in surprise and horror, unable to form a response. A cold terror settles into her chest, but Beast claws at it and sets Atae's veins ablaze with molten fury. She snarls at the hybrid prince.

"If you're going to rat me out like the spoiled little shit that you are, do it. Don't threaten me and expect me to fall in line like one of your little lackeys."

Atae's voice is brazen with Beast's confidence, and Prince Truin glares at her impudence. Jeqi covers her face in defeat; she's sure their secret from Solum is over. Sloan watches the exchange between his prince and Atae with obvious amusement. No one ever gives Truin flack, except him, of course.

Marqee's groans into consciousness do nothing to ease the palpable tension as Atae and Truin glare at each other. The dimpled purebred glances around at the stalemate.

"What did I miss?"

"We got the most points, but barely advanced to the next round of the tournament. Truin threatened to out Atae to Solum. Atae is not taking it lying down and thus commenced the stare down," Sloan says. Atae huffs and leans back in her chair to roll her eyes at the larger purebred.

"Again, with the sarcasm, Sloan?"

"That's all he is, sarcasm and bitterness," Prince Truin says. "Anyway, the point is moot. I've decided not to out you. I think you'll do it all on your own. You would have today, if not for Sloan. Either way, I'm off to gather intelligence on our enemies. Since we are one big, happy pack."

Atae frowns at Prince Truin as he strolls away with a loud cackle. Beast sneers at the smaller Kajian's retreating form before settling back into her haze of blue calm.

"He knows?" Atae asks Sloan. Then she slaps him across his wounded chest. "How does he know? And for that matter, how do you know?"

"Ow. Who doesn't know?"

She slaps him again, but this time he catches her hand in his, clutching it with a firm grip.

"I told them. You looked like you needed help. All confused and whatnot." Sloan wiggles his fingers at her, but Atae's glare prompts him to continue his explanation. "Look, Schinn is an expert at shifting."

"At least he's supposed to be," Marqee says. Jeqi glances at him in surprise.

"But to get him on board, I needed Prince Truin and Trikk on board." Sloan releases Atae's hand when she jerks at it.

Trikk? Who is Trikk? Atae frowns. Try as she might, she doesn't remember Prince Truin's second royal guard.

"So wait," Jeqi says. "If Schinn didn't tell you, how did you find out?"

"Sloan and I saw her blades and eyes shift during round one." Marqee shrugs. "They were pretty obvious. And the fact that you thought we didn't notice is really insulting."

"Why didn't you say anything?" Jeqi asks him.

"Because we want you both fighting to protect Truin in the Gridiron. Otherwise, what use are you?" One corner of Marqee's mouth quirks up into a teasing smirk, brandishing his dimples, and Jeqi fights a small smile.

"So, you're recruiting us?"

"You've already been volunteered for Team Truin. We're just making sure you follow through," Sloan says. He glances at Atae, reminding her of her faux pas in the throne room.

"But the pledging ceremony was after round one. You had plenty of time to out me to Solum. Why didn't you? And Prince Truin said you're the reason he didn't out me. Why would you advocate for me?" Atae asks Sloan. She stares at him, searching for a sign of deception in his dark face, but he answers honestly.

"Because I wanted you on my side in the tournament and the Gridiron. I certainly didn't want you on the other side."

"Another thorn?" Atae asks with a small smile. Sloan frowns, cradling his tender chest.

"More like a needle. A small, painful needle."

CHAPTER 38

"We have failed to track down the mercenary. All ten sectors have been cleared," reports the flickering image of a Kaji warrior. "We will continue surveillance at the border stations, but we can no longer maintain the Barrier. I don't know how, but this honorless scum has slipped our defenses. Nothing can penetrate the Barrier, so I can only assume that he is hiding until it falls. We will flush him out soon, Advisor Solum. He will not escape us."

Solum glares at the small hologram on his workstation. His dark hands grasping the edges of the desk, Solum struggles to control his anger as the miniature warrior flashes out of existence. Solum snarls and slams his fists into the desktop, and the wood splinters under the force of his blow. He sweeps his arms across the workstation, and crumbling metal and intricate mechanisms fly across his office into the nearby wall. He howls at the injustice of the universe loud enough for half the palace to hear him. When his rage ebbs, Solum surveys the damage to his modest office and sighs in resignation. His gaze falls to the remains of his workstation, and he grimaces.

I've failed.

A knock at the door interrupts Solum's dark thoughts, and he grumbles at the intrusion.

"Enter," he says. The door slides open, and Feku steps inside to salute his packmate.

"Solum."

"Feku, what do you want?" Solum says.

He frowns at his daughter's mentor, while Feku raises an eyebrow at the remains of Solum's workstation strewn across the room

"I came to discuss Atae, but your howling has me intrigued. It's not every day that the great Solum is rattled enough to destroy his office."

"It's none of your concern," Solum says. He crosses his arms over his broad chest, and Feku's usual scowl twists into a mischievous grin at the chance to needle his long-time friend.

"You received bad news," Feku says. He smiles when Solum growls in confirmation. "You never did take bad news well."

"We've still found no trace of that damn mercenary." Solum throws his hands into the air. "The Patrol is deactivating the Barrier. They will continue surveillance at the border stations, but that doesn't stop him from escaping our territory by standard travel."

"He must use the border stations to travel between stars. Otherwise, it will take him seasons. You've blanketed the empire with warrants for his arrest. With such a large reward, someone will turn him in."

"I've failed to capture him. I've sent warrior after warrior to find him, and each has sent word of their failure. Worthless, all of them," Solum says through clenched teeth. Anger at his poor performance plunges deep into his chest and strikes his pride.

"I remember when we were sent on missions like that," Feku says.

"We never dared to return empty-handed."

"True." Feku shrugs. "But I don't remember completing many missions within a couple of months."

"Why are you here, Feku?"

Solum doesn't appreciate his packmate's attempts to remedy his anger. Enjoying the familiarity of their discussion, Feku smiles. It reminds him of days long past when their pack was ablaze with youthful passion. A time before betrayal and loss scarred what remains of his packmates.

"Atae," Feku says.

"What about her? Is something wrong? Surely, you don't still have concerns about her turning sour?"

"No, having her confront Kandorq directly seems to have resolved most of my earlier concerns. She still seems a bit distracted at times, but nothing alarming."

"Good."

Solum also noticed a marked improvement in Atae's emotional stability, but the damage to their relationship is hard to bear. Atae spent the last few weeks training with her packmates, and Prince Truin monopolized Solum's time at Queen Sula's behest. The only time the father and daughter spent together was over meals, and Atae waffled between distrust, adoration, and resentment during each visit. She no longer seeks him out for advice or training. Solum wonders if the youngling will ever look at him the same again. Still, he does not regret his choice between their relationship and her life.

"What has you concerned, Feku? I've watched her in the tournament, and aside from her sloppy sword work, she's performed admirably."

"Yes, I agree." Feku nods his head. "But something is bothering me."

"What is it?" Solum frowns with an impatient sigh as he leans against his desk.

"There is something different about her. I haven't quite identified it, but something is definitely different."

"She and Jeqi are hiding something."

"Most assuredly. But there is something else, as well." Solum doesn't respond but waits for Feku to continue. The elder warrior places a hand to his chin in thought. "She is doing too well."

"Too well? What do you mean?"

"She is excelling in areas that should be a struggle, if not impossible."

"She surprised you." Solum pauses to consider this new information. "I've been surprised a few times, as well."

"So you've noticed it," Feku says. He sighs, glad to have Solum confirm his suspicions. "Are you certain she cannot shift?"

"Of course, I'm certain. Why would you think that? Have you seen signs?"

"Not since the attack. But hiding a shifting ability would explain her performance in the tournament."

"That's ridiculous. You honestly believe a hybrid youngling could control her brand-new shifting ability well enough to hide it from you and me?" Solum says. "Not to mention the cameras recording her every step in the tournament."

Feku opens his mouth to respond, but Solum cuts him off.

"And the beast. Do you remember how hard it was to control it in the beginning? Sloan's response to Atae in the throne room after the pledging ceremony is exactly what happens when adolescent Kaji are challenged by their beasts. And you think Atae is hiding that?"

Solum throws his arms up and glares at the other warrior for entertaining such foolishness. Feku hides a nostalgic smile as he watches Solum in his aggravated state.

The elder warrior rarely won an argument with the royal advisor. In the past, he left debates to Roga. The feisty female never hesitated to take an opposing position from her mate. Roga dug her heels in and challenged every statement Solum made, all the while boasting an arrogant smirk that drove him mad. She mostly argued against Solum because she enjoyed the challenge, but Roga occasionally argued with conviction. The difference was like night and day. One was playful and humorous; the other was passionate and demanding. When it truly mattered, Roga only ever conceded one argument to Solum. Their last one. Watching Solum's concern and passion for the youngling he fought so hard to prevent, Feku can't help but smile. Life is strange sometimes.

"What is so funny?" Solum says, snapping Feku from his memories.

"You're right," Feku says. "There is no way Atae can shift. It was a silly thought. And if we're wrong, we'll find out in the next round."

"What do you mean?"

"My students will have to contend with trestoids in the final round."

"Ouch. That won't be fun. It sounds like round four is designed to weed out those with control issues."

"Among other things." Feku nods.

"That's wise. And trestoids will definitely put this shifting nonsense to rest, one way or another."

"It should be very entertaining. Anyway, you shouldn't be so hard on Atae's skills with a hilt. Given how little time she's had with one, she's performing adequately."

"Yes, she's improving quickly with Sloan's tutoring. She'll make a decent sword handler if they don't kill each other first. I've sat in on a couple of their sessions." Solum shakes his head at the image of Atae biting off a chunk of Sloan's ear amid a heated match. "You were right to partner them. Sloan is a very skilled sword handler, and he's dominant and stubborn enough to keep her focused. It's a shame that he is a ferog. I'd be surprised if he makes it past round four, given the trestoids. Perhaps, that would be for the best."

"Perhaps," Feku says.

"Do you think he'll go feral?"

"All ferogs go feral at some point, given enough stress. Their beasts are too dominant for them to maintain control over them. That's why they avoid the Gridiron."

"Ferogs are slaves to their beasts." Solum shakes his head. "I almost pity Sloan. Do you think he knows?"

"None of them truly understand what their walking into," Feku says. Sloan's situation is a reminder that all of his students will soon enter the most dangerous Gridiron in history, and many of them will not survive.

"It won't be that bad," Solum says. "You've trained your students well."

"They've had record-breaking entries into the Royal Gridiron, and it's still six months away. I'm responsible for the data they use to project my students' survival rates. It's a very sobering task."

"And Atae's odds?" Solum asks. He twists his mouth to hide his concern for the young hybrid.

"You'll find out with everyone else when I post it to the KIC after the tournament." Feku doesn't have the heart to tell his friend that hybrids are the least likely to survive the Royal Gridiron due to Royce's growing support.

"Rest assured, Solum. Between Marqee, Sloan, and Jeqi, Atae has a solid pack on which to lean when necessary. That's probably why she's doing so well in the tournament."

"Yes, she did very well during the last half of round three. Too bad it took Sloan's pep talk to straighten her out. It's strange what a little confidence can do for younglings," Solum says.

"You're right. She was less distracted and more aware of her surroundings. Almost like-"

"She cannot shift, Feku. It's more likely that she regressed a bit toward souring before Sloan pulled her out of it."

"Okay, fine." Feku smiles and holds his hands up in defeat. "But what do you think they are hiding?"

"I don't know," Solum says with a dismissive shrug. "Honestly, I don't have time to care. They are younglings. Let them have their innocent secrets."

The door swishes open, and Queen Sula Ru-Kai rushes into Solum's office. Her long braid swings at her back as she pushes past Feku. Solum stands from his chair to greet his monarch.

"Queen Sula, what are you doing here? Feku and I were discussing-"

"Get out," Sula says. She points her finger at Feku, and he flinches.

"Sula, is everything okay?" he says. Her menacing glare and threatening growl stop him in his tracks. "As you wish, my queen."

Sula watches Feku leave then scans the room with her piercing amber eyes. She glares at every crevice in the wall until she finds a suspicious knot. Solum watches with a confused curiosity as Sula lunges at the wall behind the holographic map and jams the palm of her hand against the knot. Much to Solum's surprise, a section of the wall slides open to reveal the startled young prince.

The heavy stone creaks to a stop as dust billows out from the ancient passageway. Solum peers over Sula's shoulder and inspects the hidden entrance to his office. He notes the long path leading away and the small peephole in the wall. Solum growls deep in his chest at Prince Truin's blatant violation of his privacy, but also at his failure to notice the youngling's presence.

"Mother! How did you know?" Prince Truin asks. Stunned by his mother's keen perception, he scrambles to brush cobwebs from his face and hair, puffing a breath at the swirling dust particles. She narrows her eyes at him and speaks in a dangerous tone.

"Get out."

"But-"

"I said, get out." Sula grabs her son by the collar, jerking him from his hiding spot. "Or I'll rip your title from you. Then you won't have a reason to go charging into the Royal Gridiron. You can just stay home and watch safely from the sidelines. I truly have no qualms with that."

"Yes, Mother." Prince Truin nods his head in submission. When Sula releases him, Truin spins from her and attempts to leave through the hidden pathways from which he came.

"Not that way," Sula says. Her son rushes to the office door through which Feku exited. Once he is alone with the queen, Solum leans against his damaged desk with a sense of forced calm designed to hide his anxiety over Sula's erratic behavior. He watches the stoic female struggle against inner troubles as she swivels to face Solum. Her heated amber eyes swirl with anger, resentment, and...

And fear? What could possibly frighten Sula?

Then she blinks, and the warrior's mask slips back into place. As her hardened gaze meets his dark orbs, Solum wonders if he imagined the queen's moment of vulnerability.

"I received this just moments ago," Sula says. Her calm tone hides a whirlpool of emotions. She hands Solum a black tablet. Standing straight, he places a single finger on the touch screen, and it jumps to life with a hologram projected from the small screen. The torso and face of a slim, male alien with similar features to the Kaji, albeit scrawnier, stares at Solum. The creature's slender form and green skin give him a reptilian appearance. His long, dark green hair grows from the top of his head and past his shoulders, leaving the sides of his head bald. Solum half expects the creature to flick out a thin, forked tongue like many reptiles. Instead, the alien speaks in a smooth, silky cadence that's almost soothing.

"Queen Sula Ru-Kai, the Camille Empire extends its appreciation for the formal invitation to attend the Gridiron viewing of Prince Truin, heir to the Ru-Kai crest. His Majesty, Emperor of the Camille Empire, regrets to inform you that he will be unable to attend due to the length of the event. He is sending, in his stead, a lady of the court as his representative. She will have a small entourage accompanying her. The emperor trusts that you will see to her every need and treat her in the same respect that you would treat him. The details of her arrival are included with this message."

Solum stares at the holographic image in disbelief as it flickers out of existence. He plays it again to reassure himself that it's real and that he didn't misunderstand. When the light from the image disappears from his dark features, he gapes at Sula. She sits in his office chair with her legs crossed and back straight as though addressing the Crests of Kaji.

"You invited them to the viewing?" Solum asks.

"I did what was expected of me," Sula says. She meets his accusatory glare with a snarl. "The Camille Empire is our ally. The emperor could have taken offense if I didn't include him on the invitation list. How was I to know that he would accept?"

"But he did. He actually accepted it." Solum sets the tablet on the desk and leans against it again, this time for support. "No Camille has left their planet's atmosphere in our known history."

"Until now," Sula says. "The emperor is sending a Camille lady to stay as my guest for the length of the Royal Gridiron. She will also be present at the award ceremony afterward."

Solum glances at his queen as her words hit home, and he asks a question to which he already knows the answer. "Do you think she is being sent to spy on us?"

"Most definitely. The question is, what does she already know?" Sula narrows her eyes. "I think it may be time for the other one to join us."

CHAPTER 39

"You lied to me!" Atae points an accusatory finger at Schinn as she storms into the private training room. She marches toward him, and he retreats a few steps from her wrath. At first, he worries that Beast has seized control again, and he'll be forced to contend with a feral Kaji. But her string of curses proves that Atae maintains control.

"No, I did what I was told," Schinn says. "Where's Jeqi?"

"Don't change the subject. You lied to me. To Jeqi and me, I mean. You told me...us...whatever!"

Schinn steps closer to the irate hybrid and grasps her hands. "Atae."

His tender voice abates the flame of her anger, and his nearness sucks the air from Atae's lungs as her cheeks burn bright. But Beast reminds her counterpart of his treachery, and she rips her hands free of him. Atae steps away to free her mind of the endorphin-fueled haze that his presence incites within her body.

"You said that you heard us while you were in a recovery tank. That you overheard Jeqi and me while we were talking about my shifting ability. That's not true, Schinn."

Of course not. He lies.

Atae shakes her head at the memory of muffled voices right outside her tank after wrestling control back from Beast. She could barely hear Jeqi and Schinn when they stood right next to her tank. There's no way Schinn could've overheard them from across the medical wing.

"You lied. You didn't overhear us. Sloan told you, and you've been reporting to him and Prince Truin about me. How could you do that without telling me? You're a liar. That's why Beast doesn't trust you," Atae says. A sharp pain of betrayal digs deeper into her chest, and Beast coats her mind in an azure haze of concern with hopes of dampening the hurt.

"No," Schinn says. "I mean yes, but only because I thought it was for the best. I didn't think you'd trust me knowing that Sloan had sent me."

Atae nods to acknowledge the rationale but sneers in distaste at the lie.

"You want to out me to my father. You know he'll pull me from the tournament and the Gridiron if he finds out, and you still want Prince Truin to tell him anyway."

"Yes, I think that's the best option for you."

"How dare you!"

"Atae, this isn't fair to you. You deserve proper training. Solum can help you understand your ability in ways that I can't." Schinn throws his palms out, imploring her to listen. Atae scowls at him, and Beast applauds her.

"You don't get to make that decision for me."

"I'm trying to help you. Protect you. Sloan wants to use you in the Gridiron."

"I know. Sloan may be incredibly annoying, but he's been honest about his intentions. I wish I could say the same about you."

"You trust Sloan over me?" Schinn says. "After everything I've done for you? I've helped you control your beast and kept you from turning feral."

Beast bristles within a raging storm of red anger that fuels Atae's fiery temper. Schinn grabs Atae's arm when she turns to walk away from him.

"Don't walk away from me. I'm trying to explain."

"Explain what? That you think I'm weak and can't handle my own shifting ability? I may not look it, but I am Kaji. I can handle anything my body was created to do. With or without your help," Atae says. Beast echoes her words. "We are strong. We are Kaji."

"I know that, Atae. You are skilled for your age, but no Kajian should go through their shifting phase alone."

"I'm not alone. I have Jeqi to help me. Even Sloan has proven helpful. And I thought I had you in my corner too."

The heartbroken expression on Atae's face rips at Schinn. He reaches out for her, but she pulls away.

"I'm here, Atae," he says. "I'm here for you."

He is not worthy, Beast says. She prods her counterpart not to give in to his silent pleas for forgiveness. Atae shakes her head at Schinn.

"I have to go. I'm supposed to practice with the others today."

"We only have a few days before the final round of the tournament, and you almost shifted yesterday in the arena. We need to practice control. I've freed my whole day to work with you," Schinn says. His face twists into mild irritation, and guilt spears Atae.

"I'm sorry, I can't. Not with you. Not now," she says. "Beast and I are doing better. I think we came to an agreement during the last round. I'll practice control with my pack."

Atae shuffles to the exit, and Schinn watches her in silence. Before leaving, she glances back. Her fuchsia eyes meet his silver gaze, and a pain erupts in her chest at his look of abandonment.

"Let's talk after the tournament, okay?" she says. His face brightens a fraction as he nods an agreement, and she offers a small smile, much to Beast's dismay.

******

Later, inside a private training room, Jeqi, Atae, Marqee, and Sloan lie in a circle on their backs with their eyes closed. They all take slow, deep breaths almost in unison as Atae attempts to calm the churning waves within her. She tries to put her anger at Schinn behind her and focus on the task at hand, but the pain of his betrayal keeps digging into her heart. Beast swirls around her inner wound, leaving behind concerned azure particles. When the pain twists into anger, red rage burst from Beast to fuel Atae's fury.

Atae fidgets with an audible sigh, and Sloan grumbles next to her, catching Beast's attention. Her red anger deepens into a crimson need that sends shivers down Atae's spine.

"That's it. I'm done. This is stupid." She jerks upright and shrugs at her pack.

"I agree," Sloan says. He remains on the ground with his eyes closed. Jeqi ignores him as she shifts into a sitting position and stares at Atae with an admonishing frown.

"I thought meditating helped? This is one of Schinn's exercises."

"Well, Schinn is stupid too."

"I agree," Sloan says.

"Okay, it really creeps me out when you two agree on something," Marqee says. He sits up too, flashing a good-natured smile and his adorable dimples. Atae is surprised to see Jeqi blush before she hides it behind a forced scoff.

"What's going on? You've never had a problem with meditating before. You said it helped," Jeqi says.

"Not today. I'd rather do something else. Anything else," Atae says. Her memories of working alongside Schinn fuel her anger and, she jumps to her feet. "Actually, I know what I want to do. I want to fight."

"Finally," Sloan climbs to his feet. "Now, you're talking my language."

"You haven't mastered control over Beast yet," Jeqi says from the ground.

"I can't concentrate on meditating right now. We are too wired," Atae says.

"We?" Marqee asks.

"She means her and Beast," Jeqi says.

"Sounds like you need to burn off some energy," Sloan says. He steps away from the group to unsheathe his blade and waves a challenge at Atae to join him. "Let's see what your shift can do."

Atae and Beast smile together at the invitation, and Atae steps forward to accept. But she stops and twirls around when Jeqi protests.

"No."

"Why not?" Atae asks with an echoing growl from Beast.

"Because you have yet to shift on command. It seems to me that every shift so far has been at Beast's beckoning. Which means you are not in control."

"I'm trying, Jeqi. You act like this is easy."

"And right now, you're acting like you don't care," Jeqi says. She jumps to her feet with a snarl, invading Atae's space.

"As much fun as it would be to watch you two go at it, we have better things to do," Sloan says. "Atae, your Beast is too dominant. You can't control it."

"What?" Jeqi says. Her tail thrashes as she glares at the dark heir.

Atae isn't sure if her packmate is upset because Sloan is contradicting her, or because of the truth of his statement. Beast hums with a green pride, letting Atae know where she stands on the topic.

"How do you know that?" Atae asks.

"That she's dominant or that you can't control her?" Marqee says.

"Both, I guess."

"I know she's dominant because I saw her in the arena before the second round," Sloan says.

"I remember that," Atae frowns. "What were you doing?"

"Schinn thought Sloan's beast would be more dominant than yours. He said having an alpha to follow could help you," Marqee says. He motions to Sloan, who shrugs.

"Surprise, surprise. He was wrong."

"So," a gloating smile spreads across Atae's lips. "Beast and I are more dominant than you and your beast?"

Sloan returns her teasing with a crooked grin. "I don't know. Why don't you try making me submit?"

Atae scoffs at the innuendo and ignores Beast's eagerness. Jeqi, on the other hand, isn't in a playful mood.

"Why do you think Atae won't be able to control her beast? I know her dominance makes things difficult-"

"At her level, it makes it impossible," Sloan says. "Constantly fighting for control slows down her reaction time and affects her concentration in battle. Never mind the mental exhaustion from that kind of warfare. It's just not worth it."

"So what do you suggest? That I just let Beast take control?"

"We can't just let her go feral," Jeqi says.

"No," Sloan says. Fidgeting, he twirls his hilt in his hand as he explains. His tone is calm and nonchalant, but his gaze on Atae is stern and compelling. She can see the sincerity in his expression even as he tries to hide it. "No, you can never give your beast control because you'll never get it back. Controlling your beast is like holding onto a long rope."

"A rope?" Jeqi gapes at the dark heir, but Atae bumps her shoulder in warning, and the blonde snaps her mouth shut.

"Yeah, a rope. The tighter you hold it, the more control you have. If you loosen your grip on your control, the rope slips through your hand. It's okay to slip a bit because it's a pretty long rope. Hell, it's long enough to play some pretty kinky games." Sloan wags his eyebrows at Atae, and she huffs at him. "You can slip up. You can even drop the damn thing as long you're quick to retrieve it. But every moment counts because once you reach the end of the rope, you've got nothing left to grab."

"No rope, no control," Marqee says.

"And you go feral," Atae says. An unsettling anxiety bubbles inside her chest, and Beast watches it with curious eyes.

"That's my theory. But I'm not Schinn, and I didn't come from a family that specializes in shifting phases," Sloan says sarcastically.

"No, your family specializes in killing," Jeqi says. She sucks her cheek to hide her amusement and maintain her serious aura.

"Exactly, so let's skip to the bloody part," Sloan says. He flips his hilt into a firm grip with a flick of his wrist.

"No, wait. What am I supposed to do if I can't control Beast?"

"Don't," Marqee says, and Atae scoffs at him.

"Don't what?"

"Control her. Don't bother." Atae stares at Marqee with an exasperated expression and flips her hands out at him, demanding more.

"He means, use her, don't control her. Work together," Sloan says.

"That's impossible. We're too different. She thinks and feels the complete opposite of me."

I am right. You are wrong, Beast says.

"There's always something you can agree on, just one thing," Sloan says. When Atae shakes her head, he continues. "How about fighting? You have to both like fighting."

"We do, except she wants to kill everyone we fight. She doesn't know how to hold back. That's what's so distracting in battle. I'm always fighting against her need to use fatal attacks."

"But she's dominant." Jeqi's face lights up with a new idea. "She's dominant, so you need to redirect Beast's instincts from killing your opponent to making them submit."

"What? No one in the arena will want to submit to me. We're competing against each other."

"Exactly," Marqee says. He grins in awe of Jeqi's idea. "You'll have to physically dominate by incapacitating them."

"So, she's fighting for dominance, not survival," Sloan says. "Fine, let's give it a shot."

"You want me to make you submit?" Atae plants a hand against her hip and raises both eyebrows at the dark heir.

"No, I want you to try."

Much to Atae's surprise, Beast purrs at Sloan's invitation and doesn't lunge for control at the anticipation of a fight. The hybrid shrugs and steps away from Jeqi and Marqee to join Sloan deeper into the training room. She slips into a defensive stance and prepares for battle. As she watches Sloan do the same, calm slips over Atae, and Beast falls still. Together they analyze their opponent. Beast notes his offensive stance, and Atae finds the position of his energy blade telling. When Sloan attacks a moment later, Atae is ready.

A step before Sloan reaches her, Atae commands Beast to release her forearm blades. They erupt in time to deflect his long sword, and Atae smiles at their accomplishment. Sloan uses her hesitation and the momentum of her deflection to spin around with his elbow aimed at her nose. His elbow would've smashed into Atae's face had Beast's orange flash not warned her of his movement. Instead, the hybrid dodges low and slashes her unsheathed claws into Sloan's ribs.

He groans but doesn't slow as he twirls his sword around and toward Atae's head. Again his hilt meets her forearm blades. This time, Sloan is quick to parry, then he slams his foot into her knee. She cries out as her joint shatters under his blow. Rolling to the ground, Atae digs her claws into Sloan's thigh then dodges his retaliation. A moment later, the two younglings stand several arm lengths from each other, glaring. Atae favors her left leg as her knee swells, and a bruise encompasses the entire joint. Sloan grimaces with each painful breath as blood seeps from the wound over his ribs and his thigh. He raises his sword again, this time in defense, and Atae ignores the pain of her injury to press her attack.

Marqee and Jeqi stand on the sidelines, watching the other two younglings sword dance. Jeqi gapes at the difference in Atae's fighting style. She doesn't seem distracted by Beast's presence anymore, and she's far more aware of her surroundings. Even more than when they were all fighting the horde of clamox. When Atae dodges an incoming strike against her backside, Jeqi feels a twinge of jealousy for the advantage Beast offers Atae in battle, but she snuffs it out. Atae is pack, so any advantage she has helps Jeqi, too.

"It's amazing what a little inspiration can do," Marqee says. He watches the hybrid match the majority of Sloan's sword movements. Atae manages to hold her own against the larger purebred, but he jumps on every minor mistake and dominates the match.

"That's Atae for you. Sometimes it can take a while for a new idea or skill to click for her. But when it finally happens, she's pretty amazing," Jeqi says. Marqee glances at the blonde, enjoying the twinkle in her blue eyes as she smiles. His eyes dart away when Jeqi catches him watching her.

"It's like the blind leading the blind out there with this whole beast thing," Marqee says.

"You mean the fact that they both lack control?" Jeqi pauses with a hesitant glance at Sloan. "Does he realize what's going to happen to him in the Gridiron?"

Marqee jerks his eyes back to her in surprise. It's such a blunt question about a subject that Sloan continually evades. Finding the concern in her crystal gaze, Marqee answers with a grim frown.

"Yes, he knows."

"Then, why is he doing it? He doesn't have to enter. He doesn't have to be a citizen."

"He's an heir to one of the crests. His family…it's complicated. He has to compete. Besides, he wouldn't abandon Truin. And I won't abandon him."

"Let's hope he isn't more harm than good," Jeqi says.

CHAPTER 40

Sloan and Atae's sparring is brutal and very telling of their relationship. Neither submits to the other, so the battle continues for what seems like forever as they pummel each other. Beast is confident she could dominate Sloan, if only for his skills with the sword. As hard as she and Atae try, they cannot garner enough momentum past his defenses to cripple him. It isn't until Jeqi grows bored that she declares the fight a tie and forbids Sloan and Atae from sparring anymore. She claims Sloan would be of more help to them as a spectator that critiques Atae's technique while she fights with Jeqi or Marqee. As always, Jeqi is right.

Atae spends the next few days training with her small pack, and she learns to combine Beast's instinctual movements with the correct blade techniques. Atae learns a lot from Sloan when he isn't taunting her in battle, and Beast enjoys the touch of his rough hands on her skin when he repositions an arm or leg. At one point, he stands behind her and grasps both arms to teach Atae the movement of one difficult technique, and Beast revels in the feel of his broad chest against her back and the warmth of his breath on her neck.

Overwhelmed, Atae pushes Sloan away and picks a fight about personal space that ends with several curse words from the purebred and him storming out with Marqee in tow. They return the next day, of course, and Sloan is in rare sarcastic form. Halfway through the day, Atae grows annoyed enough with Beast and angry enough with the pompous heir that she throws her energy blade at him. Thus, Jeqi and Marqee must play referees for their respective packmates to prevent another unending brawl. And so both hybrids are glad to have a day to themselves.

Although she will never admit it, Sloan's recommendation to use the small energy blade is instrumental in Atae's success. Correctly positioned, the short, curved knife mimics her forearm blades as they glide along her arms. Defensive and offensive techniques with the dagger are almost identical to her movements with Beast's blades. Both Atae and Beast enjoy the thrill of working together, and aiming to dominate, rather than kill their opponents, calms the tension between the two.

Even now, amid a long-winded sparring session with Jeqi, Atae rides the elation of making progress with her swordplay and Beast's temperament. The weight and pressure of her life feel much lighter today, and she's looking forward to the final round of the tournament. Not even the annoying buzz at the back of her mind can bring her down. She ignores it along with every other aspect of her life. All Atae feels is the strength in her arms and legs when she slams them against her opponent. The only pain she suffers is from cuts and bruises left by Jeqi's blows. The only mental battle Atae faces is the mind games Jeqi inflicts upon her adversary. Beast is excellent at anticipating the blonde's next strike, but Jeqi is top-of-her-class for a reason. Atae enjoys the distraction of this sparring session until her blue-eyed assailant starts to fight dirty.

"Why do you think he lied to you?" Jeqi asks. She swings her lightweight sword against Atae's defenses, and Atae stumbles.

"What? Who?"

The buzzing at the back of Atae's brain thunders to the forefront as Schinn comes to mind. Beast rages against the memory of the silver heir, and Atae cringes against the mental barrage.

"Schinn lied to you. I know you haven't forgotten," Jeqi says. Then she takes advantage of an opening by slamming the hilt of her sword into Atae's side. Groaning, the blue hybrid retreats and fortifies her defenses while Jeqi shifts forward in pursuit.

"Are you still angry about it?"

Atae growls in answer and lunges toward her opponent then feints away in time to avoid Jeqi's parry. Spinning away, Atae tries to slam her elbow into the blonde's chin, but Jeqi is quick. Beast growls when her counterpart's elbow strikes a shoulder instead of the intended target. Jeqi grimaces from the painful blow but knows it could've been worse.

"What's wrong, Atae? Don't you want to talk about it?"

"Shut up. I know what you're doing."

"Make me."

Atae watches her packmate smirk and shift from foot-to-foot just out of arm's reach. Beast growls at Jeqi's taunting antics from within an orange cloud, and Atae agrees. The fuchsia-eyed hybrid shifts back into a defensive stance and waits for Jeqi's next move. The blonde huffs and pretends to be disappointed, then she launches into a rapid-fire assault. She slams her sword against Atae's defending blade over and over again, pushing her opponent backward one step at a time.

"I thought you cared for him," Jeqi says. "Of course, I thought he cared for you, too. Obviously, I was wrong."

"You don't know that," Atae says. She kicks at Jeqi's knee to stop the goading, but the blonde grins and avoids Atae's foot without pausing in her assault.

"He wouldn't have lied to you if he cared for you."

"Maybe. Maybe, not."

Liar. Beast boils red with anger at Atae's excuses for Schinn.

"Don't you feel stupid for believing him? How about defending him?" Jeqi says. She scowls with honest annoyance at her packmate.

Atae's defense of the silver heir aggravates Jeqi, and her tail puffs up around her waist. She doesn't understand why Atae can't see his real character. Schinn is a liar and born of the Fu-Kai crest, so Jeqi doesn't trust him. She doesn't trust many heirs to the Crests of Kaji. Their family dynamics are too complicated and politicized. Crests pressure their heirs to perform for the sake of appearance and sometimes force them into dangerous situations; such is the case with Sloan. While Sloan suffers the disadvantages of being born into a crest, Schinn enjoys all the benefits, like acquiring a highly coveted position in the royal guard and working alongside royalty. Jeqi believes Schinn lacks the loyalty and willpower necessary to serve the prince. He certainly isn't strong enough to stand at Atae's side for long.

"He's weak, and he doesn't deserve you," Jeqi says. She frowns between powerful blows that force Atae to stumble backward and into the wall.

Agreed. Schinn is weak, Beast says.

With her back against the training room wall, Atae realizes that she's outnumbered, and a spear of vulnerability lances her heart. Her insecurity morphs into anger, and Atae lashes out. Pressing her back into the wall with her sword guarding against Jeqi's advances, Atae shoves her weight against the stone. The friction holds her in place for an instant before she slides down the wall. During that airborne moment, Atae slams both feet under her opponent's raised blade and into Jeqi's stomach. With a surprised expression, the blonde tumbles backward. Jeqi struggles to remind her lungs how to function after having the wind knocked out of them, while Atae climbs to her feet and scowls.

"I know what Schinn did. You don't have to rub it in. I already know you don't like him. You've made that perfectly clear from the beginning. And I haven't forgiven him." Atae sighs in lost confusion. "Not yet."

"You've been ignoring the problem, Atae," Jeqi says between forced gasps. "Deal with it so that you can focus on the tournament."

"I am dealing with it. I'm angry," Atae says. Beast rallies around her in a red burst of mist. "I know it's stupid to be angry about it since he didn't know us at first. It was a lie to gain our trust. And it worked."

Jeqi tries to argue against that claim since she never trusted the silver heir. But Atae continues without noticing her packmate.

"I trusted him, only to find out that he was spying on us for Prince Truin. Ugh. And to find out from Sloan. Why wouldn't he tell us afterward? After we...grew closer? Do you really think he doesn't care?"

Jeqi stares at her friend and doesn't recognize the insecure youngling. She knows that this is the first time Atae has experienced this type of infatuation. It's also clear that the blue-haired hybrid has no idea how to handle it. Atae learns best from trial and error, but Jeqi has to advise her against giving her heart away. She has to try to make her listen.

Why Schinn? And why now? Jeqi closes her eyes and takes a deep breath before opening them again.

"Atae, he might. He might actually care for you, but it doesn't mean much because of his family. The crests won't accept you, and he-"

"I don't care what his family thinks!"

"Atae..."

Listen, Beast says.

"No. You both hate him. You always have. Neither of you gave him a chance. No wonder he lied to us."

Jeqi reaches for Atae, but the blue hybrid jerks away. She can see the blonde trying to calm her by channeling Deh's soothing tone and soft touch, but Atae won't stand for it. Instead, she pulls away and storms from the training room while Jeqi calls after her.

Atae is glad that her packmate doesn't follow her. She needs time to figure out what to do. She spent the last few days ignoring her emotions about Schinn, opting to bury them under Beast's rage. Walking along the decorated halls of the palace, Atae pushes past Beast's anger in search of her own emotions, and she finds the pain of Schinn's betrayal dulling into a fear. Surrounded by depictions of her ancestors' bravery, Atae finds it challenging to accept that she's afraid to trust. It's such a simple thing, something that's always come easily in the past. Now, Atae crosses her arms over her chest for protection, and trusting Schinn again would mean that she'd have to open her arms. She'd be defenseless, and she doesn't like it.

Don't do it, Beast says. She churns within a pale orange cloud, and Atae sighs. Of course, Beast doesn't want her to give Schinn another chance.

Big surprise. Atae muses as she wanders through the halls of the palace. Both Jeqi and Beast agree that Schinn cannot be trusted, and that should be enough for Atae. Regarding anything or anyone else, it would be enough. Atae learned several times over the last twelve seasons that Jeqi is always right. Yet, Atae can't bring herself to agree with her packmate on this. Nor does she disagree.

I care for Schinn, and I want to forgive him. I want to trust him again, but I don't think I should. Atae stops in the center of the hallway, biting her lip. She's stuck and doesn't know what to do next.

A door to her left slides open, and a burly fighter steps out. He cradles his bleeding arm and hustles past Atae in the direction of the medical wing. Grunts and groans echo from the room, drawing Atae's attention. She peeks inside to find Prince Truin brawling with several fighters at the same time. Sloan and Marqee sit on the sidelines with bored expressions while Solum studies the match. Atae's mood brightens as she recognizes the exercise and remembers the difficulty of meeting Solum's expectations. It took her longer than she'd like to admit to pass this challenge, and Atae wonders how long it will take Truin. Given his ego, it'll probably take a while. Atae smiles at the thought of besting Prince High-and-Mighty.

Atae slips into the training room with hopes of watching the match, but her eyes dart to Schinn, sparring against Truin. At the sight of him, the hybrid freezes several steps from the ring with a pit dropping in her stomach. Beast huffs red, angry bursts within a pale orange cloud of annoyance. Solum notices the quiet youngling standing back from the ring and calls out to her. Solum's voice tugs his daughter from her confusion, and she glances at him.

"Care to join us?" he asks.

When Solum motions toward Sloan and Marqee, Atae shrugs. "Sure."

"Welcome," Marqee says. He moves over to make room between him and Sloan for Atae, and she plops down next to them.

"To death by boredom," Sloan says.

Atae offers a small smile at the joke and ignores the match between Prince Truin and Schinn, along with three other fighters. She understands the premise of this exercise, and she has no desire to watch Schinn fight. Instead, she watches Solum.

Her father stands at the edge of the imaginary ring with a stern expression. He watches each strike and block with intense interest, just like he did when watching Atae. She smiles at the thought of training with Solum again. He was tough but effective. She learned a lot from him and not just during sessions; Atae would often seek guidance from him as well. Whether it was a disagreement with Jeqi, frustrations with Elder Warrior Feku, or another shouting match with Sloan at Sula Academy, Solum had the unique ability to lay everything out into a simplified pattern. No matter how multifaceted and impossible to navigate the situation seemed, Atae's father could break it down into straightforward decisions. The youngling didn't always like the choices before her nor the consequences, but she couldn't refute his logic.

When did I stop going to Father for advice?

When Beast churns with purple betrayal, she realizes the when and why of it. It was when she decided to lie to him about her shifting ability. Atae yearns to blame Beast, but she nips that in the bud. Atae chose to lie to her father.

Just like Schinn chose to lie to me.

No, Beast says. *Schinn is a liar.*

That's what I said. He lied, and so did I. It's the same thing. Why should I punish him for doing the same thing that I'm doing to Father?

No, Beast says louder. Atae grumbles at her with a sneer. How can they share a brain and not understand each other? It's exhausting.

For the first time, Atae considers confessing to her father about Beast, if only to clear her conscience. Then Sloan nudges her, and she remembers why she can't tell him. Her pack needs her in the Gridiron, so she has to hold out until then.

"What's the point of this?" Sloan asks. He motions to the five-against-one match that Truin is losing.

"Yeah, you should know how Solum's mind works by now," Marqee says.

"I don't know about that. But the point of this exercise is to figure out the point of the exercise," Atae says. She flashes a superior smirk and wonders if this is how Jeqi feels when others look to the blonde for answers.

"Well, Truin is failing," Sloan says.

"You're all failing," Atae says.

"What's that supposed to mean?"

"We're not allowed to interfere," Marqee says. "Solum told us we couldn't do anything until he gave the signal. But he never gives the signal."

"He always starts with one-on-one, then two against one, then three against one, and so on and so on until Truin is overrun," Sloan says. He waves his hand around in aggravation.

"How far does he usually get?" Atae asks.

"Usually five, sometimes six." Sloan jerks his head in a respectful nod to his friend, who finally kneels under the force of his attackers.

Solum calls off the five warriors, and they scatter from the ring to assess their wounds and prepare for the next round. Atae recognizes Truin's second guard but can't remember his name. She's surprised to see Debil and Seva, and they don't notice Atae until Schinn waves at her. The two females glare at Atae, but she doesn't notice. When Schinn waves at her, Atae meets his gaze, and his apologetic expression tugs at her heartstrings. She can also see the hope in his eyes that she's there to forgive him, but she drops her gaze. She can't give him what he wants right now. Beast dusts her mind with a blue, calming haze to help soothe her counterpart's pain, but Sloan's deep voice brushing against Atae's ear sends Beast into a crimson tizzy.

"How far did you get?" Sloan asks. Atae narrows her eyes as she twists her face to the dark purebred, finding him too close for comfort. Only a few fingers' widths apart, Atae meets Sloan's dark gaze with an overly annoyed expression, while she ignores the crimson tingles that Beast sends down her spine.

"What are you doing?" she asks him.

Atae meant to sound annoyed, or perhaps impatient with Sloan's flirtations. She didn't anticipate an involuntary shiver as she spoke, giving her a breathy voice. Sloan flashes a virile smile, and Atae rolls her eyes.

"Your beast likes me," he whispers. It's not a question, so Atae doesn't answer. Instead, she tilts her head and refuses to move away. That would be admitting he's right, and Atae refuses to let Sloan win. Of course, he's already won. A point that he proves when he licks his full lips, and Atae's eyes dart down to watch. Beast simmers crimson under the hybrid's skin, and the hair on her arms and neck stand on end.

"You're enjoying this, aren't you?" she says. Sloan snorts before something savage flashes across his eyes, and Atae recognizes it. Beast bristles with a steadfast warning, but Atae remembers seeing the same thing in Sloan's eyes before he lost control in the throne room. She smirks at him as realization dawns on her.

"Or is it that your beast enjoys it?"

Sloan blinks in surprise before lifting a shoulder. "I enjoy a lot of things."

He shines a pointed glance at Schinn, who glares at Sloan.

"You're making him jealous. Why? You don't like Schinn?"

"You just now picked up on that?" Marqee asks. Sloan leans back out of Atae's personal space, and she takes satisfaction in that tiny win.

"I'm not a very observant person."

Sloan chuckles at the understatement and rests back on his elbows, while Atae ignores him. She finally notices the death glares from Seva and Debil and wonders what problem they have with her. Sloan seems to have relationships with the two purebreds, so Atae decides to ask him about it. Before she can do that, Marqee interrupts.

"You didn't answer the question."

"What question?" Atae asks.

"How far did you get in the ring?"

"Oh." Atae shrugs. "It doesn't really matter."

"Uh, yes, it does," Sloan says. Her reluctance to answer the question intrigues the purebred, and he smells an opportunity to razz her. Sighing, Atae relents.

"Four fighters is my limit."

"That's respectable," Marqee says. Sloan says nothing, opting for a silent but smug smile. Atae considers smacking the smile off Sloan's face but thinks better of it. She'd have to face Jeqi's wrath for participating in another brawl with Sloan, and Solum wouldn't be too happy about them interrupting his exercise. She expects Truin to try again and start a new match at any point. Right now, the young prince rests on a nearby bench while Dr. Pwen fusses over a clotted cut on his bicep. While several bruises litter his face and shoulders, none of his injuries are crippling, so Solum will expect Truin to attempt the challenge again. She wonders how many times he's done this.

"It also took me five tries to complete the exercise," Atae says. "What number is Truin on?"

"What?" Marqee says. Sloan jumps up to call Truin. The prince makes a rude gesture toward his friend that illustrates his lack of patience for Sloan's antics at the moment. Sloan laughs and shrugs, then he yells across the training room.

"Oh, Prince Truin. It only took Atae five times to pass this test."

"Shut up," Atae says. She swats at Sloan with a twinge of embarrassment as Beast snickers in the back of her mind.

"No, we've been here every day since before the tournament started. I'm tired of this."

"Every day? You guys suck at this." Atae gapes in surprise, and Truin jumps to his feet, drawing the attention of everyone around the ring.

"That's not possible. There's no way she defeated that many opponents at once."

"You're right. She didn't." Solum crosses over his chest. "You've yet to identify the purpose of this challenge."

"You don't know what you're doing, do you?" Truin scowls at the royal advisor. "We've been doing the same thing for weeks."

"And we'll keep doing it until you get it right."

"It's true," Atae says from her seat next to Marqee, and everyone swivels to her. "You can't move forward without learning this fundamental principle. It's part of the foundation of Solum's teachings."

"You are not stronger than me, Blue."

Most of the fighters around the ring, including Seva and Debil, step back from the angry monarch. Beast swells within Atae at the prince's attempt to prove dominance. Atae clenches her jaw and stares into the royal amber eyes. She waffles between challenging Prince Truin or ignoring him; submitting is not an option.

Atae decides to follow Beast's lead to skirt the dynamics of their odd little pack. She stands with a resigned sigh and glances at Solum before approaching Prince Truin in a calm yet defiant manner. The royal advisor can't help a small, proud smile at his daughter's tact. She manages a perfect balance between challenging the prince and accepting his alpha status. She is not submitting to him, nor is she fighting him. Atae stops a few steps from Prince Truin, and the tension in the room threatens to drown her.

"You're making this too hard. Your ego is holding you back," Atae says. Prince Truin flinches at her comments and opens his mouth to argue, but nothing comes out. He stands hard and tense in the middle of the ring like a ball of fire ready to scorch the planet. That's when Atae sees it. She sees the confusion and frustration that smolders under the prince's anger, and the young hybrid empathizes with her prince. She doesn't like to fail, either.

"You can do this," she says. "It's much simpler than you think."

"I don't need your sympathy."

"Good, because you don't have it."

Atae returns to her seat on the sidelines next to Marqee. Truin glances at Sloan, who shrugs in uncertainty.

"Are you ready to try again?" Solum asks Prince Truin. Somehow the question sounds like a challenge. The royal hybrid nods and steps into the center of the ring while Sloan shuffles back to his seat next to Atae.

"You will stay out of the way until called upon," Solum says to Atae, Marqee, and Sloan.

"Uh-huh," Sloan says. "I won't hold my breath."

"He says that every time yet never calls on us," Marqee says.

"Then maybe you should both pay attention to it," Atae says. Beast echoes her annoyance in a dark orange burst.

"What is your problem? Solum is the one that wants us wasting our time on the sidelines," Sloan demands.

"He didn't say it was his call."

"Atae." Solum admonishes her, and she cringes at her mistake. Truin glances between the father and daughter as he considers this new information.

"Sorry," Atae says. Solum sighs and shakes his head. He'll never understand how Atae can go from aware to careless within moments.

"Trikk," Solum says. He motions toward the ring, and Truin's second guard hustles into the fight.

That's his name. Atae notes, and Beast watches the older youngling exchange blows with Prince Truin.

Impressive, Beast says.

"What do you mean, it's not his call?" Marqee breaks Atae's focus on the fight. "Does that mean that it's Prince Truin's call?"

"If so, nothing's changed," Sloan says.

"What do you mean?" Atae asks. "That changes everything."

"Not really. Prince Truin won't call for help," Marqee says.

"He prefers to do things solo." Sloan shrugs, but Atae shakes her head with furrowed brows.

"We're pack."

"So?" He says. Atae finds it odd that Sloan didn't argue her claim just the relevance since she surprised herself with the declaration. When did they become pack? Does she trust Sloan and Marqee enough to be pack?

Yes, Beast says. She swirls within a proud, green cloud, and Atae agrees with a smile.

And I guess Prince High-and-Mighty has to be pack, too, otherwise what's the point of dedicating my life to protect him?

"Whether we like it or not, we're never solo. That's just part of being a pack," Atae says to Sloan and Marqee.

"Hmm." Marqee considers the validity of Atae's statement. Though he can't argue against it, he shrugs. "It still doesn't matter. Truin would be furious if we interfered without his permission."

"Seva," Solum says. The purebred female rushes into the melee with an eager grin.

"So?" Atae asks, echoing Sloan's earlier attitude.

Sloan chuckles, and Marqee grumbles. Sloan may receive more leniency from the royal family, but Marqee has no intention of earning the prince's wrath. Sloan itches to dive into the ring if only to satisfy his beast's unrelenting need to prove dominance. When Solum calls on a third fighter and Truin stumbles under a few missteps, Sloan wonders if interceding would push past the boundaries of his friendship with the hybrid prince. Truin is his friend but not a forgiving one. When a fourth fighter dashes into the ring, Atae jumps to her feet, but Sloan grabs her arm.

"What are you doing?"

"I'm going to help him." Atae yanks her arm free.

"Truin doesn't want help," Marqee says.

"I am his packmate, not his servant." With that, Atae barrels into the ring, leaving Sloan and Marqee behind

"She's crazy." Marqee gapes as Atae brawls against Seva and Trikk while arguing with Prince Truin.

"Yep," Sloan says. His beast roars for satisfaction and the thrill of battle, sending adrenaline coursing through Sloan's veins.

"Schinn," Solum says, much to Sloan's delight. Schinn hustles into the ring and hesitates when he comes face-to-face with Atae. She doesn't notice him since she's busy sweeping Seva's leg out from under her. By the time Atae realizes that Schinn has joined the fight, Sloan is kneeing the silver heir in the groin. Atae slams her elbow into a nameless warrior then jams the palm of her other hand upward across his jaw. The young purebred stumbles back a step before crumpling to the ground, unconscious.

"The first point is mine!" Atae jumps in delight.

"Shut up," Truin calls from across the ring. "And get out. I don't need your help."

Atae ignores the prince, and Beast vibrates with excitement from within a yellow vapor. She erupts into an orange warning, so Atae spins around to face a new threat. Debil lashes out at the hybrid with wild kicks and fast punches. Atae blocks each and slams her fist into the purebred's gut.

"What is your problem?" Atae asks before Seva pounces from behind. Thanks to Beast, the hybrid spins in time to pound her knee into Seva's thigh, fracturing the bone. The taller Kaji stumbles to the ground, screaming in pain.

"That's two."

"Hey, I got one, too," Sloan says.

Truin grumbles under his breath at the obstinacy of his packmates. After he dispatches Trikk with a blow to one knee, Prince Truin glances at Marqee, who still waits on the sidelines. He paces the border of the ring, waiting for the order, while Sloan and Atae fight Truin's battle. With a resigning sigh, Truin motions for Marqee to join the fight, and the dimpled purebred doesn't hesitate. With all the fighters in the ring and four down, it's four-to-six until Sloan calls out another point. Truin frowns at the idea of Sloan or Atae earning more points than he has, so the hybrid prince rushes back into battle. Meanwhile, Atae groans under a blow from Debil.

"I'll tell you what my problem is," Debil says. She bashes her elbow into Atae's side. "It's you. Sloan is mine, and you can't have him."

Atae tries to laugh, but her lungs refused to cooperate after Debil's strike. Instead, the hybrid stumbles to the ground, feinting injury. When Debil pursues her injured prey, Atae trips the purebred and slams her knees into the taller Kaji's chest. Debil cries out and struggles to push Atae off of her.

"I don't care about Sloan," Atae says. She plows her fist into Debil's temple and knocks her senseless.

"Well, that was fun," Marqee says from the center of the ring. Atae glances up from the unconscious Kaji under her to find all their opponents incapacitated.

"Who won?" Truin asks.

Sloan chuckles. "Not Schinn."

Atae stands to search for the silver heir and finds him groaning in pain on the ground. One arm lies limp at his side, blood drips from his broken nose, and a large bruise swells around his broken jaw. Atae cringes at the sight of him; he's going to need a night in a recovery tank. Swirling in delighted yellow with bursts of crimson, Beast purrs for Sloan's accomplishment, and Atae fumes.

"Neither did Debil," she says to the dark heir.

Sloan's smug smile twists into a concerned frown until he finds Debil unconscious with minimal injuries. Seva crawls across the floor to check on her packmate, and Sloan helps her up. She grips his arm and leans against him for support with taunting glare at Atae. Beast rages against Atae's mind in a jealous tizzy, and the hybrid cringes. Solum clears his throat, demanding everyone's attention

"You all won," he says. "You are a pack. You will fail and succeed together. In the Gridiron, you will live and die within your pack."

"Then why did you say we couldn't interfere?" Sloan asks. "We could've done this weeks ago."

"Because rules don't matter in the Gridiron," Truin says. He helps Trikk to his feet. "We've all spent our lives learning to follow the rules, and now we have to learn when to break them."

"Except, Atae," Trikk says. "It seems you have a jump-start over the rest of us."

"Maybe, but this was a good reminder that some rules must be broken for the sake of the pack."

Some rules and some trusts. Atae muses and glances at Schinn. He struggles to his feet until she helps him up. Despite the blood and bruises, Schinn manages an appreciative expression, and Atae smiles back. Noticing the exchange between his daughter and the Fu-Kai heir, Solum scowls at them.

"Some rules, not all of them."

"How are we supposed to know which ones?" Seva asks. Atae spins around to face her with a bewildered expression.

We? There is no we. Seva is not a part of this. Atae wrinkles her nose, and Beast chuckles from within a bluish-green spiral.

"Honor," Marqee says. "If breaking a rule, or choosing an action, taints your honor, maybe it's not the way to go."

"And if the choice is between an honorable death and staying alive?" Solum asks the group. As expected, everyone raises their heads a little higher in response, and Solum can see that they've all considered this option. Feku and other elder warriors probably taught them at an early age that there is only one answer to this question.

"Sounds like a good way to go," Sloan says. His haunted gaze lands on the floor as he a brandishes a fake smile.

"Let's hope it doesn't come to that," Prince Truin says. He walks away from the group so that Dr. Pwen can assess his injuries. The remaining younglings scatter at Solum's command. Sloan lifts Debil and tugs her over his shoulder before assisting Seva to the medical wing. Atae reaches out to Schinn with the intent to help him, but Solum calls to her.

"Atae, Schinn can help himself. It's time for dinner."

Atae sighs at her father's blatant interference, but nods in resignation. Beast nods at Solum with approval, and Atae fights the urge to roll her eyes. Instead, she glances at Schinn and waves goodbye. He tries to say something, but his broken jaw is too painful. He waves with his good arm and watches Atae leave. Once outside the training room, Atae decides to say something that's been bothering her.

"Father, I think I should clarify something."

"What's that?"

"Seva and Debil are absolutely not part of our pack."

CHAPTER 41

"Urgh, when are they going to light this candle?" Sloan says.

He swats at his buzzing camera amid the tournament arena, and Atae shakes her head at the impatient heir, while Beast analyzes the remaining eighty students hustling to their assigned domes. She notes several potential threats and weaknesses, and Atae reminds her that they will be fighting for dominance, not survival. They must avoid mortally wounding their opponents. Beast huffs, spewing orange, annoyed particles but relents.

While her tail fidgets at her back, Jeqi scans the arena to confirm that all the starting domes are arranged along the walls. She suspects this is to allow ample room for the final challenge since the field is drastically different from the last round. The ground was filled in sometime during the week, and instead of the deep valley, a giant plateaued hill stands at the center. Unlike the valley, the mountain doesn't host any vegetation. It just looks like a giant pile of mud. Usually, Jeqi doesn't like the idea of crawling around in the mud, but after experiencing the giant clamox and the slimy, acid-covered water beast from the previous rounds, she's grateful for a little dirt.

Waiting for the few remaining domes to flash green, Jeqi fidgets between Atae and Marqee, and the purebred bumps against her shoulder.

"Why are you nervous?" he asks.

"I'm not," she lies.

"She has to get enough points in this round to keep her first-place rank," Atae says.

"Really?" Sloan says. "What's the big deal?"

"Oh, like you'd want to give it up if you had the top ranking." Atae snaps a hand to her hip and jumps to her packmate's defense. Sloan frowns, then he shrugs when he realizes she's right.

"I won't be allowed to enter the Gridiron if I don't graduate with the highest rank," Jeqi grimaces in embarrassment. "My mom won't let me."

"What?" Sloan lurches toward Jeqi in alarm. "Are you saying we've gone through all this with Atae, and you might not be able to enter the Gridiron anyway?"

"Hey," Atae says.

Jeqi is skilled, but we are better, Beast says. Atae nods in agreement but bites her tongue as Marqee speaks up.

"It's okay. We'll just make sure that whatever our objective is for this round, we do it the fastest or the most, or whatever we're supposed to do."

"We qualify individually during this round, not-" Jeqi says, but Sloan interrupts.

"Just because we have to qualify individually, doesn't mean we have to do it solo."

"Of course not. We're pack," Jeqi says. She furrows her brows at him as though she never considered the option, and Atae giggles

"They just learned that yesterday. The point is that we will make sure that you get the points you need."

"Duh," Sloan says. He winks at Jeqi, and she grins.

"Look," Marqee says. He raises his arm to point at the hologram assembling above. Skiska's round face and dark eyes peer down at the students with an excited smile, while Frack smirks with one eyebrow raised over his deep-seated eyes.

"Welcome young warriors to the final round of the twelfth seasonal Sula Academy Tournament," Frack says.

"Yes, welcome. Your performance today will greatly affect your chances in the Royal Gridiron-"

"They know the stakes, Skiska. This is the fourth time they've done this. Let's just cut to the chase."

"Good point, Frack," Skiska flashes a hard glance at her co-host. "It's time to hear the rules. Eighty students will compete, but only fifty will qualify for the Gridiron. As you know, this round will differ from all the rest in that each individual must qualify to complete the challenge."

"That means you weaklings out there that are skating by on the skills of your packmates, you're in trouble," Frack says.

"Yes, you are. This round is designed to isolate you, so I hope you're prepared. There are over eighty key bands hidden throughout the arena."

A map of the arena forms below the floating heads, and numerous yellow balls of light flicker to indicate the key band locations. Half of them cluster inside the hill, while the rest lay under the field. Atae wonders how they are meant to reach the buried keys, and Skiska is quick to answer the unspoken question.

"A massive web of tunnels exists below the surface of the arena, and at the center of it all, lies the finish line. The finish line is a simple energy platform that you must step on to complete the challenge."

A familiar energy platform assembles above the hilltop and ticks in a slow circle. From a distance, Jeqi can see tentacle-like structures sprout from the plateaued mountain top and reach up toward the spinning disk. She hopes it isn't another acid-spewing beast and sighs in relief when the constructs stay put after assembling, instead of wiggling.

"It's that simple, folks," Frack says. "Find a key, step on to the platform. The first fifty to do it wins."

"Of course, the faster you complete the challenge, the more points you'll earn. And, we all know how useful those points will be when preparing for the Gridiron," Skiska says.

"By now, I shouldn't have to warn you that just because it's simple, it doesn't mean it's easy. Beware of surprises."

"Oh, I'm certain they know that by now, Frack." Skiska flashes a brilliant smile. "Anyway, that's all the rules we have for you. I think it's time to move on."

"Yeah, time for the final round and to see who's truly the best that Sula Academy has to offer."

"Good luck, everyone!"

Wrapping her tail around her waist, Jeqi doesn't wait for the giant floating heads and the map to disappear before she bellows orders. She points to the ground several steps ahead of the small pack.

"Marqee and Sloan, you take the tunnels there to the big cave inside the hill. Find your keys, meet us at the top of the hill below the gate."

"How do you know there's a big cave inside?" Atae asks. Jeqi huffs and waves her hand.

"I saw it on the map. You and I will climb the hill from the outside, enter through a tunnel I saw about mid-way up, and grab the two keys on the way to the rendezvous point."

"Got it." Marqee nods, then the domes drop.

Eighty younglings surge from the outskirts of the arena toward the center hill. Marqee and Sloan cut to the left, push their way through the throng of competitors, and disappear. Atae and Jeqi weave through the bulk of the students, dodging a few stray punches and several energy blade swings. Neither hybrid sticks around long enough to engage the attackers, much to Beast's aggravation.

Calm down. Our goal is to reach the gate first. We can't get distracted, Atae says, to which Beast grumbles.

Atae follows behind Jeqi as she leads them through the stampede of competitors. One purebred that rushes across their path stumbles and disappears into the ground. Startled, Jeqi adjusts course around their fallen classmate. As she passes, Atae notices a smooth energy door closing shut on the trap, and she wonders how many of these surprises await them. Jeqi and Atae scan the ground as they run, hoping to avoid the pitfalls, which slows their progress. Neither hybrid spots any, but two more younglings disappear around them with surprised yelps.

Beast unleashes a flurry of orange particles, and Atae glances around to see Debil, in battle beast form, charge straight for her. Atae curses and unsheathes her blade but doesn't slow her pace toward the hill as the purebred chases her down. They've almost reached the base of the small mountain when Debil closes in enough to pounce on the hybrid. She takes one last step to gather herself for liftoff and slips through a camouflaged trap door. She flails about and squeals in panic as she plummets into the unknown.

Atae laughs out loud at the clumsy battle beast, and Jeqi glimpses back at the sound of her packmate's voice. She spots Atae just in time to see her fall into another invisible trap. Neither Beast nor Atae sees the trap door due to its perfect camouflage among the mud and dirt of the arena floor. The ground just gives way beneath her, and she falls. The petite youngling throws her hands out to find a ledge, but the trap is too big for her short reach. The momentum from her run pushes her into the darkness below faster than she expects, and Beast howls in concern at their helpless descent.

Atae slams hard into the ground at the bottom of a great pit. Stunned, she lies in the crumbling dirt, listening to Jeqi bash her fists against the door and call her name. Atae lifts her head to survey the dark cavern and comes face-to-face with a large mouth of drool and teeth. Beast flashes an orange warning to move, pumping massive amounts of adrenaline into Atae's system, and with a high-pitched squeal, she responds. She scrambles backward in a crustacean-like stance, and the creature does the same. Several clods of dirt tumble across her shoulders from the soft, dirt wall at her back, but she ignores them.

The darkness is thick enough that Atae loses sight of the creature's retreating form, although the moving shadows and the sounds of scraping claws hint at its position. Atae frowns as she realizes that it's retreating toward the only light source in the dark cave. A dim glow emanates from a small tunnel across from Atae, and the creature scuttles toward it until its body eclipses the light. When the rodent shuffles through the tunnel, Atae studies its backside. The hairless mammal pulls its serpentine-like body along the perfectly sized burrow with a dozen tiny, clawed arms and legs, and a large tail shuffles behind it. The front of the creature is buried under the tunnel, but Atae remembers the large teeth and rancid drool. Her eyes widen in surprise when she spots a yellow reflective band wrapped around the creature's slithering tail.

A key. Atae gasps. She almost marches after the creature, but Jeqi's voice calls down to her.

"Atae, can you hear me?"

"Yeah, I'm still alive."

"What was that squealing noise? Did you kill something?"

"No, it was nothing," Atae says. She'll never admit to screaming. No one will ever know, except Atae and the tunnel creature.

And everyone in the universe watching. Atae frowns when she remembers the camera buzzing around the dark cave. The camera not only caught her embarrassing squeal, but it will broadcast any shifting mishaps as well. Beast heaves with annoyance, and Atae agrees. She swats at the camera, and it dodges her flailing hand only to scrape against the cave wall. Atae can hear dirt crumbling, but the darkness is too thick to see the extent of the damage.

"Can you get to the hill?" Jeqi calls down. The cave is a few steps wide and a couple of stories deep. Atae shuffles around the dark cavern, searching for more tunnels. Finding only the lit tunnel, Atae tries to scale the wall, but the dirt crumbles with the slightest provocation.

"Uh, maybe," Atae says. "There's a tunnel, but I don't know where it goes. There's also a giant…thing…a tunnel rodent. It has a key."

Atae listens to the sounds of scuffling then a loud bang against the trap door before Jeqi responds.

"Go after it. Find a way to the hill."

"What was that?"

"Wesk bit off more than she could chew. Now she won't be able to swallow without a visit to the med-wing first."

Atae cringes at the damage she imagines Jeqi inflicted upon the purebred youngling. Wesk isn't the brightest student, nor the most skilled fighter. Frankly, Atae's surprised she made it this far. Perhaps her packmates helped her along during the first three rounds. Left to her own devices, Wesk picked a fight with the wrong hybrid. Beast beams within a proud, green mist at her packmate's skill.

"You're vulnerable up there, Jeqi. You need to move," Atae says.

"So do you. We don't have time to waste."

"So stop talking and go."

"Fine, I'm going," Jeqi says. "Just try not to scream anymore. It's embarrassing."

Atae's entire face burns bright red as she realizes that Jeqi recognized her scream earlier. No self-respecting warrior would release such a meek sound, and both hybrids knew it. Of course, Jeqi wouldn't pass up the chance to tease her packmate before she dashes off.

Beast rubs against Atae's mind with yellow anticipation, ready to move forward in their challenge, and Atae's excitement grows in response. She shuffles toward the tunnel then climbs inside. The shaft is big enough for Atae to stand on her knees, but only if she sits on her feet and bends her head at an odd angle. Her face scrapes across the tunnel ceiling, which glows with a green hue. Her skin touches something soft and wet, and she cringes. Looking down, Atae notices that only the top half of the crawl space is glowing. She shifts onto her back to better investigate and realizes that moss clings to the ceiling. She touches the phosphorescent plant, and her hand comes away covered in glowing, green spores that stain her skin. Atae wipes her hand and finds that the luminescent quality disperses with the spores, but her hands remain stained light green.

It might be cool if I glowed in the dark, Atae muses. Beast is quick to remind her of the first round of the tournament when glowing energy swords were targets in the night and easy pickings. Atae cringes at the memory and acknowledges that, for once, Beast is right. Refocusing on the task at hand, Atae shuffles back to her hands and knees and peers down the tunnel for a sign of life. Her camera uses the opportunity to buzz past her and down the shaft a bit then returns. The luminescent moss continues onward throughout the tiny passageway.

There has to be a way out somewhere. Atae just hopes she and Beast can reach it before time runs out. She sighs but soldiers onward, hoping that it's at least in the right direction. She crawls through the subterranean path and tries to ignore the shifting dirt under her weight. Every time she scrapes the side or ceiling of the tunnel, soil gives way. She wonders at the best way to collapse the burrow, and Beast paces inside an orangish-yellow ball of anxious particles.

I'm starting to think you're claustrophobic, Atae teases, and Beast bares her teeth. The hybrid chuckles out loud then gasps when the walls rumble. With the dirt shifting and falling, Atae stops in her tracks while the tunnel shakes all around her. Atae doesn't move again until the ground falls silent and still. Beast clings to her mind, pumping Atae full of adrenaline and pushing her closer to the edge of panic. Neither wants to be buried alive, but Atae knows that losing it will only make matters worse. So she takes a deep breath and continues onward at a slow and cautious pace, trying not to shake under pressure.

Atae shuffles through the tunnel until she reaches a fork in the path. She pauses, uncertain which to take, and Beast reminds her of the tunnel rodent. Atae glances around for a trail to follow, but both shafts are identical. This realization bothers Atae because every animal leaves a trail, and the tunnel rodent most certainly traveled this way. Yet even the path she's already traversed shows no signs of the odd creature, only Atae's clumsy movement.

Eager to find freedom from the tight space, Beast urges her to decide, so Atae complies and opts for the left path. She crawls down the tunnel, listening for signs of another quake, but nothing happens. As soon as she relaxes, the camera buzzes by her left ear, and Atae growls at it. Once again, the ground rumbles all around her, this time harder, and the tunnel deteriorates from the violence of it. Beast rages at Atae from within an explosion of red and gold, demanding escape. Atae tries to comply by rushing ahead, but the rumbling follows her.

A tunnel rodent explodes from the right wall of the path. It snaps its large, threatening jaws and lashes out with two clawed paws while the lower half of its body remains hidden by the crumbling tunnel wall. Atae shifts backward and shuffles away from the chomping bites. Beast searches for vulnerable attack points such as the eyes and nose and relays her findings to Atae. The hybrid pauses at a safe distance from the threatening teeth to process Beast's input. The giant rodent doesn't have any eyes; instead, a large bone protrudes above the nose and jaw.

"What the..." Atae says. Then she gasps in surprise when the rodent lurches toward her. "You can hear me, but you can't see me."

Atae shuffles back from another threatening lunge. She kicks at the tunnel rodent, tiring of its behavior, but that only angers it more. It thrashes back and forth, causing the tunnel to collapse on top of it. Atae manages to scurry out of the way and deeper into an intact part of the tube, but the rodent follows. It's unfazed by the dirt and burrows free using its multiple arms and legs.

Atae curses in frustration and uses her feet to keep the snapping creature at bay. It wasn't this aggressive in the cave. It had scurried from Atae as fast as she had retreated from it. This time, she's at a disadvantage in the tunnel where the rodent thrives. Atae kicks again, this time, landing a blow on the bone protruding above its nose in place of eyes. The creature flinches away, and Beast grins from within a yellow flurry. Atae mimics Beast's smile and kicks at the rodent again until it yelps. The tunnel rodent reels away from the hybrid then arches its slithering body upward to claw into the ceiling. Atae watches in amazement as the creature digs through the dirt above, leaving behind a perfect tunnel as it crawls away.

This thing made the tunnels, Atae says.

They made the tunnels, Beast clarifies.

Before Atae can consider what that means, she catches sight of the key band around the creature's tail and lunges for it. She grabs the wiggling rodent before it can disappear, and it squeals. Atae jumps at the ear-splitting noise but doesn't let go. She unlatches the band and yanks it off the creature. An instant before Atae decides to release the rodent, it expels a foul-smelling secretion into her face. She drops the awful animal and falls back against the opposite tunnel wall, while Beast screams in agony.

Ignoring the camera that buzzes close by, Atae gags as she wipes away the nasty substance from her face. She'd be concerned about what her father must think of this unpleasant situation, but Beast's flailing and painful squeals prevent Atae from concentrating on anything else. She sits in the green tunnel in a stunned stupor as she tries to figure out the problem.

What's wrong?

I can't see. I can't feel. I can't hear. Make it stop, Beast says.

It's okay. Everything is okay. We're fine.

But Beast wails, panic-stricken, and refuses to listen. Atae cringes and rubs her temples to help soothe the headache from Beast's fear, then she sighs and lifts the key band still clenched in one hand. The youngling straps it to one wrist and shuffles onward. After a while, Beast stops screaming but continues to fret.

What happened? Atae asks. She edges down the tunnel in complete silence so as not to attract another tunnel rodent.

I don't know. I can't see. I can't feel. I can't hear, Beast says again. She flails inside a gold, frightened orb, and Atae pities her.

But I'm fine. I can see and hear everything. What does that mean? Is this permanent? Can we still shift? Atae asks.

I don't know, Beast admits.

It must have been that gross fart. What the hell was that?

Disgusting creature, Beast says. Then she wails in despair. *We will die.*

It's not going to kill us. We'll be fine. If all the keys are on the back of those tunnel rodents, then everyone will get farted on at some point. I don't think Sula Academy wants to kill us all.

You cannot protect us. We will die, Beast says.

And we're back to this, Atae says. *I thought we were getting somewhere. Haven't I proven myself?*

No.

Not even a little?

No.

You're lying. I'm amazing, Atae says.

Beast digs into her mind with a growl, and the hybrid cringes under the pain but keeps crawling onward. She spies a corner ahead and wonders how much further she'll need to crawl. When Beast rips at her again, Atae growls.

That doesn't help either of us. Like it or not, I'm the only chance we have to get through this. The fact that you haven't tried to take control or shift means that you can't, so I'm all you've got.

Beast says nothing but sneers, so Atae continues.

Attacking me will only distract me and get us hurt or killed. So stop it.

I cannot see. I cannot hear. I cannot feel. Beast says again. She implores Atae to listen and understand the danger, and Atae nods.

I know you can't help me...us, but I can do this.

With a growl, Beast recedes into a golden tornado at the back of her counterpart's mind and, Atae sighs in relief. When she reaches the corner, Atae spots the end of the tunnel shining nearby. Excited, she rushes onward, damaging the burrow as she traverses through it.

"Yes!"

Atae celebrates as she steps out into a vast cavern, but a tunnel rodent explodes from the wall behind her and chomps into the right side of her back and abdomen. She yelps and slams her elbow into its protruding bone, and the creature reels back, releasing Atae in the process. Before the animal can retreat into the wall again, the injured hybrid unsheathes her hilt and slices the creature's head off. She rushes away from the offending wall, holding her wound as blood pours from the carcass, and the head bounces down a nearby staircase. Atae curses as she probes the injury and groans from the pain of two bruised ribs. Blood oozes from the puncture wounds along the length of her chest and back, so she applies pressure until they clot.

Had the tunnel rodent had time to rip into its prey, it might have damaged Atae's vital organs. Fortunately, Atae knew its vulnerability. Of course, the hybrid might have avoided the entire attack had Beast been able to warn her.

I'll have to be much more careful.

I cannot see. I cannot... Beast tries to remind Atae, but she interrupts.

I know, I know. I think we have more pressing concerns.

Taking a deep breath, Atae surveys the surrounding chaos. Dozens of younglings fight with others, while some seem to battle the air around them. One huge student named Rakum huddles in a corner, rocking back in forth and mumbling to himself. Another purebred, Quin, pounds at the solid wall in rage and rips out chunks of rock and clay with his bare hands. Drawn to the noise, a tunnel rodent bursts from the rubble and tackles the loud youngling.

"That's one way to get a key," Atae says. She cringes when Quin bashes the rodent's face into bits, then rather than grabbing the yellow band, he keeps wailing on the dead creature. "That's a little odd."

Several other students yell nonsense at each other as they scramble across the rough floor and rip at their uniforms. One screams about bugs crawling in her pants.

"That's very odd." Atae stares wide-eyed at the absurdity of it all until Beast growls. She glances around the cavern for an idea of where to go next.

The green moss glows on the high ceiling and damp walls, and it also lights several staircases leading in different directions. The ground under Atae feels solid like stone, unlike the unstable tunnels, and the walls feel like wet clay. The thicker mud doesn't slow the tunnel rodents. Several carcasses lie strewn across the cave, but Atae notices that none of them have keys. She realizes why when a hybrid with brown eyes and hair, named Sepkie, leaps up from a lower stairwell and snatches the key from

Quin's dead rodent. Quin doesn't mind since he's too busy pounding against the wall again.

"What is going on?" Atae yells at no one in particular.

"Atae." Jeqi peeks out from the same staircase in which Sepkie arrived.

"Jeqi." Atae rushes to her packmate's side, and Beast's golden storm lightens a bit. "What happened?"

Jeqi ascends the stairs with Marqee's arm draped over her shoulder for support. The purebred's lower leg is shattered with several bone splitters poking through the skin. It looks like Jeqi used Marqee's torn pant leg as a tourniquet, and it seems to have clotted for now.

"I broke his leg." Jeqi grimaces and hands Marqee off to Atae, who groans under the weight of him against her bruised ribs.

"Why'd you do that?"

"I attacked her," Marqee says. He cringes in pain as he follows Jeqi up a staircase with Atae's help.

"Well, why'd you do that?"

"It seemed like a good idea at the time."

Jeqi chooses another stairwell at random. Along the way, she digs her energy blade into the clay wall, scraping out a groove to mark their path.

"He was poisoned, just like the rest of them." Jeqi motions toward the insanity around them. Everywhere they go, students act out in crazy ways.

"That's what's going on?" Atae asks. Then realization dawns on her. "It's the tunnel rodent farts."

Jeqi stops to gape at Atae, and Marqee struggles to keep from giggling despite the pain from his injury. The blonde doesn't say anything for a moment then cracks a smile.

"I'm pretty sure it came from a gland, not a butt. Although it did smell awful."

"Did you get sprayed?" Atae asks as a camera buzzes past her ear, and she swats at it. Jeqi continues up the stairs with her blade digging into the clay wall.

"Yes. It doesn't seem to affect hybrids, just the purebreds."

Atae realizes then that only the purebreds are acting crazy. Most hybrids slip past everyone unfazed, although several try to calm their insane packmates. A few end up fighting the enraged purebreds. Atae, Jeqi, and Marqee shuffle past the chaos with little interference from the surrounding younglings, even when they have to double back after running into a dead end. Jeqi marks the wall next to the staircase with an 'X,' and they select an alternative.

"Were you affected?" Jeqi asks. She glances over her shoulder, and Atae notices her concern.

"No, not really," Atae says. She cringes from Beast's anger. "So when does this stuff wear off?"

"We're not sure. I don't know anything about these things."

"Really?"

"I don't know everything, Atae."

"They're trestoids. My mother told me about them once," Marqee says. "They secrete a poison that alters a Kajian's mind. It was like my beast went crazy and tried to take control. Plus, I was hallucinating. I thought-"

"You thought I was someone else, and that I was going to kill you," Jeqi says. Atae wonders if there was more to it.

"So, you broke his leg?" she asks.

"First, she tried to drown me."

"Well, it snapped you out of it, didn't it?" Jeqi says.

She glances over her shoulder at Marqee as they ascend another staircase, and he flashes a half-smile at her. Spinning back around, Jeqi purses her lips to stop the corners of her mouth from quirking upward as her tail wriggles against her waist. Atae curses when they hit another dead end. Marking the wall, they double back.

"Wait, the drowning or the broken leg snapped you out of it?" Atae asks Marqee, and he shrugs.

"I don't know. They happened right after each other, and I wasn't really in the right state of mind."

So trauma might negate the effects of this poison, Atae muses, and Beast perks up with a bit of hope.

"Have you seen Sloan?" Marqee asks. When Atae shakes her head, he continues. "We were separated when a tunnel flooded. We ended up in a nest of trestoids. I found a key, but I lost my mind. I don't know what happened to Sloan."

"We'll find him," Atae says. Jeqi glances over her shoulder at them with a knitted brow.

"Atae, Sloan already has control issues. It might not be a good idea to approach him if he's been poisoned."

"But he's pack, and he has to reach the gate to qualify. We can't leave him," Atae says.

"We'll cross that bridge when we get to it," Marqee says. "Let's get to the top and see if Sloan's there and in his right mind."

We are not leaving Sloan. He's pack, Atae says to Beast to which she agrees with a growl. How could Jeqi and Marqee even consider doing that? If Sloan doesn't qualify in the tournament, he won't have any points to help in the Gridiron. If Debil's brother is any indication, entering the Gridiron with Sula Academy without points is suicide. Sloan wouldn't compete in the Gridiron if he has no chance of surviving; that would be insane. Would Marqee enter without Sloan? Either way, why would he be okay with leaving Sloan behind?

Atae contemplates the situation as the three continue in silence up several staircases, marking each dead end, until they find daylight. After blinking off the dim light from the glowing moss, Atae sees dozens of hybrids and a few purebreds rallying among a large circle of poles. It takes Atae a moment to realize the poles are the structures they saw assemble before the round began.

"No one's on the platform yet," Marqee says. He points upward, and Atae finds the spinning platform empty and taunting every youngling on the hilltop to attempt the jump. Poles, extending from the hill, circle the gate, and each bends at the top with knotted ropes dangling down to the mountain top. At first, Atae doesn't think the poles are tall enough to be of any help reaching the spinning disk until Sepkie latches onto one rope.

The pole advances upward, and the arm stretches out toward the gate. Atae wonders if Sepkie will be the first to reach the platform until the pole ejects the other end of the knotted rope. The brunette hybrid plummets down into a giant hole in the hill below the platform. Atae steps close to the edge of the large crevice and realizes that it curves and twists like a tunnel so that she can't see the bottom. Atae watches several younglings fall then tumble down the most massive slide she's ever seen.

"What are those?" Jeqi asks. She points toward a small pipe behind them. Atae twists, leaving Marqee at the edge of the slide as he requests. He's more interested in the sounds emanating from within the discard tunnel. The pipe sticks out from the ground to about Atae's height before bending down to face a hole in the dirt that runs through the entire mountain from top to bottom.

"Look, there are several of them circling the mountain."

"But why?" Atae asks. Before Jeqi can offer an explanation, Marqee calls to them.

"I think I found Sloan."

"Where?" Atae searches the hilltop. She didn't see him when they first stepped out; maybe he just arrived.

"I think he's down there." Marqee points to the giant slide. "I can hear him fighting."

Both hybrids tilt their heads to listen, and, sure enough, his angry voice and creative curses echo through the tunnel.

"Yep, that'd be him," Jeqi says.

"Let's figure out how to get you on that platform, then we'll decide what to do with Sloan," Marqee says to the blonde.

"Well, we can see what not to do." Atae watches one student scale the pole, and when the pole extends, she leaps from the arm to the platform only to fall short of her goal. She screams as she plummets down the discard slide, and Atae can't help a small giggle. After watching several more classmates drop, Jeqi points to a hanging rope and nods at Atae.

"I see it," Jeqi says. "It's a balancing act. It takes two people to do it."

Atae's eyes light up at the realization, and she smiles. "It's so simple."

"Once we do it, everyone's going to know how," Jeqi says.

"There's only a handful left up here," Marqee says.

"Which means, I'll have some time but not much," Atae says.

"Wait, what?"

"She has to go after Sloan," Jeqi says. "It takes two to get to the platform."

Marqee sighs in resignation once he realizes what they mean. He can't go after Sloan with a broken leg, and Jeqi has to step on the gate before anyone else. Atae shrugs and swivels toward the giant slide again.

That kind of looks like fun. Atae says. Beast swirls in a golden blue confusion. *This would be a lot easier if I had your help.*

True, Beast says, to which Atae smiles.

"Atae," Jeqi says. "Be careful, Sloan might not be himself."

"Pff, are you kidding me? I'm his favorite person." Atae smirks, then she steps off into the pit.

CHAPTER 42

The giant slide is not as much fun as Atae hoped. The dirt and stones tear at her exposed arms, but the Sula Academy uniform protects the rest of her body from harm. Too bad that doesn't extend to her bruised ribs. At the bottom, Atae tumbles into the midst of pure chaos as numerous trestoids converge onto several Kaji at once within a small cavern. The tunnel rodents spring from all directions and rip into their prey. Several hybrids scream from the shock and pain of their wounds and fail to react fast enough to prevent serious harm. The trestoids snap their jaws around an arm or leg then wrap their serpent-like bodies around their victims with surprising speed. Their multiple rodent arms and legs latch onto Kaji flesh with sharp claws that were honed for digging.

A few purebreds fall victim to the creatures' poison and fall into dangerous hallucinations, as is the case with Tukk. Jent, in his second form, stands in the center of the fray with his arms stretched out toward his packmate, trying to calm the raging purebred. Dozens of cameras circle the commotion, documenting everything. Tukk seems determined to rip the head from every rodent in reach, and Atae considers it a worthy goal. Trestoid teeth shatter against Jent's armor, and he ignores their attempts to eat him.

That is so cool. Atae muses, and Beast whines at her oblivion.

Atae draws her hilt and dispatches every threatening trestoid in her path as she crosses the cavern in search of Sloan. At the back of the cave, Atae finds three connected chambers, a tiny one with a simple stone staircase, a second with several tunnels ending in a central pool of water, and a third that is littered with trestoid carcasses, a couple of unconscious and crippled Kaji, and one enraged heir. Atae suspects that the flooded tunnels dumped Marqee and Sloan in the pool, and when they were attacked by trestoids, each must have followed a different path. A mad purebred screams in terror at his pursuing camera and runs up the staircase in the hope of escaping his hallucination.

"That's extremely odd," Atae says.

As she steps into the chamber of dead trestoids, Atae grimaces at the amount of blood and innards strewed everywhere. Sloan crouches in the center of the room over a struggling purebred. Atae winces when she recognizes a beaten and bloodied Quin, and she wonders how the youngling ended up in this mess. Quin tugs at Sloan's uniform and yells nonsense while spitting out blood and teeth.

"Stop saying that. Shut up. I said, shut up," Sloan says. He shakes the other purebred and snarls.

Unnoticed by either delirious Kaji, Atae pauses at the doorway and considers her options. A sneak attack would be the fastest way to land a traumatic hit that could nullify the effects of the poison, but Atae might be able to talk him down as she did during the second round of the tournament when Sloan went berserk on the energy platform. But if she can't get through to him, a brawl with Sloan is the last thing Atae needs. Judging by their previous matches, they'd run out of time before either youngling defeated the other. Atae hesitates, unsure which strategy to choose, and frowns in frustration. Beast's insight would be beneficial right now.

A loud bang echoes down the discard tunnel behind Atae. Then water gushes from a hole in the ceiling to the left of the doorway. She glances back in concern, but no one tumbles down the slide. Several purebreds still argue incoherently, but the trestoids stop attacking. They burrow back into the mountain and disappear, leaving the remaining key bands. An instant later, Atae realizes that Kaji were falling down the giant hole non-stop since she arrived, but not anymore. Jeqi and Marqee must have made it to the gate, revealing the trick to everyone on the hilltop. Reaching the gate must have also triggered the water pipes that circle the mountain.

But why? Atae wonders as she swivels back to the tiny waterfall that flows from the ceiling and through the floor. She realizes that Sloan is watching her, and she freezes. Blood and flesh drip from Sloan's fists, and Atae can see numerous holes in his uniform from trestoid attacks.

His red eyes are the most telling aspect of his condition, and they glare at Atae with more hatred than she's ever seen from her rival. When he speaks to her, his tone makes the hairs on Atae's neck stand on end.

"What are you doing here?"

"I've come to help." Atae takes a deep, calming breath. The camera buzzing her ear is a welcome distraction, since the last time she faced red eyes, they brought her back to her nightmares. But Atae refuses to let them affect her now. She's not the same person she was in that forest with Kandorq, and she isn't afraid of monsters in the dark anymore. Atae has to prove to Beast that she can handle this, and her pack is depending on her too.

"Liar," Sloan says. His upper lip twists into a snarl, and he drops Quin in an unconscious heap. The dark heir steps forward in a threatening charge, and Atae struggles to remain in her spot. She cannot give ground to him while he's in this state. If she runs, she'll become prey. Beast cannot see or hear anything outside Atae's mind, but her counterpart's mixture of anxiety and determination worries Beast. With no other way to help the hybrid, Beast flutters around Atae's consciousness and peppers her with calming, blue flurries.

"I've never lied to you, Sloan," Atae says. Her steady voice enrages the dark heir further.

"That's all you do. Every word you speak is a lie. Just like Father."

"What?"

"Don't pretend!" Sloan stomps closer to the smaller hybrid. "You trot around the empire like you're the only heir of worth."

"Sloan, it's me. It's Atae," she says. Deep down, she's relieved that Sloan's rage isn't aimed at her but at his sister, Royce. Sloan calms at hearing Atae's name, and he blinks like he has something in his eyes.

"Atae? When did you get here? How?"

"You're hallucinating, Sloan. You need to focus on me."

"No, you're lying again. You're always-"

"Where's your rope? Do you have it? Do you still have control?" Atae asks. She tries to keep Sloan focused on her voice and not what he might be seeing.

"I have it," Sloan glances down to one bloody hand. "I have it right here."

Atae stares at his open palm and raises an eyebrow. She nods while Sloan watches his empty hand.

"That's good. You should hold it tight."

"I can't."

"Yes, you can," Atae says. She slips her hands over his larger fingers and closes his fist for him. "I know you can do it. You are Kaji."

When Sloan meets Atae's fuchsia gaze, his eyes are back to his familiar black, and she smiles. Atae isn't sure what to do next, but at least Sloan isn't on the verge of shifting. An insane Kaji in his first form is much better than a rampaging battle beast. Before she can decide on their next step, Tukk screams a battle cry behind Atae. She jumps in surprise and tries to twirl around to face him, but Sloan reacts first.

"Stay away from her," he says.

Pushing Atae to the side, Sloan knocks aside a wild punch and kicks Tukk backward on to the ground. Jent jumps in to help his fallen comrade.

Meanwhile, Atae, who was not prepared for the forceful shove, bangs face-first against the wall by the waterfall. Clutching her head, Atae stumbles into the waterfall before scrambling away. She wipes the water from her face, and Beast rejoices.

I can see. I can hear. I can feel. Everything.

Fantastic, so now we know that a painful hit is a cure. Atae flinches at the bruise swelling on her face. *We have to get Sloan to snap out of it too.*

Hit him, Beast commands. Atae rolls her eyes but does as she's instructed.

Sloan and Jent tussle in the center of the room as they slip in the mud created from the bloody trestoid carcasses. Jent's armor protects him from the dark heir's heavy blows, but Sloan's rage offers little protection from the hybrid's clawed hands. Jent slashes the purebred's chest and blood pools from the shallow cuts, but, unfazed, Sloan continues his assault. Beast growls at the sight of Sloan's blood, and Atae isn't prepared for the sensation that fuels her body.

"Don't hurt him!"

Jent glances at Atae with a confused expression, but Sloan doesn't notice her. She uses it to her advantage and launches at him from behind. She slams her foot into the side of the larger purebred's face and smiles when something cracks.

"That's my job," Atae says to Jent. Sloan stumbles away, and Beast smiles within a greenish-yellow flurry of excitement and pride for her counterpart.

"You're crazy," Jent says.

"No, he's crazy," Atae points to Tukk as he rubs dead trestoid blood over his face. Jent curses with wide eyes and rushes to stop his packmate.

Sloan climbs to his feet, and Atae watches him with a hopeful grin. Her smile slips when the purebred twists to her with enraged red eyes. He snarls and makes a guttural sound that she's only ever heard from a battle beast. Atae watches the facial bones under Sloan's skin fluctuate, and she curses.

He's about to shift.

Not yet, Beast says. *Hit him.*

Atae blitzes the dark heir with several punches, but he doesn't react, so she shifts gears. She sweeps his legs out from under him, and Sloan tumbles to the ground. Forcing him to find his footing distracts the purebred from his shift, but Atae needs to think of something else. A hand-to-hand fight with Sloan is a bad idea, but a sword fight is worse. Beast frowns in distaste at the thought of using a hilt, and Atae remembers her preference for their natural weapons. If given a choice, Beast would fight barehanded rather than handle an energy blade. Atae wonders if Sloan's beast has the same aversion.

The hybrid spots Sloan's hilt holstered to his hip and dives for it. When the purebred kicks at her, Atae elbows Sloan's shins, and he stumbles back. She snatches the unsheathed blade and scrambles out of arms reach. After Sloan finds his feet again, Atae tosses the hilt to him, and he catches it out of instinct. He stares at the device in distaste then glances up to find Atae swinging her energy blade at his head. Without thinking, Sloan activates his hilt and blocks the hybrid's attack. Atae keeps pushing against the clashing blades, forcing Sloan to take a step back. Sloan's red gaze darkens to black, and he adjusts his fighting stance.

"Sloan?"

"You helped Father do it, didn't you?"

"Ugh. Come on, we don't have time for this." Atae says. She hustles away from the out-of-his-mind purebred. "I guess I'm going to have to hurt you more."

"I'll kill you." Sloan lunges at Atae, and she parries. She shifts her weight to counterstrike, but Sloan anticipates the move and deflects it. He follows up with a jab to Atae's injured ribs, and when she flinches, Sloan slashes his sword deep across her existing injury. Atae stumbles away, clutching at her bleeding side with her free hand. Beast whirls with rage, and Sloan smiles at the pain he's caused his enemy.

"I see you haven't learned much since our last match," Sloan says. He flashes a ruthless smile that slips when Atae whines in response.

"You said I was doing better."

Sloan pauses at the disjointed response from his 'sister,' and Atae uses the hesitation to her advantage. The hybrid launches forward and sideswipes the larger purebred by slamming the hilt of her blade into his thigh. The bone doesn't break, but the pain forces Sloan to the ground with a groan. As he falls forward, Atae wrenches his arm backward. Sloan tries to turn for relief from the pressure of her hold, but the smaller Kajian shoves her foot into his shoulder and pulls. Sloan screams in pain as Atae dislocates his arm then snaps his elbow joint with a powerful palm thrust. Sloan drops the hilt from his free hand and digs at the bloody mud under him in his struggle to free his arm from Atae's snare. Hoping that this trauma might finally nullify the effects of the poison, Atae releases the dark heir.

"Jent? What happened?" Tukk says. Atae spins around in surprise to find Jent smiling at his packmate as Tukk wipes water from the pipe off his face. Apparently, the Kipp hybrid wanted to wash the blood from his comrade's face and decided to shove him into the small waterfall.

That's why the pipes were activated after Jeqi reached the gate. Atae remembers that Jeqi mentioned drowning Marqee, and Atae stepped through the waterfall before Beast was freed too.

"The water is the cure," Atae says. She smiles and twirls back to Sloan as he struggles to stand. As expected, Sloan's eyes flare red again, and he's more out of control than before. Beast flashes an orange warning to be careful, but Atae has a plan.

"That was pathetic. No wonder Father likes me best," she says, taking a stab in the dark.

Sloan flinches from a sharper pain than his broken arm, and Atae's heart aches for him. Then he snarls and lurches forward while the hybrid drops her hilt and braces for the attack. With Beast's help, Atae dodges at the perfect moment and jerks Sloan's foot out from under him. Once again, he tumbles forward, but this time Sloan lands face-first into the waterfall. Atae doesn't hesitate to jerk him free of the water and shove him on his back. When she climbs on top of his chest, water drips from his face, and Sloan struggles against her with his uninjured arm and both legs. Atae scoots across his stomach to plant her knees into his thighs then pins his one working arm with both of her forearms. Immobilized, Sloan rages against her hold even as his eyes darken back to their usual black.

"Get off me," Sloan says. The defiance in his voice riles Beast to extreme levels. At the end of her patience with Sloan, Atae embraces Beast's need to dominate and shoves her closest elbow into the purebred's neck. She presses down into his vulnerable arteries, and when she speaks, Beast speaks with her.

"Enough."

Even without the effects of the poison, Sloan's beast will not submit to Atae. The purebred continues to struggle until the pressure from her elbow causes his vision to darken. She eases a bit, and he blinks away the haze.

"Be still."

Atae's beast commands Sloan's red-eyed counterpart, and his black eyes snap to meet her fuchsia. An instant later, something happens to Sloan that he's never experienced. The creature that plagues his mind and demands control falls silent. The red eyes shrink back from Beast as he tucks his tail and drops his head in submission. Sloan's constant battle for control ends, and the shackles of his beast's dominance slip away. Sloan's beast scampers off into the shadows of his mind, and the dark heir gasps as though it's the first full breath he's taken in seasons.

As Beast pulls away from Atae's mind enough for her to feel at ease, the youngling watches Sloan's expressions change from anger to uncertainty, then finally relief. She wonders if he's still hallucinating, but Beast clarifies.

He will follow.

Atae doesn't believe Beast's claim given Sloan's history. When he relaxes under her hold, Atae grows suspicious, and more so when he raises an eyebrow.

"Say my name," Atae says. She wants confirmation that Sloan isn't still hallucinating his sister. He smirks in a way that sends Beast into a crimson tizzy and an unexpected thrill through Atae's body.

"If you insist," Sloan says. His husky voice makes Atae blush and Beast melt. "Atae."

The flustered hybrid clears her throat to gather her rampant thoughts and get Beast back on track.

"Yep, it's you." She stands up, shaking her head. Feeling Atae's weight and warmth leave him, Sloan relishes the temporary silence of his mind and takes a moment to savor it before climbing to his feet as well. He stares at the blue hybrid that somehow bested him as she searches for their hilts, and a wave of gratitude washes over him.

"Here," she says with an awkward smile as she hands him his hilt.

"Thank you," he says. Atae pauses, sensing the weight of his appreciation when Beast purrs. Then she shrugs.

"We have to go now."

"Lead the way." Sloan motions toward the door, and Atae eyes the purebred covered in bloody mud. She frowns when she realizes that Sloan is missing something.

"You don't have a key? Look at all these trestoids you've killed. None of them had keys?"

"They might have at the time. I wasn't really focused on the keys," Sloan says. He offers an unabashed shrug as he searches the mess around him. He spots an unconscious hybrid in the corner of the room. "I remember him. I think he was trying to steal something."

"You remember your hallucinations?" Atae asks. Sloan searches the youngling in the corner and nods.

"Yep," he says. Then he pulls a key band free with his good arm. "I've got one now."

"Great, let's go." Atae shuffles out the door and heads straight for the room with the staircase. Beast notes that Jent and Tukk are gone, and only a handful of Kaji remain in the main chamber for the discard tunnel. Luckily, several purebreds slip down the rough slide as Sloan and Atae leave.

"It looks like most of the purebreds are waking from the poison, but they haven't figured out how to reach the gate yet."

"Okay," Sloan says. "I don't know what that means."

"Just don't get farted on again, and you'll be fine."

"What?" Sloan tries to stifle a laugh as he cradles his injured arm.

Atae glances around when they reach the cavern where she found Jeqi and Marqee earlier. She growls at the pools of water collecting in two corners and the lack of purebreds running around in the throes of insanity. Although a least a dozen still lie on the ground, incapacitated.

"Come on," Atae ignores Sloan's choked giggle. "Jeqi marked the right path."

Sloan follows Atae up the staircases marked by Jeqi's sword during their first trek to the hilltop. Avoiding the steps with 'X' carved into the clay, the two younglings dart up the hill. When they arrive, Atae finds dozens of Kaji waiting on the spinning disk above the mountain, including Jeqi and Marqee. Beast twirls within a yellow ball of excitement at the sight of her packmate. The blonde waves at Atae to hurry, and she rushes to a nearby pole, knocking aside any dissenting classmates.

"Do you know how to use this?" Sloan asks. He pushes an angry, brunette hybrid down the discard tunnel and chuckles at the sight of

Sepkie tumbling down the dirt slide. They watch another youngling grab the rope, and the pole lifts the purebred away.

"Yeah, I think so, but we have to wait for it to reset." When Sloan lifts an eyebrow in skepticism, Atae explains. "Jeqi said she figured it out, but she also thought hitting you hard enough would snap you out of your hallucinations."

"Well, that explains this." Sloan motions toward his useless arm, and Beast smiles at Atae's accomplishment.

"This thing takes two to operate, and we are wasting time. Besides, you're just mad that I was able to do that to your arm."

"Pff, my judgment was impaired," Sloan says. He watches the pole descend back to its original position without a rope and the attached Kajian.

"So, you were still trying to kill me."

"Not you."

"Right, I know." Atae nods at him, with an assuring smile. Then a new knotted rope drops down next to her. Sloan elbows a classmate reaching for the line, and the others gathering around them back away.

"How does this work?"

"It's a balancing act. See?" Atae points toward the rope curving around the arm. "That's why it takes two. One stays here, and the other goes up, but we have to time it perfectly."

"I'll go up." He puts his hand up to stop her from arguing. "I'm bigger than you, which means I'm heavier. I'll need the shorter end, so we don't slip off the arm."

Atae huffs and shuffles over to the pole. With her back against the construct, the hybrid intertwines her fingers to form a cup and leans forward with a nod to Sloan. The dark heir steps backward and cringes in pain while he adjusts his limp arm into a more comfortable position. Then he charges toward Atae and runs into her cupped hands so that when he leaps upward, she also propels him further through the air. Sloan slams into the arm above, and Atae grabs the rope below.

When the pole and arm extend out over the discard tunnel, Sloan hooks one leg and yanks himself up. He crouches on top of the narrow beam and shuffles toward the rope dispenser in the middle of the arm. When he's in range, Sloan dips lower and waits with his one hand at the ready for the contraption to eject the knotted rope end. Sloan lunges for the free rope, and upon grasping the knot, he drops from the arm to swing on the opposite side from Atae. The momentum of his fall tugs at the rope and jerks Atae upward. One of the many knots along the rope's length snags against the arm, securing the dangling younglings on either side of the arm.

Sloan dangles by one arm just above Atae on one end of the rope while the smaller hybrid writhes on the other. Atae cries out at the pain from her wounded side but keeps both hands locked onto the line. Sloan stares out over the gate to find Marqee and Jeqi waving to them.

"You have to hurry. The others have figured out what you're doing," Marqee yells. He points to a nearby pole where two purebreds attempt the same process. The one on top misses the rope, and her partner tumbles down into the discard tunnel. When Atae's thrashing causes their line to slip again, Sloan worries that they'll end up in the same position as the failed jumpers. He descends until he's eye level with Atae, then calls out to his packmate to calm her.

"Atae, spin us."

The blue hybrid cringes at the movement but releases one hand from her rope to grab the back of Sloan's torn uniform. She tugs them around in a circle, wrapping the rope ends together to stop the slippage. With Atae latched onto his back to keep them together, he glances over his shoulder to check on her and catches sight of the giant purebred, Rakum, scaling their pole. Sloan growls in frustration at their helplessness to stop the overgrown idiot.

"Start swinging. We have to time this perfectly," Atae says. The two packmates sway their bodies toward the rotating platform, and Atae groans when the rope untwists, spinning them as they swing. "On three. One, two, three!"

Both Kaji release the tether at the same time and leap for the gate. Sloan lands in a rough tumble that leaves him splayed next to the edge of the platform as he groans at the pain from his injured arm. Atae isn't so lucky. Rakum manages to jump from the pole extension in perfect unison with the couple's leap so that the uninvited Kajian snatches Atae's ankle in mid-flight. The blue hybrid slams stomach-first into the edge of the gate, knocking the wind from her lungs. Gasping for breath, Atae scrambles to find traction against Rakum's weight, but the smooth energy field offers zero friction, and she starts to slip off the gate.

"Jeqi!"

Atae calls for help, but Seva tackles Jeqi to save her packmate from the blonde's interference as Rakum struggles to reach the platform. Fighting through the pain of his injured leg, Marqee attempts to jerk Seva off Jeqi.

Atae cries out when Rakum yanks on her thigh for leverage, causing her wounded side to rip further. She thrashes and kicks to get him to release her, but the movement only fuels his determination, and she slips farther. Sloan pushes past the pain of his dislocated shoulder and broken elbow long enough to realize Atae's trouble. He lunges for her hand from his splayed position on the platform. Unfortunately for him, Atae latches on to the first thing in reach, which happens to be his damaged arm. She grabs his wrist just as she slips over the edge, and the combined weight of Atae and Rakum tugs Sloan's head and shoulders over the side. He cries out from the pain of his broken elbow and shoulder displacing further from their rightful positions. Even so, Sloan swings his uninjured arm to grab Atae's hand and keep her from slipping from his grasp.

"Don't let go," he says through his clenched jaw, and Atae nods. Beast roars at Rakum, reminding Atae to kick him away. The blue hybrid obeys, but the large purebred won't let go.

"Rakum," Jeqi calls from the edge next to Sloan with an inactivated hilt in hand. When Rakum glances up at her, the blonde chunks the device with perfect aim, and it slams into his nose with a crunch. He flinches, loosening his grip enough for Atae to jerk free, and he falls. Sloan would've chuckled at Rakum's high-pitched screams, but the pain is too much. When he groans again, Jeqi rushes to pull Atae up.

Once on the platform, Atae lies on her back, cringing from the pain in her side. Sloan writhes on the ground next to her. Jeqi attempts to assess Sloan's injury first, but he snaps at her to leave him alone, and Marqee assures her that he'll be fine. Atae lets the Setunn hybrid check her wounded abdomen but complains when Jeqi forces her to her feet. Three more Kaji land on the platform before the gate reaches its fifty-student maximum, and the unfortunate fourth youngling passes through the energy field to tumble down the discard tunnel. Fifty cameras zoom in chaotic orbits around the platform, and the winning students celebrate.

As the platform glows gold, Skiska and Frack congratulate the winners, and Atae stares at her three packmates with pride. Beast dances across her mind with bursts of green and yellow flurries of pride and excitement.

We're going to the Gridiron.

CHAPTER 43

"Welcome," Queen Sula Ru-Kai says to the top fifty students of this season's graduating class and their families. "I am proud to announce the final rank of every student who won this season's tournament. I, along with faculty of the Sula Academy & Research Facility, am very proud to congratulate each of you on a job well done. I look forward to watching you compete in the Gridiron with my son, Prince Truin."

The room explodes into applause and shouts of hooray as Sula steps back and motions toward Elder Warrior Feku. He commands his visual visor, and every Kaji in the room receives the final update to the class rankings. Jeqi grins at the confirmation of her hard work, and Atae bumps her shoulder with a proud smile. Unconcerned with the surrounding excitement, Beast sways within a calm, blue-green haze at the back of Atae's mind. She grows annoyed when Schinn joins the two hybrids, but Atae ignores her. He motions for the blue hybrid to follow him, and she complies with a small smile. Schinn leads Atae through the crowd of younglings and family members to one of the large walls encompassing the massive event room.

Even living in the palace, Atae hasn't had the time or the inclination to explore the countless rooms, but after today, she plans to spend more time in this one. When she and Jeqi walked in, Atae was surprised by the simple design, especially when compared to the rest of the palace. Jeqi explained that Queen Sula had the room built shortly after the construction of Sula Academy finished. The space consists of two bare walls, three glorious chandeliers, a large open balcony, and a small central stage.

Unlike the rest of the palace, the engraved artwork in this room grows every season. One wall depicts the familiar logo found on each student's uniform and the unique architecture of the Sula Academy & Research Facility buildings. The names and dates of the highest-ranked student from each season surround the logo and buildings on the wall. Yesterday there were eleven names, and today the twelfth name, Jeqi, was added. The opposite wall lists the names of the other 588 students to complete the tournament over the past twelve seasons.

It's in front of this wall that Schinn stops to point out Atae's name. Ignoring the crowd shuffling past her and Schinn, she smiles at the new etching and runs her fingers across the characters with pride,

"You did really well. You've earned this," Schinn says. He slips his hand over her fingers on the wall, and she meets his silver gaze with pressed lips.

"Schinn-"

"I'm sorry," he says. "I'm sorry that I lied to you. I should've told you everything."

"Yes, you should have," she says. Her stern tone is unforgiving, much to Beast's delight and Schinn's chagrin.

"In the beginning, I was doing what I was told, and lying was the easiest way to get you to comply."

"And afterward?"

"Afterward...I was uncertain..." Schinn pauses to gather his courage, and Atae waits for him to continue. "I was uncertain about us."

"Us?" Atae asks. Her heart pounds, and her stomach flutters with possibilities.

"Atae," he whispers before pulling her into a kiss. His lips caress her, and she opens her mouth so he can dip deeper. Schinn presses her against the wall as their tongues intertwine and explore each other. Atae tugs at the silver heir for more, but he pulls away, breathing hard against her.

"You're beautiful."

"So are you." She offers a content smile. Then Beast reminds Atae of Schinn's lies with angry red spears to her mind. "You can't lie to me again. Not ever."

"I know," he says.

"You're pack now. I have to be able to trust you."

"I promise that I will never betray you again."

Atae smiles at him, enjoying his affectionate expression and the warm passion it creates within her. Atae possessively clings to the emotion as though to declare it separate from Beast and her overwhelming presence. This belongs to Atae and to her alone. Watching Schinn, she wants to kiss him again and see what other wonderful sensations he can create within her.

Meanwhile, Solum frowns at Atae's public display of affection. From across the room, he can see her lean in for a second kiss with the silver heir, and the royal advisor twists away. Affectionate displays are commonplace at these types of parties; in fact, at least two other couples celebrate against the same wall. Regardless, Solum does not wish to witness his daughter's infatuation.

"Leave them be," Feku says. He smiles from Solum's side as they stand in the center of the room, sipping on their drink of choice. "They're celebrating a job well done."

"I know what they're doing," Solum says. Feku chuckles and raises a glass before finishing his drink.

"Well, at least we have the answer to our question."

"What question?" Queen Sula asks as she joins the two warriors.

"Whether Atae could shift or not," Feku says.

"I didn't realize that was still in question." Sula raises an eyebrow at her royal advisor.

"It wasn't, but Feku had this insane idea-"

"I wouldn't call it insane-"

"It was an insane idea," Solum says. "He thought Atae might be hiding her shifting ability so that I wouldn't pull her from the tournament and Gridiron."

"That's an interesting idea." Sula glances at the blue hybrid while Schinn tugs her to the dance floor.

"And absurd. Atae wouldn't be able to hide that from Feku or me-"

"And the tournament cameras," Feku says.

"Yes, I suppose that would be too difficult for a youngling," Sula says.

"Even so, I felt it might be possible given her new association with Schinn."

"So how did you settle this?" Sula asks. She accepts a glass of her favorite drink from a servant.

"The trestoids did that for us," Feku says, and Sula nods.

"She didn't respond to the poison just like every other hybrid."

"Exactly, so it's done," Solum says.

Sula smiles at her friend before glancing at Jent in contemplation. Hybrids are odd creatures, and no one truly understands their physiology yet. The feathered Kajian stands next to Tukk as they toast to their success, and Sula notes that the one hybrid with a shifting ability wasn't affected by the poison either. Like so many other secrets, the queen keeps this new one to herself and continues to celebrate with her subjects.

On the other side of the room, near the corner bar, Debil and Seva stand to the left of Sloan with his arm wrapped around Debil's waist. Seva describes how the two purebred females avoided the trestoid poison after they observed the effects on other students. They were among the first twenty competitors to reach the gate. Debil rubs her hand along Sloan's recovered shoulder and speaks with a sultry voice.

"How's your arm?"

"All better. It wasn't anything one night in a recovery tank couldn't fix. I'm just sad that I was there all alone." He offers a suggestive smirk.

"Oh, you poor thing." Debil sticks her lip out in faux concern. "I'm sure I could make it up to you."

"Hmm, I like the sound of that."

"Good, as long as I'm the only one," Debil says. She snatches Sloan's chin, and he stares into her dark eyes, spotting the insecurity and concern hidden under her combative nature. So Sloan squeezes Debil against him, savoring her scent, and kisses her to assure her of his intentions. Without his beast riding him to pursue every female his red-eyed companion deemed acceptable, Sloan finds that he prefers Debil's company the most. Her complicated personality compliments his twisted persona well.

After a moment, Sloan slips away to the bar with a promise to return with drinks. Marqee greets him as Sloan gives the servant his order.

"It looks like you're in for a fun night," Marqee says.

"You have no idea," Sloan says.

"You seem different lately. Less…"

"Tense?"

"Sure, let's go with that."

"I'm free. I can breathe and feel and think about the things that I want. I don't fight about everything anymore." Sloan beams with an excitement Marqee's never seen from his packmate.

"Your beast submitted? How? You've been trying-"

"Not me. Atae."

"Atae made your beast submit?" Marqee asks, and Sloan nods. "How is that even possible?"

"She scared the shit out of him. Her beast is terrifying under all that blue."

"Really?" Marqee glances at the hybrid across the room with an incredulous expression.

"I know. It doesn't make any sense to me either, but I'm not questioning it," Sloan says. He accepts the drink a servant hands him before shuffling the rest of the order over to Debil and Seva.

"Do you think this will last?"

"No, absolutely not. I can already feel him growing impatient. Soon he'll grow brave and start testing my control again," Sloan says, sipping from his glass. "And I'll be back to square one."

"What are you going to do then?"

"I'm going to stick by Atae and hope she saves my ass again."

"Sounds like a solid plan," Marqee says sarcastically. Sloan chuckles at his packmate, but before he can comment, a familiar warrior with silver eyes steps up to join him.

"Sloan."

The dark heir recognizes the silver warrior's voice before seeing his round face and weak chin. Sloan remembers his companion's silver, braided hair and the scowl glued to his face. Sloan motions for Marqee to leave, and the dimpled youngling steps away to join Jeqi on the dance floor.

"Father," Sloan says. "I'm surprised to see you here."

"I've come to congratulate you."

"I doubt that."

"I see you haven't changed at all."

"And I can see that you have. You've aged."

"Watch your mouth, whelp," the older warrior says. "I've come to speak with you."

"Careful, the more time you spend with me, the more others might think we're related. Should I address you by your name instead of 'Father'?"

"Sloan," he says.

"Yes, Devun," Sloan finally spins around to face his father. "Why are you here?"

"To speak with you," Devun stares at his son with a twisted sneer, his silver gaze as cold and uncaring as Sloan remembers.

"About what?"

"About your duty to your crest?"

Sloan chuckles at the earnestness in his father's expression, and the youngling shakes his head before swiveling back to the servant at the bar. He raises his glass to ask for another, then finishes the one in his hand.

"I have no duty to the Levia crest. You made that clear to me long ago."

"Things have changed. There are opportunities-"

"You mean stealing the throne from the rightful heir." Sloan narrows his eyes at his father, but Devun shakes his head.

"The Gridiron will determine the rightful heir."

"Nah. Win or lose, I like the side I'm on now."

"I told you, Father," Royce says. She slips in next to her brother, opposite Devun. "Sloan has too much pride and honor to be swayed so easily."

"Great, now there's two of them." Sloan glances on either side of him and sighs. "What do you think is going to sway me, Royce? What could you possibly offer me that would convince me to forgive you?"

"I don't want your forgiveness. I could not care less about how much you dislike me." Royce accepts a drink from the servant and sniffs at the new glass before sipping from it.

"Oh, good, then we're done here." Sloan motions to leave, but Devun grabs his arm. The red-eyed beast growls in the back of his mind, and Sloan echoes his counterpart with a threatening snarl. He yanks his arm free, glaring at his father.

"We all know you aren't going to survive the Gridiron, no matter how well you performed in the tournament. That hybrid is the only reason you made it through the last round, and everyone knows it. Can't you see it every time someone looks at you? The pity in their eyes?" Royce says to her brother. Her sympathetic voice spills down Sloan's spine like ice. He stiffens and twists away to finish his drink. He flinches when Royce continues.

"Ferogs do not survive the Gridiron."

"What do you want from me?" Sloan asks.

"I want you to help me. I want you to fight by my side as a brother should. I can't save you from the Gridiron. You know that the family forces every heir to compete. It can't be helped. But I can honor your memory afterward. I can make sure you are remembered as an honorable warrior who fought by his sister's side when she earned the right to the throne. Isn't that better than dying at the beck and call of a spoiled, hybrid prince?"

"Why are you so certain that you're going to win?" Sloan grits his teeth.

"Because someone has to. Someone will defeat Truin. With this many entries, it's statistically impossible for him to survive. And your friends will be at the mercy of whosoever bests him. If you help me win, I'll take care of your friends afterward. I'll keep them safe. I promise," Royce says. She slips a gentle hand over Sloan's fingers on the bar. "Help me, brother."

Sloan stares into his sister's silver eyes and wonders at her sincerity. Would she keep her promise? Could she really win? Sloan doesn't have the answers, but he's never considered what would happen to his packmates in the Gridiron. His pack is much larger now, and he kind of likes each of them in their own way. Can he protect them all in the Gridiron? No. He can't even defend himself.

Sloan glances across the room at each of his packmates. Jeqi tries to teach Marqee how to tie a fruit stem with his tongue, and she laughs at his odd expressions while he tries and fails. Schinn leads Atae in a slow dance and tucks a stray hair behind her ear as she blushes. Debil and Seva chat with Trikk next to the wall of names, and Trikk points to one from a few seasons ago. Truin listens to an eager youngling speaking with animated gestures, and several other students huddle around, waiting for a chance to talk with the royal heir. The prince glances up at the perfect time to catch Sloan's eye and meet his gaze. His questioning expression makes Sloan turn away and reach for his drink again.

"Think about it, Son," Devun says. He slides his arm around Sloan's shoulders and squeezes. Sloan's stomach tightens at the term of endearment from his father, and he nods. Royce and Devun leave the dark heir alone with his thoughts, and Sloan nurses his drink in silence. Several moments later, Debil joins Sloan at the bar and slips a hand around his arm.

"What was that about?" She asks. Sloan shakes his head.

"Just the typical family drama."

"Do you want to escape into the night?"

"More than anything else in the universe." Sloan offers an empty smile, and Debil leads him away.

In the far corner of the room, Prince Truin watches Sloan and Debil leave the party, and he considers following their example. Unfortunately, his mother has some type of psychic ability that senses when he's about to do something of which she'd disapprove. Like clockwork, Queen Sula slips in next to her son.

"How is the party?"

"Boring," he says. "Why am I here?"

"These are the Kaji that are most likely to support you in the Gridiron. You must win them over now," Sula whispers around her drink. Truin rolls his eyes at her.

"They're your supporters, not mine."

"Perhaps they'd become your supporters if you mingle," she says. "Now, go."

Truin returns to the bustle of socialization and networking with the new Sula Academy graduates and their families. Queen Sula watches her son for a few moments with an amused smile before catching sight of Atae and Schinn as they step out onto the balcony. She deposits her empty glass with a servant and follows the blue hybrid. Sula slips past the dark privacy curtain that's draped over the doorway to the balcony and finds Schinn whispering into Atae's ear.

"You're not distracting my protégé, are you, Schinn?"

The silver heir jumps away from Atae as though he were doing something wrong. "Of course not, my queen."

"Good, now run along," Sula says. She waves her hand at Schinn to dismiss him, and he hustles back into the party. Atae watches him leave then salutes Queen Sula in greeting.

"My queen."

"You did well in the tournament. You and your hybrid packmate," Sula says. She frowns when she can't remember the blonde's name.

"Jeqi," Atae says.

"Yes, that's it. You both did well. As did Marqee and Sloan, of course."

"Thank you." Atae flashes a proud smile. She's uncertain what else to say when the most powerful person in the empire, perhaps the Universe, compliments her. Beast, on the other hand, bubbles with an uncomfortable suspicion and warns Atae to be careful.

"Are you certain that you're prepared for the Gridiron? It's going to be much more difficult than the tournament, exponentially so."

"We have six months to train. Jeqi and I will be ready."

"What kind of warrior would you like to become?"

"Um…a strong one?" Atae's not sure that she understands the question.

"And what does strength mean to you?" Sula asks. She crosses her arms over her chest and raises both eyebrows, but Atae shakes her head in confusion.

"Uh…I don't…"

"When you imagine the strong warrior that you want to become, what do you see?"

Atae remembers a similar exercise that Solum asked of her many weeks ago. Looking back, it feels like it was a lifetime ago. So much has changed since then. Has the image of her perfect warrior changed, too? She closes her eyes and imagines the warrior she wants to emulate. She finds her warrior beset by enemies with no escape, but still he fights. He brawls against every blow, every block, every sword, and every other attack that is thrown his way. When he stumbles, her warrior climbs back to his feet and clashes again. With every breath he draws, her warrior swings his fist or his blade. Even as he falls to the enemy, the warrior continues to fight with his last breath. Beast swirls around Atae's imagined warrior and smiles in approval.

"I want to be the warrior who never quits. She never gives up and dies fighting," Atae says.

"That's not good enough," Sula says. "I don't want you to die fighting. If you're dead, you can't help my son. Do you want my son to die along with you in the Gridiron?"

"No, of course not."

"Then, perhaps you should aim higher."

"I won't give up. I will fight until my mission is complete."

"That's better," Sula says. "I suppose I can do something with that."

"My queen?"

"Have you forgotten about my promise to train you," Sula waves her hand with a frown, "and the other one?"

"No, Jeqi and I are eager to learn from you, Your Majesty." Atae brandishes an excited grin that pleases Queen Sula.

"Good. We start tomorrow."

EPILOGUE

Queen Sula stares at the small moon that hosts her son and the other Gridiron entries. The cruiser's orbit is so close that the moon encompasses her entire viewing screen. She lies back in the cushioned chair as she envisions her son's struggles in the Gridiron. Sula sits alone in the dark, wrestling with the nightmares and fears that plague her mind. She sips from her glass in hopes of numbing the borderline panic crashing through her body. Her son descended to the surface days ago when the Royal Gridiron began, but she can't stomach the idea of watching him struggle against the enemies she set upon him. Despite her protests, Solum insists on updating her at regular intervals.

He's alive.

She clings to that simple thought like a life preserver. She wraps it around her heart and begs her drink to numb the fear and anxiety that rages against her peace of mind.

He's still alive.

A knock on the door interrupts her inner turmoil, and Sula frowns. It's too early for one of Solum's reports, so she wonders who would risk her wrath. Then a horrifying thought stabs at her heart.

What if it is Solum? What if my son is...

Queen Sula drops the glass down on a nearby table and activates the door. It slides open to reveal a petite female haloed in the dim light of the hall. Realizing the shadow could not possibly belong to Solum, Sula sighs in relief.

My son is still alive.

"Enter," she says. Her voice hides her anxiety behind a cold and controlled tone. The small form trudges into the shadows of the dark room and disappears until Sula activates the lights. It takes a moment for the youngling's fuchsia eyes to adjust to the sudden illumination. She glances around the lavish living quarters before settling on the regal form sitting in a large, comfy chair. The royal amber eyes stare at her with a placid expression designed to unsettle the young female. It doesn't work.

"My queen." Her voice is slick with false charm as she salutes Sula. "I am honored to be in your presence."

"Sit, Aniyah," Sula says. The youngling hesitates to flick a strand of her lengthy, black hair over her shoulder before obeying. She sits in the only other chair available, which places her directly across from the queen. Maintaining the proper sitting position in the overstuffed chair is difficult, but Aniyah does her best. She shines her brilliant smile to distract from her lack of etiquette. Sula watches her with a blank expression that echoes in her voice.

"Do you understand why you are here? On this cruiser?"

"Solum briefed me." Accustomed to the cold shoulder, Aniyah nods with a silent confidence.

"Good. Why are you here in my room?"

"I need some assurances from you."

"You're alive, aren't you?"

"The task you've given me is-"

"Your mother was a traitor," Queen Sula says. She picks up her glass again, and this time, she doesn't hide the hint of anger and betrayal in her voice, causing the young female to flinch. "She was the last of her line, save for you. Her betrayal tainted her lineage and your future. And your children's future."

"So I've been told." Aniyah sourly sucks on her cheeks at the reminder of her family history. "By Kaji law, it was in your right to kill me, but you chose to spare me. You graciously allowed my father to raise me on his home planet."

"I did." Sula flashes a wicked smile as she sips from her glass. "I foresaw a use for you. And look at that, I was right."

"I am grateful for the opportunity to serve you, my queen." Aniyah bows her head then raises it to meet Queen Sula's gaze. "And I hope my service is enough to restore my honor and status among the Kaji."

"Aniyah, the task I've given you may save the Kaji Empire. Complete it, and I will give you everything you've asked of me and more."

"Thank you." Aniyah sighs as relief washes over her, and she reveals a genuine smile that even Sula appreciates. The young female lies back in the large chair and relishes the hope of the future. The queen watches Aniyah with an interested gaze until the youngling collects herself and returns to the proper sitting position.

"Don't thank me. The task will prove more difficult than you think. Solum thinks it's impossible," Sula says.

"I understand the difficulties. But I assure you. I will prove my worth to you."

The determination glimmering within Aniyah's eyes reminds Sula of another fuchsia-eyed youngling that's also eager to prove her worth.

ACKNOWLEDGMENTS

There are three important people that I need to acknowledge in the making of this book. I'd like to thank my mother for always giving her honest opinion, even when I didn't like it. I am very grateful for one of my best friends in the world, Amanda. She endured my obsession with this book, and the late-night texts that accompanied it, with the patience of an angel. And she always provided insightful feedback. Finally, I want to thank my oldest friend, Suzanne. She was the first person I told when I began writing, and she's provided unwavering support since.

Without each of you, this book would've never seen the light of day.

ABOUT THE AUTHOR

Kelly A Nix is a native-born Texan from the Dallas-Fort Worth area. In high school, she competed in rodeo, earned a brown belt in Taekwondo, and strived to be an actress. After graduating with her M.B.A., Kelly enjoys her career in the veterinary industry, and she spends most of her free time with her family, traveling, and writing. An animal lover, she shares her home with three cats, Louise, Rachel, and Orange Kitty, and a Great Dane mix named Dingo.